Report from the American Forces Radio and Television Service:

Observers at meteorological stations, astronomers and geophysicists throughout the world have come to the conclusion that the great Antarctic ice sheet is undergoing destruction by unknown subterranean forces, apparently pushing hot magma and rock up through the earth's mantle. We have one icebreaker, the *Southwind,* still in the area, on a mission to evacuate the last of our personnel. *Southwind* reports tremendous numbers of glacial and tabular icebergs, dangerous swells and ocean currents flowing away from the Antarctic continent, impeding the ship's progress . . . We urge all interests in South America, New Zealand, Australia and Africa to be on the alert for rising ocean waters . . . We repeat our previous warning: if the polar ice sheet should be destroyed, the waters of the oceans throughout the world could rise as much as two hundred fifty feet, and possibly much more if the Greenland ice sheet should break up.

STOREHOUSES OF THE SNOW

Capt. Ed U. Woodard
and Heather Woodard Bischoff

LEISURE BOOKS ∞ NEW YORK CITY

A LEISURE BOOK

Published by

Dorchester Publishing Co., Inc.
6 East 39th Street
New York, NY 10016

Printed in the United States of America

STOREHOUSES OF
THE SNOW

PROLOGUE

THE MOST severe winter ever recorded held earth's northern latitudes in its frigid grip. It was December twenty-second, and in Washington, a blizzard of blinding snow swirled around the White House. Inside, in the oval office, the President faced a group of anxious men. Present were the Secretaries of State, Interior, and Defense. Also with them were two of the President's top science advisors. They were discussing a speech which the President was to make at two o'clock, before a joint special session of the Congress.

The speech was aimed at "calming the apprehensions of the populace." Certain abnormalties had been reported by astronomical observatories. News media had carried startling disclosures of strange behavior of animals especially in polar regions, and recently an alarming phenomenon described as an increase in the tilt of the earth's axis had thrown scientists and authorities throughout the world in a furor of excitement. At the United Nations, the Security Council had scheduled a special session of the General Assembly.

As the President stood before the baffled group in his office, he was visibly shaken. Leaning forward, arms rigid, and knuckles down upon his desk, he declared, "This situation is getting more serious by the minute. All hell seems to be breaking loose! I've had hundreds of calls! So have government leaders all over the world. Nobody—NOBODY—has any reasonable answers!"

Unsmiling, the Secretary of the Interior mumbled, "I wonder if the earth will topple all the way over—I mean—like this." He made a rolling motion with his hands. "Like a big snowball!"

"Who knows what will happen!" bitterly exclaimed the Secretary of Defense. "We don't even know if we'll stay in our orbit! Our ships are having navigation difficulties right now!"

A telephone on the President's desk interrupted their discussion. As he took the message, the President's countenance revealed still deeper concern. When the call was ended he faced the anxious group. "My God!" he exclaimed. "As if we haven't had enough! Great earthquakes are shaking the Antarctic! Seismographs all over the globe are recording intense earthquakes down there!" He searched the astonished faces of his listeners. "What can it all mean? What the devil can I say to the people in my speech that will help?"

Even as the President spoke, intense shock waves were radiating swiftly outward from the south polar regions. Romping through the earth's thin crust, they jolted hundreds of seismographs scattered around the globe. Also severely jolted were the nerves of the world's seismologists and geologists, observing in amazement the wild convulsions of their instruments. Richter had never devised a scale to measure such frenzy.

A buzzer sounded. The President answered, and said, "Show him in, please." To the group he remarked, "It's Admiral Gary DeLavigne, Commandant of the Coast Guard."

The admiral entered briskly. "Mr. President," he began, "here is a message, sir, the like of which no man has received since the days of Noah! It just came in from our icebreaker *Southwind* in the Antarctic, sent by the commander and several scientists who are on board the vessel."

The President opened the envelope and read the message in silence. He motioned the admiral and the others to sit

8

down, and he did so himself. He seemed to be struggling to maintain a semblance of composure. His fists were tightly clenched as he looked intently at each of the men in the room. They watched him anxiously, in silence, with mounting apprehension.

"Gentlemen," he said, with visible emotion, "I would ask that this be kept among us for the next few minutes, and that we consider it together. I must reveal it to the people in my speech, even though it will surely cause more panic."

The President then read the message aloud. As the impact of his words, and the magnitude of the calamity they implied, were fully realized by the group, they were seized by consternation and dismay.

The staggering portent of the scientists' conclusions, that the polar ice was disintegrating, and that the oceans of the world would rise and flood all coastal and other low areas, was almost beyond comprehension.

The President leaned back in his chair. There was silence for a moment as they all endeavored to regain a measure of composure. The Secretary of State was the first to speak.

"Mr. President, I presume the flooding will first occur in the southernmost land areas of South America, New Zealand, and Africa. I will have our embassies keep us informed." He was interrupted by the buzzer on the President's desk.

"Yes," answered the President. "Put him on." He listened a moment, and then said to the Secretary of State, "A message from your office. You may take it here."

While the Secretary of State listened on the phone, the others engaged in low conversation until he was finished.

He then stated, "Mr. President, messages are already pouring in from our embassies. Great ocean swells are coming fast."

"I don't doubt it," remarked the President. "Let's get busy now and revise this speech. Our coasts may be destroyed tomorrow!"

During the next hour, the speech was carefully revised

9

with the help of the science advisors and the others. The President would have the difficult task of informing the people of the United States that all their coastal cities, and much of their land, would possibly be destroyed—that the oceans of the world might rise as much as two hundred fifty feet or more—that mountainous ocean swells were rapidly coming northward.

A call came in from the naval observatory. It was the only good news of those past three days. The tipping of the earth's axis had slowed, and it was thought there could be a stabilization soon at about thirty-eight degrees. A quick calculation by the scientists and Coast Guard admiral provided the President with the information that, if the thirty-eight degree estimate was true, the sun would apparently reach nearly a thousand miles farther south, and if the earth stabilized at that angle, it would reach nearly the same distance farther north the following summer. The entire matter was conjecture at that point, and would remain to be determined as observations continued. Meanwhile, all coastal areas had to be evacuated. The President held brief, hurried conferences with members of the Office of Emergency Planning and the National Security Council.

Newcasters of the world were bombarding the ears of the bewildered and distressed populace. Scare headline type was being set for immediate extra editions to appear on the streets of the world within the hour.

Telegraph and telephone lines were jammed, and crowds surged into the streets in many large cities as the devastating swells relentlessly moved northward over all the world's oceans.

Throughout the USA, on that eventful day of December solstice, a troubled populace waited apprehensively for the President's speech. It was hoped that his warning might reduce, to some extent, the certain high loss of lives. There was scarcely any time for evacuations.

All regular broadcasting was suspended. Network and local programming was pre-empted by special news broad-

10

casts. Millions of Americans were glued to their radios or television sets. Tension mounted as two o'clock approached. Suddenly, a familiar face appeared on TV screens everywhere. His voice, usually composed and pleasant on radio and television, betrayed suppressed emotion.

"Good afternoon. This is W. L. Burton at the Capitol in Washington. The President is about to address the Congress and the nation. What he is going to say will have a profound effect upon the lives of everyone on earth. We now take you to the Congress of the United States."

The greatest human audience ever to hear or view any event in history listened or watched with rapt attention as the scene shifted to the chamber of the House of Representatives. Senators, Representatives, foreign diplomats and their families, and special guests crowded the chamber and the balconies. The uneasy assemblage awaited the President's arrival.

The President's wife, son, and daughter were the focus of attention in the balcony. The First Lady, sitting very erect, with head held high, acknowledged her friends and acquaintances with a polite nod of recognition when their eyes met. She managed a pleasant, though unsmiling countenance. Occasionally she brushed a tear from a corner of her eyes. She clasped her daughter's hand. Families of the President's cabinet members sat quietly waiting in the vicinity of the First Lady and her children.

Soft murmurs and rustling of papers pervaded the chamber. Broadcasters and television crews occupied their assigned positions. The Vice President and the Speaker of the House solemnly took their places up on the rostrum behind the lectern.

A gavel was pounded twice. The voice of the Doorkeeper, louder than usual in that hushed chamber, announced, "Mr. Speaker, the President's cabinet." Cabinet members filed in quickly and took their seats amid muffled polite applause.

Then the Doorkeeper announced, "Mr. Speaker, the

11

President of the United States." As the President entered, the assemblage rose. Applause was longer, but still restrained.

The President stepped to the platform and shook hands with the Vice President and the Speaker. The Speaker addressed the assembly.

"My colleagues of the Congress, I have the distinguished privilege, and high personal honor, of presenting to you the President of the United States."

Applause again started, but the President held up both hands in a gesture for silence. His voice was strained, but clear.

"Mr. Speaker, Mr. Vice President, members of Congress, distinguished guests and my fellow Americans. You all know, through the efforts of our excellent news services, the momentous astronomical phenomena which have taken place during the past few days. My science advisors have been constantly alert, and have kept me informed almost hourly as to what is happening, and what we may expect. I was advised today that the tipping of the earth's axis is slowing now, and is expected to stabilize very soon, possibly this week."

Some applause greeted the announcement. The President took a sip of water, and dabbed his forehead with a handkerchief.

"Now, I have something to tell you which you are not going to like. This noon we received a message from our icebreaker, *Southwind,* which is engaged in evacuation of our Antarctic personnel. The message informs us that the Antarctic icesheet is apparently breaking up. There were tremendous earthquakes at eleven this morning, and shocks have continued down there. Even now, they are being recorded at all of our seismic stations, and those of other countries. The icebreaker also reported great volcanic activity as far as they could see over the coast when their helicopter attempted to evacuate Palmer Station on the peninsula. We had already evacuated most of our other personnel by plane. We have another ship down there, the

Research Vessel *Quest*, which is now evacuating scientists from Deception Island, and will also evacuate Palmer Station.''

The President continued, speaking more rapidly, and with urgency. "Now, I must give you the most distressing and appalling news of all. My science advisors inform me that we can expect an overwhelming flood over the entire world as a result of the melting ice and snow in the polar regions. I am told that the oceans may rise two hundred fifty feet or more. This will mean the flooding of all our coastal areas, and the destruction of all our seaports. Devastating ocean swells are already moving toward us.''

The President's audience gasped.

Pausing only momentarily to mop his brow, the President continued. "I have given orders to our naval vessels, wherever they may be, to return home immediately while they have fuel. I have ordered vital government agencies to move to areas of higher elevation as necessary. We do not know how many hours we will have before the seismic swells destroy our port cities, such as Boston, New York, Philadelphia, Baltimore, Norfolk, Charleston, Savannah, Jacksonville, Miami, Tampa, Mobile, New Orleans, Galveston, San Diego, Los Angeles, San Francisco, and others too numerous to mention. Our advice to all coastal interests is to evacuate as quickly as possible!''

The President's voice rose. He leaned forward and gripped the lectern. "This is a very serious emergency! The swells will strike our coasts tomorrow morning! I have already warned the governors of all coastal states!''

The listeners became excited. Many stood and some started toward the doors.

Visibly struggling to control his emotions, the President resumed his dire warning. "Probably the entire state of Florida will be inundated, as will also much coastal land along the Atlantic seaboard, and the Gulf of Mexico. The Bahama Islands will be covered. Low countries, such as the Netherlands, will be under deep water. The Middle East oil exporting ports will be destroyed. Our western states—

California, Oregon, and Washington—will fare better, but all their seaports will be destroyed."

The apprehension of his audience, both within the Congress, and the millions of people watching television or listening to the radio, grew with each word.

Striving to be heard above the growing disorder in the chamber, the President pressed onward. "I ask all of you to take immediate steps to evacuate all areas of our coasts which are less than three hundred feet above sea level. I also ask all of you who are situated above that elevation, to show great compassion for the refugees. Your government will make all possible funds available to the states and cities for the purpose of establishing temporary places of shelter on high ground."

Holding his arms high and wide, palms outward, the President shouted for order, that he might be heard. "We will render assistance to our neighboring countries, Canada, Mexico, and the islands of the Caribbean, to the extent that our ships, both government, and privately owned, can be used. Our greatest supplies of fuel are stored at or near our seaports. They will all be under deep water, and there may be great oil spills onto the flood waters. Fuel for our ships and aircraft will soon be exhausted, and will probably not be available thereafter. Our seacoast refineries will be destroyed, and present fuel supplies throughout the land, in this coldest of winters, may not be replenished once they are expended. Many coastal power plants will be destroyed. Food supplies should be moved as rapidly as possible to high ground."

The people heard little more. They jammed the doors in a veritable stampede to get out of the chamber.

The President, determined to finish his message, gestured for attention. "The oil producing countries will not be able to supply tankers. The ships will find no seaports, nor storage facilities to which to deliver the oil." The seats of the chamber and the balconies were rapidly emptying. Seeing the futility of finishing his message, the President concluded. "To sum up," he shouted, "the

14

greatest disaster the earth has ever known is now upon us! May God help us!''

The impact of the President's speech stunned the world. His warning had been transmitted to other countries via satellite. As word spread throughout the globe, consternation and panic gripped the populations of coastal areas of all continents and islands.

The President and his family, with key members of his staff and their families, quickly departed from the Capitol. They were rushed in helicopters to the waiting Flying Command Posts, or Doomsday Planes, which took them to a prearranged destination on high ground. There they would try to carry on the most urgent functions of a confused and tottering government.

It was already dark, and bitterly cold in Washington as the frightened legislators and guests fled from the building. The blizzard lashed their cars. Traffic became hopelessly snarled. Chaos reigned in the nation's capitol as police and other city personnel abandoned their posts to join the mad rush westward to higher ground.

1

I'M JAMES Howard, a writer. My own participation in the dramatic events which I've recorded began in New York about a month before the President's historic warning.

Animals of the polar regions, the seals, whales, penguins, and other creatures, had been unusually restless and agitated. A group of scientists were preparing to go to the Antarctic on board the Antarctic Research Vessel *Quest,* and I was assigned to accompany them and provide my editors with an accurate account of their activities. I had been on dangerous assignments before, but never did I envision myself as an observer to the earth's greatest devastation to date.

I attended a briefing in our New York office and received instructions concerning the international and classified aspects of my assignment. My security clearance had already been obtained from the National Science Foundation. Next, I got a visa at the Chilean consulate, and went to my apartment to pack.

I was in a hurry, but I took time to call a few friends and say so long. I really should have said good bye, because it's probable that few of them are still alive.

Winter temperatures chilled the New York air on that late November day. As I left the building, a cold drizzle dampened my clothing and luggage, but not my enthusiasm.

I flagged a taxi on Fifth Avenue—what was then Fifth Avenue. I reached the check-in counter at Kennedy Airport just as my flight was being announced. Next day, after a change of plane at Santiago, I arrived at Punta Arenas, Chile, on the Magellan Strait. I took a taxi to the port.

When I reached the pier, I was glad to see that *Quest* was still at her berth taking on provisions and supplies. There were visitors on the pier, and when I drew near I heard one of them ask why such a large quantity of provisions was being loaded.

"We're going to the Antarctic," a seaman said. "We must have enough to last through this summer, and next winter too, in case we get stuck in the ice."

A woman moved closer and asked, "Isn't it dangerous to go down there?"

"Yeah," the seaman replied. "It takes experience. We been workin' there a long time. Th' skipper knows that ice."

The cab driver who had brought me from the airport put my gear near the gangway. The seaman came toward me. "Let me help you," he said, and took my ditty bag, typewriter and valise. "You must be a photographer." He was looking at the cameras.

"Yes, ah, no, I'm a journalist. My name is Ja—" My introduction was interrupted. The skipper had come across the gangway.

"I'm Isaac Pack. Glad to meet you," he said quickly, "You must be—"

"Howard, James Howard," I said. He pumped my hand with a strong and friendly grip. I tried not to wince.

"Well, you're just in time. We had given you up for lost. We're about to get under way soon," he said. He then told the seaman to take my baggage to a cabin. I gladly surrendered everything except the cameras and tripod. I wanted to go to the cabin too. I wanted a hot meal, a hot shower, and to crawl into bed. I was bone weary. The captain must have read my thoughts.

"You must be exhausted after such a long trip. But we'll have you fixed up in no time," he said.

"No," I lied. "Just a bit tired, that's all."

I followed Captain Pack over the gangway and along the starboard side of the wheelhouse. He introduced me to a small group of tourists and friends who were visiting the ship, then said, "Well, here you are. Welcome aboard! You go down and get some rest. I'll see you later—after we get away from the pier. I'm just showing my visitors around the ship." He motioned to a companionway with a short flight of steps, beyond which another stairway led down to the deck below. The man who had taken my baggage below was coming back up. He beckoned and I followed him down to my cabin on the deck below off the mess room, port side.

The cabin was small but comfortable. There were two bunks, not quite wall to wall, but nearly so. There was still room for a small, built-in desk and chair. There were two clothes lockers, and four drawers under the lower bunk. I was told that I would have the lower, for which I was thankful. There was a shaded reading light on the bulkhead above my pillow, and a high board along the outside edge of my bunk to keep me from rolling out. This was not new to me. I had been on many ships in my travels.

Some heavy clothing and a battered suitcase had been tossed on the upper bed. I read the name on the tag: M. Vogt. I was curious as to who my roommate was. I was informed that he was ashore at the warehouse with some of the other scientists getting additional heavy weather clothing and boots. I wondered where we would stow all our gear. I had plenty myself, what with my cameras and all. I put some of my stuff in one of the lockers.

I located the midship head. It was across on the starboard side of a short alleyway between the mess room and the engine room nearly opposite the door of the midship laboratory. It was a combination type head with a high commode and a shower stall with a high sill in front to keep the water from spilling out on the deck. It often did anyway. I found out later that one hardly knew which way was up in the Drake Passage sometimes! There were hand-

19

holds on the bulkheads near the commode and in the shower. I never knew until that voyage below the Horn how important they were.

I showered, shaved, and tried to rest. But I was too keyed up and overtired to sleep. I seemed to have gotten my second wind. So I decided to go up on deck, roam around, and interview some of the crew. I pulled on an old sweater and was loading a camera when someone flung open my cabin door. An immense, bearded bear of a man filled the doorway. He scowled as he surveyed my gear. His eyes narrowed. He clenched his fists.

"You in here?" he growled. "I was suppose t' have dis cabin wit' Mike Vogt." Then he peered intently into my face. I was about to reply when he drew in his breath sharply. His jaw dropped. He turned away quickly and left the cabin, slamming the door.

I got on deck with time to spare before *Quest* sailed, but decided against trying to talk to the crew. They were at their stations and involved with getting underway. So I busied myself taking pictures of the pier and what could be seen of Punta Arenas from the ship. As I looked around the vessel, I didn't see anyone resembling a scientist. I assumed they must all be in the laboratories busy doing whatever it is that scientists do. When I looked up from the deck I saw Captain Pack at a wheelhouse window. He saw me and waved.

Pack was a punctual man. Indeed, *Quest* departed Punta Arenas on that day, November 26, at exactly 1400.

I marveled at the synchronization between captain and crew, and the care and patience applied in maneuvering the vessel away from the pier. Not only was Pack punctual, he was obviously very careful.

The research department in our office in New York had supplied me with some background on the skipper before I left. Captain Isaac Pack was a veteran of many polar voyages. He was known to his friends by the nickname "Icepack." Some members of the crew had other names

20

for him, but generally he was liked by the crew and scientists.

As *Quest* departed from the pier, a small group of wives, relatives and friends stood in the cold wind and waved as long as the ship could be seen. Backing slowly away from the long pier into the harbor, Pack turned his vessel northeastward into the Magellan Strait. When he was clear of the pier, he motioned to a Chilean naval officer to take over and give instructions to the helmsman. The officer was on board *Quest* to act as pilot through the Magellan Strait.

Passage through the reaches of the Strait was made without incident. The pilot was taken off by a ferry, the *Barcaza Concon*, and *Quest* proceeded into the Atlantic southeastward along the Argentine coast of Tierra del Fuego or "Land of the Fire." I was exhausted from my plane trip, so I went to my cabin for a nap.

At dinner that evening, Captain Pack introduced me to the scientists and various crew members who were to be featured in my story. He said that there was a complement of twenty-nine persons on board. That included the captain, eleven scientists, three deck officers, three engineer officers, one electronic technician, a cook, three able seamen, an ordinary seaman, two oilers, a wiper, a messboy, and, of course, myself.

The scientific group included Dr. Elbano "Elbow" Larsen and his two assistants, Mike Vogt and Per Thysen, Dr. Arnold Varany and his wife, Dr. Nancy Varany, Arthur Allen and three graduate assistants, Dr. Belle B. Abbey, and her young and pretty assistant, Miss Carol Moore.

The cook had rendered a sumptuous meal. The air was filled with genuine conviviality and excited anticipation of the upcoming expedition. By the end of dinner, we were all on a first name basis.

I listened intently to the conversation, which centered around the various activities of the scientists and what they hoped to accomplish on the trip. I asked questions and made some preliminary notes on each one.

Dr. Larsen was designated Chief Scientist and acted as head of the scientific group. His assistants, Vogt and Thysen, were mountaineers. Thysen was the big man who had burst into my cabin claiming he should have been its occupant with Vogt. I had an uneasy feeling that I had seen him before, under less pleasant circumstances. I caught him staring at me once or twice, but he said nothing.

Dr. Larsen was an authority on glaciology, having made numerous expeditions to both Arctic and Antarctic regions. He was a strong and hearty man who seemed to be forever bursting with enthusiasm and anticipation for his next adventure into the world's great storehouse of snow and ice. *Quest* would put Larsen and his assistants ashore at various places where they would remain for several days until the ship could return and take them to other predetermined areas. Their first stop was to be at Livingston Island in the South Shetlands. They would also go down into deep ice caverns on Deception Island and several places on the Antarctic Peninsula.

Dr. Varany and his attractive wife, Dr. Nancy Varany, were specialists on the behavior of penguins and seals. They would be put ashore at some large penguin rookery, where they would resume a study of penguins begun on previous voyages. They had several publications to their credit concerning animal behavior. On the cruise, the Drs. Varany intended to give special consideration to the amount of encroachment upon the penguin population by leopard seals and other predators, and determine if possible the reason for the new and strange behavior of all the other Antarctic animals and birds.

The Varanys had complete confidence in their ability to endure the arduous sub-zero environment of a penguin rookery, and expected to remain about a month in some isolated region close to the largest penguin rookery that could be found, where leopard seals were also present.

Quest was to put them ashore and crewmen would help in setting up their camp and radio antenna. There would be a daily radio schedule. They could expect storms and blizzards.

Arthur Allen, a very well known and highly regarded Antarctic personality, was on his way to Palmer Station at Arthur Harbor, located on Anvers Island near the coast of the Antarctic Peninsula. He was to be laboratory manager. The three graduate assistants were also going to Palmer Station where they would assist in laboratory investigations. Arthur Allen was a remarkably capable individual, and a devoted electronics expert who had rendered years of service to the success of polar programs in that remote and rigorous environment.

Dr. Belle "Beebee" Abbey was a most interesting, efficient and charming widow, of strong character and remarkable ability in her field, the collection and study of benthic biological specimens.

Beebee was ably assisted by her companion and coworker, Carol Moore, a tall, active, intelligent girl in her mid-twenties. Beebee and Carol were to remain on board for about half of the five month cruise. Certain male members of the scientific party, as well as the crew, were quite happy to have lovely Carol on board, even though she gave them no attention whatever. When she was bundled up in her heavy weather clothing, sweaters, boots, and red flotation jacket, she almost succeeded in hiding her attractiveness, but not quite.

As the evening wore on, the number of scientific notables dwindled in the mess room. One by one they begged off to return to their cabins. The hour was late and it had been a long day. I wanted to question the Varanys about the disturbances in the rookeries, but they were the first in the group to excuse themselves. The captain, Beebee, and I lingered over second cups of coffee.

"Beebee, what do you think is causing the disturbances in the rookeries and among the seals and other animals?" I asked.

"Well, I don't know," she answered. "I suppose it could be any number of things. Besides, I hate to speculate, especially in front of a journalist," she laughed. "It's really not my area of expertise, you know."

"You'll find scientists, at least in this part of the world, to be very non-committal," teased the captain.

Beebee laughed again. "Oh, Captain, that's not necessarily true." She turned to me. "But seriously, Jamie, you should ask the Varanys about it. It's their field. Perhaps they'll have some answers for us after they visit the rookeries." She changed the subject. "You've been asking all the questions. Now, tell us about yourself."

Being an egotistical, self-centered male, I was instantly flattered. The captain seemed to be enjoying our mild flirtation.

"Well," I responded, "I was born in Britain. My mother was British and my father an American diplomat. He was recalled to America shortly after I was born. I was schooled in the States and I've worked there ever since."

"But you've travelled back to England many times, haven't you?" Pack asked.

"Yes, I have," I said, "but only on assignment. I never made it my home."

"Where is your home? Where do you base your family?" Beebee asked.

"An apartment in New York, but no family," I answered. "I'm a loner."

"Oh?" Beebee said with a slight lilt in her voice, and then quickly changed the subject again. "You've certainly written some fascinating accounts of events around the world. I was particularly interested in your coverage of the Apollo lunar landings, the Viking studies on Mars, and the space shuttle program. I suppose it was scientific curiosity on my part, but really, they were marvelous."

"That's very kind of you," I said, beginning to feel slightly embarrassed by her continued flattery.

"Well, if you'll both excuse me," Beebee said finally, "I must check on a few things in the lab before turning in.

It's been a pleasure meeting you, Jamie. I hope you'll enjoy our trip. It should be very exciting." Yes, indeed, I thought, very exciting. She left the mess room.

Half aloud, I said, "Admirable woman. Charming."

The skipper laughed, and with a twinkle in his eye, said, "That she is, that she is." After a moment's silence, Pack asked, "Any regrets at never having married?"

My dossier, I thought. I hadn't remembered telling him I'd *never* married. Perhaps it showed or perhaps he was just guessing. "I'm a confirmed bachelor. With all my traveling over the years, I never felt it fair to have a family stuck away somewhere at home." My answer seemed to satisfy him.

"I know what you mean," the captain mused.

I sighed and said, "I think I'll go on deck for awhile."

Out there I found the air had turned colder. I quickly went to the lee side of the ship. I folded my arms and leaned against the bulwark. Beebee's lovely features and pleasant smile filled my thoughts.

Daylight waned about 2200. I was not yet used to the short night periods in those latitudes. As the sky darkened I saw many natural gas flares along the Argentine coast of Tierra del Fuego. Their reflections danced upon the night waters. I was reminded of my cruise, two years before, on the *M.S. Sinbad* in these seas, and to the Antarctic. I wondered if the paths of *Quest* and *Sinbad* would cross on our voyage.

There was a light southwest breeze. *Quest* boldly advanced through the darkness, her running lights brightly shining. Small feathers of vapor from the stack drifted off our port quarter. The engines purred and *Quest's* bluff armored bow cleaved the water, disturbing myriads of tiny luminescent creatures glowing in the bow wave and shimmering astern in the turbulence of the wake. *Quest* seemed eager to reach her icy destination.

The incident of Per Thysen, the burly mountaineer, arrogantly invading my cabin and claiming I had displaced him, kept returning to my mind. An encounter with him at dinner had proved to be still more puzzling. His dislike for me was evident. I could not recall any previous knowledge of the man, but a feeling persisted that he knew me. I suspected he had an aversion to something I had written. He was a big man with large powerful hands. I shuddered. Suddenly footsteps interrupted thoughts. My pulse quickened. I turned and peered through the darkness, but it was not Thysen. Just a member of the crew on his way forward.

I stayed on deck for a while, watching the Argentine coastline. The sea air made me hungry again, and I went below where I found cake and hot coffee in the galley. Soon, feeling refreshed, I decided to get acquainted with the crew members in the engine room and in the wheel-house, before I turned in.

In the noisy engine room I visited briefly with Jesse "Crankshaft" Lytel, *Quest's* Chief Engineer, and with Oiler Bill Kiernan. Talking in all that noise was difficult, so I didn't stay long. I went up to the bridge where Third Mate Jim Lefevre gazed wearily through the rigging at the horizon ahead. I stayed up there conversing with Jim, and later with Second Mate Paul Shelley when he came on watch at midnight. It was a pleasant night, and I wasn't sleepy, so I stayed right through Paul's watch also, to get better acquainted with him.

But when Chief Mate Harry King came up just before 0400 I decided to end my bridge visit, especially when King said to me, "You'd best be getting below, Howard. You'll be needing some shuteye. It'll be time for breakfast before you know it." I knew he was right, and I left the bridge with Paul Shelley as he went off watch. I made my way to my cabin and undressed in the dark, trying not to disturb Mike Vogt, sound asleep on the upper bunk. It seemed that I had hardly touched my head on the pillow when it was time to turn out for breakfast. I found out later that the AB on watch always called the cook at 0530. Soon there were noises from the galley, and pleasant breakfast aromas spread through the ship.

Breakfast started promptly at 0730, a fast moving operation of eggs, hot cakes, bacon, grapefruit juice, coffee and rolls, juggled from the galley to the mess room table by Pete Fortunato, a tall, curly headed messboy. Pete's hair was too long to suit the mate, who accused him of tossing his curls over the food as he brought it along the passageway from the galley. The mate finally got the boy to wear a white rag around his head. It came loose one day at dinner, and fell into the mate's soup. The boy went back to the galley and wrung the rag out into the soup and brought it back to the table, whereupon the mate said it had a strong flavor.

So the voyage progressed. Gradually the weather changed. As *Quest* approached Le Maire Strait, which separates Isla de los Estados from the toe of Tierra del Fuego, the sky became overcast. Long wispy citrus clouds stood upwards from a dark area of the southwest horizon in fan-like formation, indicating a stormy low was moving eastward. Icepack was concerned about the change in weather. I accompanied him to the wheelhouse. "How does it look?" I asked.

"Not good," he said with a frown. "Our ET should be getting another weather report soon."

Perky, hatchet-faced, black-eyed Enrique Salaverry was the radio operator and electronic technician. Sometimes he was called "Symbol for Period" by the skipper, and sometimes, just "Period," by the mate. He came to the wheelhouse with a radio weather message. The skipper read it and handed it to the second mate who was picking his teeth and scowling at the darkening horizon. The skipper turned to the ET. "See if Palmer Station has a position of that storm from the satellite."

Enrique replied, "I have just been talking with them. They don't have it yet, but expect it soon."

The skipper thought for a moment. "Hmmmm," he mused. "Well, see if you can get something from the Chilean Navy, or try Don Marsh. He might have a late report from the Argentine Navy. I would like a late position on that storm.''

"Yes, sir," said Enrique, and returned to the radio room.

"Who is Don Marsh?" I asked.

After a pause during which Captain Pack studied the sky, he replied, "The Marsh family owns a large *estancia* on Tierra del Fuego. He's an expert radio technician. We've had him here on *Quest* as ET occasionally." Pack didn't offer any more information about Don Marsh, so I decided against asking him further questions.

As time went on, I learned that Marsh was a man of the land, that fertile and superbly scenic land which was Tierra del Fuego. His family's splendid ranch, carefully tended by several generations of his forebears, bordered on the Beagle Channel fringed by numerous islands. Not far to the west along that waterway was Ushuaia, the world's southernmost city, and the very threshold of the Antarctic.

Animals of many kinds roamed the hills, valleys, and plains of Tierra del Fuego. With its thousands of hardy people and its many large sheep ranches called *estancias,* it was indeed an important and productive territory. Chile and Argentina shared the region. Within its borders were over a million sheep and thousands of horses and cattle. It was also home to many species of wild animals and birds. Its coasts were frequented by many seals and whales.

Tierra del Fuego, "Land of the Fire," with snow-capped peaks its sentinels, and Cape Horn, its stormy outpost, had much in common with the Antarctic. Even as that austral winter ended, it shared with Antarctica a mysterious phenomenon.

Don Marsh was greatly concerned about the strange behavior he had noticed among his flocks of some twelve thousand sheep, and the unusual activity of his dogs, horses, and cattle. He observed peculiar actions also of the guanacos, foxes, otters, beavers and rabbits. Animals and birds seemed unable to settle down. He wondered why they never seemed to rest or sleep. What was wrong? What could be disturbing the creatures?

Don discussed the abnormal behavior of the animals with several of his ham radio friends scattered around the territory, and with others on mainland Chile and Argentina. The news reached the rest of South America and other lands. The news media of the world soon picked up on the stories. The strange behavior of the animal kingdom at the earth's southern extremity quickly became general knowledge in and out of scientific circles.

Within the hour after Pack asked the ET for a weather report, Palmer Station gave Enrique the position of the low, indicating it was moving rapidly northeastward, and would soon pass south of Cape Horn. The skipper reasoned that if we kept going, by the time we reached the area of the storm's path, it would have passed. He decided to keep on rather than seek shelter. He said it would be better to go on right after the storm, and get well south of it, before the next one came along.

No longer preoccupied with plotting courses, Captain Pack turned to the ET. "Did you reach Marsh?" he asked.

"Yes, I did," said Enrique. His face clouded. "But he wants to talk to you."

"What?" Pack exclaimed. "Now, I wonder what he wants to talk to me about. Okay, call him back." He followed Enrique into the radio room and closed the door. When he came out his face was grim. "They have had to abandon the *estancia*. They can't stay there. The stench of dead whales and seals along the shore is unbearable. He's flown his family and others to another ranch in the hills, well back from the coast. Don said that a lot of the coastal people have done the same. The Varanys and the other scientists here on *Quest* will be interested in all this. We'd better go down and tell them."

We went below, where we found the Varanys and Beebee in the mess room. Some of the crew gathered around as Pack recounted the story he had told me about Don Marsh. There was great interest among the scientists.

The Varanys were most anxious that we make all possible speed so they could get to work in the Antarctic as quickly as possible.

"We're doing about eighteen knots right now," said Pack with a grin.

Carol Moore came out of the cabin she shared with Beebee. "Did I hear you say we are doing eighteen knots?" she asked.

"You sure did," replied the skipper.

"That's grrreat!" she exclaimed. "That's wonderful! We'll get to Palmer Station in a couple of days, won't we?" Evidently Carol was in a hurry.

I wondered about Carol. I quietly said to Beebee, "Carol seems anxious to get to work." Beebee looked at me with a wry smile, but made no comment.

"We won't be doing eighteen very long," explained the skipper. "Just for a few hours. We have a strong current with us here, but it won't last long. Sorry, Carol."

"Oh, that's all right, Captain," replied Carol. "I'm in no hurry." Beebee gave me that sly smile again.

After passing through Le Maire Strait, Pack set course for Livingston Island in the South Shetlands. It was rough the first two days crossing the notorious Drake Passage with a high confused sea left over from the storm. Except for some fog, as we passed the convergence area and entered the colder waters, the next two days were fairly good going.

Art Allen weathered the Drake Passage very well, considering that he had refused to occupy a berth when he learned that there were not enough for all persons aboard. I learned that I was the cause of Art's displacement. He, and not Thysen, had been assigned the cabin with Mike Vogt. When Art found out I was joining the expedition, he told the mate he would give up his bunk for me. When I tried to reverse the situation and insist on his sleeping in the bunk, he would have none of it. As the weeks passed, I learned that Art Allen was a genuine, kindhearted person, always trying to help someone.

Art found a place to sleep on the deck in the midship lab. When *Quest* was rolling and pitching South of the Horn, he wedged himself between some large canvas bags of weather clothing. He slid across the deck the first two nights from one end of the lab to the other. Like an old sailing master, he went to sleep anyway, oblivious to the motion. One night a large plastic bottle of alcohol fell off a shelf and burst open, spraying him and his surroundings. He said he woke up chewing on a felt boot insert. Art thought it was one of the mate's boots.

I can vouch for the mariner's usual designation of the Drake Passage as "the roughest seas in the world." Few of us "shore types" on board *Quest*, especially the three graduate assistants and myself, had any appetites the first day after the ship left the Cape Horn latitude and headed southward across Drake Passage. The rolling and pitching never stopped. The only possible place for me was in my bunk, where I stayed nearly all the first day and night. My infrequent visits to the head were perilous adventures involving short dashes and grabbing of pillar and post as the deck spurned my feet, and the overhead collided with my cranium and my shoulders. I had been on many ships, but I'd never experienced anything like that trawler in those heavy seas of the Drake Passage. I swore that if I ever put my feet on solid land again, I would never look at a ship as long as I lived.

By the second day, I felt a little more accustomed to the motion, and decided to try eating something at the noon meal. Beebee and some other scientists, Per Thysen, and a couple of mates were at the table. Chief Mate Harry King grinned and said, "Come on, Howard. Sit right down and git y'r nose in the trough. Only hold on to y'r plate. Pete, bring Mr. Howard some a' that salt pork ya got out there, and some a' that good bilge water to wash it down." I shuddered and precariously slid into a chair, holding tightly to the edge of the table and bracing a knee against the table leg nearest to me. Fiddles were in place and the table cloth was wetted down to help keep the dishes from sliding around. We had to hold onto our plates and cups as we ate. Every few minutes, the ship would lurch in a heavier sea, and we would grab everything we could hold down.

Suddenly, our world was turned upside down. *Quest* was struck by a heavier sea than usual. The ship rolled violently to starboard. The mess room turned into immediate chaos. Carrots and peas ascended into the air as though shot from miniature cannons. Beverage containers spewed their contents like geysers. Plates of food and all utensils clanked, clattered, and plummeted to the deck, or into our laps. The mates, engineers, and some of the scientists just laughed and went on eating whatever they could hold onto, bracing themselves and swaying with the ship. Not so with us "shore types." Within seconds we were thrown to the deck. On my way down, I saw my dinner plate jump the fiddles into Beebee's lap. Chairs and settee cushions flew across the mess room and crashed against the starboard bulkhead. The mess room became a confused scene of thrashing torsos and flailing arms and legs. As the vessel rolled violently back to port, I tried to get to my knees and help Beebee up, but Per Thysen got to her ahead of me. I'm not sure, but in the confusion, I think he pushed me aside. I was thrown back down on my stomach. Swimming in a sea of gravy, coffee and salad dressing, I went sliding and sloshing across the deck toward the open door of Beebee's and Carol's cabin. There I managed to grab the door frame and hang on until *Quest* steadied a bit.

From my humiliating position on the mess room deck, I caught a glimpse of big Per Thysen lifting Beebee in his strong arms. I felt an immediate sting of jealousy, an emotion I had not experienced in several years.

Chief Mate Harry King and Dr. "Elbow" Larsen got up laughing from the table and began assisting the others. Within minutes we determined that, aside from a few knocks and bruises, there were no serious injuries.

Quest continued its violent antics for several hours. I

could only remain braced in my cabin with my chair against the bunk and my feet against the bulkhead. Vogt didn't disturb me. He and some of the other scientists thought nothing of the rough seas, and spent the time in one of the labs.

I finally managed to get to the head, where I showered and made it back to the cabin. I turned in for the night wondering what would happen next. I soon got my answer. Just as Vogt was climbing into the top bunk, *Quest* lurched again. Vogt lost his footing and stepped squarely on my face. "Oops! So sorry," he declared politely. And with that grand finale, *Quest* had passed through the last of the rough seas left over from the storm.

We made an early evening landfall and anchored off the south shore of Livingston Island where it was low with sloping hillsides. There "Elbow" Larsen and his two assistants were taken ashore in a zodiac. Someone remarked that they must be getting off there just for the skiing. It took three trips to get all their gear ashore. I busied myself with taking pictures of the entire operation. Finally, the ship pulled away and left them, three sturdy red-clad figures, tramping off up the slope over a deep blanket of snow. I was glad Thysen would be gone from the ship for a while. We stood on deck watching them. I glanced frequently at Beebee's face to see if Thysen's absence was causing her any concern. If it did, she didn't show it.

It was still daylight when the ship left Livingston Island. The sun was low in the west making a long oblique slant toward the south where it would disappear for about three hours around midnight, still close enough below the horizon to give light to the sky. *Quest* headed northeast toward Nelson Island where the Varanys were to be put off the ship. They had chosen to set up their camp on the shore of a small embayment called Harmony Cove. Anchoring there early the next morning, the Varanys were ferried ashore on one of the zodiacs through loose ice. During the day, Enrique and other crew members set up their camp and radio antenna. Then the ship left for Palmer Station.

Palmer Station lay on a low rocky point at the entrance to a narrow inlet on the east side of Arthur Harbor. Girded by boulders worn smooth by glacier ice, the anchorage was in a protected cove between some nearby offshore islands and rocky Bonaparte Point. There was a small dock and two large buildings up a short rocky road, where a group of men known as USARPS (U.S. Antarctic Research Personnel) had wintered over. They had been without mail for the past eight months. As soon as *Quest* could reach the dock through the loose pack ice in the harbor, the mate handed the two sacks of mail to the station manager amid shouts of welcome and much tossing of snowballs between the crew and the gang on the dock. About five inches of snow covered the decks and the shore.

During the excitement, Carol Moore was furiously waving to someone on shore. She was all bundled up with a parka hood over her head, and the man on the dock didn't recognize her. She shouted, "Larry! Larry! It's me! Carol!" At the sound of her voice, the entire group of men, who hadn't seen a woman in eight months, surged toward the edge of the dock. The biggest among them was Larry Field, a biologist, and one of the three scientists who had wintered over at Palmer Station. Larry, who hadn't known of Carol's coming on *Quest*, began to shout with glee, wave his long arms, and dance around in his big boots.

"Hey! Carol! Carol!" he shouted over and over again. "How come you're here? Jumpin' Jupiter, am I glad to see you!"

The crew soon had a ladder set up to the rail and a cargo net rigged below for safety. Larry pushed his way to the ship's side in his hurry to get to Carol. The edge of the dock was slippery with ice. In his excitement, he slipped and fell into the net. The others laughed and went on board ahead of him. He clumsily climbed up the net with his heavy clothing and boots. He had lost his cap in the

34

slushy water, and his blond wavy hair was covered with snow. Larry clambered over the rail and threw his arms around Carol. Their faces were wet with snow and tears as they hugged and kissed over and over on the forward deck.

Some of the gang danced around them shouting, "Kiss her again, Larry!" "Give her another for me!" "How's about passing her around?" "Give us all a chance!"

So that was the reason Carol had been so quiet during the voyage, especially when asked about romance in her life. No, she had no intentions of marrying. No, she felt that she would devote her life to her studies. Yes, worms on the ocean bottom were more important than any man. But she had seemed so eager that the ship make all possible speed. She blushed. The crew laughed. Icepack, who took it all in, remarked, "Looks like there'll be a wedding around here one of these days."

Larry held out his big hand to the skipper. "I hope there will be, but it's still a long way off."

Carol laughingly said, "Some day, maybe, after we get home."

That, then, was a fleeting glimpse of the lives of Larry and Carol; a worthy couple they would make, pondering their insects and worms together. Larry, the biggest man on the station, studied the smallest creatures in the Antarctic. The men present shared, in a way, the romantic moment of their reunion. Carol and Larry had met years earlier at an atmospheric and marine science laboratory, where the science of romance quickly flourished. After a few weeks, Larry had gone on a research vessel for a cruise to Africa. They corresponded when possible, but hadn't seen each other again until that snowy day when *Quest* arrived at the southern rim of the earth. I soon found out that such was often the course of life in the world of ocean science.

Welcoming activities ended abruptly as the station men hurried ashore to get their mail. Most of the crew went along. The skipper, Art, Beebee and I were invited to supper by George Reszke, the station manager. We had a couple of drinks at a small bar in the lounge before eating. George, a civil engineer, was a physically sound, psychologically "safe" and well adjusted individual in his early forties. The son of Polish immigrants, he made a worthy contribution to the U.S. Antarctic presence.

Louis Berg, the station cook, had prepared a feast. He was a rotund, jolly individual, with a smile and a joke ready at all times. He was called "Bitsy Berg" by his mates, and played a most important role during the long, dark winter, since mealtimes were the high point of their grim life, surpassed only by the evening movies.

After supper, we sat in the lounge chatting and gossiping. Our conversation soon got around to the unusual animal behavior.

Captain Pack recounted the conversation he'd had by radio with Don Marsh on Tierra del Fuego a few days before. "The people are alarmed," he said. "There seems to be some sort of sinister influence affecting all kinds of animals, both ashore and in the sea."

I added, "And apparently in the air too. These matters have been noticed in New York, and elsewhere around the world."

We continued our discussion until the manager set up a projector, pulled down a screen at the other end of the dining room, and ran a film. Another film was sent to the ship and shown there. Some of the men watched the movies. Others went off to their quarters reading and answering their mail.

Larry and Carol took a stroll arm in arm, up the rocky road toward the helicopter pad, a steel plated deck overlooking the station buildings, the harbor and the glacier. They were accompanied by Princesa, a young husky dog, the station mascot, playing and cavorting in the snow around them.

Larry said, "We've always had a lot of fun with

36

Princesa. She's one spoiled pup. But lately we have noticed something peculiar. Our M.D. has been watching her carefully. She seems normal enough tonight, but sometimes she just stands and growls at nothing at all.''

Carol replied, "Animals are acting strangely everywhere, but tonight let's talk about us.''

The sun was still above the horizon in the southwest, casting its bright rays on the snow covered hills, high peaks, glistening icebergs and glacier cliffs across the harbor. Carol and Larry sat huddled together on a big, smooth boulder and talked of their future. The soft roar and splash of massive chunks breaking off the end of the glacier, the distant squawking of skuas and gulls, and the occasional laughter and music from the station faintly floated through the cold air to them.

Knowing that they might have only one evening together, Larry suggested they seek more privacy. "Why don't we go over there on Bonapart Point, across the inlet?'' he asked.

"You mean, way up there over the glacier, and around to that point? That's too much walking for me, and anyway, we'd need snowshoes, wouldn't we? And it looks dangerous,'' said Carol.

"Not at all,'' Larry replied. "We don't have to go that way. I'll show you. Come with me.'' He led her toward the inlet, and they climbed together over the rocks.

Access to Bonaparte Point was by a cable stretched across from one rocky bank to the other over the ice filled water. There was a seat, like a simple chair lift, or boatswain's chair, hanging from a block with a pulley by which the rider could pull himself, or be pulled, across the inlet.

Larry assured Carol it was safe, so they went over. There they found a secluded place, behind the boulders, out of sight of everyone. Larry tied the chair to their end, so nobody could intrude, and there they spent several peaceful and happy hours as the daylight waned, making up for their long separation. Oblivious to the cold, they surrendered to the strong urges of their love and passion, and to the natural gratification of their desires.

The short austral night had nearly passed when Larry brought Carol back to *Quest*, and returned to his quarters in the station.

Quest was scheduled to leave next morning. Carol would be helping Beebee for the next few weeks. Larry was to leave with his group upon the arrival of the icebreaker *Southwind*, which would bring the scientists and support personnel who would occupy the station during the months ahead. Larry's group would be transported to McMurdo and from there the men would be flown to New Zealand on their way to the U.S.A. Larry thought he would ask the manager, George Reszke, to let him stay over and go back in a couple of months when *Quest* would make a mid season trip to Punta Arenas. In that way, he could see Carol occasionally during the next two months when *Quest* made stops at Palmer. It was a daydream, but it might work. In the morning, Larry and Carol found out it could be done. Larry was given permission to remain at Palmer and continue his investigations. It was a welcome break for the young couple.

Quest left early, backing slowly away from the dock, avoiding large chunks of ice and small bergs floating in Arthur Harbor. Carol stood on deck and waved to Larry until the station was lost to view behind Bonaparte Point.

During the next two weeks, *Quest* stopped at coves, inlets and bays along Gerlache Strait, then moved on toward the South Shetlands. Beebee and Carol were very busy. Day after day and far into the nights they toiled, sorting and recording samples of marine biological specimens brought up from the bottom along the way. There were holothurians, sponges, tunicates, polychaetes, small white clams, euphausiids, scaphopods, starfishes, anemones, snails, and many other creatures, all thriving in that frigid environment. The ship's officers and crew were busy with trawls and grabs, often in severe cold wind on deck at the winch. Beebee worked as hard as any man, helping to pull the nets in over the rail, with hands cold and wet, transferring the hauls into the lab. She recorded depths at the fathometer, converting them to meters and, always smiling and pleasant, worked far into the wee hours sorting out her collections. Carol, often cold and weary, but enthusiastic and excited, helped with all the details. The skipper and mates, busy with the navigation in the dangerous and often uncharted waters, maneuvered to achieve the best results for the important scientific studies.

As *Quest* made one of the short runs northeastward between working areas, a red-hulled passenger vessel appeared some distance off our port side. It was the cruise ship *Sinbad*, slowly moving in the opposite direction. The ships exchanged courtesy signals by sounding three long blasts, first *Sinbad*, then *Quest*. Those were followed by one short blast by each ship.

I stood, with several others, on *Quest's* main deck. I listened to the greetings of the ships with a sense of nostalgia, recalling the cruise I had made on *Sinbad* two years previously. I thought about those wealthy, pampered tourists, enjoying their Antarctic visit in extravagant comfort, and compared them with the hard-working, often cold and exhausted scientists and crew on our modest research trawler. I didn't envy the tourists. Surely my shipmates were much happier, involved in their scientific achievements, and ignoring their discomforts. It was, nevertheless, a pleasure to meet another vessel in Antarctic waters. There were so very few. I watched *Sinbad* move southward until the luxury vessel was lost to view among large icebergs.

As I observed Beebee at her work, my admiration for her kept growing stronger. I was becoming so interested in her that I sought excuses to be in her company as often as possible. I'm sure she noticed, but she didn't seem to mind. I knew that, sooner or later, I must tell her of my feelings for her.

2

INVESTIGATION OF the bottom dwellers went on. Beebee and Carol busily sorted net hauls of copopeds, serolid isopods, tunicates, and other small specimens, some juicy, some slimy, all useful in determining the nature of the local benthic populations.

For a while I listened to a news broadcast in the radio room. It was disturbing, to say the least. Energy shortages, unemployment, starvation, nations at war—the world seemed fraught with problems. I went up to the bridge where I found Paul Shelley, the second mate, scowling at some figures in his navigation work book. I said, "You look like you're fed up with the whole world."

Paul looked up, still scowling. "It's worse than that, Jamie," he replied. "I'm fed up with myself. A while ago I was showing Carol how we navigate by the sun. I took a sight with my sextant, but I couldn't get the figures to work out. Something's screwy. I can't take another sight— too many islands—no horizon. I'll show her tomorrow."

I sympathized with Paul, and went down to the after lab. There I spent a couple of hours watching Beebee and Carol at their work. It was nearly 2300, and the long daylight hours were ending when they finished operations off Hoseason Island. We then went back to the mess room for a snack before turning in.

After getting the ship underway toward Livingston Island, Captain Pack joined us around the table. "We have a message from the Varanys at Harmony Cove," he said. "They want to be picked up and moved to another island. They say the birds are acting peculiarly. We'll pick up Dr. Larsen and his assistants at Livingston Island, then get the Varanys."

"All this strange animal behavior," I said. "What does it mean?"

Almost angrily, Carol said, "I don't know, but if it keeps on much longer, we'll all go wacky!"

I could see that Beebee and Carol were both very tired. I said, "You better get some horizontal, both of you. Before you know it, you'll be acting like the rest of the animals."

Beebee sleepily replied, "Speak for yourself, James. Come on, Carol, it's midnight. This is no place for us poor working girls."

They retired to their cabin. Pack moved closer to me, and in a solemn tone said, "I was listening to an international news broadcast this evening. I didn't get all of it, but something very serious is going on. Scientists and environmentalists are up in arms. They want more money for crash programs to determine what is happening. There are alarming news reports, and great numbers of people are nervous. Even the astronomers are having some sort of hassle."

We were joined by Chief Engineer Jesse Lytel. "I heard some of that broadcast, too," he said. "Someone in Congress said the nations of the world are spending a total of four hundred billion dollars a year on armaments, but not enough on research to cure a sick billy goat. And they go right ahead and vote to send several billion dollars worth of additional arms to some foreign country."

"Arms inevitably lead to war," I said. "Over fifty million lives were lost in World War II alone, and millions more in Vietnam and other conflicts since then. So you can imagine what the next world war will cost in lives with all the new, sophisticated weapons."

Captain Pack remarked sarcastically, "They provide billions of dollars for arms, yet *Quest*, tight little trawler that she is, should have been replaced long ago by a fine, large modern research vessel like the Russians' *Professor Viese,* with many laboratories and some two hundred scientists and technicians on board.''

"Right," echoed the chief, "and that's not the only big, modern ship Russia has on worldwide research.''

"Well, that's enough philosophizing for one night. See you in the morning," said the skipper. "Good night."

I soon followed his example and went to sleep thinking about those four hundred billion dollars a year, and what tremendous good it could be doing if it were used for peaceful pursuits. It seemed that I was hardly asleep, when I was awakened by a strange knocking, or thudding, against the hull of the ship. At first I thought we were going through a loose ice pack. I tried to dismiss it from my mind, and go back to sleep, but suddenly I was wide awake. I heard people shouting, and running through the mess room. I slipped on my pants, grabbed my jacket, and hurried up to the main deck. There before my eyes appeared a scene I shall never forget, a scene which made me shudder.

Quest was not going through any ice pack. We were plowing through a seething pack of killer whales. Hundreds of the sleek, black and white creatures were rampant in the sea around us. They seemed to be in a sort of angry frenzy, dashing headlong against the sides of the ship, and leaping into the air. Some of them nearly made it onto the deck.

We kept on at full speed, but the whales stayed right with us for about an hour. Their bodies churned the water in a spectacular display that was, in the semidarkness, both fascinating and frightening. Nearly all the ship's company had come on deck. We watched with apprehension while the bizarre scene lasted. Finally the whales disappeared.

We all turned in again. I couldn't sleep. I was sure that others were also troubled. It was a weird and alarming phenomenon, and I wondered what the future would bring.

Quest arrived at Livingston Island early in the morning

and took Dr. Larsen and his two assistants, Mike Vogt and Per Thysen, aboard.

I watched Per Thysen unobtrusively. Neither his demeanor nor his attitude toward me gave me any clue to the cause of his continued anger. If his hostility was the result of something I had written in the past, he kept quiet about it. And I had no desire to disrupt the scientific program in which Thysen was involved by confronting him.

We departed Livingston Island as soon as Dr. Larsen, Mike Vogt, and Thysen were on board. There was a slight swell, and *Quest* swayed a little after we got away from the anchorage. Mike and Thysen were busy stowing and recording some ice samples and cores which they had brought out in the zodiac, bringing them in from the forward deck and stacking them in a big reefer, or walk-in refrigerator, just off the port side of the after lab. I stood near Mike, taking some notes as he described some of the ice samples.

"This core could be several thousand years old," he said. "And some of these chunks of ice may have been formed way back in time, possibly just after the great flood of Noah's day. We'll preserve them here in this reefer at temperatures below zero, and later take them ashore and analyze them, and also study whatever fossils we may discover in them."

I stood with Mike inside the reefer. Per Thysen was outside passing the samples in to Mike. I was engrossed in making notes and bracing myself against the slight roll of the ship. I didn't notice when Mike went out. Suddenly I heard a swishing sound behind me. I quickly turned and saw that the big heavy insulated door of the reefer was swinging shut. I lunged toward it to keep it from closing, but I was too late. The door closed and the latch clicked. I was in total darkness. I stumbled and fell over chunks of ice. I shouted and struggled to push the door open, but my shouts were in vain.

I searched around the door trying to find the safety ring

which I could pull to unlatch the door. I was getting cold. My hands were numb. I wore thermal underclothing, but I hadn't put on any warm jacket, thinking I would be in that cold temperature only momentarily.

I groped for the emergency release ring. Finally I found it, but when I pulled with all my might, nothing happened. Something was wrong with the mechanism. I shouted again, but I heard no reply through those thick insulated walls. I was trapped. My whole body began to feel the penetration of that sub-zero chill. I decided that I must keep moving. How long could I survive? How long would the oxygen last?

And what about Per Thysen? I was certain that he had been there on the outside. Would Mike come back? Had they stowed all their samples and left? These thoughts raced through my mind as I tried to move around and stamp my feet which were beginning to feel like the chunks of ice around me. My teeth chattered and I began to shiver. I shouted again and again, though I feared it was useless. I suspected Per Thysen had deliberately slammed the reefer door. I began to despair and fear for my life. Gradually I sank to the deck and lay across some of the chunks of ice. I became drowsy.

What seemed to be hours later, I heard voice, far away. Just soft murmuring. Gradually I regained consciousness. I vaguely saw faces looking down at me. In a few moments, I recognized Beebee's face close to mine. She was saying my name. "Jamie—Jamie, can you hear me? You're going to be all right, Jamie! We got you out just in time! Do you hear, Jamie?! You'll be *all right!*"

I couldn't reply, but I tried to nod my head. Slowly I began to recall what had happened and I realized that I'd been rescued and was lying stretched out on the long table in the after lab. I heard the voices of Captain Pack and Dr. Larsen questioning Per Thysen and Mike Vogt. I heard Thysen mumbling contemptuous responses.

"I to't he shut d'dam door 'imself an' went away f'm dere," Thysen growled. "W'at d'hell biznus did 'e have goin' in dere anyhow?''

Elbow Larsen cut in, "Let's get this straight. From the beginning—Mike, how did it happen?"

"I've been wondering myself," replied Mike Vogt. "When I left, Thysen was standing outside, and Jamie was just inside the door taking some notes. I went to see if we had left any ice samples in the zodiac."

"Yeah," interrupted Thysen, "an' I went after 'im t'help bring 'em in."

Captain Pack's tone was sharp and scornful. "You mean to tell me you left Howard alone in that reefer?"

"So w'at—'e could come out by 'imself, couldn' 'e?" Thysen sullenly asked.

Mike continued his account. "There were no more samples in the zodiac, so I started back to the reefer. I met Thysen coming along the passageway and told him there were no more samples. He said he would go back and close the reefer if Jamie was finished. Then I went to my cabin."

"Yeah," said Thysen, "an w'en I got back 'ere d'door was shut—so I t'ot d'guy 'ad shut it 'imself an' gone away. D'damn lashin' musta come loose."

"It was broken," said Dr. Larsen. "It must've parted from the roll of the ship, and let the door slam shut."

"After a while I went looking for Jamie," Mike added. "I looked in the lab and didn't see him there. I opened the reefer to see if our samples were all stowed properly—and there was Jamie, lying on the deck almost dead. He wouldn't have lasted much longer."

Finally I regained my full senses, due in part to Beebee's tender care. They put me on a stretcher and carried me to my cabin to recuperate. I kept murmuring, "Dear, dear Beebee," over and over. She stayed by my side until I fell asleep.

When I awakened I resolved that I would have an understanding with Captain Pack about Thysen's attitude. I strongly suspected that he had deliberately broken the tieback and slammed the door of the reefer in an attempt to kill me, but I really couldn't prove it. When I got an opportunity to talk with the captain about it, he was sympathetic.

"I'm certain Thysen intends to do away with me," I said. "I think he's dangerous, and possibly mentally unbalanced."

"I've had suspicions myself about Thysen," replied the skipper. "I'll have a talk with Dr. Larsen about him." Then as an afterthought, he added, "All these people who come to the ship are supposed to have been carefully screened in Washington, but it's not beyond comprehension that some characters who should never be allowed to come do squeeze through. Meanwhile, I'll try to keep an eye on Thysen, and I'm sure you will be careful, after what has already happened." There was no doubt in my mind about that!

Quest proceeded to Harmony Cove at Nelson Island to embark Dr. Varany and his wife, Dr. Nancy Varany. We anchored in the cove and sent a zodiac to pick them up. There was much ice floating along the rocky shore, and it took a lot of maneuvering to get the zodiac through it. Four trips were made to bring all the Varanys' gear out to the ship.

Arnold and Nancy Varany had spent their time during those past three weeks recording data about the Adelie penguins on and around a point of land at the west side of the cove. They estimated there were some ten thousand nests in that rookery.

At supper that evening, Dr. Varany and his wife entertained us by talking about the penguins. They showed us some of the small stones and shells with which the male birds form the nests on the ground in November.

"We had a good opportunity again this year," recounted Dr. Varany, "to observe the hatching of the chicks. The parents take turns incubating the eggs, each one staying on the nest for a couple of weeks while the other goes into the ocean for food. The female leaves first, right after laying the two eggs. By the time she returns to the nest to take over the incubating, the male has been ashore without food for about five weeks. Sometimes the rookeries are snowed in and covered over by blizzards—nests, eggs, birds and all. They huddle down under the snow keeping just a small hole over them for air.''

"You can see their heads down in the hole," added Nancy. "They stay on the eggs no matter how deep the snow gets."

Dr. Varany continued, "After the chicks are about three weeks old, the parents start to take off. The chicks gather in groups which we call creeches. The parents bring them food, and the young huddle together to keep warm. Some time next month, those chicks will start molting, and their waterproofing process will begin. The downy baby coat is exchanged for feathers which have a natural oil, and they also develop fat under the skin, all of which helps them in the cold environment, the snow and the water."

"Did you notice any strange behavior?" I asked.

"Yes," Nancy replied. "We noticed unusual behavior of the adult penguins this year. For the past week or more, they have been extremely restless. Large groups of birds, coming in from the sea, seemed disoriented. Some came in eastward along the island and then made their way here. They would go back into the water and swim along the coast as if looking for their rookery. We've never seen such odd behavior."

"That's true," agreed Dr. Varany. "The whole rookery was strangely upset by something. The birds were unusually noisy, and it seems to me that large numbers of them haven't come back yet to relieve their mates. This is certainly most peculiar. They are usually very precise about such things."

Beebee asked, "How do penguins find their way around? We see them so far out on the ocean, they certainly can't see their way back. Have they got some kind of built-in compass or direction finder?"

"They sure have," confirmed Varany. "It's not a compass exactly. It has been well established by various experiments that they go by the sun. They can guide themselves in a general direction toward their home areas by the sun, even allowing for its constant change all day long, until they get close enough to find the right island or point of land.''

Captain Pack said, ''When it's overcast or snowing, I suppose they must occasionally get lost.''

''No, not for long,'' countered Dr. Varany. ''They are quite sensitive to light and stay fairly well on course.''

''How about durin' the' winter when it's dark here all th' time?'' asked Paul Shelley, the second mate.

''They go farther north in the winter, riding the ice floes and swimming,'' said Varney. ''They stay away from the breeding grounds for about eight months, then come back for the nesting season in October, so they're mostly in the pack ice during the months of total darkness.''

''Why do you think they are getting lost now?'' I asked.

''There you have me stumped, Jamie,'' replied Varany. ''I never saw anything like this before. We haven't had any real darkness. As a matter of fact, it has seemed lighter than usual during the two or three hours each night that we usually have some darkness.''

Paul Shelley carefully considered the last statement. He later said that in thinking back over those past few nights, he was inclined to agree. He wondered if there might have been some auroral display which we hadn't seen because of the high mountain range on the peninsula, but which might have been reflected into the sky by the icecap over the continent. It was just a fleeting thought which he dismissed as unlikely. Sometimes strange things occurred in polar regions. He thought about the false result he had gotten the evening before, when he had tried to demonstrate a simple sight reduction to Carol.

''Anyway,'' Paul said to Carol, ''th' penguins aren't th' only ones who have navigation problems.''

Carol asked, ''Did you ever get the observation figured out?''

''Nope,'' replied Paul.

After supper *Quest* trawled and grabbed near Harmony

Cove for a few hours, to fill Beebee's jars and bottles with bottom dwellers. Snow had fallen all afternoon and evening. The decks were covered in white when we anchored for the night to rest.

Unknown to us, some events had taken place in Washington during those past few days related to a mysterious world-wide phenomenon which had scientists and political authorities baffled. Later I learned the details.

We were aware the radio news had carried some brief comments about it, but little was yet known, and the information given by astronomers seemed so highly technical that the signficance was generally overlooked by the media. There were some vague reports about a "celestial phenomenon" which astronomers classed as "significant." Others reported that astronomers were "evaluating" the situation to determine whether or not it might have some effect on world temperatures. Nothing specific could be determined for a few days.

The "few days" had passed, and we on board *Quest* hadn't long to wait for something "specific" indeed.

In Harmony Cove on that strangely luminous night of December solstice, a shimmering tableau of cresent shore and violet shadows appeared in illusory perspective. Headland and strand, ice cliffs and drifting floes, were richly adorned as with emerald and pearl. Umber sentinel rocks boldly guarded the bank, their sculptured ridges silhouetted sharply against a hillside coverlet of snow. A refuge hut with white-topped roof stood lonely vigil upon a deserted shore. Restless penguins in the nearby rookery made uneasy sounds as if disturbed by some mysterious invader.

Quest lay quietly at anchor with nearly everyone asleep. Faint crackling of floating ice was heard as the tide carried it slowly along the sides of the ship.

Midnight had passed. In the wheelhouse, Second Mate Paul Shelley entered the new day's date, December 22, in the log book, and perched himself on a stool to keep his weary watch. I couldn't sleep that night, and kept Paul company. He wondered why the sky remained so light. At 0330 the wheelhouse Seth Thomas clock softly struck its "three pair and one." Paul and I started to go below, I to my cabin, and Paul to awaken his relief. But suddenly we heard Palmer Station calling. Paul stepped into the radio room and picked up the mike. "Research Vessel *Quest*," he answered.

Palmer's ET, Ira Mason, didn't conceal his excitement. Almost shouting, he said, "I have a very urgent and important message for Captain Pack. Please call him, and your ET, Enrique. This is urgent! Over."

"Roger," replied Paul.

"What the—" I didn't finish my sentence.

Paul glanced at me. The look on his face was grave. He immediately rang the phone to Icepack's room. "Sorry to disturb you, sir. There's an urgent message from Palmer. They want to give it to you personally, an' want Enrique to copy."

The skipper wearily answered, "Okay, Paul, I'll be right up."

I stayed in the wheelhouse while Paul went below and roused the ET and Chief Mate Harry King.

At Palmer Station nearly every one had been asleep, but George Reszke hadn't yet turned in. He was in the radio room with Ira Mason listening to traffic between the Icebreaker *Southwind* and McMurdo Station. Reszke was tired, and he had finally started to leave for his room.

"Wait a minute, George," said Mason, "here's something for us." They listened in growing amazement as an urgent message was slowly and carefully spelled out, a message for both Palmer and *Quest*. Reszke grabbed the intercom mike.

Suddenly, the tranquility of Palmer Station was shattered by the manager's urgent voice. "Attention all station personnel! Report immediately to the lounge! I have an important announcement!"

In a few minutes all the men, some in pajamas, some in shorts, gathered around George Reszke as he read the most astonishing message ever heard by modern man.

On board *Quest,* the skipper and Salaverry reached the radio room at the same time. Salaverry answered Palmer, then Ira Mason transmitted the message slowly and precisely, spelling out some words letter by letter and symbols for punctuation. As the message unfolded, all of us in the radio room stiffened and held our breaths, hanging on each word. We couldn't utter a sound. This is what we heard, and this is the way the message appeared as it was typed by Enrique and handed to Captain Pack:

INCOMING MCMURDO
22 DEC 0610Z
07 0557Z DEC 22
FM NSF POLAR WASHDC
TO MASTER RV QUEST
INFO NSF REP ANT/NSF REP NZ/PA
LMER STA
BT
UNCLAS
NR 16
SUBJ SAILORD
1. WORLDWIDE ASTRONOMICAL OBSERVATOR-
IES REPORT UNKNOWN FORCE APPARENTLY
CAUSING INCREASE IN OBLIQUITY OF ECLIPTIC.
PROBABLE RISING TEMPERATURES POLAR RE-
GIONS.
2. QUEST TO EVACUATE ALL USARP LIVINGSTON
NELSON ISLANDS AND PROCEED IMMEDIATELY
EVACUATE ALL PERSONNEL PALMER STATION.
3. MAINTAIN CONSTANT CONTACT PALMER
STATION FOR LATER ADVISORIES.
BT

At Palmer, there was complete silence as the men watched the manager lower the message to the table. The impact of the situation had robbed them of speech. Then they all began at once in excited voices to exclaim,

"Where's *Quest*?" "Yeah, where the hell is *Quest*?" The answer came quickly.

In *Quest's* radio room Pack made a fast calculation, then scribbled a reply, which Enrique immediately transmitted:

LARSEN, VOGT, THYSEN, BOTH VARANYS EMBARKED. PROCEEDING TO PALMER. ETA TOMORROW TWENTY THREE DECEMBER ABOUT 0300 ZULU.

The skipper rushed outside and gazed into the sky. The sun was very close above the southern horizon. It was broad daylight in all directions. The temperature had risen noticeably. Rays of sunlight were showing through distant peaks along the Graham Coast to the east. The skipper went back to the telephone. "Chief!" he called. "Chief!"

In a moment, Jessie Lytel's voice came through as if out of a deep cavern. "Yes, Cap?"

"Jesse!—Jesse—we have an emergency!" The skipper tried to subdue his emotions and speak in a calm voice. "Jesse, something's happened to the world. Get the engines warmed up fast. Let me know just as soon as we can move. Jesse—we must evacuate our people at Palmer! Come up here when you can."

Jesse said later the skipper sounded as if he had swallowed his upper plate. He didn't lose any time. Within thirty seconds, he had both main engines warming up.

Pack called on the intercom. He had switched to ALL SHIP, and raised his voice. "Attention, all hands! Hear this! We have an emergency! Stand by to heave anchor. Stand by to get under way. We must evacuate our people at Palmer. Get moving! On the double!"

There was great excitement throughout the ship. The crew and scientists scrambled out of their bunks as the skipper's voice resounded throughout the quarters. Within fifteen minutes we had the anchor up and were moving out of Harmony Cove, still warming up the engines. Soon *Quest* was up to full speed, heading toward Gerlache Strait and Palmer. As we passed Greenwich Island, the sun came to view through the snow covered peaks across Bransfield Strait on the peninsula. We watched with awe as it moved upward, casting long shafts of light through the clear atmosphere. The temperature rose unseasonably, becoming exceedingly warm. We discarded our jackets.

At Palmer, excitement mounted. "When will *Quest* get here?" "Are we in danger now?" "How about *Southwind?*"

Some went to the windows to see if the whole world was turning upside down.

"It's lighter than usual."

"It's getting warm!"

"Will all the snow melt?"

Ira Mason spoke up. "I relayed the message to *Quest* a few minutes ago. They're at Nelson Island. They've already picked up Dr. Larsen's group and the Varanys. They're coming immediately and should be here late tonight. McMurdo says they are also evacuating. Several planes are already there from New Zealand removing men from McMurdo, Pole, Byrd and other areas—general evacuation of all polar stations. Russia and England are going out too. Haven't heard from the Chileans nor the Argentines yet."

The babble of voices rose in crescendo as the baffling situation began to strike home. Again someone exclaimed, "How about the *Southwind?*"

Mason answered, "I don't know exactly. I know they're near. They left Punta Arenas four days ago. They must be here tonight, unless they get diverted to McMurdo."

"That means we'd have to go back to *Quest,*" Larry said hopefully.

"Yup, looks like it. She'll be crowded," Mason said, and returned to the radio room. Art Allen and George Reszke went with him. They listened to messages being transmitted in rapid order between McMurdo and other polar stations, and between *Southwind* and McMurdo. They heard one message which confirmed their earlier conjectures: *Southwind* was close, but would be diverted to complete evacuation of McMurdo. They would have to depend on *Quest*. During the morning, they overheard considerable activity on the Argentine frequency, apparently between Orcadas, Buenos Aires, and Deception stations. They didn't understand it, but something very serious was happening. It wasn't a mystery for long. McMurdo called Palmer.

"Palmer Station," answered Mason.

The voice over the radio said, "Relay following to RV *Quest:*

ARGENTINA REQUESTS FIVE MEN BE EVACU-ATED FROM DECEPTION IF QUEST IN VICIN-ITY. INTENSE SEISMIC AND VOLCANIC ACT-IVITY AT DECEPTION.

"Roger," replied Mason. He called *Quest* to relay the message.

Quest was bowling along at top speed toward Gerlache Strait and Palmer. Suddenly, ahead and slightly to starboard, a low dark spot appeared near the horizon. The skipper, mates and myself, and others who had come on deck, stared spellbound at the dark widening spot as we watched it slowly rise, forming a column of black smoke, expanding like a cloud at the top. Three more columns were forming and rising near the first.

"Good grief!" exclaimed Pack. "That's Deception Island! That's an eruption! Look! It's spreading north! I wonder if anyone is at the Argentine Station. Enrique, have you been talking to any of your friends at Deception? Do you know if the station has been occupied yet this season?"

"Yes, Captain," replied the ET. "Last I heard, there

were five men there. They're still there. I'll call them." As he spoke, we heard *Quest* being called again. "*Quest* here," answered Enrique.

"*Quest*, this is Palmer. Argentina requests you evacuate five persons from Deception Island. Increasing seismic activity reported there. Fear new volcanic eruptions. Over."

The skipper grabbed the microphone. "Roger! Roger!" he answered excitedly. "We have Deception in view. Eruptions are now going on! High columns of smoke are rising from the island. Looks like four or five separate eruptions. Big black cloud forming over Deception. Wait one!" He turned to the second mate. "Paul, give me an ETA at Deception." Paul quickly took a radar range. The columns of smoke stood out clearly on the screen.

"Twenty-one miles, sir," Paul calculated. "About 1100."

"Palmer, this is *Quest*. ETA Deception about 1100. I won't know until I get there if I can go in or not." Pack's voice revealed his anxiety. "It looks bad from here—we'll do the best we can to get those men out. Over."

"Roger, Captain Pack," replied Mason's voice from Palmer. "Please keep us informed. Palmer out."

"Enrique, see if you can contact those guys at Deception, and tell them we're going to try to evacuate them," ordered the skipper.

The ship advanced rapidly toward the island. The black clouds grew larger, expanding as we drew nearer. The island was almost obscured by the smoke which also extended northward over Livingston Island. *Quest* had been inside the crater many times, and Pack was thoroughly familiar with the hazards involved.

He told Enrique to ask the Argentines if they could go over the hills behind the station so *Quest* might pick them up outside on the west shore of the island. That would make it unnecessary for *Quest* to go inside the caldera. Pack knew that area, having climbed over those hills on a visit to the station long ago. He recalled there were small crater ponds up there. The Argentines replied that it was impossible for them to attempt to go over the hills. The craters there had suddenly become active, and were spewing forth fire. Burning fragments were falling all around, even onto the roofs of the buildings. There was no other way they could go. *Quest* would have to pick them up inside the caldera. They urged, "Please hurry! We're afraid the buildings will burn!"

In Palmer's radio room, Art Allen, George Reszke, and Ira Mason listened with apprehension to Pack's announcement that he could see columns of smoke at Deception. They then heard McMurdo and *Southwind* discussing a possible change in *Southwind's* orders. In view of *Quest's* diversion to Deception, *Southwind* was again ordered to Palmer. *Southwind* was close to Palmer, and the ship was expected to arrive in three hours. George Reszke picked up the radio room intercom microphone.

"Attention, all station personnel." His voice betrayed his excitement. "*Southwind* is due at Palmer in three hours! All hands prepare to evacuate and board *Southwind!*"

Most of the men needed no second invitation. Their baggage had been packed for hours. There were whoops of joy as they scurried around getting their belongings down the stairway. Only Larry Field felt despondent. When would he see Carol? He went to the radio room in hope of talking with her, where he learned that *Quest* was heading into Deception amid volcanic eruptions, and his anxiety mounted for Carol's safety. Art and George left the radio room to get their things together to leave the station. George spoke to engineer Hugh McGregor and others about shutting down the station generators, closing fuel valves, and draining water lines. Station shutdown procedures had to be followed. The station would be carefully secured, and familiar abandon procedures observed. Everyone had his duties and set about them with utmost speed.

A large mobile hydraulic crane was moved from the dock area and parked at its usual place in front of the main building, just beyond the steel flag pole. Hank closed it up and secured it. It was a heavy piece of equipment, standing high on its big, deep treaded tires, which were taller than a man.

Princesa the husky chased excitedly around, puzzled by all the sudden activity. Larry Field, who had always taken special care of Princesa, said, "I'm going to take her with me. We're not going to leave her here. I'll look after her on the icebreaker."

Deception Island was thought to have once been a group of volcanoes partly superimposed on each other in an arc of some seven or eight miles outside diameter. Eruptions of the group, and subsequent collapse of the large central crater, or caldera, had left a sea level basin surrounded by hills of lava, cinders, and ice.

Beyond the narrow entrance, past a high cliff, and on the right, or north side, was a small embayment skirted by a beach and a short expanse of flat terrain. That was Whalers Bay, behind which black hills rose abruptly, their summits encrusted with ashes and snow. Near the beach stood some old buildings, the ruins of long abandoned try-works which had weathered a century of blizzards and eruptions.

Beyond Whalers Bay, the caldera opened out to a sheltered tidal basin, some six miles long and four miles wide, called Port Foster. It was well protected from the sea by the surrounding cinder and ice covered hills, the highest of which were Mount Kirkwood on the south, and Mount Pond, on the east. Lower hills formed the rest of the rim around the crater. Several of them had erupted individually and collectively at various times through the years, some more recently, attesting to the continued volcanic proclivity of the region. Station personnel at the Chilean base in Pendulum Cove on the northeast rim of the caldera, had to flee toward Whalers Bay under a shower of hot ashes and volcanic particles illuminated by volcanic flashes during an eruption on December 4, 1967. Several eruptions had occurred since then, and earthquakes, or tremors of varied intensity, were registered almost daily. Steam rose constantly around the edge of the caldera indicating to some volcanists that a molten magma chamber deep below was heating a superficial aquifer, giving rise to the fumaroles around the basin at the water's edge. That activity had never ceased through the years.

The Argentine base calling for help was located on the southwest rim of the caldera facing a wide cinder beach where there were several low buildings and radio towers. Snow-covered hills of rock, cinders and ice rose gently behind the buildings. There were also some small crater lakes among the hills. The station personnel at that time consisted only of the four Argentines and one Britisher. They were seriously engaged in a study of the volcanic and earthquake activity. No other people were on the island.

Pack turned to the intercom. He spoke rapidly. "Elbow and Harry, please come to the bridge." He then called the engine room. "Jesse, please come to the bridge."

"Aye, sir," the chief crisply answered.

Soon the four men and I stood in the chart room. The temperature had climbed to the mid fifties. We had discarded our customary thermoclothing and were in shirt sleeves and T-shirts. The sun was higher than it had ever been in that region in the recorded history of man.

"I want to have a short conference," Pack hurriedly began. "You all know the dangers of going into that inferno to get those men out." He pointed to a chart of Deception Island. "Dr. Larsen, you are familiar with the geology of Deception and the previous eruptions. The Argentines tell us that these new eruptions are mostly over where they were last time—on the north and east side." He indicated the area of Pendulum Cove, Telefon Bay and Yelcho Island. "But," he continued, "they also say there have been some explosions closer to their station at *Primero de Mayo*," he pointed to the location of the

Argentine Station on the west side of Port Foster, "the one the Chileans call *Fumarolas Bay*."

"Yes, Cap," Dr. Larsen spoke soberly. "That *is* bad! There are probably some new fissures up through those fumarolic vents along the beach. From what they say, it looks as if a larger area is erupting this time, but the wind is blowing the smoke northward."

Harry spoke up. "That, at least, is in our favor, but it's only a light breeze, and we could get a shower of hot ashes in there."

"Yes," said Jesse. "And some big burning chunks might fall on the ship."

Captain Pack spoke with determination. "We'll have to keep her wet. We'll need plenty of water on the deck. Chief, I hope you can give us a lot of pressure on the fire line."

"I'll stand right over that pump."

"Have all extinguishers ready, and the CO_2 system for the engine room."

"All hands'll be on it, Cap. Just get us in and out before the whole shebang goes up in there."

"The eruptions are an hour and a half apart," calculated Dr. Larsen. "How long will it take you to go in, get the men, and get out?"

"I can get into the Argentine Station in about half an hour. Same time out. That will give us about half an hour to get the men aboard," the skipper said. He knew it would be a close call, with the risk that an eruption might occur off schedule at any time. The fact that new eruption locations had been observed by the men inside added much greater peril to the undertaking.

Harry said, "We'll keep 'er wet down and close 'er up tight. It'll be hot below."

"Harry, get all hands up here so we can explain what we want each one to do." The skipper's voice was firm. "Dr. Larsen, please talk to all the scientists and assign duties. Have the three women and Dr. Varany take care of any casualties. There may be burns."

The mate's voice boomed over the intercom. "Attention all hands! We are goin' into Deception. Come to th' after deck right away! Th' Captain'll give you instructions there."

While we waited for the group to assemble, I took the opportunity to consult with the skipper. "Captain Pack, I'd like your permission to remain on deck when you go into Deception."

Pack frowned. "It's going to be dangerous! You might get hurt!"

I wouldn't back down. I persisted, "I'm here to take pictures and do a story. I've been in tight spots before! Lots of them!" I managed a forced laugh. "Besides, if this is the end of our world, someone has to record it for posterity, right?"

Pack drew a sharp breath. He thought for a moment. Then he slowly exhaled, and reluctantly agreed. "OK! OK, you've made your point. You stay on deck. But be careful! That's an order, Howard!"

Soon the entire crew, except the engineer on watch and the second mate in the wheelhouse, were assembled on the after deck.

Captain Pack spoke quickly. "You all know what has happened. We have been asked to go in and evacuate five men from the Argentine Station at Deception. We'll be going into an old sunken crater, or 'caldera.' That means 'boiler' in Spanish. As you can see from here, there's a lot of volcanic activity. The Argentines tell us the whole area is shaking with earthquakes, with the main eruptions occurring about every hour and a half. I think we can go in and get them out between eruptions. We'll keep the decks wet down, but there is risk of fire—and even loss of the ship. On the other hand, we have a good chance of getting the men out." The skipper paused for a few seconds. He glanced quickly at each member of his crew. When he spoke again, his voice was low and deliberate. "Now, I don't want to *force* anybody to go in there."

Big Harry King, Dr. Elbow Larsen and Chief Jesse Lytel

instinctively moved closer to Icepack as he spoke. A ship master's life is a lonely one at times. When danger looms, he alone must make the decisions, often hard ones. The burden of human lives rests upon him alone. Right or wrong, the responsibility is his. Mistakes are too costly. He can't delegate final authority. The impulsive movement of big, usually dour Harry King, ebullient Elbow Larsen and able Cranky Lytel, all veterans of ice and storm, nearer to the skipper as he faced the ship's company, didn't go unnoticed by Pack. Their gesture spoke louder than words, as if to say, "We're with you, skipper."

Captain Pack continued. "If any of you would rather not risk it, we'll arrange to put you off in a zodiac and you can wait outside. We'll pick you up when we come out."

The oiler, Bill Kiernan, who was standing behind the others, spoke up first. "What if you don't come out?"

"That's a chance we'll all be taking. If you decide to stay out in a zodiac, you could try to get ashore at Livingston or some other island, but with this heat, there must be torrents of melt water flowing down those hills. The peninsula would be worse, even if you could reach it against the strong current." We looked toward Livingston Island. We could see a cloud of vapor rising from the snow covered island.

Dr. Larsen declared, "The ice must be melting over the whole Antarctic!"

Harry faced the group. "We're in a strong nawth'ly current here. Y're prob'ly safer on th' ship." He added, "I'd rather take my chances on th' ship than git off on any dam' zodiac. We got about a four mile set here right now. If y'break down, or run out'a gas, or try t'find a place t'git ashore, this current'll carry y't'sea along with all this ice."

The skipper concluded his speech. "You have to compare the two risks. If we get caught inside the crater in a really big eruption, the vessel will be destroyed, and all of us along with it. The choice is yours. Anybody who wants to take a chance in a zodiac, get together with Mr.

King within the next ten minutes. Harry, get a zodiac ready just in case. Put some food and water in it and fill the gas tanks.'' The skipper left the group and returned to the wheelhouse.

Big Harry shouted, ''Come on, you guys! Let's go! Git that zodiac ready! Git a bunch of fire extinguishers up on deck, an' a coupl'a you guys drag out all th' tarps y' can, an' get'em wet down! Now, if any a'you fat heads wants t'git off, step over here!'' He indicated an unoccupied part of the deck with a sweep of his arm.

The group began a heated discussion of the pros and cons of staying or leaving the ship. To Harry's surprise, the third mate, Jim Lefevre, was the first to decide to get off *Quest*. He avoided Harry's cold stare, and mumbled under his breath, ''I'd rather drown than burn. I'll go in the zodiac.'' He stepped over to the starboard side near the mate. Kiernan, the oiler, followed suit.

Harry said to us later, ''At least, they'll have a navigator and mechanic. That may help!''

The group started to break up, and as we moved off the after deck, Peter Fortunato, the messboy, held back as if he couldn't make up his mind. Finally, he decided to join the oiler and third mate.

Harry looked on the three as cowards and didn't try to hide his opinion. There was irritation in his voice as he barked, ''OK, you three! Get down there and help stock up y'r boat! We got no time t'lose!''

Soon the zodiac was ready. The ship was stopped and the three men, wearing orange life jackets, were left behind, bobbing in the choppy sea, surrounded by loose ice, and floating northward off the starboard quarter as *Quest* moved away. They had been instructed to remain as close to Deception as possible to be picked up later. The trio had a battery radio and could keep in contact with the ship.

Down below, Larsen held a hurried conference with the Varanys, Beebee Abbey, and Carol Moore. They readied bandages, salves and hypodermics. The cook brought out a quantity of towels and clean sheets. Beebee suggested that they take a lot of wet towels topside to be wrapped around the heads and faces of anybody having to work in smoke. She had been in a fire or two herself. A bottle of whiskey was opened in case someone in pain would need a drink.

In the engine room, the slow throb of the fire pump told of the pressure on deck where the men assigned to hoses were already playing streams of water over everything. They drenched the wooden decks, bulwarks, sails, booms, tarpaulins and the clothing of the seamen themselves. Vogt and Thysen were ready with shovels and axes to toss burning fragments overboard. At orders from the mate, all hands had heavy weather oilskins ready to put over their clothing. It was too warm to wear them until necessary. Fire extinguishers were on deck, and the remote controlled CO_2 system was ready for the engine room and hold compartments around fuel tanks.

I had gone to my cabin, and loaded two of my cameras. I put extra film in my pockets, and took my gear back up on deck.

In the radio room, Enrique was talking with the Argentines, reassuring them that the ship would soon pick them up. At the skipper's suggestion, he told them the ship would go as close to the cinder beach in front of their station as possible. There, they would put a zodiac over and run it to the beach. He would blow quick blasts on the ship's whistle as the zodiac left, and Enrique would also inform them by radio. The men were to run out of the protection of their roof, and with some metal sheets or other hard cover over their heads, they were to run to the zodiac. They said the beach was boiling, and that steam from the fumaroles was blowing up all around the basin. They feared the hot steam would scald them, but there was no other way, so they agreed.

Just before Pack brought *Quest* close to Neptune's Bellows entrance, he ordered the two gasoline drums to be released and anchored. While that was being done, there was a tremendous eruption which sent clouds of black smoke high in the air. *Quest* trembled from the intensity of earthquake shocks. It seemed as if the whole island was going up. Large chunks and incandescent rock fragments were blown up and came raining down to the north of the entrance. Some fell outside near the ship. Ashes came down like black snow. Most of the material was blown off the north hills by the breeze, which, although slight, was sufficient to carry the smoke away from *Quest*. That was certainly a break. We wouldn't have much success if we had to suffer from smoke inhalation.

The pyrotechnics of erupting volcanoes close at hand was an unnerving experience, considering the ship had to go into the crater itself. If Captain Pack had any last minute qualms, he succeeded in concealing it. To say that he, or any of us on *Quest* weren't afraid, would be to say that we were inhuman. The prospect of heading our ship and ourselves into a quaking inferno was absolutely terrifying!

Pack kept *Quest* at top speed through the narrow entrance. Paul kept his eyes glued to the radar and gave the skipper constant ranges off the cliff. We moved rapidly past Whalers Bay and on to the inner caldera, pushing aside the loose ash-covered pack ice. The air was hot with smoke and choking black dust. Burning cinders rained down on the ship and we brushed them off our wet clothing. We stopped close to the beach off the Argentine Station amid a shower of incandescent fragments and turbulent sea caused by continuous shocks of the earth beneath us.

The zodiac was quickly put over. Two men held a wet tarpaulin over the boat and their heads as the craft moved rapidly toward the shore and the curtain of steam at the water's edge. The five station men came running toward the boat with pieces of sheet roofing over their heads. They were black from head to foot with smoke and volcanic dust. Earthquake shocks were so strong that they were nearly thrown into the steaming water as they clambered aboard the zodiac. The boat was pushed off and returned at top speed to *Quest*. All the men crouched under the wet canvas. Once aboard, and the zodiac recovered, the men were taken below where their burns were cared for by *Quest's* medical staff, Dr. Varany, Nancy, Beebee, and Carol.

On deck, great activity was taking place. An explosion had thrown huge chunks of porous molten rock into the air which had fallen on deck in a fiery shower. Two fire hoses had been scorched and were nearly useless. The men were filling buckets and trying to dodge the burning rocks while throwing water on the smoldering pieces on deck. Others were trying to shovel them off the deck, but they were coming down too fast. The deck was ablaze at several spots as the shower of fire continued.

I was snapping pictures as quickly as possible. I had used up the film in one camera, which hung around my neck, and had almost finished with the second camera in my hands. Just at that instant, I suddenly had the wind knocked out of me and was thrust to the deck. A chunk of molten rock had hit me squarely in the chest and knocked the camera out of my grasp. The blow had thrown me down. I saw my camera slide across the deck and smash against the hatch coaming. Fiery fragments from the rock burned my hands and splashed up on my face. I was stunned and gasping for air as I tried to get to my feet. Strong hands grabbed both my arms on either side, pulling me up.

Mike Vogt on one side, yelled, "Jamie! Are you all right?"

Before I could answer, Harry King, on my other side, shouted, "Come on! You're going below!"

Breathlessly, I managed, "No! My camera!" I tried to look back, but they dragged me across the deck.

Mike, his voice more controlled, said, "It's smashed, Jamie! It's ruined!"

They got me below to the hospital area, and then went back up on deck. Beebee rushed to my side and attended my wounds, which turned out to be only superficial burns. As Beebee finished applying ointment to my face, she said, "You don't know how lucky you are! It just missed your eyes!" I was grateful for that, and also for her attentions.

I looked down at the remaining camera hanging around my neck. It was broken. The fall, I thought. I must have crushed it. "I'm going back up!" I said to Beebee as I scrambled to my feet.

Arnold Varany overheard me. "No, Jamie, don't!" he advised. "You've had a shock and the wind knocked out of you. Stay put!"

"Dr. Varany is right. Please don't go up there!" begged Beebee.

"I have to!" I replied. "I want to see what's going on and I want to help!" I staggered up on deck and made my way very carefully to the wheelhouse as *Quest* rapidly moved away from the explosive area and out of the lava hail.

All hands were ordered to bring extinguishers and hoses from other parts of the ship, but before the glowing fragments could be removed, some surface holes were charred in the deck planks, though none burned through them. Several persons besides myself suffered minor burns and lacerations. The hospital below was kept busy with ointments and bandages.

Heading for the opening at full speed as the decks were being cleared, *Quest* was an appalling sight. Covered entirely with black ashes and charred by many fires, the plucky vessel pushed through the dirty loose pack ice, toward the opening still some three miles away.

In another five minutes, the opening was only two miles away. At that moment, a violent earthquake lifted the waters of the caldera and *Quest's* bow, high into the air. The stern sank beneath the sea, flooding the after deck. All hands were violently thrown against bulkheads and decks.

Mount Kirkwood, on our right, only about a mile and a half from our position, erupted with a deafening explosion which sent great columns of black smoke and hot pumice over the ship. We were in complete darkness except for fiery volcanic flashes. The ship finally righted itself after violently rolling and pitching several times. Pack got to his feet and stopped the headway. He tried to peer through the volcanic dust and smoke to get some idea of which way we must head. If we were sinking, he must try to beach the ship.

Finally the breeze cleared the air enough to see the opening through Neptune's Bellows. All of us in the wheelhouse gasped at the terrible sight ahead. The opening was completely blocked to several feet above the water by an avalanche of rock. Part of the cliff had broken away and fallen across the entrance, completely blocking the exit. *Quest* was trapped! There was no longer any way out for the ship. We felt the end had come. Nevertheless, we were alive. The ship didn't seem to be sinking, at least not fast enough to be seen from the wheelhouse. There was still hope, even though we were in an active volcano.

Mount Kirkwood continued to belch forth ashes and smoke and new lava flowed down its ice-covered sides, causing vast clouds of steam to rise with loud hissing and sputtering. It seemed that the earthquake shocks had reached their maximum intensity with that last great convulsion. The turbulence of the ice-filled caldera slowly diminished. *Quest* lay still, a wounded ship, blackened as if in mourning.

Pack sought an anchorage. He moved *Quest* toward Whalers Bay. We had to collect our wits and try to contact the outside. After anchoring, Pack went below to inspect for damage. He had to know if there was any breach of the integrity of the hull. He told Enrique to call Palmer as soon as he could get the radio transmitter back in operation.

Sounding the bilges and examining all compartments,

Captain Pack and Jesse Lytel determined there were no serious leaks. Some water had come into the ship when the stern submerged, but *Quest's* rugged hull was intact.

We settled down and went about the business of cleaning up inside the ship as much as we could. When all wounds had been attended to for the time being, the hospital duties were suspended, and all the scientists assembled in the labs to assess the damage and salvage whatever hadn't been broken.

I finally had time to inspect the camera which had been hanging around my neck. It was jammed and broken beyond repair. I couldn't remove the film without exposing it. I was damned sorry I had no pictorial account on record of the nightmare we had experienced. Fearful of forgetting even an instant of it, I immediately set about recording our ghastly experience on Beebee's cassette recorder. I would later transcribe the tapes into written form.

What we had just witnessed took me back to World War II. I was reminded of my assignment to cover a British bombing mission of the strategic dams in the Ruhr River Valley in Germany. Enemy machine gun fire and flak were aimed directly at the British Lancasters as we came in low to hit the targets. The fiery chunks of molten rock hitting *Quest's* decks in rapid succession were reminiscent of the machine gun fire. Given my choice, in comparing the two incidents, I would have taken my chances on the British Lancasters any day than do a repeat performance on *Quest's* deck battling molten rocks. I shook the dim past from my mind, and forced my thoughts back to the present.

I began counting my blessings. I was alive. I had my eyesight, my injuries were minor, and I was receiving careful attention from Beebee, whose tenderness and solicitude thrilled me. And I was very grateful that I hadn't used the third camera which I had brought along on the trip. It was in my cabin and still intact.

Raymond, the cook, managed to put together a hot

meal, but few hands on board had any appetite and the mess room was practically empty. Uppermost in everyone's mind was our present plight. How and when would we get out? And what of the three we had left outside in the zodiac? LeFevre, Kiernan, and Fortunato—how would they survive? We were prisoners in a bubbling cauldron—the caldera of Deception Island.

The radio room was a shambles. Transmitters and receivers were damaged, antennas were a charred and tangled mess. Enrique and Asst. Engineer Earl Trant were making repairs as fast as they could. We had no communication with the world outside.

We were deeply concerned about our men at Palmer Station. Had any of them survived? Carol Moore was understandably anxious and fearful as to Larry's fate.

And what of the cruise ship *Sinbad* with its large crew and all those passengers? Were they all dead? Eventually we learned the full story of *Sinbad's* ordeal, and the details of the disaster at Palmer.

Below deck, those of us who could do so were still attending injured, or attempting to restore order. The hatch cover over the mess room had been opened and covered with a tent-like tarpaulin to permit air to enter, even though it was somewhat smoky. *Quest* had no interior air supply other than that carried through the ventilation system which wasn't cooled. In the area of *Quest's* operations, the outside temperature seldom rose much above freezing. At that time, in the caldera, it had risen to about fifty degrees Fahrenheit.

In spite of the shambles of the galley, Ray, the cook, came through with a bang-up breakfast, which he served with little help. Ray had lost his messboy, but there was only one mishap. When pouring out the grapefruit juice, Second Engineer Bennett L. ''Slim'' Park dumped a piece of pumice about the size of a hen's egg into his styrofoam cup. He drank the juice and fished out the pumice, shook the juice from it, rinsed it, wrapped it in a napkin and put it in his pocket.

"First time I seen a ship's cook use anythin' like that for flavorin'. Anyway, I'll take it home for a souvenir." Slim was a down-easterner accustomed to the rough and hardy life on the banks. A little burned rock flavor didn't bother him.

"Did you mention home?" asked Jesse. "How do you know you'll ever *get* home?"

The question started a conversation about a subject on everyone's mind. The skipper thought it would be a good time to have a talk about our situation.

"You know, Jesse, you may have a point there." Pack spoke seriously. "Suppose we all try to get some idea what we're really up against here. Let's take an hour or so right now and talk about it. Then we can see what we come up with. Paul, you may have some ideas about what's happening with the sun. You go first."

The second mate began slowly, his Alabama accent coming through once in a while. "Wale, from what we heard on th' radio before the dam' thing went out on us, it may be that th' polar regions will warm up. When we swing around in orbit to th' other side of th' sun, th' Arctic is gonna git much more heat, jus' like we're gittin' it now. I suppose that's what'll happen. When Enrique gits his doohickeys workin' agin with th' radio, let's see if they've found out any more about it."

Enrique responded with enthusiasm. "I'm gonna get on it again right away."

Elbow Larsen cleared his throat and put down his coffee cup. "I've been listening to those loud noises over on the peninsula. To me, it sounds like more volcanic explosions. We have this heavy cloud cover and frequent blowing smoke, rain and hail. I'm wondering if the whole Antarctic is heating up from below. Those continuous clouds coming from the southeast could be caused by great explosions boiling up the melted ice and sending up hot steam. I wonder how far down the peninsula it is hap-

71

pening. I'll be glad when we can talk with Palmer."

Beebee said wistfully, "I wonder what has happened to the zodiac?"

Enrique replied, "I have tried to call them several times. No soap. They don't answer."

Big Harry, the mate, said, "I wouldn't be surprised if they were dead by now. Anyhow, it was their own choice!"

Captain Pack grimaced. He felt that he shouldn't have let them leave the ship. Actually, if he had known what really had happened to them, he would have felt no remorse whatever. I learned many months later that strong currents, along with pack ice, bitsy bergs, growlers, and many large icebergs, had carried them far to the north, hundreds of miles away from the Antarctic. They managed to get off the zodiac onto a large iceberg. It had a broken sloping spot where penguins were climbing on and off. They pulled their zodiac up the slope and rode the berg for about three weeks, until it became unsteady. Fearing that it might capsize, they got off again in the zodiac, and were picked up a few days later by a disoriented German freighter off the coast of Brazil. The freighter was having a difficult time navigating due to changes in declinations of celestial bodies. They finally reached Fortaleza, Ceara, Brazil. There they found the breakwater and the city under water. The freighter continued northward and eventually they reached high land in Venezuela.

Carol couldn't keep her mind off Palmer and wondered what could have been the consequences of the earthquake there. Beebee, reading her thoughts, said, "We'll probably hear from Palmer soon." Actually, none of us knew whether we would ever hear from Palmer or anybody else.

While those comments and thoughts were passed around in the mess room, Enrique and Third Engineer Earl Trant were in the radio room tinkering with the equipment there. Enrique finally got some results with the receiver. They heard *Sinbad* calling them, but they couldn't answer. Later, they heard the British Antarctic Survey Vessel *Bransfield*, and learned of *Sinbad's* predicament. Enrique called Captain Pack. "*Sinbad's* icebound in Lemaire Channel," he said. "They have some injured people on board, but none dead. The ship isn't badly damaged, but they can't move. They're surrounded by icebergs."

"Too bad we can't help them," declared Pack. "I'm sure glad they didn't sink!" In a moment he continued. "The sooner you get that transmitter working, the better. I want to talk with somebody—Palmer—*Sinbad*-*Bransfield*—anybody—and let the world know we're still afloat." The skipper clicked off his squawk box, and then switched it back on again. "I'm coming up there and listen to some of that traffic. Tell the chief and Dr. Larsen about *Sinbad*."

"Right, sir," answered Enrique. He turned to Earl Trant. "The skipper sounds edgy," he said. Earl agreed. He went below and passed the news around that the receiver was working, and told us about *Sinbad's* plight. Soon, several of Quest's company crowded around the radio room, including Carol Moore, Beebee and myself.

"What about Palmer?"

"Is Palmer Station okay?"

"Any news about the men at Palmer?"

Questions were fired at Enrique all at once, questions for which he had no answers. He hadn't heard a word from Palmer.

"I'll let you know as soon as I hear anything," Enrique promised. He resumed working on the transmitter, and some of the others left. Carol lingered, wondering how Larry and the others at Palmer had fared in the terrible earthquakes. She kept hoping that she could talk with Larry and assure him that she was safe. "Please, Enrique, ask about Larry, whenever you get in touch with Palmer."

"Yes, Carol, I'll let you know. I'm trying to get this transmitter working as fast as I can. We got quite a jolt."

73

"Yes" Carol sighed. "I know—I know." She slowly went below.

Enrique had to make repairs to the antenna as well as the transmitter. It was late afternoon before he was able to use the set. He finally got things in order and called Palmer Station, but Palmer didn't answer. Captain Pack came and sat in the radio room. Enrique called Palmer several times. Finally *Sinbad* answered. Ole Magnussen's voice was clear. "Research Vessel *Quest*. This is *Sinbad*. How do you read? Over."

"Read you loud and clear," replied Enrique.

"It's good to hear you. You are weak, but clear. Are you all right?"

"Affirmative," answered Enrique. "We had a hard time, but we're all alive. We are trapped in Deception, anchored in Whalers Bay. Some fire damage—some people burned—none critical. We got the five men from the Argentine Station. Can you tell us anything about Palmer Station? Are the men all safe there? We haven't had any word about them since the earthquakes. Over."

Ole's tone softened. He spoke slowly, almost reluctantly. "I don't know all the details, but there were injuries and some were killed. I heard a coast guard helicopter reporting to the icebreaker *Southwind*, but I did not copy the names. There were four dead. The helicopter is still at Palmer, but it is damaged and could not evacuate any of the men. The last I heard from them is that they are trying to straighten up the helicopter with their crane, and they will not be using the radio for a few hours. You can try calling them on 2182, but you will not get any reply for a while. The station buildings are in ruins. Over."

Captain Pack closed the radio room door. "Call *Southwind*," he whispered to Enrique. "Get the names. Keep it low."

Enrique replied to Ole. "Roger. I'll try to call *Southwind*. Thanks. Over and out." He then called *Southwind*, but could get no response. After calling several times,

Sinbad answered. "Your signal is too weak," said Ole, "I'll call *Southwind* for you."

"Okay, thanks," agreed Enrigue. "Please tell *Southwind* we're not badly damaged, and all our people are alive. Ask for the names of casualties at Palmer."

"Roger," replied Ole.

Enrique and Captain Pack listened in silence to an exchange of messages between *Sinbad* and *Southwind*. They heard Ole report that *Quest* was trapped at Deception Island, and learned the names of the men killed at Palmer. Larry Field was one of the dead. Shocked, they silently stared at each other.

The skipper made motions to Enrique to turn down the sound. He spoke hastily, in a low voice. "Tell *Sinbad* you copied the message so Ole doesn't repeat those names. It's a good thing Carol isn't up here. Don't say anything about this—at least, not until we get confirmation directly from Palmer. Keep calling Palmer—I mean, the helicopter. I suppose we're all using 2182 in this emergency. Anyway, get them as soon as you can. If you get a confirmation about Larry Field, keep it quiet. Just let me know, and I'll figure out the best way to break the news to Carol."

"Okay, sir," agreed Enrique. He then called *Sinbad* and told Ole that he had copied the traffic between *Sinbad* and *Southwind*. The skipper went below, saddened by the news of the deaths at Palmer Station.

We had plenty to do, taking care of the burns, and straightening out the shambles in the quarters. Captain Pack was in no hurry to have the decks cleared. Little notice was paid to the top side. Pack avoided Carol Moore. He was concerned that his own lowness of spirit might cause her to suspect that he had heard bad news.

Just before 1900, Paul Shelley was in the wheelhouse looking at a chart of Deception. He glanced at the mud flat shown at the entrance to Whalers Bay, then went to a wheelhouse window to look at it. It was completely covered by water! He looked toward the abandoned buildings and saw that the water had risen to their ground level. The whole beach was covered by the high water.

"Hey!" Paul shouted down the companionway. "Hey! Come up here! Look how high th' water's gittin'!"

The skipper and several others clambered up to the wheelhouse. Icepack said right away, "That's certainly no normal tide! It looks like something is happening again! We'll have to watch it. Paul, keep an eye on things and let me know if it continues to rise." Pack then went to his cabin.

Shortly thereafter, Enrique heard the helicopter at Palmer calling *Quest*. He picked up the mike and answered, "This is *Quest*. Are we glad to hear you! How do you read? Over."

"Your signal is weak, but I can read you. Where are you, and are you all right?" It was Ira Mason. His voice was deeply troubled.

"Yes, we're all alive, but *Quest* is burned topside. We're trapped inside Deception! Anchored at Whalers Bay! Wait one, I'll call Captain Pack. Over." Enrique couldn't suppress his emotion.

"Roger," replied Mason. "George Reszke is here. Over."

Enrique closed the radio room door and called Captain Pack's cabin. "I've got them," he said softly. Soon the skipper was by his side.

"Palmer—this is Captain Pack. George? Over."

Reszke's tone was guarded. He slowly answered, barely audible. "Captain Pack, this is George Reszke. It's good to know you're all safe. We were worried. We have this helicopter here, but it has two damaged rotor blades. Our buildings are wrecked." Reszke paused. He seemed reluctant to continue. His voice was even lower when he spoke again. "Captain Pack—before I can give you any more details, tell me—is anyone else listening? Anyone besides your ET, I mean. I suggest you take this message with earphones. Over."

Pack glanced at Enrique, and motioned toward the door. Enrique looked outside and shook his head. He plugged a set of earphones into the receiver and switched off the speaker. Pack answered Reszke. "No, George, only Enrique and myself. Go ahead. Over."

There was another short delay. Reszke falteringly continued. "Captain—we've had a terrible time. It's really a wonder any of us are alive." Reszke paused. "Captain Pack, four of our men are gone. Two of the boys you brought, and two of our men." It seemed that George was about to stop talking. The skipper called him.

"George, are you there? George?"

There was no respone. No doubt George Reszke found it very hard to deliver his message. When he finally responded, his voice trembled. He sobbed, "Albert Steel's head was cut off—cut right off." There was another long pause. "And Captain, I hardly know how to tell you this. Larry—Larry Field is gone. He went into the wreckage to help the boys. That's the last we saw of him. We've been working as best we can, trying to get the helicopter up out of the water with the crane. That's why we weren't using its radio today. We haven't had a chance yet to look for Larry's body. I'm sorry to have to give you this bad news. Maybe you'd better keep it from Carol Moore until we have a chance later to look for Larry's body. We'll do that right away, and get back to you within the hour. Over."

The skipper answered, "Roger, George, I understand. We'll wait for your call. We already knew about Field and the others. *Southwind* gave us the information through *Sinbad*." Pack started to say "over," but thought better of it and said, "George. One thing more. How long do you estimate it'll take to repair that helicopter? Over."

"Repair it? I don't know," replied Reszke. "Our shop was destroyed. I don't know. It may take weeks. Maybe we can't do it. The water is rising fast. We're going to try to get some of the shop equipment out of the wreckage before the water gets up to it. Over."

"Roger, George. *Quest* out, and standing by on 2182."
Pack put down the earphones and spoke quietly to
Enrique. "We'll just keep quiet about this until they call
us back. Let me know when you get the call."

Pack left the radio room, but didn't go below. He went
out on the after deck and sat on one of the bollards. He
needed time to collect his thoughts. Carol would have to
be told sooner or later, but he didn't want to tell anybody
about Larry until he found out whether his body had been
found. He didn't have long to wait. In less than half an
hour, Enrique got a call from Ira Mason on the helicopter.

Ira said, "Enrique, please take a message for Captain
Pack from George Reszke. 'No bodies found in wreckage
of Palmer buildings. Field, Taylor, Rankin and Steele, all
apparently washed down into open chasm beneath
wreckage.' Message ends. Sorry. Palmer out. Standing by
on 2182."

Enrique acknowledged the message and went out to the
skipper. "Reszke advises no bodies found." He handed
the skipper a message form on which the names had been
typed. Captain Pack looked at it, and put it in his pocket.
He went below and asked Dr. Larsen and Beebee to come
with him to his cabin.

Beebee told me later that she knew the skipper had
some bad news about Larry Field the moment he asked her
and Elbow Larsen to his cabin. Elbow said he had thought
so all afternoon because Pack looked so glum. They both
received the news calmly, but, Beebee, knowing she would
have to be the one to tell Carol, murmured, "I feel almost
as if I had lost a son. It's not going to be easy, but Carol is
well adjusted. She'll get over it in time. At least, I hope
she will."

Later, as I passed Carol's door, I heard her sobbing. I
knew that Beebee had told her. I guess we all shared
Carol's grief. I know I did.

The next day, December 24, passed slowly. Everyone
tried to relax. Jesse Lytel showed a couple of films in the

afternoon to "celebrate" Christmas eve.

I had spent much of the time during that day recording and transcribing the events of the past two days. I hadn't seen, nor heard from Carol Moore all day. She hadn't made an appearance at meals. Nobody did much talking. Off and on, we got bits of news from Enrique about the world outside our caldera. He monitored whatever traffic the radio waves brought our way. The men at Palmer said that they were still trying to get the helicopter rotor blades repaired. They also said they were planning to put together a large raft with empty drums and planks under the helicopter so it would float in case the water rose up to it.

Enrique occasionally spoke to Ole Magnussen, the radio operator on *Sinbad*. Ole said he had many messages to transmit for the passengers to their relatives in various parts of the world, but that only a few were actually getting through because of widespread international turmoil.

Before turning in for the night, I went up to the after laboratory. Beebee, Elbow, the Varanys, and Carol were there. Carol's eyes were red and swollen from crying, but she managed a wan smile.

I put my arms around her and held her close. "I'm so very sorry, Carol."

"I know—I know." Her words were muffled against my shirt. "I can hardly believe Larry is gone. Somehow—I'll—I'll have to—I hope—he—he didn't suffer." She paused, looked up at me with tear-filled eyes, and added, "We are very fortunate that we all didn't lose our lives."

I admired Carol's courage, and I knew Beebee had been a source of strength in her time of need. In fact, Beebee became a source of strength for all of us during those trying days. But for the first time in my long career of journalistic adventures—I was truly afraid.

Soon Carol and the others retired to their cabins. Beebee and I found ourselves alone for what, I realized, was the very first time. She started to leave the laboratory, hesitated, then moved over to me. "I'm glad you're with us," she whispered. "I'm so sorry for Carol. You're helping me ease her burden—and mine too."

It seemed that Beebee had cast aside her customary reserve. She too, was troubled by fear and apprehension. Instinctively I drew her close to me. Which of us may have been the most in need of that embrace is hard to say. As our lips eagerly met, we realized that mutual danger and adversity had inspired a deep affection and desire for one another.

I soon began to realize too that we had need for a measure of restraint. Perhaps a time would come when we could freely express our devotion. I had no wish to distract Beebee from her important scientific work. I was sure she had relaxed momentarily only because of her weariness.

We parted smiling and comforted, with a lingering kiss. Visions of happiness with Beebee filled my thoughts as I returned to my cabin.

On my way, I saw Per Thysen in the passageway ahead of me. I wondered if he had been listening outside the open lab doorway. Thysen did not look around, and I lingered a moment to let him get out of sight. The last thing I wanted just then was a confrontation with the big mountaineer.

Quest still lay at anchor in Whalers Bay. The once smart, well-kept vessel reflected the terrible bath of fire through which we had passed. Lying in the grey half-light of the strangely overcast sky, hidden by frequent showers of sleet, and covered with black ashes and piles of cinders, *Quest* presented a grim and awesome spectacle.

Volcanic activity had subsided to a degree, although clouds of steam rose from old and new fissures around the perimeter of the caldera. Grey smoke swirled upward, or at times was blown downward from the smoldering volcanoes. Subterranean rumblings and tremors continued, causing *Quest* to tremble. From across the strait, toward Danco Coast on the peninsula, came a continuous rumble like distant thunder, punctuated by loud explosions.

3

THE LUXURY cruise ship *Sinbad* had departed from Buenos Aires about two weeks before we passed her that day in Gerlache Strait. A modern passenger vessel, the M.S. *Sinbad* was well suited for cruises to polar regions. Spacious cabins, comfortable lounges, intimate bars, and excellent cuisine made the vessel seem like a large yacht. Passengers were limited to one hundred, but on that first cruise of the season there were only ninety-three. Included were people from England, France, Germany, Canada, the United States, and other countries. The cost of the cruise was high, and the majority of the passengers were wealthy. They were accustomed to, and demanded, the best accommodations and services that could be obtained.

Dr. George Barry, a former polar explorer, was cruise director on the *Sinbad*. I had first met him on my cruise aboard that ship. Dr. Barry had spent a lifetime investigating the polar regions. He and the passengers later recounted to me the following remarkable and dramatic story of their experiences.

The first cruise of the *Sinbad* each austral season was usually light. There were always a few unoccupied staterooms. On that particular trip the owner had planned to use those accommodations for a good advertising gimmick. Invitations, offering a free cruise to single women between the ages of twenty and thirty-five, were sent to travel agencies in several large cities. Each woman had to be a bona fide travel agency employee with at least one year's experience in the agency. Her employer had to approve, of course, and give her a month off. It was called a "Familiarization Cruise," and was common practice in the travel industry, providing first hand knowledge of the cruises offered. In all, there were twenty-three young women on board *Sinbad*, representing travel agencies all over the world.

During the outward voyage, Dr. Barry invited the passengers to the main lounge where he gave a lecture about the great continent they were to visit. He gave his first lecture before the vessel reached Estrecho de Le Maire, and the rough Drake Passage.

"Ladies and gentlemen," he began with a smile, stroking his short beard, "you may have noticed that we are being followed. We'll be followed all the way to the Antarctic. Sometimes I think I recognize some of those albatrosses, I've made so many trips down here. I've seen you watching them soar around the ship, gracefully riding the breezes, hardly moving their long wings. Some have spans of over eleven feet between wing tips. Someone asked me if they follow all ships. 'H'm,' I said, 'the birds follow the ships that throw out their galley scraps. If you see a passenger ship without birds following it, beware! We say they feed the scraps to the passengers.' " There was some polite, scattered laughter. "*Sinbad* had plenty of birds!" Barry tried a little joke now and then as a warmup.

Mr. and Mrs. Philip Cavige sat in the front row, hoping his jokes would improve. They had traveled widely, seen everything, and heard all the seagoing yarns. Dr. Barry sensed their thoughts by their unsmiling faces. "You can't please everybody," he said to himself.

Emma Cavige was a wide, stone-faced woman with a double chin, hay-stack hairdo, and a figure like a can buoy. She wore blinding diamonds on both hands and a double strand of large pearls around her ample neck. She exuded an aura of money from top to bottom. Her husband was rotund and bald, and constantly chewed on a cigar. He had a loud voice. They were from Texas.

Barry continued his lecture. "Some of the other birds we may see during the voyage are Wilson's petrels and Cape pigeons. They are active ocean flyers and will be with us all the way across Drake Passage. Here, along the coast of Patagonia, you may occasionally see penguins swimming in groups and bobbing up for air. Sometimes an Arctic tern may be sighted passing the ship. They fly each summer all the way from the Arctic to the Antarctic, then back north to the Arctic for the summer there. It's a long flight of some eleven thousand miles each way."

A passenger who had just drifted in from the adjoining bar interrupted Dr. Barry. "Hey, Doc," he drawled, "any cuckoo birds down there?"

"Sure," quipped Barry. "They fly around in smaller and smaller circles until they fly into their own tail feathers." Phillip Cavige grinned. His wife sneered. Amiable and unperturbed, Dr. Barry continued. "There are penguins of several kinds. We may see the Magellans, the Adelies, Chinstraps, Macaronis and Emperors. The Emperors are the big ones. They hatch their chicks on the ice. I've heard that if a skua robs their eggs they'll get a stone or even a chunk of ice and sit on it."

Brenda Clarke, of the South Travel Agency in New Orleans, asked, "Dr. Barry, what is a skua?"

Dr. Barry replied, "The skuas are scavengers about the size of large gulls. You can see pictures of all these birds on the walls of this lounge." When the lecture ended, some of the passengers drifted into the bar while others went on deck or to their cabins. Brenda and her shipboard roommate, Marjory Dumont of the Dumont-Chester Travel Service of London, lingered in the lounge to look at pictures of the birds and ask Dr. Barry more questions. He was delighted to have two very bright, attentive young women to talk to after what had seemed to be an indifferent audience during his lecture. Soon they thanked him and left the lounge. He wished that more passengers could be as enthusiastic as those two.

Brenda and Marjory shared a cabin on B deck across

from the Beauty Shoppe. They were both twenty-four. Brenda was a brunette, small and pretty with an oval face and mischievous brown eyes. Marjory was a redhead, taller than Brenda, with a high forehead, straight nose and narrow chin. Her figure was not her major asset, but she had a charming voice and pleasant smile. Her uncle owned the agency in which she worked. From the start of the cruise, the two became good friends.

One morning, after *Sinbad* had crossed Drake Passage, Brenda and Marjory were walking around the main deck. It was cold and they wore winter coats. They walked briskly toward the stern on the windward side, and forward on the lee side.

The girls were having a discussion about the population explosion, a topic of much interest to the travel industry.

Brenda said, "I don't think young people now coming into the work force are going to travel much. They're having a hard time enough just making a living."

"I don't wonder much at that," Marjory said crisply. "We were caught up in a lot of activities which were really a waste of effort. All those protests and demonstrations! I know that in my case, more study and less idealism would have been a lot better for my education. If my uncle hadn't given me a job, I wouldn't have had much of a chance."

During their brisk walk around the deck, the girls were joined by Gerald Connally, a young clergyman making the cruise with his wife, and out on deck for a morning stroll alone.

"Hi, Reverend," Brenda said cheerfully, "join the marathon. The sign says ten times around the deck is a mile."

"OK," Connally answered, as he fell in step. "Only don't call me 'Reverend.' I don't use titles. Just call me Jerry."

The girls were a little surprised. Marjory said, "Your talk Sunday morning was very interesting. It was like selling a trip to some beautiful scenic land. A bit different from our preachers at home. Too bad there were only about half of the passengers there. I suppose people are getting sort of sour on religion."

Brenda, whose legs were on the short side, stopped and said, "I'm tired, let's go into the lounge. I'd like to sit down awhile and have another cup of coffee."

"Suits me," said Jerry.

"Me too," echoed Marjory.

They entered a small lounge near the library. The trio was cordially greeted by four other passengers, Dr. and Mrs. Clarence Dearborn and Mr. and Mrs. Alfred Norwood, sitting at a large round table. Dr. Dearborn was a retired physician from Cleveland, Ohio, and Mr. Norwood was a retired official of a large chemical company in the United States. This was to be the highlight of their cruise experiences; a trip to the unknown, the mysterious, the perilous.

"Why don't you join us?" said Dr. Dearborn. "We could use some help doing nothing." To Connally he said, "Where's the missus?"

"She was a little tired this morning," answered Jerry.

"Well, it's no wonder, poor dear," declared Helen Norwood. "I can't understand why you would bring her on a trip like this when she's expecting a baby in three months! Didn't her doctor object?"

"Now dear," Alfred Norwood cautioned his wife.

"No, it's alright, Al," said Jerry. "Yes, the doctor was concerned at first. But we checked with the cruise line and were assured the ship is well equipped for any emergency. There are a physician and a nurse on board." He turned to Dr. Dearborn, "And I'm sure Dr. Dearborn would come out of retirement and give us a hand if we needed him, wouldn't you, Doctor?" Dearborn smiled and nodded. Jerry continued, "But we don't foresee any problems. The cruise is only about three weeks long and with a few days of air travel we'll be home within a month. That gives us two months to spare. I guess Lucille will be along pretty soon. She's not too good a sailor. That rolling yesterday—"

87

"Before we came through the convergence area," Al Norwood knowingly interrupted. "Dr. Barry explained that to me. He said that's where the cold water from the Antarctic meets the warmer waters of the Atlantic Ocean. The cold water sinks down. They say the weather is often better after passing the convergence." Al added magnanimously, "Anything you want to know about the Antarctic —just ask me!"

"OK, Eskimo," said his wife, Helen.

"Speaking of Eskimos," said Marjory, "why don't they live in the Antarctic as well as the Arctic?"

"I asked Dr. Barry that same question," said Helen. "He said it's due to lack of food animals, such as caribou, and fur animals like bears and such. The weather is another reason. Winters are more severe, with temperatures down to one hundred twenty or more below zero, and winds over two hundred miles an hour!"

"Not a very cozy place to live," said Marjory.

The lounge steward brought a tray with cups of coffee.

The minister's wife, Lucille Connally, entered the lounge. The group expressed concern about her health. Jerry pulled out a chair for her and said, "Feeling better, honey?"

"Yes," she replied weakly. "Guess I'll live." The steward brought her coffee.

Brenda wanted to continue talking about the population problem. "What do you think," she asked of Jerry, "about the population explosion?"

"Well," replied Jerry, "as I'm the sky pilot on this expedition, I'll refer you to my best source of information. In Genesis it says: 'Be fruitful and become many and *fill* the earth!' It was to be a paradise—all of it—east, west, north, and south. *All continents.*"

Jerry was on board at the invitation of the cruise line, to conduct nonsectarian services on Sundays, a custom on cruise ships. He and Lucille were popular with most of the passengers. Even those who had no use whatever for religion found Jerry likeable. Phillip Cavige was among a group which entered the small lounge while Jerry was speaking.

"There's Jerry, sounding off again," said Phil in a loud voice.

Jerry said, "Sit down and join us. Brenda's worried about the population explosion. We think there's still some room. What do you say?"

"That's a lot of hogwash," replied Phil. "There's plenty of room." He spread his arms out wide. "You people ever been t' Texas? Y'd *never* fill Texas up!"

"Yes, I guess it would take a big explosion at that," quipped Dr. Dearborn. "Anyway, the latest statistics indicate the population increase has slowed down considerably, so don't worry."

Al said, "You mentioned *all* continents, Jerry. How about Antarctica? Was that to be inhabited? It is covered with ice. Dr. Barry says it's as large as the United States and Mexico together. That's quite a big hunk of real estate."

Jerry replied. "I can only go by what is written. When it reads 'the whole earth' it must mean the Antarctic too."

Marjory said, "I have a brother in England who speaks like you. He speaks about a 'new earth' or 'new world.' He thinks we are headed for what he calls a 'great tribulation.' If you ask me, I would say we are already in plenty of trouble, but he says this is nothing compared to what's coming."

The small, intimate lounge became filled with passengers, and the chatter increased.

Dr. Dearborn said to Jerry, "We'll have to talk again sometime. Anyone for a walk?" He and Al and their wives made their apologies and moved off toward the promenade deck. Jerry and Lucille left for the library, while Brenda and Marjory joined some of the other "travel girls" having a gab session out in the main lounge. After a few minutes, several rushed over to the starboard windows. *Sinbad* was passing the first iceberg on the trip. It was a long tabular berg only a couple of miles away. It was flat on top and looked like an island. There was seldom a dull moment for *Sinbad's* passengers. The hostess and lounge stewards were busy decorating a large Christmas tree in a corner of the lounge.

Brenda excused herself from the group, saying she was going to her cabin. She was curious about a handsome man she had met on board the ship, named Tony Destefani. She had learned his stateroom number from a steward. She hadn't seen Tony in the lounge with the other passengers, so she decided to see if he was in his stateroom.

Standing outside stateroom 206, Brenda could hear a man and a woman in subdued, but animated discussion. She recognized Tony's voice, but who was the woman? Brenda didn't know at the time that the couple inside the stateroom was traveling as Mr. and Mrs. Anthony Destefani of New York. At least, that was how their names appeared on the passenger list. A well-groomed couple in their late twenties, they exhibited a façade of grace and culture. They played bridge well and sought the association of the most opulent passengers. Their fashionable attire, obviously by *haute couturiers,* gave credence to their assertions that they were enjoying a fortune recently inherited.

Almost inaudibly, Brenda heard the woman say, "Tony, if you blow this one, you might just as well stay in the Antarctic."

"I won't blow it," Tony snapped. "Stop worrying and get off my back!"

"I'm warning you," the woman countered. "Your life won't be worth a dime in New York if anything happens. And keep away from that Clarke girl. We don't know who the old man may have sent to spy on us. Don't get too familiar with any of them."

At the sound of her last name, Brenda gasped. There was silence from inside the stateroom. Brenda thought they must have heard her. She wanted to run, but was frozen to the spot. She held her breath. Tony raised his voice and said, "Another thing I like. This ship is steady. Doesn't roll too much."

There was silence again, and then Tony, resuming his conspiratorial tone, said, "I'm not getting involved. Don't worry about me blowing my cover. Look out for your own. I saw that woman we played bridge with— Mrs., uh, Helen—what's her name?—Norwood—she looked you over pretty close. You made a couple of slips when you talked about Washington. I don't say she noticed, but you never know. You talk too damn much anyway."

It was the woman's turn to lose her temper, but at that moment the breakfast chimes began to sound and she didn't reply.

Brenda, fearful of being discovered if the door opened, ran from the scene. The sound of her footsteps was covered by the chimes. She was badly shaken. Was the woman Tony's wife? If so, why hadn't Tony told her he was married? And what were they arguing about? It didn't make any sense. Brenda's mind was racing. She needed time to sort out her thoughts. Instinct told her to keep the matter to herself. Perhaps she would confront Tony later, after she had time to think.

As Mr. and Mrs. Destefani entered the dining room, they exchanged nods with the Norwoods seated at a small table for two on the port side. After they passed, Helen Norwood leaned toward her husband, "You know, Al, I have an odd feeling about those two. I don't know why, but she impresses me as being a phony."

"Yeah?" Al said, with a mouthful of toast.

"Uh huh," said Helen.

Al put down the rest of his toast "Well, they looked okay to me. Play bridge well."

Helen mused, "I can't explain exactly. Somehow they seem too perfect. You know. Like they were chiseled out of a block of platinum."

Al picked up his coffee cup and then put it down again. "Come to think of it, they dropped some pretty big names."

"Yes," said Helen, "that's another thing. She never spoke about common ordinary people. It was always 'Sir this' or 'Lord that,' or some ambassador or senator."

"Maybe so—anyway, it doesn't matter to me." Al picked up his cup and finished his coffee. "Maybe they think I'm a retired bartender. After all, I was telling how to mix that Pisco Sour. So what? There are a lot of phonies in this world, so if there are a few on this cruise it's okay as far as I'm concerned."

Helen batted her eyelashes. "Oh, I was just curious."

They finished their breakfast and stepped out on deck, but it was cold, so they went to get their coats. As they walked through the main lobby, or "Pursers Square," they met some of the "travel girls" on their way to the dining room.

Brenda had made her way back to the dining room and joined the others. She spotted the Destefanis, but pretended not to see them. Helen, who never missed a trick, turned and caught a glimpse of Brenda's reaction. When Helen was well out of earshot of the group of girls, she remarked to her husband, "Another thing, I've seen that Destefani guy hanging around that Clarke girl a lot."

Helen Norwood was not the only passenger on *Sinbad* who took notice of Brenda's reaction to the Destefanis in the dining room that morning. Seated directly across from the Destefanis was Mme. Victoria Degrelle, a tall, striking, middle-aged blonde from Belgium. Mme. Degrelle was a widow and traveled alone. Her fifth husband had left her a sizeable fortune when he mysteriously passed away in their chalet in the south of France. She had taken the cruise to help her get over her sorrow, but more importantly, to avoid too close an inquiry into her husband's untimely demise. During the entire cruise, she adorned herself with an endless array of black mourning clothes from her very expensive European wardrobe. She had a knack of appearing suddenly and joining whatever group happened to appeal to her fancy on board the ship. Victoria was not exactly disliked, but nobody seemed to get very friendly with her, although she was occasionally seen in the company of Dr. Barry. She had taken a liking to him and often engaged him in conversation.

Like the Norwoods, Victoria Degrelle was suspicious of the Destefanis and she had also taken note of the apparent attachment of Tony Destefani and Brenda Clarke. She made it her business to keep an eye on them whenever she saw them together.

During the night before *Sinbad* was due to arrive at King George Island, light snow filled the air and swirled gently around the ship. There were icebergs in the area. Speed was reduced and all outside lights around the decks were switched off for better visibility on the bridge. Most of the passengers had retired, but a few lingered in the lounge. Tony Destefani and his attractive brunette wife, Teresa, were having a nightcap.

At a nearby table, two men, who had apparently consumed several nightcaps, amused themselves with clamorous remarks and laughter. They were similar in build and appearance, although one seemed a little older than the other. The men furtively eyed Teresa from time to time, and occasionally she caught the younger one's appreciative glance. The men finally left their table and walked unsteadily to the door leading to the promenade deck.

Teresa told Tony that she wasn't feeling well and wanted to go to the powder room. While Tony waited for her, he strolled out on the promenade deck for a few minutes. In the dark, there was a struggle, a man's scream, and the sound of a splash. Tony quickly stepped back into the lounge.

When Teresa returned, Tony exclaimed, "A man just fell overboard! I saw it! And I think I saw a woman push him, too. It was you, wasn't it! You thought he was—"

Teresa interrupted him.

"Me? I went to the powder room!"

"Then where did you get the water spots on your dress? It's snowing outside."

"I told you I wasn't feeling well. I splashed some water on my face and neck. That's all. Besides, Tony, maybe you didn't *really* see anything. Or—maybe—who knows. Maybe it was a lover's quarrel. And who cares, anyway." Her tone was caustic.

"I know what I saw! Teresa, if it *was* you, and you bungled this, you know what will happen to you. We were supposed to try and make a deal with—"

Teresa cut him off again. "I don't have to listen to your damn accusations! I told you it *wasn't* me! I'm going to bed!" She left the lounge.

On the bridge, the second mate, who had relieved the watch, was checking the green starboard side light when he heard the victim's scream and splash of a body in the water. He shouted. "Man overboard!" and released two life buoys. Their lights flashed on when they hit the water. The emergency lifeboat crew was immediately summoned, and the ship was put into a "Williamson Turn." In less than five minutes, *Sinbad,* on a reciprocal course, was back at the lighted buoys. The area was searched for three hours, until after daylight, but no one was found. It was finally ascertained that the victim's name was Gorden P. Bailey. And it was assumed, after much discussion and investigation, that he had committed suicide. *Sinbad* then resumed the voyage toward King George Island.

All of us on board *Quest* were oblivious to the drama that was already unfolding on *Sinbad.* I had enough to do taking notes and writing about our activities on R. V. *Quest.* Several weeks later I was able to interview some of the survivors of the luxury cruise ship *Sinbad,* and write this story.

Sinbad reached Admiralty Bay at King George Island about mid-December. There were few places visitors to the Antarctic could go ashore. At King George Island, calls were made at the Chilean Meteorological Station, Presidente Frei, and nearby Russian Station, Bellingshausen. Arrivals of *Sinbad* passengers at those lonely Antarctic stations were occasions for great celebrations. Occupants of the stations made them welcome indeed. Hospitality knew no bounds. Those men, isolated for months during the long winter of darkness, greatly appreciated such occasions. Passengers and crew returned their hospitality by having the men out on the ship for relaxation and entertainment. When the ship was ready to leave, there were, except for ship's officers and crew, few sober individuals, ashore or afloat. It took them at least a day to recuperate.

Sinbad left King George Island in the late evening and headed southwestward toward Deception Island, a distance of about seventy-five miles. The ship moved slowly to delay arrival until after breakfast so the passengers could view and photograph the spectacular entrance to the inner caldera which formed Port Foster.

Sinbad's lanky, grey haired, fifty-one year old skipper, Ivan Gilbert, took his vessel in slowly and cautiously. He passed the towering cliff carefully and headed into Whaler's Bay so that the passengers could see the old buildings of the whaling station. It had been a lively rendezvous of seal and whale hunters in the past century, but had long been abandoned. Gilbert didn't anchor there because the bottom of the bay was said to have been fouled with old cables and chains. He stopped *Sinbad* for a half hour, and then slowly moved out. Gilbert made a turn around the sunken crater to show the Argentine Station, and let the passengers get a good view of the fumaroles spouting steam around the northwestern shore line. The activity attested to the existence of a large magma chamber deep below which was capable of erupting into active volcanoes at any time. The fumaroles were very action. Some of the passengers were thrilled that they were in the crater of a volcano belching forth steam.

The occupants of the Argentine Station came out in their own boat while *Sinbad* stayed close to their side of the bay. The group of five men included two Argentine volcanists, an Argentine cook and a mechanic, and a British geologist. They were royally entertained by the passengers in *Sinbad's* luxurious main lounge.

Curious about men who lived and worked in such a forbidding environment, the passengers crowded into the lounge and plied them with questions. Philip Scott, the British geologist, acted as interpreter for the group. Toward the end of the visit, his interpretations became spiritedly scientific.

"There's been a g—great increase is seis—*hic,* seishmic activity here," he said, as he drained his sixth glass of champagne. "We have re*hic*—recorded over hunc—hundred light earthquake sh—shocks a day."

"What? Earthquakes?" several exclaimed.

"Yes. Jus' light tr—*hic,* tr—tremors. Nothing to—nothing t' worry ab—about. These hish—" Philip got unsteadily to his feet, leaned against the table, and waved his arm around in a wide circle. "These hills all 'round us —ol' volcanoes—*ehup*—erup' every couple years."

Philip's Argentine companions, also well lubricated by the excellent wine, stood around the large table. Several of the passengers spoke Spanish and the party was getting noisier by the minute.

Among those getting somewhat boisterous were Tony Destefani, Emma and Philip Cavige. They were joined in singing by several of the travel girls. Their voices sounded like the howling of sea lions. The Norwoods, Dearborns and Connallys remained at a safe distance. Al Norwood had cornered one of the Argentine volcanists, and, aided by one of the passengers who spoke Spanish, Al asked, "What would you do if there was a big volcanic eruption here at Deception Island, and no ship around to take you off?"

"We would run away, along the shore," was the reply.

"It's happened before, and it could happen again, any minute. The Chileans had to run for it in 1967. They used to have a station over across the caldera at Pendulum Cove. They had to abandon it in a hurry."

Suddenly Marjory Dumont shouted. "They have over a hundred earthquake shocks here every day!"

Victoria Degrelle, standing apart from the group, exclaimed, "Let's get out of zis place—QUICK!"

"That's a lotta hogwash!" shouted Phil Cavige.

His wife yelled, "Shut up! We gotta get outa here!"

Victoria turned to go out of the lounge and collided with a lounge steward bringing in a tray of drinks, scattering the filled glasses on the deck. Dr. Barry helped the steward pick them up.

Loudly, Victoria shouted, "Zey got enough drinks! Get zem off z'bode!"

The sentiment soon spread, and was shared by the more sober passengers on the outer fringes of the party. The two hours that Captain Gilbert had scheduled for the visit to the Argentine Station were over. The five men were escorted to the gangway and poured into their launch. They chugged away to shore waving and laughing, and pulled their small boat up on the beach past a thin curtain of spouting fumarolic steam. Slowly *Sinbad* moved outward, and soon the cinder and ice-covered hills of Deception Island were far behind.

The weather was good, and Dr. Barry was chatting with a group of passengers on the after promenade deck. "The icecap over the continent hides many mysteries. It is believed that Antarctica was once a warm continent with vegetation and prehistoric animals roaming its forests. The ice is fourteen thousand feet thick at one known place. At the South Pole it is nearly nine thousand. There are about seven million cubic miles of ice. The burden is so heavy, the continent is depressed by it. Scientists believe that if it were removed, the continent would rise nearly three thousand feet. Its present elevation averages about a mile above sea level, but there is also much below sea level.

There is so much ice on this continent that if it all melted, it would raise the level of the oceans of the whole world by about two hundred fifty feet.''

"So I've heard!" Al exclaimed. "That's nearly halfway up the Washington Monument!"

Helen asked, "Since there was a temperate climate here at one time, could it ever become temperate again? What keeps it frozen?"

Dr. Barry replied, "The sun's rays reach the polar regions obliquely. They don't come far enough south to warm it up much here. It's a good thing it doesn't, because we would have much colder winters in the north if it did. Let's leave the ice right here!"

"You bet," said Al. "And the cold too. How cold does it get down here in the winter?"

"One hundred twenty-seven below zero Fahrenheit has been recorded over on the ice plateau. It's warmer than usual here on the peninsula today," said Dr. Barry.

The ship passed a tabular iceberg about a mile to starboard, and someone in the group asked how big those icebergs were.

"One has been seen over twice as large as the state of Connecticut," Dr. Barry replied. "They break off from ice shelves. That is why they're so flat on top."

Sinbad slowly moved through the picturesque Neumayer Channel between Anvers and Wienke Islands. Passengers lounged along the rails in their red flotation jackets, enjoying and photographing the splendid scenes. It was December 20th, a beautiful clear day. Meager radio newscasts from various countries briefly referred to possible changes in weather patterns thought to be due to certain undefined and poorly described astronomical phenomena. But nobody gave it much thought. Weather was always changing somewhere, and as far as astronomical phenomena was concerned, NASA could take care of that problem. So reasoned Phil Cavige, who was standing with a group on deck as the ship entered Port Lockroy.

Captain Ivan Gilbert slowly and skillfully maneuvered

Sinbad toward the inner anchorage, passing close along an ice cliff on the port side. *Sinbad* was anchored in a cove skirted by the blue-green and white ice of the glacier face. There, the passengers had a close view of icebergs breaking off into the water, which happened every few minutes at some point around the frozen rim of the cove. A large block at the top, near the ship, leaned outward as if it would break off at any moment.

"I'll bet anybody fifty bucks that chunk will fall within ten minutes," challenged Cavige. The piece looked as big as a city block and was already tilted outward at a wide angle from the edge of the cliff with a deep shadowy crevasse behind it.

"I'll take your bet," countered Dr. Dearborn.

Destefani joined in, "Why don't we make a pool? I'll say between ten and twelve minutes."

"OK," agreed Norwood. "Fifty bucks. Twelve to fourteen minutes."

A number of the others joined in the bet. In a few minutes, there were over three hundred dollars in the pool. Word got around and soon everybody on deck was watching the big block of ice at the top of the cliff. Every few minutes small pieces dropped from the edges and the onlookers shouted, "There she goes!"

"Come on, baby!"

"Hang in there another three minutes!"

An hour later, when *Sinbad* left Port Lockroy, the big potential iceberg was still up there in one piece. Several small chunks sloughed off at other places and slid down the face of the cliffs into the water with a big splash which sent a swell out to lap against the steel sides of the ship, but Cavige's chunk never budged. He grumbled, "Ah, hogwash! I'm gonna complain to the captain."

It was nearly noon when *Sinbad* left Port Lockroy and headed for Lemaire Channel. Marjory Dumont said, "These news items about changes in weather patterns— now the crew tell us that even right here in the Antarctic, they think the temperature is higher than usual. I've heard for years weather is changing all over the world. Maybe the poles will thaw out and the rest of the world freeze up, like another ice age. I know that in England, it was much colder last winter. Every year it changes someplace.''

"Yes, and there were more tornadoes than usual," said Brenda, who had joined Tony Destefani, and the rest of the group.

"I think it's due to more pollution. Jet planes are spilling out exhaust fumes into the atmosphere," declared Helen.

"Naw," Cavige loudly sneered, "that's a lotta hogwash!"

Helen, ignoring Cavige, turned her attention to Marjory and agreed. "Yes, we must be causing some change in the atmosphere with all those cars and planes."

After lunch, the group gathered again on deck, taking in the sights. They were joined by Dr. Barry and a few others, including another young man, Edward L. McCaughlin, Jr.

Ed had decided at an early age to give his all to the electronic media. A promising student in broadcasting, Ed had graduated with top honors. He had a wealthy uncle who owned a chain of radio and television stations, and had made him a graduation gift of the *Sinbad* cruise, after which Ed was expected to assume the position of account executive in his uncle's empire. He was intelligent and witty, and well liked by the other passengers, especially the "travelettes."

Ed amiably remarked, "You're huddled here in such serious deliberations. Are you plotting a mutiny?"

"Worse than that," replied Al. "Join us and get some macabre ingredients for a radio program." Al then addressed a question to Dr. Barry. "You remember when we were back there in that bay? You know, the first place we stopped."

"You mean Buenos Aires?" interrupted Tony Destefani.

"No," said Al, "I mean down here. The first stop we made—Admiral Island."

Dr. Barry corrected him. "I think you mean Admiralty Bay."

"Admiralty Bay—that's it," replied Al.

"King George Island," added Barry, "just before we went to the Russian and Chilean Stations."

"Yes. You remember those graves we saw on the hill?" asked Al.

"Those piles of stones with crosses on them?" Tony casually inquired.

"What about them?" asked Dr. Barry.

"Well," continued Al. "I think you said that the ground was rocky, or frozen, so they couldn't dig any graves."

Barry reflected for a moment and then replied. "They just covered the bodies with what little soil they could find, right on top of the frozen ground. Then piled those stones over them to keep skuas or seals off and stuck those crosses on them. That's all."

Ed McCaughlin remarked, "I suppose in this climate, the bodies would just remain frozen solid."

"Yes, probably they would," replied Dr. Barry, "although here, on the peninsula, it thaws a little each summer. Sometimes in January and February it will go up into the forties for a few hours in the middle of the day."

"So those bodies probably didn't remain frozen," said Tony.

"I think they did remain frozen under the rocks," stated Dr. Barry. "All winter, at least for, say, ten months of the year, it stays below freezing here, so probably they never did thaw out. They may have been there for many decades. I never inquired about them. There are other places, up on the plateau, where nothing ever thaws out. A body left there in the ice would remain frozen forever."

Helen said, "Suppose some scientist found a body that had been frozen like that. Could he bring it back to life?"

"No," Barry laconically replied.

"Why not?" Helen persisted.

"For one thing," commented Barry, "Life is more than just a body."

"A soul?" asked Ed. "You mean the body had a soul that flitted away somewhere, and it can flit back into the body again?"

"No," said Barry. "I believe when a body dies, the soul does, too."

Marjory joined in the discussion. "What do you mean? What goes to heaven—or to hell?"

"Nothing," Ed emphatically said. "I don't believe there are any such places. Does anybody believe in a resurrection anymore? Do we die and come alive again sometime? How about those bodies back there at Admiralty Bay? Would they be resurrected?"

Dr. Barry was beginning to think the conversation was getting out of hand. He was tired of fielding such questions. Helen took up the ball. "I don't know," she said. "Some of my folks believe in a resurrection. They think *new* bodies will be given to dead people, and they'll start walking around again."

"Oh sure," said Al dubiously. "I've heard that one, too. I wonder what it would feel like if one of them came down here and saw a frozen corpse—say, one of those back there under those piles of stones."

"For one thing," said Ed, "he would have a funeral, and bury himself. But he would have to chop a grave out of the ice or frozen ground. He'd need an ax. You've heard the expression, 'Let the dead bury their dead'? Maybe, if he were a scientest, he might try to revive himself. Then he would be twins." Dr. Barry winced. "Or," continued Ed, "he might start blaming himself for what happened. Suppose he were one of those seal hunters who killed hundreds of seals in the old days—fur seals, I mean —until they were nearly extinct."

"Yes," said Helen, "I heard about that. I heard one

ship left here with thousands of seal skins. The ship was lost in a storm. All that killing for nothing.''

''You said it,'' agreed Al. ''Suppose this scientist, and his revived body, got into a fight, and one killed the other. Would it be murder, or suicide?''

''Both,'' offered Helen.

''Would he be tried for murder?'' asked Tony Destefani.

Dr. Barry answered Tony's question. ''There aren't any courts down here in the Antarctic.''

''You mean if someone commits a murder here, he can't be tried?'' asked Tony. His tone was casual.

Dr. Barry deliberated. ''No country has political jurisdiction here. The Antarctic Treaty, signed by twelve countries in 1959, makes this an international area for scientific research. I suppose there would be some question as to in what court a murderer could be tried. If a murder were committed on board a ship, the trial would be held in a court of the country in which the ship was registered. If committed ashore, that's another matter. It might then be just a question of the murderer's nationality.''

The sunlit sky slowly merged into a strangely luminous twilight as *Sinbad* moved steadily southward among snow-capped isles and glacier-vested peaks. A magic lantern moon rose obliquely along the northern horizon, a pale round disc slowly moving westward close to the rim of planet Earth. As it came into view between the distant islands, it cast a delicate reflection upon the shimmering waters.

A December night in polar seas, so mild and light, made *Sinbad's* captain and officers uneasy. But their passengers were cheerful and contented. They strolled the decks, or gathered in the bars and lounges, enjoying the music of the ship's orchestra. Some were playing cards.

In addition to Tony Destefani's attachment to Brenda Clarke, passengers were beginning to notice his ''wife,'' Teresa Destefani, in the company of another passenger, one Victor P. Daly. They had been spending a lot of leisure time together.

In his early days as a young lawyer, Victor Daly had, like some other legal beagles, subsisted on sordid divorce cases. Later, by adroit manipulation of his colleagues and peers, and aided by his wealthy brother, Hugh P. Daly, a New York tanker operator, Victor had gained an appointment as a federal judge. After a few years, his financial situation had vastly improved. He had accumulated a fortune. Daly had made some enemies, but the wealth that he had magically acquired gave him the means to travel extensively, thereby avoiding confrontations with miscellaneous ex-convicts whom he had sentenced.

Tony didn't seem to object to Daly's constant attention to Teresa. In fact, he seemed to encourage the shipboard affair much to the delight of the gossips on board.

Marjory Dumont was concerned about her roommate, Brenda. On one occasion Marjory had seen Brenda in Tony's brief but ardent embrace. Later she warned Brenda about getting involved with a married man. Brenda merely said, "Don't worry, Marge, I can take care of myself." Marjory was sure she could, but she hoped the infatuation would not get out of hand.

Romances were budding all over the ship. Marjory herself had received the attention of a few male passengers, but so far, she had remained impartial. She had a slight preference for Ed McCaughlin, but she kept it to herself.

Except during meal times, and at occasional bridge games, Tony's "wife" Teresa, and Victor Daly were seen very little. They were often together in Daly's stateroom. Nobody minded, Tony least of all. If the facts were known, the affair between Teresa and Daly was well suited to Tony's schemes. It not only gave him an excuse to pursue Brenda, but he was sure that Teresa would soon tire of Daly, and fulfill a certain purpose for which they had gone on that cruise. He felt that whatever suspicion might result would be directed toward Teresa.

At first Brenda was afraid of getting involved with Tony. But as time passed, and she realized that Tony had no regard for his "wife" Teresa, she put her doubts aside, and succumbed to his urbane and artful seduction. To Tony, Brenda was just a delightful and luscious dish, to be sampled in passing, but he grew more fond of her than he had intended.

That evening, Victor and Teresa had been playing bridge with Victoria Degrelle and Emma Cavige for about two hours. There were occasional outbursts of profanity on both sides. The four had frequently played bridge together, and the other passengers in the lounge paid little attention to their squabbles. Victoria and Emma were loaded with jewelry which they displayed to good advantage at the bridge table. Teresa was smartly dressed, as usual, but given to wearing less conspicuous hardware. She was, otherwise, well endowed, which hadn't been overlooked by the male passengers, especially Daly.

The game proceeded uninterrupted for a while until finally they reached an impasse. They had asked a lounge steward for a fresh deck of cards. Teresa won the bid in spades. Victoria, in her usual distracted manner, was looking around the lounge, when her partner, Emma, played the ace of diamonds. Teresa, aware that Victoria wasn't paying attention, quickly drew the last cards in the suit, the jack and queen of diamonds, from Daly's dummy hand on the table, and her own. She covered Emma's ace with the two face cards. Victoria, who saw only the two top cards, immediately drew a low spade trump from her hand, and proudly displayed it on the table. She was unaware that she had commited the classic *faux pas* of bridge.

Emma Cavige screeched, "You blind? You just trumped my ace!" She was on her feet, leaning across the table toward Victoria, her red face distorted in anger, her pudgy fists clenched. "I'll bust that moldy puss a'yourn! You lousy tramp!" Emma's careful diction had dissolved with her rage.

Victoria pushed back her chair and scattered everything on the table. With the cunning of a cardsharp, she flipped the rest of the cards in her hand toward her partner's head. The sharp edges of the new plastic cards stung Emma's face like tiny daggers.

All heads in the lounge turned toward the scene. When she stood up, Victoria's chin was on a level with the top of Emma's haystack hairdo. Vic Daly got up and tried to intervene, but Victoria pushed him aside with a sharp elbow jab. He led Teresa to one side. Some of the other passengers crowded around, but none tried to stop the scrap. Victoria screamed vulgarities in a mixture of French and Flemish with a few choice English phrases thrown in. The other passengers applauded and urged them on in various languages from Low German to Greek. Emma held her ground in high-octane Texan, and swung one fat fist toward Victoria's jaw, but missed.

In retaliation, Victoria grabbed at Emma's hair. To her surprise, she lost her balance and was thrown backward. Emma's haystack hairdo wig had come off in Victoria's hands. In an instant, Emma was on her, pounding her with her fists. Like two wildcats, screaming obscenities, and kicking and clawing at each other, they rolled over and over on the floor of the lounge. Victoria finally freed herself from Emma's grasp, got up, and pulled her fat opponent to her feet. With long, red lacquered nails, Victoria scratched Emma down both sides of her face. Emma screamed in pain and lunged at Victoria, tearing the front of her filmy black gown down to the waist.

A large, very elaborate and expensive diamond brooch which had adorned the front of Victoria's low cut dress, came loose and went flying under a table near the starboard side where Brenda Clarke and some other passengers were sitting. Three persons, including Brenda, got down under the table to look for it. But the brooch had slid past their table toward Teresa Destefani. While all eyes in the lounge were directed toward the search under the table, Teresa stuck out one foot in the path of the brooch, stopped it, leaned down, and scooped it up in her hand. She closed her fingers around it and said nothing.

Meanwhile, Victoria had torn herself loose from Emma, and started after the brooch. She saw Brenda and the others rising from under the table. She shouted at Brenda, "Geeve me zat brooch!" and held out her hand.

"I didn't find it!" Brenda shouted back at her.

Victoria looked at the others. There were blank stares all around. None would admit finding the brooch. Victoria got down under the table herself, as did some of the others, but the brooch had disappeared. She was certain Brenda had it. They looked under nearby tables and along the near side of the lounge with no results.

Victoria accused Brenda again. "You better geeve it to me!" she threatened with a menacing tone. "I will make you geeve it to me! I want it now!" She started to reach for Brenda.

Emma Cavige shouted, "Leave her alone!"

Tony Destefani was nearby. He came over and stood between Victoria and Brenda. He smiled and winked at Brenda. She gave Tony a grateful glance. He quietly said to Victoria, "If she says she hasn't got it, then she hasn't got it. So just calm down." Brenda thanked Tony. She walked over to Marjory Dumont, who had been seated at another table.

Victoria suspiciously eyed everyone, especially the "travel girls," whom she considered far beneath her station. Emma Cavige, somewhat mollified by the thought of Victoria losing her brooch, plopped her mangled wig back on her head, and straightened her clothing. Emma and Victoria started to leave the lounge by separate doors, shouting insults and threats across the room as they went, each in her own language, only partially understood by the other, but bringing forth peals of laughter from the other passengers.

As Victoria left the lounge, holding up the shredded front of her gown, she shouted, "I want zat brooch back! I will report zis to ze captain! I am going to see Dr. Barry!"

With that final outburst, Victoria, her head held high, turned in a huff, and left the lounge.

Victoria was unaware of Dr. Barry's presence in the back of the lounge. He had arrived in time to see the fight, and was the only witness to Teresa's theft of the brooch. Dr. Barry was undisturbed by the scene, and not at all surprised by Teresa's actions. He, too, had suspected the Destefanis of some ulterior motive on *Sinbad's* cruise, but he couldn't prove it. Rather than report the incident to Captain Gilbert, Dr. Barry thought he would try to handle the matter himself. He would bide his time, and then later discreetly confront Teresa Destefani. In that manner, he hoped to avoid further scandal.

The infamous bridge game fight, culminating with the missing diamond brooch, became fuel for instant and intriguing shipboard gossip. The story spread like wildfire. Little by little, many of the passengers began to believe Victoria Degrelle's accusations. Perhaps Brenda Clarke *had* stolen the diamond brooch.

Leaving the picturesque Neumayer Channel and Cape Errera, *Sinbad* was carefully guided through Butler Passage with due respect for ominous, well-named Hazard Rock, on the left, and Heed Rock, on the right. On *Sinbad's* spacious and quiet bridge, the navigators were blissfully oblivious to the chatter, laughter, quarreling, feuding, intrigue, thievery, and other forms of knavery flourishing within the merry stack of decks beneath their calm sanctuary. Steadily and smoothly, *Sinbad* moved south toward the majestic peaks of Cape Renaud and the Graham Coast during the early hours of December 21st.

Radio news items continued with frequent comments about possible changes in the weather patterns. There were occasional references to "astronomical events." Such things had occurred in the past, and, as no celestial navigation was done while among the islands and along the Antarctic Penninsula, Captain Gilbert assumed the "events," whatever they were, to be temporary, and that normal conditions would soon return.

Ole Magnussen, *Sinbad's* radio operator, and Ira Mason at Palmer exchanged brief comments on the weather. Ira joked, "If this keeps up, we'll have to get this station airconditioned."

"By next trip, maybe you'll have some palm trees around there," contributed Ole. "We've got our air-conditioning going right now on the ship. Maybe when we visit Palmer in a couple of days you can come aboard and cool off."

During the morning, *Sinbad* proceeded slowly through gorgeous Lemaire Channel and into Penola Strait. It was Captain Gilbert's intention to take his vessel close to the British base at the Argentine Islands, and then on to Adelaide Island. There was much pack ice and many icebergs of all sizes and shapes in Penola Strait. Their progress was slow. Frost smoke rose from the icepack as far away as they could see. At times they were closed in by fog so dense they could barely see the bow of their ship from the promenade deck or from the bridge. At such times, they stopped the ship and waited for the fog to clear. Some of the icebergs could be seen on the radar screen. Others, with sloping sides, covered with soft snow, didn't make good radar targets. The ship wasn't moved ahead at such times.

While stopped in fog, the passengers often listened to sounds from sources they couldn't see. Occasionally, if near an iceberg, they could hear the faint cracking of the surface and feel a coolness on their faces. The lapping of small wavelets could be heard against the berg at the waterline, and sometimes a "swoosh," as a swell came up under an overhanging ledge, or ice "foot." Sometimes they heard small chunks break off around the edges and drop on the loose pack in the water. Big icebergs had their own voices.

At times, unseen gulls could be heard plaintively calling

overhead. Sometimes the sea and ice around *Sinbad* were obscured by the fog, and the polar sun caused a misty glow to surround the ship as if it was shrouded in a giant cocoon floating alone in space.

Occasionally a group of penguins would appear in unison out of the depths near the ship. Together they would breach, making a short dive into the air in a small upward curve and down again, excitedly and tempestuously, into the ice water with just a flash of their black and white coats and yellow feet. Dr. Barry remarked that their actions were very strange.

Now and then, a flat white "pancake" of ice would drift by with two or three dark grey seals riding on it. If it came near enough to the ship, the passengers would shout at them, but the seals would merely swing their pudgy heads. If the ship came too close, they would clumsily move to the edge and dive off. Often, they just went back to swaying and fighting.

At one place, *Sinbad* was near a large iceberg which capsized. It rolled over, majestically and slowly, then continued to roll from side to side like a big ocean liner in a long beam swell, until it finally stabilized. It caused a swell which made our icebergs roll a little, and bitsy bergs and growlers pitched in unison around it. The swell even caused *Sinbad* to roll a little. The deck steward jokingly said that Captain Gilbert had arranged the demonstrations.

They finally reached a point off a narrow inlet between small islands near the British Station, but found it still frozen over with flat winter ice from shore to shore. They had intended to send in a launch so that some of the passengers could visit the station. Marjory and others from England were disappointed when they learned the launch couldn't go in to the station.

Some of the station personnel could be seen on a hillside waving to the passengers. The ship blew three long blasts as a courtesy salute and turned slowly away. *Sinbad's* radio operator talked with the station personnel and wished them all happy holidays. They said the British Antarctic Survey Ship *Bransfield* was anchored nearby, and they would be having a party on board.

4

SINBAD PROCEEDED slowly southwestward through "Grandaddy" Channel toward Adelaide Island. The passengers, tired from a long day of sightseeing, retired to their cabins for the night. Captain Gilbert stopped the ship off Larrouy Island, and lay down on a settee in the chart room for a short rest. He intended to take *Sinbad* through to Adelaide Island next morning, then back to Palmer Station for a short visit.

Just before 0400, the tired skipper was awakened by radio operator Ole Magnussen. Ole had copied a message which Palmer Station had sent to *Quest*. The message was about the change occurring in the angle of the earth's axis, and the evacuation of Palmer Station. Captain Gilbert's reaction was immediate. He was wide awake even before he finished reading the first line. This was indeed something serious!

"Evacuations!" he exclaimed. "They must think there is great danger—but from what? Is the Antarctic going to drop off the earth?" He became increasingly concerned as he read the message again. It was certainly true that the temperature was above normal.

When the chief mate came to the bridge to relieve the second mate, Captain Gilbert and the two mates, all good polar navigators with many years of experience, discussed the important message at great length. Celestial navigation wouldn't be possible. They wouldn't have precise declinations for any celestial bodies. Their return to South

America would have to be by dead reckoning. The radio operator continued to copy messages between Palmer, *Quest,* and *Southwind.* Soon *Bransfield* joined in with additional information. The ship had orders to evacuate the British Stations. *Bransfield* had already started evacuation procedures.

Captain Gilbert sent a message to the ship's agent in Buenos Aires, advising that he was cognizant of the phenomena, and would keep them informed of *Sinbad's* movements. He decided that, as stations were being evacuated, he should cut the cruise short and take *Sinbad* back to South America, and told Ole to so advise *Quest* and Palmer. Captain Pack informed him that *Quest* was already underway to evacuate Palmer Station, and Captain Gilbert turned *Sinbad* northward.

At 1100, *Quest* and *Sinbad* exchanged messages again. *Quest's* ET, Enrique, told Ole that *Quest* was going to attempt an evacuation of the men at the Argentine Station in Deception, that there were new eruptions there, but *Quest* was going in anyway and try to get the five men out of the caldera.

Ole passed the information to Captain Gilbert. His only comment was that Captain Pack was taking a big risk, but that if anyone could pull it off, he was the man. The eruptions didn't surprise Captain Gilbert. He was glad they hadn't occurred when *Sinbad* was there a few days earlier. They were far from Deception, and he considered his vessel to be in safe waters, but the report of the increase in the tilt of the earth's axis and the evacuations of Antarctic Stations made him uneasy. He decided his ship should depart Antarctic waters and return to South America without delay.

Sinbad continued northeastward toward Lemaire Channel. There were many icebergs and growlers and much loose pack in the channel. Progress was slow. The polar sun was hidden behind the lofty peaks of Danco Coast. Sheer, nearly perpendicular masses of rock, ice and snow rose abruptly on both sides of the vessel, stark walls making a narrow canyon. Great glaciers filled steep gorges and ravines between the peaks.

Unaware of any problem, many delighted passengers were out on *Sinbad's* deck after luncheon, enjoying the beautiful fjord-like passage. Chatting, joking and laughing, their voices echoed off the rocky walls of the canyon. Some took their noonday meal in the comfort of the main lounge, watching the ship's progress through large picture windows, while others remained in the main dining room. The crew was discharging their duties with customary efficiency.

At 1300, *Sinbad* was in the narrowest part of Lemaire Channel. Suddenly the vessel shuddered, lurched violently, and seemed to crunch down hard on something beneath it. Several tremendous impacts came in rapid succession with thunderous subterranean explosions.

Sinbad pitched and rolled, first to one side, and then the other. Terrified passengers and crew were violently thrown to the decks, against bulkheads, and out of chairs.

Deep rumbling earth shocks followed one after another. *Sinbad* shook as if struck by massive gunfire. The ice-filled waters of the channel rose and lifted the ship on enormous swells. Avalanches of ice, snow and rock plunged, with deafening crescendo, down the steep slopes of the canyon, dashing great waves of water and ice over the ship. Everyone on board was stunned and bewildered. Some were struck by flying chunks of ice. As soon as they could stand on their feet, the captain and bridge officers tried to regain control of the vessel. They knew they were in deep trouble. They realized that an earthquake of great force and intensity was taking place. Fortunately, *Sinbad* was in deep water clear of the channel banks on each side. Was it damaged and likely to sink? Captain Gilbert called the engine room. The answer came that there seemed to be no damage to that part of the vessel, but two men were injured. Slowly, reports were obtained from other parts of the ship. There was no apparent damage to the hull, no visible leaks. What had seemed like impacts against the hull had been strong earthquake shocks. Immediate attention to the needs of the passengers was ordered.

Lemaire Channel was filling with icebergs, large and small, rapidly breaking off from several glaciers. The channel northward became completely blocked with icebergs. Captain Gilbert decided to go back toward Penola Strait. He tried to turn the vessel with twin screws, but as he did so, he was dismayed to see that the channel southward was also becoming blocked. It was getting increasingly difficult to move the ship against the mounting jam of bitsy bergs and growlers. Unable to turn, *Sinbad* stopped. The bergs crowded closer around the vessel. The ship lay across the channel completely bracketed in on all sides. If Gilbert and his men had known, they would have realized they were better off between the high mountains than outside of the channel.

Bismarck and Gerlache Straits were also full of icebergs rapidly moving northeastward in strong currents. Some bergs were grounded near the islands. Others were slowly turning between opposing currents. It was no place for any ship. The vessel could have been crushed by the monsters. *Sinbad* was in great danger, but less than if the ship had been outside the channel.

Frightened passengers clamored for information. During a lull in the earthquake, Captain Gilbert spoke to them over the ship's public address system.

"Attention, please. This is the captain speaking. We have been advised of a very powerful unknown force which has caused the earth to change the angle of its axis with reference to the plane of its orbit around the sun. In other words, it has tipped a little more, causing the sun to appear farther south. In addition to this, as you all well know, there are strong earthquakes which we are still experiencing. We are now trying to communicate with other stations, and the Research Vessel *Quest* was going into

Deception Island to evacuate five men. So far, we have no reply from *Quest* nor from Palmer Station. We believe there may have been damage to their radios or antennas. As far as we have been able to determine, there is no serious damage to *Sinbad*. We are doing all we can to attend to the injured, and we are making every effort to proceed northward as the ice may permit. We don't anticipate having to abandon the ship, but I suggest you read over your instructions for such an emergency, so as to become familiar with survival on ice should it come to that. The bergs surrounding us are jammed in this narrow channel and aren't moving much. We may be safe here for the present. Please keep your flotation and life jackets on or near you at all times."

After a brief pause, the captain continued. "We have advised our Buenos Aires office that we have no fatalities, but that we are in danger, although our vessel hasn't been seriously damaged yet. They will in turn advise our agents in all countries so that inquiries from your relatives and friends may be answered. Meanwhile, our operator will transmit messages you may wish to send."

Gradually the alarm among passengers and crew was abated by the skipper's calm voice. He himself didn't feel calm, however. No one in charge of the safety of a ship, with a hundred and seventy-five persons on board, surrounded by great menacing icebergs and trembling from continuous shocks, could feel exactly calm.

Meanwhile, officers and stewards went among the passengers giving advice, helping them understand the abandon ship procedures which were given in pamphlets handed to them at the start of the cruise. They were urged not to panic, but to obey the instructions which would be given over the ship's public address system. They wouldn't abandon ship unless it was certain to become crushed. Procedures for survival on ice were clearly spelled out. Other vessels, in the past, had been abandoned and persons saved. But those were hardy Antarctic explorers and mariners. All of *Sinbad's* passengers were inexperienced, and more than half were women. Some were injured.

Large bergs, many higher than *Sinbad's* bridge and boat deck, were moving closer to the vessel from both sides, driven by pressure of other icebergs breaking off from glaciers. Pressures against the ship were increasing. Overhead, the sky had become overcast obscuring the sun. Captain Gilbert and the officers grew apprehensive and constantly had the hull checked for pressure leaks. All lifesaving equipment was made ready, and plans for leaving the vessel were discussed in detail. It appeared that they would all have to get onto one of the large icebergs if they were forced to leave *Sinbad*. The berg would float, but *Sinbad* would sink.

Along the coasts of the Antarctic Peninsula, the earthquake shocks gradually subsided. The great glaciers, descending faster toward the sea, filled the straits, bays, and fjords with countless icebergs. Rocky heights, worn smooth by glacier ice, appeared on the façades of Graham land.

Awesome avalanches of ice, snow, and rocks continued to roar down the steep slopes in a deafening crescendo, overwhelming the plaintive cries of bewildered birds and animals seeking refuge in the strange turmoil.

Copious masses of vapor were swiftly borne northward by strong upper winds. Driven by forceful katabatic gales, a fine mixture of volcanic ash and snow filled the lower atmosphere forming greyish drifts against the lee side of the rocks and cliffs. Gerlache and Bransfield Straits were filled with huge icebergs rolling and colliding in the current. Lemaire Channel offered no means of escape for *Sinbad*. An immense iceberg was seen slowly moving in from the Deloncle embayment carried by current and wind, its movement fequently checked by radar. Before long, it was observed to have stopped moving, apparently hard aground and completely blocking the narrow channel. Many glacier icebergs were also crowding in on the other side. *Sinbad* was surrounded.

Because of frequent squalls, most of the passengers remained inside to avoid the smoke, rain and sleet. Ole Magnussen posted a notice on the bulletin board that a speech by the President of the United States of America would be broadcast throughout the world and could be heard in the main lounge at sixteen hundred, or two P.M., Washington time.

Many of the passengers whose injuries weren't too severe assembled in the main lounge, carrying their red flotation and life-jackets, which they piled on deck or on chairs near them. Damaged furniture had been stacked in a corner of the lounge, and broken bottles and glasses cleared away from behind the bar. Debris of broken Christmas tree ornaments was swept away, and the tree was standing again with a few decorations still intact. Lounge stewards, some with bandaged heads or hands, served drinks and did their best to attend to the needs of the passengers. The lounge became quiet when the President's speech was announced.

Reception was poor, but enough was heard to cause some consternation. Those with homes in coastal areas were most vociferous. After the President's speech, the radio operator was swamped with messages to be transmitted to relatives and associates. The passengers' anxiety about their people and properties at home was added to the anguish of their own perilous situation. It was a sleepless night for most of *Sinbad's* passengers, as well as for Captain Gilbert.

During the early morning hours, the officer of the watch notified Captain Gilbert that *Sinbad* was being pushed toward the big grounded iceberg. Watching the ship's movement closely, they determined the vessel would be forced against the berg by the pressure of two smaller bergs already against the fenders of the starboard side. There was an ominous grinding and crackling of those masses of solid ice against each other and against *Sinbad's* fenders and hull.

The smaller bergs weren't high. Early rising passengers could see over them as they stood along the rails on the promenade deck. Some passengers were merely curious, others were greatly alarmed. During the day, the ship's officers and crew concealed their own anxieties and endeavored to assure the passengers that the vessel would be extricated from its perilous situation. A program of games and entertainment was announced, and free drinks were made available at the bar. There was to be a "besetment" party until the ship got out of the ice jam. The orchestra played request music with only brief intermissions. Nevertheless, many passengers were apprehensive and some became hysterical.

Sinbad closed slowly with the larger grounded berg. All available fenders were already in place on the port side. Loose pack ice was squeezed out or crushed between the hull and the iceberg. The flat top of the berg was about ten feet above the boat deck, a solid wall of white against the port side. The two pale green and white glacier bergs were close along the starboard side, apparently with underwater protrusions against the hull. Lemaire Channel was completely filled with large masses of icebergs from shore to shore, tightly jammed, not moving. *Sinbad* was imprisoned in a massive girdle of ice.

On the evening of December 24, Emil Angstrom, chief engineer of *Sinbad,* had casually made his way up through the ship to the master's quarters. He had felt a great urge to race up several steps at once, but he didn't want to arouse the curiosity of passengers or crew, even though what he had to tell Captain Gilbert had quickened Emil's pulse and brought beads of perspiration to his brow. His knock on the captain's door was louder than usual and brought a quick response. Emil entered, carefully closed the door, and spoke in a low tone.

"We've got trouble, Captain. Water is coming in at

three places on the starboard side about four feet below the water line. Ice pressure is crushing the hull. We hear it cracking in several places. So far, the bilge pumps are holding it, but if the crushing increases, we may not hold it long.''

Captain Gilbert slipped on his jacket and the two men left the quarters. They nonchalantly walked along the deck to the service stairwell, and, with forced smiles, greeted passengers as they passed. Within moments, they were in the engine room examining the leaks in the hull. By that time, a leak had also developed on the port side. It ruled out the possibility of listing the ship to bring the starboard leaks above the water.

Gilbert needed no further convincing. He went to the bridge and summoned the cruise director, chief purser, and chief steward. After a short briefing, and a quick conference with deck officers, he scribbled a *Mayday* message and handed it to Ole Magnussen, the radio operator. It was transmitted at 1900. Then Captain Gilbert made an announcement to the passengers over the ship's public address system.

Speaking calmly in an effort to hide his emotions, he said, ''Ladies and gentlemen, this is the captain. I have decided that, for the safety of all persons on board, it is necessary to establish a camp on the iceberg alongside of us. We will endeavor to secure *Sinbad* to the iceberg by means of ice anchors and cables. We have several small leaks in the hull caused by pressure against the ship; therefore I consider the iceberg safer than the ship for the present. The ship may sink if the pressure becomes too great. Please go to your cabins and pack only essential items, including two outfits of warm clothing. Do *not* rush or panic. The pumps are easily holding the water at present, and this is only a precautionary measure.''

Captain Gilbert paused for a moment, then continued, ''We will transfer a motor life boat and several inflatable rafts to the iceberg, and spread tarpaulins underfoot. I do not know how long you will have to remain on the iceberg. *Sinbad* may not sink. Some crew members will remain on board, and we will keep the pumps and other systems going. Possibly the ice pressure may weaken and some of the cracks may close to a small extent and lessen the flow of water. We will also make every effort to stop the leaks and keep the vessel afloat. Possibly you will be able to return aboard, but that is only conjecture at this point. We will try to make you as comfortable as possible in a camp on the iceberg. We will take ample supplies of food and beverages. As soon as you have had dinner and have packed your essentials, please go to the boat deck where you will be assisted up a ladder to the soft top of the iceberg. Take your flotation jackets and life preservers. Wear your thermal overshoes and your boots. The top of the iceberg will be wet. Fortunately, it is fairly flat.''

Meanwhile, the deck crew had hung a Jacob's ladder on the side of the iceberg from the top edge down to the level of the boat deck and rigged a safety net below it. They imbedded ice anchors in the surface of the iceberg and attached cables with which *Sinbad* was made fast. Seven of the ship's inflatable life rafts and one motor lifeboat were hauled up and placed about fifty meters back from the edge. There the rafts were inflated and securely anchored. They were to provide covered shelter for all one hundred seventy-five persons on board *Sinbad*. Four heavy plastic tents with plastic floors were also set up and secured. Two of them were improvised as rest rooms and set up near the far side of the berg with suitable drainage ditches to the edge. Another tent was to be used as a galley, and the fourth as a mess room.

The top surface of the iceberg was soft and wet from melting. It was a slushly operation due to the abnormally warm temperature. Some runoff canals were chopped in the ice to drain the camp area. All equipment was securely anchored. The improvised habitats were placed close together with lifelines passed between and all around them. Lifelines were also made ready to be fastened to passengers whenever they moved outside the covered life rafts or tents. The danger of the iceberg suddenly becoming loose and listing or capsizing had to be kept in mind. It was of medium size, composed of stratified layers of snow pressured into hard ice. The side against the ship was nearly vertical. It appeared to have broken away from an ice shelf or tongue.

Continuous rumbling, as of distant thunder and loud explosions, was heard. Clouds of smoke and vapor rapidly drifted northward driven by strong upper winds. Frequent squalls with rain and hail made the work hazardous. Nevertheless, *Sinbad's* willing and hardy crew managed to set up the camp with surprising speed.

Dr. Barry assured the passengers that a camp on an iceberg was feasible. "In our scientific programs, we have purposedly set up camps on drifting icebergs. Some of them have been occupied by scientists for months at a time for the purpose of studying currents and atmospheric conditions."

Frank Lundstrom, the chief purser, tried to dispel fear among the passengers. "*Sinbad* is especially well supplied with lifesaving equipment. We have two motor lifeboats and ten inflatable life rafts. Captain Gilbert is very strict about drills. The crew has been well trained in these matters."

The passengers had received Captain Gilbert's pronouncement with varied degrees of emotion, from mild apprehension to abject terror. Among the latter was Teresa Destefani. At the captain's instructions to leave the ship, she paled and shook with fear. She collapsed in a lounge chair and shouted obscenities. Gone was all pretense of refinement or culture. Tony Destefani tried to calm her, and threatened to use his fist on her makeup-smeared and noisy face if she didn't shut up.

Phil Cavige clutched at his chest. His knees weakened and he slumped to the deck. His fall was eased by his wife and another nearby passenger. His heart attack was mild. The ship's doctor, Hector Raymond, was called, and Phil was taken to the ship's hospital. Two other men were also hospitalized with heart attacks, one of them quite serious. Dr. Raymond and the nurse, Lorraine Jackson, had a busy night.

Helen Norwood tightened her hold on her husband's arm and gasped at the captain's words. She breathed heavily for a few minutes, but quickly recovered. Al comforted her, and they went to their cabin to pack their "essentials."

"I don't know what to take," Al mused. "I can't shave without electricity. I'll have to grow a beard."

Helen said, "I'm just going to wear this warm pants suit and take another with me."

"Me, too," added Al.

"And my books and flotation jacket," continued Helen.

"Tooth brushes," said Al. "Gloves and sun glasses." Helen had completed the list.

"Yeah, let's get dinner now." Al tried to be jovial. He squeezed his wife's hand as they left their cabin.

After dinner, they donned their flotation jackets, and took their life jackets and overnight essentials to the boat deck where they were joined by the Dearborns.

"There's a rumor some of us can sleep on the ship every night. I mean—take turns," declared Dr. Dearborn.

"Oh, yeah?" exclaimed Al.

Chief Purser Frank Lundstrom's voice sounded above the noisy babble. "Ladies and gentlemen, may I have your attention, please. The captain has decided that, as the leaks aren't getting any worse, and the pumps are holding the water down, it will be possible for some of the passengers to sleep on the ship. We will divide you into three groups of about thirty-one passengers each. The crew will also be divided in such a way that they can carry on their duties. We will start by asking you to move to three separate locations in the following manner: all those whose surnames begin with the letters A through H, please stay near the ladder to the iceberg. You will be called group A. Those beginning with letters I through P, please step to the starboard side, the side opposite the ladder. You are group B. Those with letters Q through Z, please go into the main lounge. You are group C. After you have done this, we will even up the groups. It's not our intention to separate relatives or friends, so we will adjust the groups as best we can after the first division.''

"We'll be separated,'' said Joyce Dearborn.

"I don't think so,'' answered Helen Norwood. "We can ask them to change us to your group. He said they wouldn't separate friends.''

"Okay now, come on, Joyce,'' urged Dr. Dearborn. "It looks like we may have to go onto the iceberg first. We're in the A group.''

"We're in B,'' said Al. "We stay right here on this side. Go ahead. We'll try to join you on the next go-around.''

Clarence and Joyce Dearborn moved off toward the Jacob's ladder. Al and Helen Norwood stepped to the starboard side. Everyone carried his or her orange colored life jacket over an arm or slung from a shoulder. It was too warm to wear them. There was some confusion because a number of people weren't sure to which group they belonged. It was soon evident that group B had more than either of the other two groups. The assistant purser appeared with a passenger list and addressed group B.

"Please respond when I call your names,'' he said. After all B names were called, four people had to move to A and C groups. Still the B group had too many.

"Our friends are in A group,'' said Al Norwood. "May we change?''

"Yes, Mr. Norwood,'' said the assistant purser.

The Norwoods moved to the A group at the ladder and joined the Dearborns, to the relief of all four. Soon the groups were nearly equal.

The chief mate, Eric Sorensen, and four seamen took places at the top of the ladder. The second mate and two other seamen stationed themselves on the railing, halfway up the ladder. They held its rope sides to keep it steady. The chief purser, Frank Lundstrom, and the assistant purser stood on deck at each side of the ladder.

The people in group A were instructed to don their life jackets and start up the ladder. A lifeline was looped around them under their arms and they were almost hoisted bodily by the seamen at the top. Some of the passengers went merrily, taking it all as a great adventure. Others nearly fainted, while some were too busy taking pictures to worry. Some struggled and had to be forcibly persuaded to step over on the flat wooden steps. A rope ladder hanging on the side of an iceberg was a fearsome thing to many. Group B followed group A up the ladder and onto the iceberg.

As the operation proceeded, the voice of the captain was heard again. "Ladies and gentlemen. We have decided on the following arrangements. Group C will remain on the ship until midnight, then go up on the iceberg, and group B will come aboard. At eight in the morning, group A will come aboard and B will go to the iceberg, and so forth. Each group will stay eight hours on the ship, and sixteen on the iceberg. In this manner there will never be more than an average of thirty passengers on board *Sinbad* at any one time. We believe that, in case of possible sinking of *Sinbad*, we will have ample time to transfer this small number to the iceberg. This will give all passengers an opportunity to sleep in their staterooms during their eight hours on board. Of course, those who do not feel safe on the ship may stay on the iceberg under cover, in the inflated life rafts."

After a short pause, Gilbert continued, "This channel is now completely filled with icebergs, many of which are aground near the banks. With the current setting in, and with this big grounded berg hard against the bank, the ship may possibly be held without much greater pressure than it has already had. We really cannot tell what may happen, but if that is true, there is a good chance we may save the ship and eventually have all of you back on board. I have a plan of action in the event the ship should sink or become separated from the iceberg. I am sending our chief mate, Mr. Eric Sorensen, to take command on the iceberg. He will have navigating instruments with him. Each passenger raft will have one of our officers in charge. If you have to abandon the iceberg in the rafts, Mr. Sorensen and a crew will try to launch the motor lifeboat and tow the rafts to whatever land may be accessible. Dr. George Barry, our cruise director, will also be with you. He is well experienced in camping on ice. I hope you will find these arrangements beneficial. In the event of separation, my duty will be to remain with my vessel and do all in my power to save the persons on board, and to keep the ship afloat so that we may, if possible, get all of you back on *Sinbad*. We are hoping that Palmer Station will be able to get a disabled helicopter repaired and take everybody ashore, but the personnel there is having much difficulty. Rising water has made it necessary for them to abandon their station and establish a camp on the hill above where they think will be the highest level of the water. The rising water may affect us also, causing movement and release of icebergs, but possibly the wind and current will hold them in the channel and only push harder against the ship.''

Captain Gilbert cleared his throat before continuing. ''You will have our radio operator, Ole Magnussen, and the portable radio transmitter up on the iceberg at all times. Meanwhile, I will keep you well informed as to our situation. Our chief steward, Carl Peterson, will work out a schedule of meals so that each group may eat on board. Please keep your flotation jackets and life preservers with you at all times, both on the iceberg and on the ship. Thank you.''

Bill and Jean Bush were the first passengers to climb

over the top edge of their frozen refuge. Bill was a New York architect. "Welcome aboard," said Bill, helping to pull the eye of the rope over Jean's head. A seaman fastened them together with a short length of heaving line to which he was also attached and led them toward the cluster of covered plastic life rafts. They sloshed through an inch or more of melt water, slipping and stumbling over the uneven mixture of ice and melting snow. They tightly grasped the lifeline which was stretched between upright ice spears from the edge of the camp. Assisted by the seaman, Bill and Jean climbed onto the nearest life raft, Raft One. Opening the flap which formed the end of the plastic "cabin," they found themselves in a dry, dimly lit space surrounded by grey plastic curtain-like sides, a curved plastic roof, and a heavy inflated double hull.

The raft contained survival food, water and first aid supplies as well as oars, tools, signal rockets and other safety equipment. All the items within the rafts had been carried in large cylindrical cases on the ship. When transferred to the iceberg, the rafts were inflated simply by pulling on a line which released compressed air. There was room inside each raft for twenty-five persons to ride in safety protected from weather and heavy sea.

A team of four had been assigned to each of the seven rafts on the iceberg, an officer and three other members of the *Sinbad* crew. They were charged with the care and safety of the passengers who occupied the rafts. The passengers, averaging sixty in number on the iceberg at any one time, were divided among three rafts. Another raft was used for extra provisions. The remaining rafts, two of which would be occupied by the rest of *Sinbad's* passengers in the event they had to move off the ship, were used by various other members of *Sinbad's* crew, including Ole Magnussen, who had lugged his radio equipment to one of them. All the rafts and the motor lifeboat were secured close together by their painters and other ropes.

Bill and Jean Bush sat down on the inflated tube-like

bulwark which extended the full length of the raft on each side. The next arrivals were the two "travel girls," Brenda Clarke and Marjory Dumont, who sat on the opposite side. They were followed by the Norwoods, Dearborns, Destefanis, Caviges, and Connallys. Next came Victoria Degrelle, Victor Daly, Edward McCaughlin, and two more girls. In addition to the Norwoods, Ed McCaughlin had switched from group B to group A. Marjory was pleased about that.

Last to enter Raft One were Dr. Barry and the nurse, Lorraine Jackson. Dr. Barry wanted to see if everyone was comfortably seated, then left to check on the other two passenger rafts. Later, he returned and again took a seat in Raft One. Including the mate, Eric Sorensen, and three seamen, there were twenty-five people in the raft. The rest of group A, and all of group B, were similarly accommodated in Rafts Two and Three.

Al and Helen Norwood spent their first minutes in Raft One adjusting themselves to their strange surroundings. Accustomed to comfort, they found themselves inside a plastic capsule with over twenty people with whom, other than the Dearborns, they had only short acquaintance. They all sat on the large inflated tubes on each side of the raft, facing each other, wearing their life jackets. Despite being on top of an iceberg, it was warm inside the raft. One of the crew opened the flaps at each end. As the people accommodated themselves, and adjusted their mental attitudes, there was a babble of voices.

"Sixteen hours in here," remarked Al. "That's a long time to sit this one out!"

"I'd rather be in here than sitting out on that iceberg," reflected Joyce Dearborn. "I wonder how long this will go on."

"I'm going to see if we can go out once in a while and get some exercise," declared Clarence.

"In this weather?" cautioned Al.

"Maybe we four can tie ourselves together and walk

129

around a bit between squalls," suggested Helen.

One of the ship's seamen was making his way down the middle, stepping over inflated thwarts, and trying to avoid tripping over the feet of the passengers. Al stopped him and asked, "Can you tell us if we may go outside for exercise once in a while?"

"Right now it's dangerous with this wind," the seaman replied. "You might stumble on this uneven slippery surface. Mr. Sorensen will advise us when it's safer to go out."

After they all had become somewhat familiar with their assigned places, they were told by Eric Sorensen and Dr. Barry that they could move around outside whenever the weather permitted, provided they kept secured to the lifelines. There were short lanyards with snap hooks by which they could secure themselves and move by sliding the hooks along the lines.

Because of the slushy top of the iceberg, some remained inside a good part of the time, but others moved around visiting the passengers and crew in Rafts Two and Three. Their sixteen hour sojourn on the iceberg wasn't comfortable by any means, but it wasn't unbearable.

Emma Cavige called the *Sinbad*, the ship's owners, captain, mates, engineers, cooks and room stewards every name in her extensive vocabulary of profanity. She beat on the inflated seat and shook a pudgy fist in her husband's flushed face. "You made us take this cruise, you— crumb! I'd never have come on a lousy trip like this!"

"Aw—hogwash," muttered Phil Cavige under his breath. He rubbed his chest, still feeling discomfort from his mild attack. Although Phil's condition hadn't been serious enough to warrant his confinement in the ship's hospital, Nurse Jackson had been assigned to Raft One to keep an eye on him.

And so the drama of survival was carried out on board *Sinbad* and on the iceberg. The passengers and crew were deeply concerned with their own problems, and the fate of their families at home. Radio reports about the devastating ocean swells were received with growing anxiety and anguish, but even the most apprehensive and alarmed among the passengers and crew couldn't imagine the awesome terror and suffering actually taking place throughout the world.

5

After Quest's departure, Palmer Station settled down to a measure of tranquility. Except for Larry Field, the men who had wintered over busied themselves with preparations to turn over their duties and investigations to the next group, due to arrive on the Icebreaker *Southwind*. Art Allen, Larry Field, and three graduate assistants, Norman Gingell, Jon Rankin, and Andrew Taylor, would remain. The group arriving would man the station during the austral summer which was just beginning. They would number over twenty. There would be more scientists to take advantage of the milder temperatures, which would average about zero degrees Celsius on the peninsula.

Those to depart on the icebreaker were George Reszke, Palmer Station manager; Stanley O. Schaeffer, M.D., medico and surgeon; Hank Osborne, mechanic and crane operator; John Powell, meteorologist; Hugh MacGregor, mechanical engineer; Enrico Monelli, geologist; Ira Mason, electronic and radio technician; Albert S. Steele, maintenance man; and Louis "Bitsy" Berg, cook.

Although those men had enjoyed all the comforts of the most modern station, with its adequate facilities, which included private rooms, recreation hall, library, lounge, and well equipped laboratory, all were impatiently awaiting their departures.

Suddenly the tranquility of the station was shattered by the message from Washington ordering *Quest* to evacuate them because of the mysterious and alarming increase in the earth's "tilt." The excitement of evacuation, the eruptions at Deception, the daring attempt by *Quest* to rescue the Argentines, the pending arrival of the icebreaker *Southwind,* and their yearning to get home were almost too much for some of those who had wintered over. They paced the floor, consumed coffee, or hit the bottles at the bar, then impatiently completed packing their baggage and securing the station. Darkness and cold had taken the usual toll. The noon meal was a tumultuous affair. Some of the men were torn between getting their food on their trays and going off to crowd around the radio room and listen. Others watched on the balcony for *Southwind.*

Quest had entered Deception at about 1200. As the noon hour passed, suspense increased. Ira Mason and Arthur Allen were glued to the radios. Others stood around trying to keep quiet. Each minute dragged slowly by as their imaginations carried them to Deception Island, their friends on board *Quest,* and the perilous mission.

At 1230 Ira called *Quest.* There was no response. Tensions mounted. George Reszke stood beside Larry Field and gently slipped his arm over the big man's shoulder. Larry's face was drawn with anxiety over Carol, but he managed a grateful smile at George. Carol was on the minds of others too. Arthur gave Larry a reassuring pat. Nothing had been heard from the ship since it went into the crater, but Arthur Allen had known Captain Pack a long time. He felt confident that the skipper would bring *Quest* safely through its dangerous undertaking. Arthur tried to reassure Larry, "Remember, no news *can* be good news."

Ira Mason briefly spoke with *Sinbad*'s radio operator, Ole Magnussen. Ole told Ira, "*Sinbad* is now proceeding northward in Penola Strait, approaching Lemaire Channel. The passengers are having a good time, enjoying the cruise, but we are all disappointed that we can't visit Palmer. Captain Gilbert has decided to leave immediately for South America on account of this tilt business, and the evacuations. Over.''

"Roger," replied Ira. "I'll pass your message to the manager. Have you heard anything from *Quest*? Over.''

"Negative," answered Ole. "Nothing since *Quest* entered Deception. I will advise you immediately if I hear from *Quest*. Over, and standing by on 2182.'' Ole stayed glued to that radio frequency.

Finally, the noon meal was over at Palmer. All except four of the men busied themselves outside, taking their baggage down to the dock to put it on *Southwind*'s launch for transfer out to the ship when it anchored. Arthur Allen had a length of nylon rope with which to lower the baggage to the launch.

Two of the graduate assistants, Andrew Taylor and Norman Gingell, assisted Palmer's cook, Bitsy Berg, in cleaning up the galley. When the galley was in order, they went to their rooms to get their baggage. Bitsy, whose bags were already on the dock, went outside and joined the others. Ira Mason remained in the building trying to call *Quest*.

As the men busied themselves with preparations to depart, those who had wintered over were cheerful that they were soon to be on their way home. Those who had recently arrived were despondent that the station was being evacuated.

Suddenly, they all became aware of an amazing scenario developing in the surrounding waters, along the rocky banks. Hundreds of leopard seals and killer whales had invaded Arthur Habor and the inlet in front of the station. They swam excitedly, breaching and diving, in what appeared to be attempts to evade some unseen enemy. Many leaped in apparent terror onto the rocks near the dock, and along the banks of Bonaparte Point across the inlet. The seals laboriously climbed over the boulders, swaying, fighting and bellowing. Such a wild display of sea animals had never been seen by the men at Palmer. Penguins, uttering strange, timorous squawks and cries, their flipper-like wings stretched wide, scurried in panic over the boulders.

"Look at that!" shouted Hugh MacGregor, who stood near the dock. Three leopard seals, fighting among themselves, leaped into a zodiac tied between a corner of the dock and the bank. There ensued a veritable melee as several killer whales streaked up from below and capsized the zodiac. So loud was the turmoil and clamor that the men became alarmed. They gathered in a group in front of the main building.

"I never saw anything like this!" exclaimed Arthur. "Look at the dog!" Princesa scrambled along the bank, furiously barking at the seals and birds. Suddenly, she raced toward the group of men, savagely growling.

"Look out!" yelled Doc Schaeffer. "Don't touch her! Don't let her bite you! Maybe she's got rabies!"

George Reszke ran into the building and got a rifle, but when he came out, Princesa had gone off again, and was barking at the skuas and gulls which were making a raucous cacophony on the rocks west of the building.

All at once, the animals became silent. At that instant, the men felt a slight tremor in the ground beneath their feet. After a moment, they felt it again, stronger the second time.

"Earthquake! Earthquake!" they shouted, almost in unison.

The ground shook again and again, each time with greater force. The buildings trembled and rattled. The tremors rapidly grew into a great roaring earthquake, throwing the men to the ground.

Ira Mason came stumbling out of the building as the walls cracked and glass shattered. With a terrible crash, the west wing and center section of the main building buckled and collapsed. The east wing swayed and twisted, but remained standing, leaning sharply toward the rest of the wrecked structure. The large building at the rear also buckled and slumped, becoming in seconds a grotesque heap of twisted framework and rubble.

A great fissure, like a crevasse, opened in the ground across the point, from the dock area to the opposite bank, right under the wreckage of the main building. Much of the wreckage slid down into the wide gap as the earth continued its violent quaking. The interlocking sheet piles of the dock structure were twisted and dislodged. Piles and fill disappeared into the turbulent water.

The men scrambled to stay clear of the wreckage and the perilous ground and rocks caving into the yawning chasm. They crawled, yelling and screaming in terror, not knowing which way to move to avoid the bewildering maze of structural pieces and rolling boulders.

The tall flagpole fell, its cross piece striking and breaking Hugh MacGregor's right forearm, as he crawled on the rocky ground. He moaned in agony, and pulled himself clear.

"Look out!" shouted Ira Mason as he saw the big tractor crane toppling toward men crawling on the ground near it. They scrambled to get out of its way, but one was too late. Albert "Stainless" Steel didn't quite make it. Bitsy tried to pull him clear, but failed. A heavy steel edge fell squarely across Bert's neck like the merciless blade of a guillotine. His legs flew upward, and his arms flailed wildly as the swift blow severed his head and silenced his scream.

Blood spurting from the stump of Bert's neck stained the surrounding water and ice a bright crimson as it splattered around the area and over the crawling men. Bert's round, partly bald head rolled and bounced among chunks of ice and boulders as the ground continued to shake.

Arthur Allen, on his knees, roped himself to the toppled crane. His hands and face were bloody from a deep gash across his forehead. He grunted and groaned as he reached for Bitsy and tied him to the crane. He half-moaned, half-screamed to the others. "Over here! Come here! Get over—!" A great swell of water and ice swept

137

over the area and drowned out Arthur's words. George Reszke and Doc Schaeffer dragged themselves toward the crane and away from the widening chasm in the ground.

Screams of the two young graduate assistants, trapped under the wreckage of the west wing of the building, were briefly heard as the wreckage sank into the fissure.

Larry Field crawled toward the wreckage. "I'm going in!" he shouted. "I'm going to help them! I'm—" his words were drowned out by another great crest of icy water. He dragged himself in toward the place from where the screams had originated. The dog, Princesa, whimpering with fright, followed him into the shaking ruins.

A large plastic zodiac boat and an empty oil drum came hurtling down on the crest of the next swell. The zodiac fell into the wreckage of the building, but the oil drum struck Dr. Enrico Monelli, dashing him against the upended concrete base of the flagpole. He shrieked as he heard the shin bone crack in his left leg. He clawed at the concrete base, but couldn't hold on against the pounding of the swells. He was being washed toward the gaping fissure in the ground. Hank Osborne crawled as fast as his bruises would permit, the end of Arthur's rope in his teeth, toward Enrico. He reached him just in time to keep him from being dashed into the wide rift. Hank managed to get a turn around Enrico's right leg. The men dragged Enrico and Hank back to the crane.

Finally, all the ten remaining men got themselves lashed together and to the crane. Swell after swell washed over them. Large chunks of ice, driven high over the toppled crane, struck them. They were constantly battered and drenched by the icy brine, severely injured and frightened.

"Where's Larry?" shouted George Reszke, when he was able to look around. "Hey! What's happened to Larry?"

"He was crawling toward the building," yelled Arthur against the roar of the water. "He went after the boys!"

"He'll never make it!" screamed Mason. "He'll be knocked into the rift!"

With all the water and spray over the area, the desperate men could hardly see the wrecked building. They caught a glimpse of Steel's headless body being washed across the clearing. They didn't see his head anywhere. Schaeffer yelled, "I guess his head has been washed into the rift!"

The roar of large icebergs breaking off from the glaciers and plummeting into Arthur Harbor and the inlet, and the great swells crashing against them, made all attempts to communicate very difficult. The earth shocks continued. Ice and slush flowed down from the higher ground, carrying mud, debris and oil from the fractured tanks. There was no respite for the men huddled by the crane. Southward, mountainous swells rolled toward Palmer and the offshore islands.

If it weren't for the barrier provided by those offshore islands, the accumulation of large icebergs grounded against their shallows and between them, and the protection of the high ramparts of Graham Land, the Danco Coast, Wiencke Island, the mountains of Anvers Island itself, and Bonaparte Point, all the Palmer men and every vestige of Palmer Station would have been swept into the sea.

In terror, the men held fast as each foaming wall of water and ice swirled over and around them. They struggled and writhed, grasping whatever they could reach, to keep from being snatched away from the tenuous shelter of the toppled crane. Drenched and cold, battered and bruised, they were a wretched crew. The two large storage tanks were ripped apart and dashed across the rocky point like egg shells, spraying the area with the remaining oil.

When finally the ruthless swells subsided, only two of the men were able to move or stand. John Powell and Doc Schaeffer laboriously propped the heads of the severely injured on stones, out of the swirling icy water, oil, and mud. Larry Field was nowhere to be seen.

Overhead, a black haze filled the sky, obscuring the

high sun. A strong odor of sulphur and diesel oil permeated the atmopshere. Torrents of melt water cascaded down the slopes, bringing avalanches of ice and mud. Large glacier bergs continued to break off in rapid succession, jamming Arthur Harbor and the surrounding waters.

Arthur Allen and George Reszke gradually regained enough energy to move. They helped drag the groaning injured to safer positions. Dr. Schaefer, his face lacerated and bloody, limped with the help of George from one man to another, feeling arms and legs for fractures. He found two had broken bones, and many others had deep cuts and agonizing bruises.

After making the injured as comfortable as possible, the doctor and George, with great effort, waded toward the wreckage of the main building to search for medicines and whatever they could find for bandages. It was a difficult and dangerous task, but they succeeded in finding a couple of metal first-aid boxes, the contents of which provided the doctor with the means to give some assistance to the injured.

Shortly, they had Hugh MacGregor and Hank Osborne on their feet. The doctor fashioned a sling for Hugh's broken arm and cleaned and bandaged Arthur's head wound. Arthur and Hugh set out for the wreckage to look for more medicines and Larry Field's body. They found some cans of food and a couple of unbroken bottles of whiskey, but no trace of Larry.

Gradually the survivors' morale began to improve. Groans gave way to more natural utterances and discussion of their plight. Within two hours after the momentous disaster, all those fortunate enough to be alive were awkwardly moving around, trying to make their position less perilous.

Suddenly, Bitsy shouted, "Quiet! Listen!"

Above the noisy rush of water and clatter of ice, they heard the welcome sound of an approaching helicopter.

George and Hugh, followed by Arthur and John, made their way with great difficulty toward the helicopter pad. They found much debris, boulders, large chunks of ice, mud and oil on the pad. Icy water flowed around and over the area. They set to work as best they could in their bruised condition, clearing a spot for the helicopter. The steel-plated platform had a few cracks across it. One flat side was slightly slanted down, but there appeared to be room for the bird to set down.

The men moved off to one side after they had made a clearing. Hugh MacGregor gave signals to the pilot to help him avoid the debris around the cleared area. Lt. Harvey Thompson, USCG, brought his orange-red helicopter slowly and carefully down on the pad. The landing seemed perfect. As the rotor slowed, and the full weight of the helicopter came to bear upon the cracked deck, the men were startled by a sudden sharp snapping of steel, bending bars, and grinding of boulders. Instant failure and sinking of the deck tipped the helicopter's port side down. The rotor was still turning. The ends of two blades struck sharp glancing blows against the top of a high chunk of solid glacier ice, one of many which had accumulated beside the pad. Damage to the blades was certain, but it couldn't be immediately determined. The sunken place was full of water up to the under side of the helicopter's fuselage. Lt. Thompson and co-pilot Lt. Jg. Mike Stefano had been violently jerked against their safety straps toward the low side. Unhurt, they unstrapped themselves, and climbed out along the upper side, down onto the high part of the pad.

The seas crashing over the point had washed out a large portion of gravel and soil from beneath the deck at the north side. The washout was hidden from view by the pile of boulders and ice at that end. It had gone unnoticed by Reszke and MacGregor, who, but for their injuries, would have made a closer inspection of the pad before the helicopter put down.

As soon as Lt. Thompson could stop swearing and calmly survey the situation, he saw the impossibility of flying his chopper out of there for some time to come. He could easily see that the Palmer Station buildings were totally wrecked. Thompson said that on his flight in from *Southwind*, he had seen what appeared to be violently erupting volcanoes over the Danco Coast for many miles. He had also seen great columns of smoke and steam rising at many other places, when he had gained some altitude.

Weather at Palmer was rapidly deteriorating. Smoke, haze, and flurries of hail blew over the area. Movement became increasingly hazardous. *Southwind* had been unable to approach closer to the coast because of the great accumulation of large icebergs and heavy hummocked pack out beyond the islands. The strong earth shocks had swayed and staggered *Southwind*, but fortunately the ship was well offshore, in water deep enough to cushion the shocks. The great swells which followed the earthquakes passed in awesome succession beneath the vessel.

Lt. Thompson described the action. "*Southwind* didn't roll much more than usual—which is plenty. We didn't make any headway either. What movement we *did* make was straight up and down. I think we must have been lifted over three hundred feet on those monsters! They were like mountain ranges and valleys coming toward us, then sliding under us. That's why we were delayed getting in to you. But if we had been closer to the coast, in shallower water where the crests were breaking, we would never have made it. *Southwind* would have foundered."

Thompson could see that the evacuation effort was now a mess. *Southwind* had to be advised of the situation. He climbed back into the chopper and called the ship. "*Southwind*—Helo One Six. Do you read? Over."

"Go—One Six." The answer came quickly.

"Reporting damage to rotor blades due to failure and cave-in of pad plates while landing. Visible damage shows no possibility taking off from Palmer. Station buildings wrecked. Four men killed. Over."

"Helo One Six—*Southwind*. Roger. What's th'chances of gettin' One Niner in there at this time? Over."

"Negative," Thompson bitterly replied. "I say again—*Negative!* No landing sites in view. Fog, sleet, and smoke. Visibility nearly zero. Whole area flooding. Boulders, wreckage of buildings, and large chunks of glacier ice over the whole area." Thompson was shouting into the microphone. He went on, "I consider it inadvisable to make any further attempts to evacuate, even by hoist, at this time. We're still talkin' to the station manager and engineer. They say a generator and some shop equipment may be salvaged. Suggest we try field repairs to One Six instead of risking another bird. I will pass medicine chest to station medical officer. Station manager thinks we can get enough chow out of the wreckage for several days. Do you concur? Over." Thompson put up the mike and waited for his reply. Reszke had managed, laboriously and painfully, to climb up beside the pilot.

"One Six—*Southwind*—wait one," came the radio reply. In a few minutes, *Southwind* continued. "One Six — *Southwind* Commander Dillon concurs. *Southwind* will proceed to McMurdo. Hope to catch you on our way back. Copy following message for Palmer Station and Research Vessel *Quest*. I quote: McMurdo Station reported great earthquake damage. Aircraft unable to land that area due breakup all runways and fracture Ross Ice Shelf into thousands of icebergs. Nearly all US personnel evacuated by aircraft before earthquakes. Eight men still at McMurdo. Mount Erebus and many other volcanoes in violent eruption. Personnel in great danger. Request *Southwind* come ASAP. Evacuate by helicopter. End of message. Over."

"*Southwind*—Helo One Six," Lt. Thompson replied. "Roger your message. Will pass to Palmer. Over." He glanced quickly at Reszke by his side.

"Helo One Six. *Southwind* now proceeding to

McMurdo. Conditions critical there. Can you give present location R.V. *Quest?* Over.''

Thompson hurriedly consulted with George Reszke before replying to *Southwind's* question. "Negative," he answered. "Palmer manager states no contact with *Quest* since 1400 zulu. Palmer's radio capability zero since earthquakes. Last message *Quest* reported twenty-one miles northeast Deception Island, which message you copied. No further communications since *Quest* entered Deception. Wait one." George was making motions to Thompson. They exchanged words for a few minutes, and then Thompson resumed talking with *Southwind.*

"The station manager wants you to give the names of the men killed here to National Science Foundation. I spell: Albert S. Steele, Andrew Taylor, Norman Gingell, Laurence Field. Others injured, but none critical." Thompson then added, "Station wrecked, but manager Reszke hopes that with two vessels, M.S. *Sinbad,* and, if still afloat, the R.V. *Quest,* still in the vicinity of the Antarctic Peninsula, relief for the Palmer survivors may come soon. End of message. Over."

"One Six—*Southwind.* Roger your last. Will pass to NSF. Standing by on 2182. *Southwind* out."

"One Six out."

Southwind had intercepted *Sinbad's* message to Buenos Aires soon after the earthquake and before Lt. Thompson had left with the helicopter, so he knew *Sinbad* to be afloat. But what about *Quest?* He tried to call *Quest* several times, without result.

Before he climbed down to the group waiting below, he passed down the chopper's well-stocked first aid chest. He was obviously shaken by the news he had received about McMurdo, but he assisted Reszke in getting out of the chopper and down onto the pad. Then the group moved, some limping, others helping, down among the boulders and chunks of ice, slowly picking their way to avoid the rushing icy water and mud.

The sun was still high. It didn't go below the horizon, but its rays couldn't penetrate the haze and sleet. All the men were acutely aware of the tremendous events taking place: the change in the angle of the earth's axis; the great earthquakes which had apparently occurred throughout the vast regions of the Antarctic Continent; the sudden eruptions of many old and new volcanoes; the breaking up of the great Ross Ice Shelf; the torrents of melt water, and evident speeding up of the flood of glacial ice tossing thousands of giant icebergs into the sea. What did it all mean? Would they survive if they couldn't get away? Would *Southwind* return? What had happened to *Quest?* They had to try to get information about *Quest* as soon as possible. They also had to try to get their tractor crane right side up, and take it up to the pad and try to straighten up the helicopter. And they had to try to repair the rotor blades.

George realized the need for rest and food. He had those who were least injured collect materials to fashion a shelter against the weather and moved the others under it. Hank made some crude crutches, and they all helped with the tasks. MacGregor and George examined the crane. They brought some tools out of the east wing, which was still standing, although precariously slanting as though it might collapse at any moment. Lt. Thompson supplied some survival kits which the helicopter carried. Bitsy and Jon Rankin set about searching the wreckage for more cans of food. Jon was shaken by the death of his two companions, Taylor and Gingell. As he and Bitsy searched through the rubble, Jon was sickened by the thought that they might trample on the lifeless bodies of the two young men. However, they saw nothing of them. They did find a good supply of food. Making several trips, they brought out many cans. Some of them were dented, but for the most part the efforts of the two men were highly successful. Unfortunately, there was no dry wood with which to make a fire, and no dry place to start one.

Ira tried to contact *Quest,* calling frequently, using the helicopter's transmitter. He made all the adjustments possible, but *Quest* didn't answer. He and Thompson copied traffic between *Southwind* and McMurdo Station. They learned, among other things, that they at Palmer and the eight men at McMurdo were the only US personnel remaining in Antarctica, except those on board *Southwind, Quest,* and *Sinbad.* All others had been evacuated by aircraft before the earthquakes. The British Antarctic ship *Bransfield* was en route to the South Orkneys to evacuate the British Station at Signy Island. All other nations had also removed their Antarctic personnel by ships or aircraft prior to the earthquakes.

Southwind's Commander Charles Dillon reported that great columns of volcanic steam and ash were being blasted with terrific force high into the sky, forming a thick overcast which obscured the sun far out to sea. Rain and hail were being driven against the ship by constant violent gusts. At Ira's request, *Southwind* frequently tried to contact *Quest,* but with negative results.

On Palmer, the men saw great clouds of water vapor rapidly moving northward at high altitudes. Frequent squalls dropped pellets of hard packed snow and ash, apparently driven from the peninsula plateaus by katabatic winds. Earth shocks continued and hampered the preparations to build a shelter.

Southwind reported tabular bergs more numerous as the ship progressed. The vessel had to keep farther off from the coast than usual, in order to make headway against the growing agglomeration of icebergs. The commanders of *Southwind* and *Bransfield* exchanged several messages which were copied by Lt. Thompson. Both commanders agreed that a great upheaval was taking place on the Antarctic Continent. Commander Dillon, of *Southwind,* dispatched a message to US Coast Guard headquarters. It stated that vast quantities of Antarctic ice were flowing northward on exceptionally strong ocean currents. He also

146

reported that great quantities of high, fast-moving clouds of vapor and smoke seemed to indicate the disturbance was widespread over the continent.

On board *Southwind*, there were over twenty scientists and support personnel who had been scheduled to relieve their colleagues at Palmer Station—geologists, glaciologists, volcanists and biologists. The scientists, experts in their respective fields, were excited and fascinated by the startling sequence of events which they observed. They continuously exchanged comments and views to the extent that the pitching and rolling of the icebreaker would permit, and concluded that the earth's mantle beneath the Antarctic Continent had suddenly become heated by a great molten chamber below it, causing the eruption of countless volcanoes which released great quantities of heat from the magma. They also concluded that the earthquakes were causing the disintegration of the ice mass, and that intense heat was boiling the melt water, and throwing up great volumes of vapor which they could see blowing northward away from the continent high overhead.

Reports from McMurdo that the immense Ross Ice Shelf had fractured into countless tabular bergs, and messages from Argentine, Chilean, and Russian ships, and the British Station at Signy Island, overheard by *Southwind*, indicated that the Filchner, Larsen, and other shelves and tongues in the Weddel Sea area and around the entire coast were disintegrating. Glaciers were rapidly flowing seaward due to the heat below them. Countless glacier bergs were breaking off into the sea like ore pouring out of giant sluices.

Whales, seals, penguins, and other birds were fleeing the area on the icebergs and floes, in the waters and the skies.

Southwind encountered greater difficulty hourly as the turmoil of strong current and fast-moving ice made progress hazardous. *Bransfield* reported the same conditions on her course northeastward. Reports from

Sinbad indicated the ship was unable to move and was trapped by icebergs in Lemaire Channel. There was no communication with *Quest*. The only contact with Palmer Station was through the disabled helicopter. At McMurdo, the eight men were fearfully waiting for *Southwind* to rescue them.

Southwind's commander dispatched another long radio report to USCG headquarters in Washington with a copy to the Division of Polar Programs of the National Science Foundation. His report set forth in detail the difficulties confronting *Southwind* in its attempt to navigate the turbulent ice-strewn seas toward McMurdo Station. He not only reported on the weather and sea conditions, but also included the opinions of the group of glaciologists and other scientists on board the icebreaker. They believed that the great polar ice sheet was disintegrating, and would eventually release some seven million cubic miles of ice into the oceans.

Immediately upon receipt of *Southwind*'s message, the Commandant of the Coast Guard in Washington personally took it to the President, who was reviewing the speech he was to make to Congress at two o'clock.

As the afternoon wore on at Palmer, thick black clouds of smoke and steam continued rolling overhead toward the north. The USARPS there also observed that the ice-laden water surrounding their small peninsula was higher than usual. If the dock hadn't been destroyed, the water would have covered it. It was starting to creep up the slope toward the wrecked buildings.

Another anxiety began to arise in the minds of all the men. Would the waters continue to rise and cover the whole of Palmer area?

In the helicopter, Lt. Thompson amplified a relayed American Forces Radio and Television Service broadcast. The announcer reported, "Observers at meteorological stations, astronomers and geophysicists throughout the world, have come to the conclusion that the great Antarctic ice sheet is undergoing destruction by unknown subterranean forces, apparently pushing hot magma and rock up through the earth's mantle. We have one ice-breaker, the *Southwind*, still in the area, on a mission to evacuate the last of our personnel. *Southwind* reports tremendous numbers of glacial and tabular icebergs, dangerous swells and ocean currents flowing away from the Antarctic continent, impeding the ship's progress. The British Survey Ship *Bransfield* is evacuating the personnel from their stations. They fear they may not reach their station at Signy Island, due to the overwhelming flow of large icebergs from the Weddell Sea area. We urge all interests in South America, New Zealand, Australia and Africa to be on the alert for rising ocean waters. All vessels in southern waters must take great precautions against icebergs which may be carried by ocean currents far to the north, even as far as the equator. We repeat our previous warning: if the polar ice sheet should be destroyed, the waters of the oceans throughout the world could rise as much as two hundred fifty feet, and possibly much more if the Greenland ice sheet should break up.''

Art Allen listened to the broadcast with growing excitement. ''Good grief!'' he exclaimed when it was over, ''We're getting it here first!''

They began to take closer note of the ice bound shores around the point. ''Sure!'' shouted Arthur. ''That water is higher than it's ever been!''

Everybody was talking at once.

''I wonder how fast it's rising?''

''Oh, boy! Haven't we had enough?''

''Now we gotta move up higher!''

''Gotta get that lousy helicopter repaired!''

''I wonder how long before *Southwind* gets back? Why th'hell didn' that dam' icebreaker stay here?''

Art declared, ''They reported a heavy flow of large icebergs moving north! Maybe *Southwind* can't get back! I wonder what happened to *Quest?*''

George instantly took charge of the situation. ''All right, now, let's have volunteers to get that tractor going!''

Amid groans, nearly all volunteered, and, except Bitsy, Art, and Ira Mason, they painfully made their way over to the big tractor crane which was still on its side. Hugh MacGregor and Hank Osborne brought jacks and bars from the wreckage; others moved wood blocks. Noise around them was deafening.

Bitsy and Jon Rankin were busy trying to put together a cold meal. Enrico Monelli couldn't help them. He lay on a plank, his left leg in splints, but that didn't stop him from making disparaging remarks about the food. Bitsy and Jon managed a meal of sorts, served in cans, and eaten with sticks and fingers. They had to shout at one another to be understood.

Bitsy hollered, ''I don't know if we're going to find any dishes or pots, so hold on to your cans.''

The men polished off the rest of the whiskey they had found and hoped there would be more to salvage from the wreckage. It wasn't long before morale was on the mend.

After the men had eaten, they resumed trying to stand up the crane. With blocks and jacks and a lot of agonizing effort, they managed to get it upright onto its big tires. They found some drums of fuel which had become jammed in the wreckage. Hank filled the crane's tank, and soon he had the engine clicking away, a very welcome sound. The crane was a formidable piece of equipment to which they owed their lives. It was rugged, and hopefully dependable, considering the punishment it had taken during the violent earth quakes.

Once in a while someone would mention Larry Field. They were also mindful of Carol Moore on board *Quest,* and the sad news that, sooner or later, would reach her.

Art Allen made a suggestion. ''When we get in contact

with *Quest,* let's not mention anything about Larry. We'll try to find his body first. I'm sure he's dead, but when we do tell Carol, I hope we can at least say we looked for his body. We haven't had a chance to search that part of the wreckage yet—and another thing—nobody has seen our dog, Princesa since she followed Larry in there."

George Reszke agreed, and added, "We don't even know whether *Quest* is still afloat. We don't know if anyone on the ship is alive." He decided not to belabor that point. The sad, exhausted faces around him were enough to make him quickly change the subject. "Now, I propose that you try to get some rest. We've got a lot to do in the morning."

It was past midnight, although broad daylight. The men sought whatever comfort they could find in the shelter and in the helicopter. Ira Mason and Lt. Thompson kept a radio watch. They frequently called *Quest,* but received no reply.

The night was stormy. Earth tremors, distant shocks, and constant rumbling attested to the continued breaking up of the ice. Sleep was fitful, frequently broken by groans of pain. The next day would bring more hard work. The waters continued to rise, creeping higher each hour around the banks of their small point of rocky land.

What the scientists had believed, and the President of the United States had stated in his broadcast warning, was indeed true. Even as the President delivered his dire message, the relentless seismic ocean swells swept rapidly northward from all parts of the Antarctic coast. After the devastation of Palmer and all other Antarctic stations, the next land mass to receive the impact of the enormous swells was the southern tip of South America.

Travelling northward over four hundred miles an hour, the first great seismic swells broke against Cape Horn and Tierra del Fuego. The inhabitants of Ushuaia, the world's southernmost town, and other Fuegian towns and villages,

151

had little more than an hour to flee to high ground. Fortunately, they had also felt the earthquakes, and warned by Don Marsh and other ham radio operators, many persons reached the nearby hills, including numerous tourists visiting Ushuaia. A large part of the Tierra Del Fuego sheep, numbering nearly a million, were also saved due to their habit of grazing in the uplands during the austral summers, but many were lost. Don Marsh flew his family to safety at a ranch in the hills, but their comfortable home and all their *estancia* buildings were demolished, and soon would all be deep below the surface of the rising water.

Excitement had been high for several days among the populace along the Magellan Strait. News media had carried reports by astronomers of the tilting of the earth's axis. In Punta Arenas, Chile, there was great apprehension as to the meaning of the mysterious phenomenon. Fear turned to outright panic as the mighty swells approached, ravaging everything in their path as if possessed by some powerful unknown force.

Although *Quest's* company had a good breakfast on December 23, the day following the earthquakes, that same morning the breakfast at Palmer was another tin can affair. Despite the injuries, everybody knew that no time should be lost in salvaging as much equipment as possible, and in moving to higher ground. The men decided that the best direction to go was toward the foothills of Mount William, some six miles eastward. There they hoped to reach an elevation higher than they expected the waters would rise. Wind, sleet, and the constant roar of water and ice flowing down the slopes around them made talking and working difficult. There was much ice above, but patches of rocky ground were beginning to show along the shore of Biscoe Bay. They had to follow the coast, staying just above the rising water, hoping one of the ships would pick them up before they had to move very far over the rocks.

Bitsy had managed to make a fire in a small drum, using some oil-soaked rags and some sticks had been dried off in the helicopter. The smell was awful, but the hot coffee was delicious, amply laced with slugs of whiskey. After the men got their cans filled around Bitsy's "galley," they took a short break while George Reszke outlined a plan of action. "Now, listen," he shouted. "First, we get out all the provisions, medicines, and tools we can from the buildings. Then straighten up that chopper with the crane so we can build a raft under it before the water gets too high." The men huddled closely together as they discussed their plight and plans.

Hugh MacGregor motioned with his good arm toward Mount William. "When we start moving," he yelled, "we'll have to carry everything up there by hand. We better move in stages."

"It's gonna be tough," bellowed Hank Osborne, "but we got no choice."

"I'll carry all the medical supplies I can find. Maybe we'll hear from *Quest*," shouted Dr. Schaeffer. He motioned toward Enrico Monelli stretched out under the small shelter. "We'll have to take turns lugging him."

Monelli beckoned. Doc bent over him. "Make me crutches—crutches—make me a pair of crutches," he pleaded. Doc nodded, but he knew Enrico would never make it over the rocks. The USARPS would have to carry him on one of the stretchers that Doc had seen in the helicopter.

Reszke resumed in a loud voice, "Art? Art?—What is the sea water situation? The rise, I mean. How fast is it rising?" Arthur had set up a pole, marked in centimeters, for a tide gauge. He had it sticking up in the water between some boulders to keep the ice from knocking it over. Art hobbled over to it and noted the height of the water, judging an average mark between waves. He returned to Reszke.

"The water has come up about twenty-four centimeters

153

in the last four hours,'' Art shouted in Reszke's ear. ''That would be about a meter and a half a day, give or take some for tide. I don't know how much is tide, if any.'' Arthur was very tired. He hadn't slept more than a couple of hours since the earthquakes. He had stood watch at the helicopter radio, relieving Mason and Thompson and had done a hundred odd chores, making several trips into the wreckage, bringing out provisions, and he had searched for the bodies of Larry Field and the two graduate assistants. Art Allen had just about had it, but he kept going.

George continued, ''Thanks, Art. It looks like we'll only have about two days before the water gets up to the buildings. In another couple of days, it'll be up to the chopper.''

Bitsy yelled, ''Come on, damn it! Let's get a move on, then!''

George called to Doc Schaeffer. ''Doc, you and Bitsy and Rankin get all the provisions you can. Bring them up here to the pad. While you're in the wreckage, keep an eye out for the bodies of Larry, Taylor and Gingell—and Steele—but I guess he got buried down in that rift. Anyway, have another look around.''

Doc exclaimed, ''And Princesa! We haven't seen her around! I guess she got washed into the rift too!'' The dog hadn't been seen since she disappeared with Larry Field inside the shaking building.

During the morning, the other USARPS gathered planks and oil drums which had become lodged in the wreckage. They fashioned a large raft under the helicopter, hoping to float it when the water got to a high enough level. Even their shouting at one another tired them as they worked, but they kept on going, spurred by the knowledge that the helicopter might be their only means of transportation to safety. Lieutenants Thompson and Stefano assisted the USARPS. They were the only uninjured men in the group, and they pitched in with all the tasks. Ira Mason kept a watch at the radio in the helicopter, hoping for word from *Quest*.

At noon, they knocked off for a short break and to see what Bitsy had conjured up in the way of a feast. It was some more of the same, more cans and coffee. But nobody complained. They knew they were lucky to have any food at all. At least they weren't starving. They ate amid the sonorous roar around them, and the constant reverberations of earthquakes which kept jolting the mainland beyond the peninsula. They took a few minutes to rest after eating. Conversation was impossible in the noise.

Suddenly, Mason shouted from the helicopter. The men moved as close beneath him as possible. "*Sinbad* is stuck in Lemaire Channel! They can't move! Surrounded by icebergs! Ship is still afloat!"

"Holy smoke!" exlaimed Hugh. "That's not far! We could fly over there in less than half an hour with this bird!"

George yelled to Mason, "Is *Sinbad* in trouble? Will they sink? Maybe we can move their people to land somewhere, if we get this chopper going." Mason went back to the radio, and George climbed up onto the helicopter near him.

Mason shouted in Reszke's ear. "The *Sinbad* operator is sending messages for the passengers. I'll try to talk with him when I can. I don't think they're sinking, from what I heard, they are jammed in there by icebergs, and can't get out of the channel. Maybe we can get over there and stay on the ship. I haven't heard anything from *Quest* yet."

At 1230 on December 23, Mason got through to Ole Magnussen, the radio operator of *Sinbad*. "Palmer, this is *Sinbad*," said Ole. "Ira Mason? How do you read, Ira?" Mason had his earphones on again, and George stood by him, braced against the lopsided fuselage of the chopper.

"*Sinbad*, this is Palmer—Ira Mason. Read you five by five, Ole. Glad to know your ship is still afloat. I've been

155

listening to some of your traffic. Our buildings are wrecked, and I'm using the radio of a Coast Guard helicopter. That's damaged too, and we can't fly it. Are you in danger where you are? Over."

"Yes. We're in danger, but we're not sinking—yet. Not much damage to the ship so far, but we have some injured passengers and crew. We're stuck near Glandaz Point in Lemaire Channel. We'll try to get around to Palmer if possible. This whole area is blocked with icebergs. Have you heard from *Quest*? Over."

"Negative," replied Ira. "Not since they went into Deception. We've had a hard time here at Palmer. Both buildings down. We're camping alongside the chopper. Lost four men. Everybody is injured more or less. Over."

Ole responded. "Yes. I intercepted your helicopter's message to the icebreaker. I knew about your troubles, but I've been busy sending messages for the passengers. Over."

"Roger," answered Ira. At that moment, George Reszke nudged Ira. Ira removed the earphones.

Reszke shouted, "Tell him you'll be closing down for a few hours while we try to lift this chopper back up straight."

Ira nodded his head. "*Sinbad*, this is Palmer. We'll shut down here for a few hours, starting in a short time. We're going to lift the helicopter. Please try to raise *Quest*, and if you hear from them, advise our situation. We'll call *Quest* again when we get back on the air. Over."

"Roger your message," replied Ole. "*Sinbad* out."

"Palmer out."

The bedraggled Palmer men were occupied with lugging provisions, tools and blocks of wood all afternoon, stopping only long enough to refresh themselves with a scanty meal at supper time. Then they struggled with the crane, getting it in position and blocked so they could use it at the helicopter site.

Reszke found the rifle he had lost when the earthquakes

began. He knew there was another rifle and some side arms in the helicopter, which would be needed to hunt food if the USARPS ran out of provisions.

Shortly after the men had eaten, they got the chopper lifted and blocked up straight and level. At about 1900, George, Mason and Lt. Thompson climbed aboard. It was at that point in Palmer's timetable that Ira got through to *Quest* for the first time since the earthquakes began. Enrique's gritty voice had filled Ira's earphones like the notes of a beautiful symphony. George and Thompson could tell by Ira's short gasp and brightening countenance that he had heard from *Quest.* Ira listened to Enrique's excited account of *Quest's* condition and the situation. He beckoned to George Reszke, and handed him the earphones. "They're at Deception! Trapped there! Can't get out!" Ira yelled to the men below outside the helicopter. George put on the earphones. On *Quest,* Captain Pack took over from Enrique, and George gave Pack the sad details about the loss of the four men.

As soon as the helicopter was level, some of the men lifted Enrico, and helped Hugh up into it. The others kept on building the raft under it until nearly midnight. Finally, exhausted, they all climbed into the chopper and went to sleep. Thompson, Mason, and Arthur kept radio watches, their earphones muting the roaring turmoil outside.

The next day, December 24th, was another busy and frustrating time for the USARPS. They continued working on the raft all day. Their movements were painful and their work hampered by their injuries. But at least they had a dry and relatively comfortable place to rest inside the chopper. Gradually the noise of the wind and ice subsided, and by supper time, the men were able to talk without shouting. Bitsy and Jon had managed to improve the meals a little, and there was enough whiskey to go around. After supper, the USARPS took a short break. Then, just as Reszke said, "Let's go," Ira held up a hand.

He heard *Sinbad* calling.

Ole Magnussen, *Sinbad's* radio operator, sounded weary and tense as he transmitted the emergency message given to him by Captain Gilbert at 1900. "Mayday—Mayday—Mayday—Motor Vessel *Sinbad* calling for assistance! Now being nipped by icebergs! Position, in Lemaire Channel, near Deloncle Bay. One hundred seventy-five persons on board. Preparing now to abandon ship and camp on iceberg." Magnussen paused a moment, and again repeated the Mayday distress call and the ship's location, adding, "Iceberg alongside *Sinbad* apparently grounded now. Ship is secured to iceberg by cables and ice anchors." After another short pause, Ole resumed his call for help. "Palmer Station—Palmer Station—do you copy? Palmer—do you copy? Over."

In the helicopter at Palmer, Ira Mason and George Reszke listened intently to Magnussen's distress call. Ira answered, "*Sinbad*, this is Palmer. Roger your emergency message. It's been passed to our station manager." Ira and George agreed that they must advise Magnussen of their exact situation. "*Sinbad*—this is Palmer. We're unable to render any assistance. Helicopter still under repair. Over."

"Roger," replied Ole. "Calling Research Vessel *Quest*. *Quest*, this is *Sinbad* calling. Do you read? Over."

Enrique and Captain Pack were in *Quest's* radio room. "*Sinbad*, this is *Quest*," Enrique responded. "Roger your distress call. Your message passed to Captain Pack. Regret we can't give you assistance. *Quest* is trapped at Deception Island. We'll make every effort to reach you if we get out, but we can't estimate when that will be. Over, and standing by on 2182."

Ole Magnussen continued the Mayday distress call a few more times. The British Antarctic Survey Ship *Bransfield* responded, but the vessel couldn't approach the coast due to heavy concentration of icebergs. The Icebreaker *Southwind* replied with the same message as *Bransfield*. Later,

Ole heard from the Argentine ship *General San Martin,* and the Chilean Naval vessel *Piloto Pardo,* with much the same result. The great masses of large icebergs crowding off from all sides of the Antarctic Continent prevented any vessel from giving assistance to *Sinbad.* The people on the luxury liner would have to depend upon their own resources for whatever protection they could gain.

At Palmer, George Reszke and Ira Mason heard the exchange of messages between *Sinbad* and the other ships with growing anxiety for the safety of the *Sinbad* passengers and crew. Ira called *Sinbad* again. "Palmer calling *Sinbad.* Advise your situation. Over."

Ole immediately answered. "We have several injured. Our pumps are holding the leaks at present. We're setting up a camp on the iceberg. Over."

"Roger," replied Ira. "Please advise your situation every half hour. We'll stand by, and advise you of our progress in repairing the helicopter. Palmer out."

"Oh, brother!" exclaimed George, and turning to Thompson, asked, "Do you have any idea how long it can take to get those rotor blades fixed? *Sinbad*'s in deep trouble, and they're about to abandon the ship and camp on an iceberg. If we can get this chopper going, we can put them ashore somewhere."

"To be honest," confided Lt. Thompson, "considering what we have to work with, it'll take a long time. And believe me, I don't see how we can get this helo in operation before the water gets up to it."

George called Arthur. "Art, how much time have we got?"

Arthur's reply confirmed Thompson's statement. "Not over twelve to fourteen hours," he declared.

"That all?" George asked with dismay.

"Yes, it's rising faster now," replied Arthur.

The urgency of their own situation, augmented by *Sinbad*'s perilous emergency, spurred the USARPS to their utmost effort. It wasn't long, however, until they were all convinced that they were fighting a losing battle with the water. Reszke ordered a stop to all work on the rotor blades, and had the men make preparations to take care of the helicopter once it floated upon the raft. Thompson and Stefano were to stay with the chopper, and the others were to lead out the hoist cable along the shore. Thompson was to heave in on the cable as required, and in that way, haul the raft and its load along with the men as they made their way toward Mount William. Arthur termed it "kedging" and he was the one responsible for suggesting it to Thompson.

While the preparations were being made, Bitsy said to Enrico, "I wonder if the Lieutenant and Hank can really fix those blades."

Enrico frowned, "I don't know," he murmured. "It's complicated, the way those blades are made. The hub of the rotor needs repair too. That may be the hardest part. I heard them talking about it. They call it an 'articulated hub.' There's this 'pitch cone coupling'—complicated to repair—blades actually flap and feather."

"You mean something like this?" Bitsy held his hand horizontally and twisted it, like feathering an oar.

"Yes. Something like an albatross gliding. They make small adjustments to their wings," Enrico replied.

"You're kidding! Can a chopper do that?" Bitsy asked with disbelief.

"I don't know enough about helicopters to explain all the details. Go ask the pilot. I just heard a few words. He also said something about repairs to the control linkage." As Enrico was about to offer some additional information, Reszke gave orders that he was to remain in the chopper while it was being rafted along the shore so that he wouldn't have to be carried by the men. "Okay," commented Enrico. "I'll be taking a joy ride!"

The Palmer USARPS worked long into the night on Christmas Eve to finish the preparations for their move. By Christmas morning, the water was high enough to float the raft with the helicopter, and the tired men started their trek toward Mount William.

6

R. V. QUEST was still anchored in Whalers Bay on December 25. It was another day of apprehension and frustration for all of us. A small, table-size Christmas tree was taken out of the box in which it was stored from year to year. It was moth-eaten, and smelled bad, but Ray stood it up on the mess table anyway. I helped him hang some dirty tinsel and a few cracked ornaments on it. I hoped it wouldn't collapse into our food. Elbow and Icepack made a few wisecracks about our efforts, but we shrugged them off.

We sat around the mess room for a while, expressing some of our thoughts about Christmas, and the events that were taking place around us and in our homeland. We all felt pretty despondent, and having that crummy-looking tree on the table didn't help much. Elbow and Icepak were deeply concerned about the situation into which we had been so unexpectantly thrust. The trembling and rumbling, like distant thunder, continued, and we didn't know what was in store for us.

"What *can* be the meaning of this great unheaval?" asked the skipper. "Can it really be that the whole damn ice sheet is breaking up?"

"It would take several years to do that," was Elbow's thoughtful reply. "It would take much more than the seasonal warmth of the sun to melt it, even though the sun is relatively higher here now."

"How about the earthquakes and eruptions?" I asked.

163

"Now, that's another matter. Apparently, from what we have heard by radio, some great molten mass has shifted in the interior of the earth, and is pushing outward against the mantle under the ice with extensive earthquakes and volcanic eruptions. If that's true," Larsen theorized, "then, yes, it might break up and melt the ice away."

I took notes on Dr. Larsen's comments. "Maybe that's exactly what's happening," I said.

"Could be," he mused.

"Why don't we climb up one of these hills," suggested Captain Pack, "and look out over the rim of our crater to see what things look like outside?"

"Okay. Let's go," agreed Larsen.

I asked permission to go with them, and when the skipper said, "By all means," I got my camera. We were put ashore in a zodiac. With much effort, we slowly trudged up the black slope covered with fresh cinders. At the top, a frightening scene lay before our eyes as we viewed the sea surrounding Deception Island.

Icebergs, larger than city blocks, plunged and crashed against each other, scattering huge chunks with thundering echoes, as they were borne northward by the strong currents flowing away from the glaciers of the Antarctic Peninsula. As far as we could see, through the haze and smoke, the massive bergs tossed and rolled as if some terrific force was jolting them like ice cubes violently stirred in an enormous punch bowl. Had *Quest* been out there, she surely would have been ground to bits. I was indeed glad that I had one good camera left.

In the ever threatening volcanic crater of Deception, *Quest* had, temporarily at least, a haven of protection from the raging monsters outside. The blocking of Neptune's Bellows by the avalanche had prevented *Quest* from leaving, but it had also, in reality, saved our lives. From the hilltop, we could see the that the water had risen and covered the obstruction at the entrance.

"Maybe the water will rise enough to let us take the ship

out over the obstruction," suggested Pack.

"Who knows," observed Elbow. "If enough ice melts off the continent, perhaps, but that's a big 'if.' "

We stood on the hilltop a long time, three rugged but weary men, our figures silhouetted against the stormy sky. In awe, we watched the tortured sea full of great white monsters, realizing that, but for our ordeal of eruptions, earthquakes, and fire, we might have been crushed and lost in that terrifying stampede. We looked back down at our charred but still sturdy ship anchored in the quiet bay. Pack became silent, lost in deep reflection. Later, he said he had been thinking of the sailing vessels which had sought haven in Whalers Bay in times long past, and of the small, forty-seven foot sloop *Hero*, which young Nathaniel Palmer had sailed there from New England. Doubtless *Hero* had anchored in Whalers Bay, with other seal hunters and whalers, in the early part of the past century. The skipper pensively gazed down at *Quest*. I sensed, and shared with him, a sudden feeling of deep admiration and affection for that scorched and blackened trawler. What meaningful testimony such vessels were to the skills of their builders, and of the mariners such as Palmer, who brought them safely through tumultuous seas! What a miracle it was that *Quest*, and our small group of mortals, had survived the terrifying ordeal of those past few days. How grateful we were to have been prevented from leaving Deception. If we had escaped the caldera, we would have been smashed to splinters in the maelstrom of ice in Bransfield Strait. Slowly and silently, we made our way down the slope to the zodiac waiting to take us back to *Quest*.

On board again, we were informed by Second Mate Paul Shelley that he had been making some observations and calculations. Occasional fleeting azimuth bearings of the sun, for which he had patiently waited, coupled with his known position and Greenwich mean time, had shown him that the sun's declination was then decreasing. Paul concluded that the earth was no longer increasing its tilt and had apparently stabilized. He wasn't sure, but he assumed we were still in the same orbit, and the sun would appear a little farther north each day. He surmised that we might possibly expect the unusual warmth to give way gradually to more normal polar temperatures, although there was no indication of it occurring at that time.

"This means," said the skipper, "that unless we get out of here, we may have to winter over."

"Oh, no," groaned Carol who overheard the conversation, "please, not that!" She was, understandably, low in spirit.

"I'm with you," the skipper soothingly assured her. "We'll certainly try to get out, but it'll take some time for the water to get high enough. Besides, it's too dangerous out there now." He called Enrique. "Get me Palmer. I want to find out some more about that helicopter. That may be our only hope. I wonder how the *Sinbad* people are making out on the iceberg."

Ira Mason answered Enrique's call. Pack took the microphone. "Ira, this is Captain Pack. I need some good, reliable, happy information, Ira. Do you feel like giving me some?"

"Okay Captain. I'll do my best."

"When are you going to send us that chopper? When? Tomorrow? Next week? Next month? Never? Don't answer, Ira. We're just getting a little edgy, sitting here alongside these volcanoes, with a murderous sea condition outside. It looks as if that bird may be our only hope. Over."

Ira's reply was not exactly the "happy information" the captain had requested. He said, almost bitterly, "Captain, I can only say this. We're doing our best. The water rose very quickly and we couldn't possibly get the helicopter repaired before the water reached the pad. We had to stop the repair work, and we're moving to higher ground. We have the chopper on a raft now and it's floating. Everybody worked as hard as he could, but it's a complicated job to repair these rotor blades. Sorry. Over."

"Roger, Ira," answered the skipper. "Thanks anyway. I know you're doing your best. When you can stop moving and get the helicopter repaired, I will expect you to rescue those *Sinbad* people first. Tell George Reszke and the others we wish them all the best. We have a measure of protection here in Deception at the present time, but we don't know for how long. Over."

After a short pause, Ira's voice came through again. "Captain, George Reszke wants to have a word with you. Here he is."

"Captain Pack? George Reszke here." He spoke slowly. He sounded hoarse. It was the voice of a weary man. "Captain—I just wanted to say, merry—what I really want to say is—we all hope to see you—to see you again—soon. I just can't see anything very merry for any of us, but we haven't lost hope yet. Let's hope the new year will bring us all safely through this trouble. Over."

"Roger, George," replied Pack. "We're alive, and we'll find some way. Just keep on hoping, and do the best you can. I think we'll be seeing you soon. I'm worried about those *Sinbad* passengers on that iceberg. They're worse off than any of us. Over."

"One more thing, Captain," George's tone softened. "Please tell Carol Moore—for all of us—we send her our deepest sympathy. Over and out."

"Roger, George. I'll deliver your message. *Quest* out."

As the day passed, we became more optimistic about our chances of survival. With much interest and curiosity, we viewed the constant rising of the water level which was then up to the old buildings on shore. Earthquakes and volcanic activity had subsided to some extent at Deception, but distant rumbling and loud explosions could be heard from the peninsula across Bransfield Strait.

In the late afternoon, I spent a little while in the galley with Ray. I got myself a cup of coffee, and did some snooping into the pots on the stove. Just forward of the galley was the fo'c's'le with rooms on each side and a mess table in the center. Taking a breather at the table were

Oiler Philip Kenosheta and Wiper Orville Simpson. They were having a profound discussion of the events which were happening around us. Ray and I listened with amusement to their sagacious remarks.

"You know what I was thinkin'?" said Simpson.

"I can't imagine." Philip rolled his eyes upward.

"They say the crust of the earth is like a thin skin. That where the mountains are, like the Rockies, Andes, an' such, are really only wrinkles of the skin," Simpson explained.

"Sure is wrinkled a lot down here in the Antarctic."

"Yeah. That long range extends all the way down from Alaska along the west coast of North and South America, across the Drake Passage and into this Antarctic Peninsula." As an afterthought, Simpson added, "Sorta like y'r spine."

"Uh huh. It musta got a slipped disc here. An' at other places like where I come from—California. It bounces around there too, sometimes." Philip drummed on the table with his fingers.

"What gits me," continued Simpson, "like I said, I read somewhere—the crust, or mantle of the earth is so thin, it would be like if you stuck your head in a barrel of beer. The beer that sticks to your head would be like the crust of the earth."

"Hell! That sure is thin. I don't like beer anyway. Let's use your head. It's fatter!"

"Yup," said Simpson, "an' they say it's fulla molten rock, nickel and iron."

"Y'know, Ollie, it's a wonder that stuff don't fall out through such a thin crust."

"It does push out sometimes, like volcanoes and such."

"Some places, I guess, the crust is thinner than others," reflected Philip.

"It's a good thing gravity holds it all together." Orville Simpson changed the subject. "Sure have been a lot of earthquakes lately."

"Maybe somethin's shiftin' around in there, like a ship

168

when its cargo shifts."

"I was on a ship once," observed Orville, "we had a load of grain. The stevedores put up the shifting boards, but some musta come loose. In a blow, some of that grain in number two hold shifted, an' we come into port with a list to starboard."

"Yeah," said Phil. "Like once I worked on an ore carrier, up on the lakes. She was about six hun'erd feet long. When we loaded iron ore in Duluth, the mate had to stand on deck an' watch a pendulum at each end. If not, they'd get a twist in the ship, like the forward end to starboard, and the after end to port."

"You sayin' the earth's takin' a list?"

"Right."

"Well, anyhow, the earth must be pretty well balanced, to have all that hot stuff inside an' still keep goin' around steady."

Philip's oriental grin disappeared and he assumed an air of superior wisdom. "Some of us scientists think the core in the middle is hard nickel. If that ever shifted, we might start to wobble."

Simpson gestured toward Kenosheta's shining straight black hair neatly tied back from his face. "You suppose too much. That'sa matter with you. You sure git some wayout ideas. Wobble! *You* got hot rocks in your head!"

With a smile at Roy, I left the galley and went up on deck to look around and wait for supper. For some time, I had been aware of ill feelings between Per Thysen and Mike Vogt. I could see that the situation disturbed Dr. Larsen. That afternoon they had a loud argument, which I had overheard. It took place in the forward laboratory which they used as a storage area for their mountain climbing gear. I could hear their voices as I walked on deck, but couldn't understand what they were saying. It was mostly in Swedish or Norwegian, with an occasional English word. I did hear the name "Beebee" several times, so I assumed the argument had something to do with her. Before long I heard Dr. Larsen's voice, and soon the quarrel ended.

Thysen and Beebee were often on my mind. We had all seen him making passes at her. He would often seat himself beside her at the dining table. On more than one occasion I had observed him hanging around her cabin door. I was sure that Mike Vogt and Dr. Larsen had noticed.

Thysen loved to use the language of the scientists, especially in Beebee's presence. His brief, boastful, utterances were sprinkled with words like "disciplines," "parameters," "petrographically," "geonomy," "stratographically," which he dropped into his conversation whenever he thought he could impress Beebee. His forcing his attentions on her infuriated me. How did he ever get security clearance? I decided to ask Mike Vogt a few questions about him.

"Thysen," said Vogt, "is a louse!" I wondered if that was all he was going to say, but he continued. "Thysen's people were Danes. He comes from the Atlantic Avenue section of Brooklyn, New York. He lived in Montreal for a while, and later moved to England, where he married an English woman, and they went to Denmark. When the Nazis occupied Denmark, he and his wife escaped to Sweden, where he met Dr. Larsen. They were afraid the Nazis would put his English wife in prison. We all got along fine the first few years. I can't tell you what our troubles are about. All I can say is—Thysen is a louse!" I didn't pursue the matter any further. I saw that Vogt wouldn't either.

I went to my cabin to rest, but I was unable to sleep. A remark that Mike had made kept coming back to mind. The word *Nazi* had opened up an avenue of conjecture. Vaguely I began to recall my various assignments during World War II. I had written a lot about the Nazis, and their occupancy in European and Scandinavian lands. Suddenly the face of a Nazi collaborator, about whom I had written, flashed across my memory. That face—yes—it was Thysen! But the name was different. His beard had been shorter, and his hair had been neatly trimmed, but I remembered a scar across his cheek, which was now only partly hidden by his heavy beard. Yes—it must be the same man! I was sure of it.

As the moments passed, I recalled more details about Thysen, or whatever his name had been. Vogt's story was not entirely correct. Thysen had undoubtedly concealed the truth. Yes, he had been living with an Englishwoman in Denmark. When the Nazis occupied that country they went to Norway, not Sweden. In Norway Thysen became a Nazi collaborator, a "quisling." The woman had been arrested, and probably killed. I began to ferret out the sordid details, and filed my story in Sweden. As a result of my reporting, Thysen had fallen into the hands of anti-Nazi elements and was beaten almost to death. He finally got out of Norway and into Sweden where he assumed the name Thysen. There he met Dr. Larsen and Vogt.

So there was Thysen, and there too was I, on that small ship in the Antarctic, much too close for comfort. After careful thought, I decided to keep quiet about Thysen. He was undoubtedly very useful to Dr. Larsen. I was certain now that he had recognized me immediately as the author of the articles about him. I felt sure also that he would try to do away with me again if an opportunity came along. I had to continue my vigilance.

Supper that evening was somewhat of an event. Ray had been assisted in the galley by the cook who had been rescued from the Argentine station. His burns were a hindrance, but he managed, with Ray's help, to prepare a tasty "*puchero*," a favorite Argentine dish. Philip Scott, the British geologist, and the Argentine volcanists were able to join us at supper, but they needed some help in eating because of their bandaged hands.

After supper, we sat around the sorry-looking Christmas tree on the mess room table, and tried to cheer one another. A few bottles of wine appeared. We were really thankful for many things—our lives, for one. Carol sat with us, silently suffering.

Beebee told about how she and a colleague had once collected specimens in a small boat in the waters of Panama. They pulled up a little iron box encrusted with barnacles. Its lid was slightly open, and inside they found what remained of a left hand. There was a large diamond ring on one of the fingers. Beebee was horrified, and quickly took it to the police.

"Maybe it belonged to some murder victim, and the murderer couldn't get the ring off the finger, so he cut off the whole hand," suggested Elbow Larsen.

"Was it a woman's hand?" I asked.

"Yes." Beebee shuddered.

"I wonder why he didn't just cut off the finger?" asked Chief Jesse Lytel.

"I don't know." Beebee sipped her wine. "It was an . . ."

"Maybe," said the chief, "someone was coming, and he had to get away in a hurry, so he put it in the box and dropped it overboard."

"Was the woman left-handed?" asked Paul Shelley.

"Why'nt you guys shut up? It's Christmas! Don'cha know that?" Harry King's voice was a little thick.

"So what?" mumbled the chief.

As the hours passed and the wine diminished, we tried some old fashioned singing. Oh, brother! What harmony! It was like everybody was singing a different song.

I had been sitting on the settee with Beebee. I got up to fill the glasses around the table, emptying the bottle. At that moment Thysen, who had evidently been drinking something stronger, came in and plopped himself down alongside Beebee where I had been sitting. He put his arms around her and tried to pull her to him. She struggled to free herself. Thysen's action was too much for me. I shouted, "Leave her alone," and with that I swung the empty wine bottle. It broke in half against his head. I held the jagged top half of the bottle menacingly toward his bearded face and blood-shot eyes.

172

Thysen was stunned for a moment. Then he slid his big frame around the end of the table and started to lunge at me. Beebee and Carol screamed. I moved toward Thysen. Vogt and Elbow came around the other side of the table and grabbed Thysen before he could reach me. The mess room was in an uproar of cursing men and screaming women.

Thysen, bleeding from a wound where the bottle had broken on his head, was dragged away from me shouting obscenities. "I'll kill dat cheap, pen pushin' summabish," he yelled. "I'll t'row dat bastid ova' board." And with strength like a bull, he shook off Mike Vogt and Elbow Larsen. With head down, shielding his face from my broken bottle, he charged at me, ramming his head into my stomach. To avoid falling, I grabbed the table, but dropped the broken top half of the bottle. Thysen's big sledgehammer fists slammed into my face and my head jerked back. I beat him off with all my strength, but his hands closed on my neck and throat.

"Get off me, you stinking idiot," I yelled, gasping and choking. We both went crashing down onto the deck. My fists were no match against my tough assailant. I struggled to escape him.

Thysen's drunken rage and abuse went on. "Ya doity scum!" he bellowed. "Ya t'ink ya so dam' smart! I'll bust ya crummy mug!" He doubled a heavy knee, and was about to plant his whole weight on my chest. Everyone was yelling, but suddenly I heard the mate's booming voice louder and closer than the others.

Although big Harry King, the chief mate, was far from sober himself, he apparently decided that he didn't want a clumsy, unsavory homicide, especially there in front of everybody in the mess room, on Christmas. He had no use for "shore types" in general, and "dam reporters" in particular, but he detested Thysen.

Harry pulled Thysen to his feet, waving off Vogt and Larsen, who tried to help. I scrambled up too, and tried to resume my fight, but the mate brushed me aside.

"I'll take care a' this," Harry yelled. "I'll fix this bum." The two big men seemed evenly matched as they squared off in the middle of the room. But knowing of Harry King's past history as a boxer before he went to sea, I was sure Thysen would get what he deserved.

The brawl that followed made a shambles of the mess room. Chairs were broken, dishes and glasses smashed, and blood splattered on deck and bulkheads. In the middle of the fight someone turned out the lights, but the battle went on between the two giants in the darkness.

When the light was restored, Thysen, who had pulled a knife, lay lifeless on the deck with a fractured skull. Harry was on his knees, mopping his own bloody face. He was bleeding also from several cuts on his arms and legs where Thysen's knife had slashed in the darkness. But Harry had, as he had promised, "fixed that bum."

Of course, that fixed my troubles with Thysen too, although I would never have wished so harsh a solution. However, I suppose it would have been necessary to eliminate him eventually, if I was to stay alive. We buried Thysen immediately right there at Whalers Bay, well up from the shore, where we assumed the water would not reach him. We didn't have a coffin, but the ground was no longer frozen so we dug a shallow grave and covered him with cinders and rocks. We built up a cairn to mark the spot, and Captain Pack read a few verses from the Bible.

Harry King's wounds were superficial, and he was easily patched up by Dr. Varnay. His recollection of the fight was somewhat hazy, but he said he thought Thysen fell and hit his head against a fire extinguisher bracket in the darkness. We verified that statement by examining the extinguisher and finding it dented and bloody. Paul Shelley, the second mate, made the necessary entry in the deck log book, and Captain Pack entered an account of the altercation and Thysen's death in the Official Log.

At about 2300 while we were trying to restore order in the mess room, Enrique suddenly burst into the room.

"*Sinbad* is sinking!" he shouted. "We just got another

174

Mayday message! *Sinbad* is being crushed by icebergs in Lemaire Channel! A hundred and twenty-eight people are off on an iceberg! There are still twenty-two passengers on board, and twenty-five of the crew trying to save the ship!''

7

FAR FROM the Antarctic, the Florida winter season was in full swing. Despite the unusual cold in Palm Beach on December 22, the John Hadley mansion was in festive holiday array. The Hadleys had invited their friends to a luncheon, and the guests began arriving about twelve ten. Cadillacs, Rolls-Royces, Imperials, and other status wheels, a Bentley, a Maserati, a Ferrari, and a Facel-Vega entered the grounds and rolled around the circular driveway to the portico, and parked near the Hadley motor pool which included a Continental, a Jaguar sedan, and a Mercedes-Benz sports car.

The occasion was John and Bernice Hadley's silver anniversary. There was also another reason for the gala affair. The guests were nearly all wealthy Florida land developers and their wives. Also included were a couple of influential politicians. John Hadley headed a consortium which had recently acquired, after much difficult negotiation, a large portion of central Florida for development, promotion and sale.

The deal was potentially highly profitable, and the Hadleys chose their anniversary to celebrate. John had invested their entire fortune in the venture. He also persuaded his friends that the vast territory they had purchased was too good an opportunity to miss. His friends agreed and had plunged as deeply as their assets allowed. John had also revealed plans to his political friends by which they, too, could become millionaires without even trying.

John told Bernice that this would be their last venture. "I'll retire," he promised, "when the profits start to roll in, and we'll take a cruise around the world."

The Hadleys' three children were married and raising families of their own. One of the Hadleys' sons was on John's board of directors, and the other was a bank official. Their daughter, Susan, was married to geologist Philip Scott of the British Antarctic Survey. He had been working with Argentine volcanists at Deception under the auspices of the *Instituto Antártico Argentino*. Susan had closed their apartment in London for the duration of the austral summer and was visiting her parents in Palm Beach with her six year old son, Johnnie.

The palatial Hadley mansion was often the scene of social events which had a remarkable effect on the trend of Florida land development. On December 22, the mansion resounded with laughter and gaiety. The Hadleys' reputation as hosts was legendary.

A huge and gaudily decorated Christmas tree stood in the center of the spacious foyer, the first object to meet the eye whenever anyone entered through the front doors. Beyond, and to the right, was a large drawing room where cocktails were served.

Conversation over cocktails was largely about the important land purchase which the group had made, and the excellent potential for high profits under the Hadley plan, mingled with talk about the unusually cold weather. There was also much heated discussion about the government's so-called lack of leadership in the oil crisis. Gasoline rationing was denounced as ineffective. Prices at the pump had reached $2.50 per gallon. Gasoline had become a scarce commodity, and many service stations had closed.

The Hadley group operated a company plane which was used to take prospective purchasers to their land. Someone said, "If this keeps up, we'll soon have to ground our plane for lack of fuel."

While still partially sober, someone mentioned a news item which was causing a furor among astronomers and scientists. "The last I heard was a broadcast this morning. They called it 'tipping of the earth's axle.' They say it might affect our climate. Maybe the north will stay colder and our southern states—Florida, and the tropics—will become temperate."

"I'll drink to that," avowed another.

John laughed, "That should increase the value of Florida land. More snow birds will buy in Florida. Maybe we bought this piece just in time. Looks like maybe we gave ourselves a real good Christmas present."

"I'll drink to that," said the voice again as the caterer's waiter appeared with another tray of full glasses.

Bernice announced, "The President's speech will be at two o'clock, so let's go in to lunch now."

Soon the thirty guests were seated around a long and sumptuous table. John explained that the governor had sent his congratulations and apologies at the last moment due to an urgent message from the President, something to do with the scientists' reports. The governor hadn't given John any details, but merely said the message had come unexpectedly.

As fine food and wines were consumed, the guests engaged in animated chatter. After a couple of brief, highly saturated speeches of congratulations to John and Bernice, John Hadley pushed back his chair and rose unsteadily to his feet, a partly filled champagne glass clutched in his hand.

"Ladies an' gempl'men," John sputtered.

"Sit down, John," admonished Bernice from the opposite end of the table.

"This is one of the—"

"Sit down," Bernice pleaded.

"You all know—" persisted John.

"John, will you *please* sit down!"

"—how much I love Bernice." John walked unsteadily toward his wife, laughing and waving his glass. He intended to embrace her, but he only succeeded in spilling the rest of his champagne down her front.

"Oh, B'nice, I'm sorry, honey."

"John, *will you sit down!*" He sat down.

After luncheon, they all went to the TV room for coffee and liqueurs, and to hear the President's speech to Congress. Seated in large comfortable chairs, they continued their prattle until nearly two o'clock.

At last, the television screen was graced by the handsome face of broadcast journalist W. L. Burton. Hadley's party quieted as Burton announced the President's speech.

As the urgent and alarming message fell upon their ears, apprehension and dismay began to infuse those gathered in the room. When the President stated that the whole state of Florida would soon be under water, consternation gripped the Hadleys and their guests. Wealth, as measured by Florida land, had, for the majority of them, suddenly vanished. Word by word, the President's speech struck like hammer blows. Some of the guests jumped to their feet and started cursing whatever and whoever came to their minds. Some sat silently, hoping it was just a bad dream. Suddenly, most of them weren't only penniless, they were also badly in debt. One summed up the situation by exclaiming, "My friends, as of this moment, we couldn't sell a split level outhouse! We couldn't sell a square inch of that land! We couldn't even *give* it away!"

"That goes for the whole state of Florida!"

"The Bahamas too! Last year I bought an island. It won't make a shoal spot in the ocean when this flood covers those islands!"

"I wonder how long it will be until the flood gets here!"

"Who knows?"

"There will be a rush to get to high land!"

"What high land?"

"*Not* in Florida."

"I'll bet the highways will be jammed! I'm getting out fast!"

"Before the stampede!"

With the sudden realization that there would be a grand exodus from the Florida peninsula, the guests started to leave. Some stopped just long enough to thank John and Bernice, but most rushed for the door to get their cars out first. In their haste, they knocked down the Christmas tree and scattered the lights and decorations over the floor. Others trampled over the tree and the ornaments.

John turned on a radio to get further information. He found that only the powerful Emergency Broadcast System stations were in operation, disseminating information in accordance with standard "imminent disaster procedures." Although EBS was created specifically for use in case of a war emergency, the federal government had obviously switched to the alert system because of the gravity of the flood situation.

John slumped as he realized the great devastation ahead. Suddenly, they had nothing; even their home was valueless. Bernice came over to him and sat on the arm of his chair. She pulled his head over and held it close. He patted her hand and said, "It looks as if we're going to have to start all over again. In the last few minutes, Florida has become worthless."

Bernice murmured, "We have each other. We'll muddle through."

"Daddy!" Susan said excitedly. "I wonder if Phil is in any trouble down there in the Antarctic. From the earthquakes, I mean."

"I don't know about Phil," said John. "I'll call the National Science Foundation tomorrow, and see what I can find out."

Bernice asked, "Where in the world can we go? Everything we have is here."

John answered, "When you come down to it, we haven't got anything except our furniture, the cars, and the boat. There's no use trying to move our furniture until we get another house on higher ground."

Susan anxiously inquired, "Where is high enough ground?"

"Not in Florida!" exclaimed her father. "We may have to go to Georgia or Alabama."

Bernice brightened. "We can go to my folks." Her parents, both still living, had a small farm in Monroe County, southwest Alabama.

John grimaced. Neither of them had visited her folks for over five years. John had offered to provide for them on several occasions, but they had constantly refused help. Poor, but still confident of their ability to work their farm, they kept themselves going by their own toil. They had a few cows, a couple of corn fields, and a vegetable garden. They had given up cotton, since they couldn't grow enough to make it pay. They had sold most of their cows, keeping one for milk and a few more for beef for themselves. The big home was old, but comfortable, and they spent most of their time in the large kitchen near the fireplace and their television set. Temperatures were lower that winter than ever before, so they didn't go out often. The old man brought in wood for the fireplace and fed the cows. An old car, which neither of them drove, stood in the driveway. A neighbor did some grocery shopping for them once a week. They got a small social security check each month.

When Bernice called her parents, her mother answered. "Hello? Oh, hello, Bernice . . . Okay, I guess. I never saw such cold weather. . . . Yes, we did. We heard the flood probably won't git much farther north than Atmore. Maybe they'll have to release all the prisoners there . . . Yes, I know—the whole state of Florida. Whacha goin' to do? Y'all got any high land? . . . Sure. Why not? He's all right. Just bringin' in some firewood. Wanna talk to him?

Here, Bill. John wants t'talk with you—they say they're thinkin' about comin' here.''

"Hello, John. How are you? . . . Yes, we been listnin' to the President. Guess we're around five hundred feet here . . . I dunno exactly . . . Sure—come on. Susan with you? . . . That's fine . . . No, it's real cold. Colder'n I ever seen . . . Yep, we got plenty, canned a lot last fall. G'bye.'' Bernice and Susan then spoke with the old folks for awhile.

Not a moment was lost. John hurried to the bank to withdraw the small amount of cash they kept for day-to-day expenses. He checked the passbook. The balance was only thirty-two hundred dollars. A few weeks earlier, he could have written a check for over a million, and could easily have borrowed another million or more. Now they were down to thirty-two hundred dollars in cash, over fifty-thousand dollars' worth of furniture, and over three hundred thousand in the yacht and the three cars. John thought he could borrow on them if he could get everything to Alabama.

The President's speech had sobered John, but he was now suffering from the aftereffects of too much champagne. His head throbbed and his stomach felt queasy. He fought the nausea and tried to put it out of his mind. He glanced at his watch. It was after banking hours. Perhaps the bank was open anyway. He muttered to himself, "I'll draw the thirty-two hundred and see if I can get a mover to take some of our furniture to Alabama. I'll sell some of it there, and sell one of the cars. We'll hang on to the yacht. There'll be plenty of water, and maybe I'll have to move some of our stuff by boat."

He drove immediately into town, but when he turned into the block where the bank was located, a crowd was in front of it, clamoring to get in. Only a few people were allowed in at a time. There was a "run" on the bank. John had dealt with that bank for years, and at times he had millions on deposit, but he couldn't get near the door. He went to a telephone booth to call the bank president. Eight persons were ahead of him. John went home to call. All the bank numbers were busy. He tried to call his son, the president of a bank in a nearby city. The result was the same. John was edgy and very pale.

"It's so cold out," said Bernice. "Better have another cup of coffee."

"No! No more coffee! I'll soon need a stiff drink if this keeps on!" exclaimed John. "I'll see about a mover." He tried several moving and storage companies. Their telephones were also busy. He decided to go to one mover personally.

"John, you don't feel well and you don't look well. Let Plato drive," urged Bernice.

John slipped on a sweater to wear under his jacket. He had seldom felt so cold in South Florida. "Must be down around freezing," he groaned. Plato Kim, his chauffeur, had the heater on in the Jaguar.

The first movers they visited informed John they couldn't take any more orders. They had many more jobs than they could ever handle, and were about to get out of the state anyway. John thought of a van. Plato took him to a station that rented them. He made a deposit on two vans. When John and Plato went back to the bank, the crowd was still there. Some of the people were angrily shouting and threatening to break the windows. One man was up on the balustrade, yelling at the mobs, "Let's break in!" Someone came with a couple of two-by-fours, and the crowd let him pass.

John saw a sign on the door of the bank which read "Closed for the Day." In his wallet he had less than a hunded dollars, but he remembered that there probably were three or four hundred in a small safe at home.

He said to Plato, "Let's go home."

"I can drive one of those vans," Plato volunteered.

"Good, Plato, I'll drive the other. Bernice can drive the Continental, and Susan can take this car. Take me home,

184

and then get the cars filled up with gas and ready to go. What are we going to do about the Mercedes?"

Plato said, "Maybe Daisy and Juby will drive it," referring to the cook and maid. "Daisy likes the Mercedes anyway," Plato continued. "Who we gonna get to load the vans?"

"I don't know, Plato. I'll make some calls and see who I can round up. Guess we'll all have to help."

"Okay, boss. I know a coupla guys. I'll call 'em too."

Plato had some trouble getting gas. He took the Continental first, and had to get on a long line of cars. When he got to the pump, the price had shot up to $5.00 a gallon. The attendant said the station would close for good as soon as the present stock was sold. They couldn't get any more. Plato got the car's tank filled and went home with the news. They all realized there would be no gas for the vans or the other two cars. John started to get angry. Bernice poured him a drink. After much thought, he finally said, "Okay. Get everybody into the Continental."

John called the airport to inquire about the company's plane and was informed that the pilot had already been there, but had gone, saying there wasn't enough gas to fly the plane, and none would be delivered to the airport.

John decided, as had millions of other Floridians, that he had better get his family out fast.

"Everybody get your clothes packed. Take warm clothing. We've got to get out of Florida before all the roads are jammed with cars. Bernice, take all your jewelry. We only have about six hundred dollars. There'll be a wild scramble to get land or houses on higher ground. I'll take you all to Alabama, then I'll come back and see if I can get some fuel for the yacht and load it up. Plato, how's the gas in the Jaguar?"

Plato answered, "Well, it was almost full this morning."

"Good," said John. "Now, Daisy—"

Daisy interrupted him. "Naw, suh, I ain't goin' nowheres! I'm goin' over to my sister's an' I'll take Juby with me. Y'all go ahead. We'll catch up before the flood comes."

John said to Plato, "Leave some gas in the Mercedes. Daisy, you keep the Mercedes here and look out for the house. I'll be back in three or four days. C'mon now! Let's get moving!"

In less than an hour, they left their magnificent but worthless mansion. Plato drove the Jaguar, loaded with clothing, and John drove the Continental with Bernice, Susan, Johnnie, and whatever items they had been able to pack. Bernice couldn't conceal her tears as they left their beautiful home, looking back until it was out of sight. She was also very worried about their sons. She had repeatedly called their homes, but there was no answer. John kept reassuring her that the boys were all right. He felt they were smart enough to get their families out of Florida.

The Hadleys' progress northward from Palm Beach was slow. As the cold afternoon wore on, they began to wonder about where they could stop to rest. They were on the Sunshine State Parkway, and at each access road, more cars moved onto the turnpike. The Hadley family saw crowds and many cars lined up for gas at the service plazas. Plato had a hard time keeping track of his employers in the heavy traffic. By the time they reached Ocala, it was nearly midnight, and both cars were getting low on gas. They decided to pull out and try to fill up, but they couldn't find any. It was a very cold night, and they finally stopped to rest. There were many cars where they stopped, several abandoned. Some people were seen trying, without success, to siphon gas from the abandoned cars.

John began to wonder if they would ever make it to Alabama. He decided they would have to abandon the Jaguar and some of the clothing, and put the remaining gas from the Jaguar into the Continental. Plato insisted on staying with the Jaguar, hoping to get some gas the next morning. That was the last the Hadleys saw of him.

They made one more gas stop before reaching Alabama in heavy traffic, and paid $13.00 a gallon for their next tankful. They reached the old farm in Alabama in the evening. Around the big fireplace in the old house, they found a measure of peace, but all that night, and for days following, many thousands of cars and people, fleeing from Gulf Coast cities, drove into and through Monroe County. The old farmhouse and fields were overwhelmed with frightened refugees.

John tried in vain to call his sons in Florida. He couldn't get through to them.

Within an hour after the President's speech, the White House, Capitol, and all Washington offices were deserted. Because of the uncertainty as to how far the ocean swells would reach up the Chesapeake, the nation's Capitol suddenly became Washington D'Ceased. When John tried to phone the Division of Polar Programs at the National Science Foundation, he again got no answer. He tried without success to get through to anyone who could give him some information about Susan's husband.

Philip, with a few scratches and burns, but safely on board *Quest,* hadn't heard anything as to the fate of Susan, his son, or his in-laws. He hoped they had escaped from Florida in time, and wondered if they had gone to Alabama. He was very concerned. The news reports were alarming.

Enrique tried to get through to Susan's parents. On a couple of occasions, he succeeded in getting a ham operator in Kansas to set up a phone patch, only to learn that many telephones were out of order in coastal states.

Months later Enrique was able to get Philip in contact with his family in Alabama through the assistance of other ham operators. It was thus that I learned the details of the Hadleys' escape from Florida.

187

In addition to our own precarious situation on board *Quest*, we were all extremely concerned about the terrible circumstances in other parts of the world reported by radio.

The northern hemisphere was in the grip of the most severe winter in modern history. Chilled by gales to temperatures below zero, the northern part of the USA and also much of the south was plagued by shortage of heating fuel. Snow covered the country as far south as Texas and the Florida Peninsula.

While energy barons and bureaucrats were locked in endless debate over pipelines, power, and profits, the nation's supplies of fuel dwindled. Rivers were frozen and highways closed. Precious fires that warmed millions of homes went out completely. Water in pipes turned to ice. Many lives were lost as the bitter chill crept into the bones of young and old alike.

Parts of Florida, the Sunshine State, had already been declared disaster areas. Valuable crops of citrus and vegetables had succumbed to the freezing temperatures. The imminent calamity proclaimed by the President—the approach of the great seismic swells—had suddenly thrown the population into utter panic. Consternation and terror seized the inhabitants of Florida. Wild and tumultuous throngs struggled and fought in their desperate attempt to flee northward to higher elevations of Georgia and Alabama. Highways and fields were jammed with vehicles of all kinds, loaded with cold and frightened people. Similar scenes occurred in coastal areas throughout the world.

Hospitals, power plants, stores, police and fire departments, banks, schools, jails, asylums, airports, army, navy, coast guard and other institutions were abandoned in the mad rush for survival. Fires raged unchecked. Prisons were forced open, and looters, murderers, and mental patients mingled and fled with the crowds. Animals escaped from abandoned zoos and attacked helpless people.

Tourists poured out of plush Miami Beach hotels, already abandoned by their employees. Multitudes jammed the streets and causeways seeking to reach the mainland. Miami International and other airports were in utter confusion as crowds filled the buildings clamoring for transportation and pushing out onto the runways. Airline and airport employees crowded to the planes demanding to be taken aboard. Control towers were abandoned, their personnel seeking to board the airplanes. Aircraft collided on the runways, scattering debris and bodies. As flames rose from burning planes and smoke blew across the airfields, hope vanished for the throngs seeking escape by air. Crying and moaning in despair, trampled and dying, the frightened horde struggled in vain to flee from the low, flat, vulnerable peninsula of Florida.

Since the first alarming news of the earth's increasing tilt, ships of all kinds, large and small, began filling the seaports and harbors of the world. Those already in port didn't venture out, and those at sea quickly sought refuge.

Harbors, anchorages, and docks of South Florida became crammed with vessels. Large luxury cruise ships were moored two abreast at Dodge Island in Miami Harbor. Cargo ships, tankers, yachts, and thousands of small pleasure craft swarmed throughout the area. Maritime interests were apprehensive and confused. Their activities had come to an abrupt halt.

R. V. *Alert,* a sleek, fast research vessel, lay at a dock in Port Everglades. She was fueled and provisioned for an extended period at sea, but her departure had been reluctantly cancelled by Mark L. Dover, vice president of the organization of scientists and engineers which operated the vessel.

On December 22, Captain Dover and Captain Seth Fulton, *Alert's* skipper, were in the ship's mess room discussing the tilt and the resulting invalidation of celestial and satellite systems of navigation.

"We'll have to depend mostly on loran," said Mark.

Loran C, an electronic long range hyperbolic navigational system, had become most important to navigators in northern hemisphere oceans where the shores were dotted with pairs of loran stations, some two hundred to four hundred miles apart, transmitting synchronized signals. Unaffected by the tilt, the electronic system was a reliable means by which positions of vessels could still be determined.

"Right," said Captain Seth. "At least we still have loran. And, assuming the earth's rotation hasn't changed, our gyro compasses shouldn't be affected." Seth and Mark were both showing signs of strain because of the mysterious situation. Seth bitterly declared, "This sudden shifting of the earth is getting everybody unhinged. I wonder what the hell is going to happen next!" He didn't have long to wait.

Alert's officers, and several members of the crew, joined the captains in the mess room to hear the President's speech. Seth switched on the television set, and Captain Mark moved back to view it better. He took out a notebook to jot down whatever he might wish to recall later. His memory needed no prompting however, for the rest of his life. They listened with increasing horror to the President's warning of the approach of the great seismic swells. Their reaction was immediate.

"Deep water!" exclaimed Mark. "We must get away from the coast!"

"Beyond the continental shelf—in deep water!" echoed Seth. "Let's get *Alert* out there! How about over the Abyssal Plain?"

"Anywhere outside the Blake Escarpment," replied Mark. He started toward the bridge. "I'll call our families! We'll take them with us!"

Seth turned to the second mate. "Get Captain Mark a position—nearest point in deep water—around a couple of thousand fathoms, toward Bermuda." Then to the others he said, "Call your families, your immediate relatives! Tell them to get here fast if you want them to come with us!

We'll get away within two hours! We don't have a minute to lose! Some of you call from the phones on the dock. We can't all use the ship's phone." He addressed the ship's chief engineer. "Chief, we'll need all the speed we can get! We'll light off the turbine, but only for a short while, to get away fast! We must watch our fuel. We don't know how long we'll have to stay at sea."

Captain Mark tried to call the families concerned, but all the lines were busy and turmoil was so great onshore that he had much difficulty reaching anyone. Not all those he was able to contact accepted his invitation to go to sea on *Alert*. While talking with one of the wives, he overheard loud remarks by someone else in the room with her. "Holy mackerel! Is he off his rocker? That's right smack in the Bermuda Triangle!" Another said, "Taking families out there? He must have lost his marbles! Tell him no! Not on your life! No Bermuda Triangle for us!"

In less than two hours, *Alert* was ready to depart. On board were members of several families of *Alert's* crew, including Mark's and Seth's. Also on board, at Mark's invitation, was Marilyn Allen, Arthur Allen's wife, and their children. Apprehensive as to Arthur's fate at Palmer Station in the Antarctic, and fearful that she would be unable to escape from Florida by land, Marilyn had gladly accepted Captain Dover's offer.

Many others had declined in fear. Some had already abandoned their homes and were attempting to drive out of Florida. Others were aghast at the thought of deliberately going out into the ill-famed Bermuda Triangle. Some had come to the dock, but hesitated to go aboard. "Too dangerous," they said, "out there!"

"Dangerous?" retorted Mark. "You're damn right there's danger! But the greatest danger is right here on the coast! You stay here and you'll all die!" Still they held back. "Come on!" he snapped. "Make up your minds! We can't wait any longer!" A few more stepped aboard.

"Let go all lines," Captain Seth ordered from the

bridge. He backed *Alert* slowly away and headed for the open sea, leaving a small group standing on the dock, arguing about the dangers of the Bermuda Triangle.

"You know," Mark reflected later as he and Seth stood together in the wheelhouse, "this myth about the so-called Bermuda Triangle—this big fairy tale—this fake invention, gives me a large pain. You and I have crossed that area hundreds of times, worked all over it for months at a time, day and night. This is the result of irresponsible rumors. Those people back on the dock will probably lose their lives just because they're afraid of a ridiculous myth."

"Yes," said Seth, "the situation ashore is terrible. Everybody's fighting to get north. The airports are closed. Our people had a hard time getting to the ship because of the confusion and the traffic jams everywhere. I'm glad we're out of it."

"A disaster, that's what it is," continued Mark. "As far as the Bermuda Triangle goes, it's just like any other area of ocean, or, for that matter, any place where traffic is heavy. You take automobiles, for instance. Where there are a lot of them, there's where most accidents happen. Same with ship traffic—more ships, more accidents, especially where it's not regulated, and where you have a lot of amateur yachtmen. Bermuda Triangle—baloney!"

The mate added his thoughts. "Even the Russians are tryin' to get in their two cents worth, to confuse shippin' on our coast. Some guy over there says the positions of the earth, moon, and sun are havin' somethin' to do with the Bermuda Triangle. As if that wuz somethin' new! Sure they do! Tides! The same as everywhere else. We bin workin' out there—how long? For the past three or four months and years before. Las' time we wuz out there, we talked about that Triangle bunk. We never had seen anythin' strange out there—never—in all these years!"

Captain Seth Fulton put *Alert* on a northeasterly course

and increased speed. The vessel was powered with twin diesels for cruising, and a thirteen thousand shaft horsepower turbine for high speed. *Alert* was capable of forty knots. None of the people on board had ever seen a ship move through the water that fast. With the additional help of the Gulf Stream, *Alert* was making about forty-three knots. But Seth wouldn't keep the turbine going very long. Guzzling great quantities of fuel, it consumed too much of *Alert*'s precious supply. Seth changed over to the two diesels as soon as he was sure they would get beyond the continental shelf in time. Speed was then reduced to about eighteen knots, fast enough to make it.

All night, as they sped northeastward, the people on *Alert* listened with increasing alarm to radio reports continuously broadcast from EBS stations in the interior of the United States. Accounts relayed from South America described in frightening detail the terrible destruction as the mighty swells ravaged the shores.

The low coastal plains of Argentina were quickly devastated, their seaports destroyed. Sweeping northward to the River Plate, the swells grew in height and destructive force. Rolling into the wide estuary with great speed, they lifted ships and cast them onto the land. The cities of La Plata, Buenos Aires, and Montevideo had scarcely four hours advance warning. They couldn't be evacuated in time to save their people.

Uruguay, Brazil, French Guiana, Surinam, Guyana, Venezuela, Trinidad, and Colombia received, in turn, the terrible impact of the swells. Their ports were destroyed and millions of their people killed.

Diverted slightly westward by the earth's rotation, and the Coriolis force, the impact was greatest against the eastern coasts of all continents. Along the west coast of South America, Chile, Peru, Ecuador, and Colombia rapidly lost their seaports, but their populations were more fortunate. They had the nearby foothills and lofty Andes Mountains for refuge. Many were saved, but those who failed to heed the warnings or were unable to reach high ground in time lost their lives.

Increasing in height and power, the gigantic seismic undulations curled their massive crests over the islands fringing the Caribbean. Some of the islands, including St. Thomas, Puerto Rico, Hispaniola, Jamaica, Cuba, and others, had mountainous areas to which some of their inhabitants fled, but the majority drowned.

Slightly impeded by the islands, but still moving with great force, the monstrous swells glided across the Caribbean and swirled around the Gulf of Mexico, bringing devastation to the littoral of Central America, Mexico, Texas, Louisiana and Alabama.

The offshore oil rigs of the Gulf Coast were mowed down like weeds, lifted and flung violently, one against the other. They had all been rapidly evacuated, but their crews were caught in the coastal ports, and along with millions of others, they perished.

Spreading up the Mississippi and other great river valleys, the surges devastated a wide swath, throwing their awesome power against the rivers and causing high bores which raced inland, ruining cities and towns along the banks.

The first mighty undulations struck the Pacific coast of Panama at eleven P.M. They rolled over Panama City and Balboa, and their enormous crests knocked down the Thatcher Ferry Bridge as if it were mere sticks. They demolished Miraflores and Pedro Miguel, and plunged swiftly across the Isthmus, driving their towering summits over Gatun Lake and locks. They hurled large ships on their crests from the Pacific over fifty miles into the Caribbean.

The Atlantic swells took several hours longer to reach Panama, having farther to travel because the coast of Brazil juts far to the eastward. They struck the Atlantic coast of Panama about five A.M., carrying many ships upon their crests, and leaving others wrecked upon the mountains. As swell after swell continued to batter the Panama Canal, first from one ocean, then from the other, those fine works of man were reduced to rubble and mud. Thousands of persons perished, but some were saved by flight to high ground. Emergency radio warnings by canal authorities and the Panama radio stations were broadcast continuously and emphatically, beginning with the first hour they had been received from Don Marsh at Tierra del Fuego.

Before dawn, R.V. *Alert,* well battened down, awaited the arrival of the swells on the safe waters of the Bermuda Triangle. Anxiety and despair, tempered by fascination and hope, were etched upon the faces of the men and women. Weary but sleepless, they waited for—they knew not what.

Captain Seth Fulton's calm voice instructed everyone to keep life jackets on, and to find stanchions, or other fixed parts of the vessel, which they could grasp and use to steady themselves. All, except members of the crew, were to remain inside or below. All movable objects were secured.

The height of the swells had been reported as over three hundred meters on the Argentine coast, and about five hundred meters at Rio de Janeiro, indicating an increase in height and volume as they moved northward. That was, indeed, baffling to everyone. They should have decreased in size as they moved farther from their source.

"What powerful force is driving those monsters along higher and higher as they come? They'll be half a mile high by the time they get here if that keeps up!" exclaimed Captain Dover.

The eastern sky began to lighten, gradually revealing the dark, level rim of the ocean's early horizon. Suddenly, on *Alert's* bridge, there came a call from the ship's laboratory. Captain Dover answered.

"PDR shows a rapid increase in depth, sir. Are we moving?" The voice from the lab was startling.

"No. We're not moving," replied Mark. "How much increase?"

"About thirty-eight meters, but increasing faster now. Maybe we've drifted over a hole," said the voice.

"No change in position," said Seth, who was watching the loran.

"We're getting a lift!" exclaimed Mark. "That's what it is! The first swell! Leading edge of it!"

Fascinated and excited, everyone stared toward the southeastern horizon which was then clearly visible against the faint tones of morning light. They watched with awe as the horizon ascended, and the summit of the first mighty rise came toward them. The voice from the lab reported that the precision depth recorder showed a rapid increase by hundreds of meters. Higher and higher *Alert* was lifted, to nine hundred meters—over half a mile—as the summit glided beneath her.

All day, and far into the night, *Alert's* passengers and crew steadily rode the rhythmic heights and slopes, safely cradled in the Bermuda Triangle.

The towering undulations swept onward. Reaching the continental shelf, their massive summits broke into angry cascading crests which would have dwarfed Niagara Falls. Rolling swiftly over the Bahamas, they cast their tremendous weight against the Florida Peninsula. Obliterating the low Keys, they struck the shores with a deafening roar, more fearsome than a dozen hurricanes. The lethal surges ripped asunder the harbors and the cities, casting ships, buildings, and helpless people across the coastal fringes into the Everglades. Within two short hours, the shores of Florida were inundated beneath a sea of foaming turbulence.

The sumptuous resorts were devasted, one after another. The tall towers of Cape Canaveral were toppled like toys. The swells rushed swiftly inland and surged up the river valleys on their frightful journey northward.

As the surface of the ocean gradually resumed its normal

state, the people on *Alert* began to take courage. Radio continually brought appalling accounts of the destruction on the coasts. Far at sea, the doughty research vessel had come through the world's greatest ordeal without harm.

Captain Seth remarked, "I didn't have any great fear of the swells. I've been in swells before; in the Pacific. They call them '*tsunamis.*' They cause damage along the shore. We never worried much about them out in deep water. But I never saw any tsunamis like these! What I'm concerned about now is where we're going with this ship. All the Florida seaports are destroyed."

"Yes," said Captain Mark, "and all the rest of our coastal cities and ports are gone. The whole state of Florida will be under water. We may have to look for an anchorage way inside Georgia or Alabama. All our coastal plains, from Texas to Maine, will be flooded." Mark looked at the radar scope. "Nothing within range."

The mate was loud in his priase of *Alert.* Boastfully, he exclaimed, "Those swells were a mile high! That's what they looked like when we were down in the troughs between 'em. I never seen anythin' like it! Sometimes we were up on a high rise, then way down, lookin' up! We didn't roll much. Just went up and down. It was weird!"

The people on *Alert* were saddened by the loss of their homes, and the probable loss of many of their relatives and friends, but thankful for their own survival, and thankful that Mark Dover's quick decision to bring them out into the "dangerous" Bermuda Triangle had saved their lives.

Seth tried to adjust the Loran C receiver, and scowled at the digital readout. "Nothing!" he exclaimed after a few minutes. "No more loran. The stations have probably all been washed away! So we're back to—what? No celestial, no satellite, no loran! We'll have to feel our way by soundings! But where the hell will we go?"

Mark examined a bathymetric chart. He said hopefully,

"Let's go in toward the coast and find a shoal spot where we can anchor and wait for more news from—from Washington? No, from someplace, wherever the government is set up now. Who knows? We'll just have to move in carefully, get our anchor down, and save fuel until we can find out something. Maybe we'll just have to play it all by ear, and find some high land where we can get on shore. I wonder where our people are—our company people. I suppose they had to get farther west. Maybe they went to the Blue Ridge Mountains. Sooner or later, we'll have to get in touch. I suppose they think we're sunk."

Nearly all navigational systems were useless. Loran stations, radio beacons, charted radar targets, satellites, stars, planets, sun, everything customarily used to determine a ship's position at sea had been made unreliable by the earth's increase in tilt, and the coastal devastations. Lightships, lighthouses, and buoys were all swept away. But the experienced oceanographic research navigator had something else up his sleeve. The ocean bottom was still there!

Less than a couple of miles below them were well-charted geological features of the earth's crust. Hidden from view beneath the deep water were aids which would serve, to a limited extent, in the navigation of vessels equipped with precision depth recorders, like *Alert*'s. Great ridges, or mountain ranges, reaching high above the ocean bottom, and extending hundreds, some even thousands, of miles along their rugged length; plateaus, knolls, rises, cones, seamounts, escarpments, fracture zones, slopes, trenches, continental shelves, rift valleys, basins, canyons, and abyssal plains, were all distinct but hidden formations of the oceanographer's world. The navigators of *Alert* would find their way. The ocean bottom would serve as their guide.

When Mark Dover was interviewed many months later, he said, "It was like walking through an obstacle course blindfolded. But, with our sensitive transducers, and our

PDR tracing the contours below, we made our way. Our 'tiptoes' did the walking.''

"I wonder what we'll find when we get to the coast," said Seth.

The mate had an encouraging answer. "Maybe just a lot of dead bodies floatin' around."

They finally found a shoal spot near the Florida shore. The mate had been right. There were many bodies, and the Gulf Stream was carrying thousands northward. *Alert* anchored to await more news, or instructions—or something.

Months later, Art Allen at Palmer communicated with his wife, Marilyn. Art gave me the account of the actions taken by Captains Mark A. Dover and Seth Fulton. Eventually, they got their passengers safely ashore on high land in Georgia.

In Manhattan, near the shore of the East River, the tall, domino-like structure of the United Nations stood steadily upon its crumbling foundations, foundations poured with a weak aggregate of human imperfections, futile aspirations, nationalism, religious intolerance, and greed. A fitting tombstone to its predecessor, the League of Nations, it was a disgusting "last straw." As a preserver of peace and security, it was, indeed, a "man of straw."

On December 22, within the shell, a typical debate was in progress. The Security Council had hurriedly summoned an emergency meeting of the General Assembly right after the President's speech to Congress. There ensued several customary harangues by delegates from emerging nations, blasting the United States of America for what they called, in effect, "lack of worldwide lifesaving facilities."

Someone said that the USA, with all its technical ability, should have foreseen the coming flood, and should have taken the necessary measures to prevent it. As usual, they blamed the USA in general, and the CIA specifically, for all the world's troubles. They were just about to accuse the USA of deliberately melting the polar icecaps, when the U.S. delegation picked up their papers, shoved them into their attaché cases—slammed them shut, and shuffled out into the cold polluted air of New York City.

Incredible chaos followed. Delegations, finding air services to their homelands suspended, were trapped in New York. Fearful of oncoming ocean swells, they remained in the building with their families and employees. Order collapsed as crowds pressed in from the streets.

In other areas of the city, media reports of the oncoming disaster were received with varied emotions. In a dimly lit tavern on a street near the Battery, two men sat watching television. Their drinks and several dollar bills lay on the bar in front of them. The skinny one's name was unknown, but in certain midtown circles he was called "Chintsey." His companion, the heavy one, was Coco Solare. Coco was enjoying freedom, of which he had been deprived for some two years, with a year off for good behavior and some well planted "lettuce."

On television the governor was urgently repeating, "tidal wave" warnings. There weren't many people at the bar, but those who listened became increasingly excited. The tavern grew noisier with their chatter, but Chintsey and Coco, seated at the far end of the bar, didn't participate. Chintsey leaned over and spoke softly into Coco's cauliflowered left ear. "What about Vic Daly on that cruise ship *Sinbad*?"

Coco put down his glass and straightened up. A shiny bald spot on the top of his head reflected the dim yellow light above them. He sneered at Chintsey. "Tony'll get 'im. If he don't my daughter Teresa will. Last I heard, they left Argentina on a cruise to the South Pole. Maybe they'll all git swallowed up in the earthquakes the President was squawkin' about. I couldn't care less—so long as Daly don't show back here. Anyway, from what we been hearin', this town is gonna be flooded over an' nobody'll do any more business here. I think I'll go back to the coast."

"How about Tony's old man?" Chintsey asked.

"At least another year before parole," said Coco.

"Maybe they'll have to parole a buncha cons on accounta th' floods," remarked Chintsey.

"Look at all the jails an' pens around the coast—where they gonna put all them guys?"

"Shoot'm—if they turn a buncha bums loose an' they start operatin' on banks an' other grabs, a lot are gonna git shot."

"Ha! Who's gonna shoot 'em?" sneered Coco.

"Fuzz."

"Oh, yeah? The fuzz's already pullin' out for high ground."

"Why don't we find out if old man Rossi is gonna git out? Maybe we can pull a coupla jobs durin' all this excitement."

The tavern was getting crowded. Excited patrons, pulling off overcoats and mufflers, were pouring in and pouring down drinks as if the town was going dry instead of wet. New Yorkers, for the most part, took world-shattering events in stride. But not this time. The governor continued his warning of immense "tidal waves" coming up the coast.

Coco and Chintsey made their plans. They would try to spring Tony's father, old Mike Rossi, who was somewhat of a bank expert. Amid all the turmoil, they thought they could make a few significant "collections" and get lost in the grand exodus to the west. But they knew they had to scramble for a high spot in their vicinity to spend that night.

Coco looked over his shoulder and then lowered his voice. "You packin' heat?"

"Yeah."

"C'mon. Let's git outta here."

They left the bar and made their way unsteadily along

the chilly crowded street toward South Ferry and across Battery Park. They were jostled and shoved by the press of an angry and frightened multitude rushing to get into high buildings. Chintsey kept his arm pressed against the small bulge in his zipper jacket. They made their way slowly toward a tall building. Thousands of New Yorkers had the same idea. Battery Park, between Broadway and the river, was a solid mass of shouting, struggling humanity pushing toward the entrances to high buildings. The ferries disgorged throngs fleeing Staten Island.

After an hour of struggle, during which Chintsey was sorely tempted to slip his hand inside his jacket and produce his "persuader," they entered the great twin tower structure of the World Trade Center and started to climb the stairs. Elevator service had long since ceased to function. By midnight, the large, new building was packed with a seething, terrified horde. Those who were able to reach only the lower floors were fighting to get higher, while those above were fighting to keep them down. Frequently the forms of pitiful victims came hurtling down from high windows to splatter upon the screaming crowd below.

If doors were made to keep people out, that function was futile on that eventful night. And if bridges were built to bring people together, they were succeeding as never before. All the great bridges from Brooklyn westward toward Manhattan were jammed from end to end with cars and angry people. A clawing, fighting, screaming mass of humanity on foot and in bumper-to-bumper cars crawled over the George Washington Bridge in a great exodus toward New Jersey and westward. Flight from the oncoming ocean swells had thrown the entire populace into an increasingly dangerous panic.

As Chintsey and Coco fought their way slowly up through the mass of sweating flesh in stairways and corridors, they filled their pockets with loot easily taken from wallets and purses. Some of it was, in turn, lost to colleagues with superior skills. Coco, out of practice for a couple of years, and being the heaviest, was the jostler making the openings. Chintsey kept close behind taking up the "collection."

They were cursed and threatened in many languages. Gathered from the streets of New York City and packed into the great structure were natives of several countries speaking many tongues and dialects including some English. Nationalities, cultures, ideologies and religions were forgotten. The crowd was imbued with the one great desire—to survive. Throughout the city, similar scenes were enacted wherever tall buildings offered escape from the streets below.

Coco and Chintsey climbed higher, using their own rough tactics to push their way up. Finally tiring, they began to look for a place to ride out the disaster. They chose a spot in a plush but crowded office on the south side near the top. Coco managed to shove some occupants off a large executive desk near a window which overlooked the Battery and New York Harbor.

Beside the desk, in a high-backed upholstered executive chair, sat a man whom, had he been shaved and spruced up a bit, Coco and Chintsey should have recognized. They had undoubtedly seen his picture in newspapers and magazines many times; a man of great wealth and power. He was Hugh Peter Daly, president of a large oil tanker operating corporation, and brother of former judge Victor Daly who was, at that moment, on board M.V. *Sinbad* trapped in Lemaire Channel in the Antarctic. Hugh's family, and associates with their families, were part of the crowd which then packed the oil magnate's plush offices. Unaware of Daly's identity, Chintsey and Coco forcefully made themselves room on the ample carved mahogany desk. Daly was a large strong man, but he made no effort to remove the intruders, suspecting from their remarks and actions that they might be armed. Eavesdropping,

Hugh was able to hear the two men call each other by name.

The weary crowd in the building slumped down on every inch of the floor and desks. During the sleepless night, many more crowded in trying to find room to sit or lie down. Still more jammed themselves into every cubic foot of space within the walls of the structure. Climbing, stepping, or falling on others, a mass of humanity kept pushing upward from lower floors. Chintsey and Coco held on to the big desk as did its owner, Hugh Daly, and others, to keep from being pushed out through the window beside it.

For several days, ocean vessels had been acumulating in New York Harbor. Since the first announcement of the strange astronomical phenomenon, many ship masters had refused to start their vessels on long ocean voyages. Some coastwise vessels departed, counting on loran and radar. Some shipping companies ordered masters to stay in port until more information could be obtained as to the safety of navigation. As a result of those measures, New York harbor was crowded, as were many other harbors around the world, with large ocean cargo vessels and passenger liners. Hundreds were occupying berths or anchored in both lower and upper New York Bay. They had been joined each day and night by new arrivals.

In that impressive fleet of the world's largest and finest ships were two deeply laden oil tankers of Daly's corporation riding impatiently at anchor off quarantine, awaiting *pratique* and customs entry before proceeding to berths at Bayonne. When daylight came, Hugh Daly saw them through his binoculars from the crowded office.

"Too late, too late," he murmured softly. "All those men, too late."

Daly noticed several other loaded tankers anchored or moving on the bay. "There must be a couple of million barrels of crude afloat on that bay," he thought. Near his two ships, he also saw three large transatlantic passenger ships, one of which appeared to be a thousand feet long, nearly as long as the height of the Empire State Building. Other large ocean liners were anchored or moving in that busiest of all harbors. They would have been safer at sea.

There were many transistor radios among the people in the crowded tall buildings. Emergency news bulletins provided information as to the progress of the seismic swells. The people listened fearfully as city after city succumbed during the night. As the disaster neared New York, those who had been able to reach only the lower floors began to scream and claw their way upward over others. Many died of asphyxiation or heart attacks. Others were kicked or mauled until they dropped and were trampled underfoot.

In Daly's office, all who could do so, tried to see through the windows toward the south.

About eight o'clock in the morning, they became aware of a faint rumble like distant, low thunder. Within minutes, they saw what appeared as a foaming mountain range advancing up the lower bay. A monstrous wall of water, with an angry curling and cascading crest, extended across the entire bay and as far as the eye could see from Brooklyn to the east and New Jersey to the west. In seconds it buckled the Verrazano-Narrows Bridge, crowded from end to end with cars and people. With awesome might, the towering sea swept over Staten Island and onward over Governor's Island. The frightened people gasped as the Statue of Liberty toppled and plunged intoi the sea. Relentlessly, the gigantic swells came toward them.

Torn from their moorings and tossed high upon the soaring crests were hundreds of ships with their passengers, crews and cargoes. With a roar like a hundred tornadoes, they were dashed against the buildings and bridges of Manhattan. The great passenger liners and oil tankers were flung against the skyscrappers. The doomed watchers in

Daly's offices shrieked as a big ocean liner and a tanker crashed against their building with an impact so powerful that the entire structure plummeted into a mountain of rubble and mangled bodies. Ships and buildings disappeared beneath a massive oil spill which spread over the doomed city.

Within minutes, much of Manhattan and low areas along the Brooklyn and Jersey shores were devastated. The Palisades on the New Jersey side provided some protection for that shore, as did the Heights from the Brooklyn side. Spared was the famous and historical old "fruit salad" section of Brooklyn Heights with its Pineapple, Orange and Cranberry Streets where Captain Pack of *Quest* had lived as a boy, and Columbia Heights where young Jerry Connally, then on board *Sinbad*, had studied and preached before his marriage. Those ramparts saved many lives and formed sides of a wide channel through which the angry seas surged from side to side up the East and North River valleys with Manhattan caught squarely in the middle.

The slab-sided United Nations building was felled by the great might and power of the sea like a clay pigeon struck by a cannon ball. In seconds it was a pile of waste. The angry brine, swirling in and around the debris of that erstwhile great tower of Babel, was mingled with the blood of delegates representing the nations of the world. Death found those who sought refuse within the crumbling walls. Crumbling, also, were the nations the delegates represented.

The bridges, jammed with humanity, were toppled like fragile toys. Tunnels and subways with hundreds of loaded trains were inundated for miles. Within minutes, millions of people perished.

The lethal waves swept on toward more conquests, and the dead swirled around in the oil and rubble. Here and there, a live blackened body clung to some floating object, bur survivors were few, and rescuers, none.

Miraculously, Hugh Daly and Coco Solare found themselves clinging to the big mahogany desk floating bottom up on the gooey mess. They were badly cut by broken glass and covered with black crude oil. Hugh helped the nearly unconscious Coco to get a better grip several times when he was about to slip under. The desk, with some six persons clinging to it, had crashed through the window when the building fell. Only Hugh and Coco were left. The others had lost their grasps and their lives.

Daly and Solare held precariously on to the desk. As they swirled around the turbulent oil-covered water over the flooded streets of Manhattan, they knew they could easily slip off and go under at any moment. Strong men as they were, there was a limit to their endurance.

Coco was in bad shape. His teeth had been knocked out, and blood flowed from a nasty gash on his right leg below the knee. Hugh had numerous lacerations, but he managed to secure himself to the overturned desk by sticking his legs through drawer openings. All the drawers were gone, which gave both men hand-holds. Hugh tore off a shirt sleeve. Maneuvering Coco's leg up, he fashioned an oil-soaked tourniquet around it to check the loss of blood.

The two men, numb with cold, whirled dizzily around in the turbulence among the debris and floating dead. Coco was getting weaker and Hugh tried to encourage him.

"Don't give up! We'll—we'll try to get off onto something!" Talking was difficult. Hugh struggled to concentrate on his grasp. After a few minutes, he said, "My God! I've lost my family—friends! You've—you've lost your friend—Chintsey—wasn't it? I heard you talk—your first names. You're—Coco. What's your last name, anyway? I'm Hugh Daly."

"You mean—you're *the* Hugh P. Daly, the—oil company boss?"

"Yeah."

"I'll be damned!" mumbled Coco.

"Why?"

"You—you Judge Victor Daly's father?"

"No. His brother. You know him?"

"Yeah! He put me in the slammer!"

"No kidding!"

"He sure did—for two years. Jus' got out last week—an' now *this!*"

They stopped talking for a while. Their floating desk, at which the "interview" was taking place, made them dizzy, whirling in the strong eddies. The flood waters dashed them against the blackened walls of buildings and hulls of capsized ships. They seemed to be moving toward the North River. Frequently, they nearly lost their hold on the desk as it caromed from side to side. At times it would pause, then turn rapidly in opposite currents. Both men had little hope of surviving the ordeal. With their faces covered in thick black oil, clogging eyes, ears, and nostrils, breathing was becoming more difficult each moment.

Coco managed to ask, "Your brother went to the South Pole—didn't he?"

"Something like that. What did he send you up for?"

"Oh, nothin'. I was jus' takin' a li'l vacation. 'Workin' over the public' in midtown, an' some wise dick wasn't gettin' his cut."

Hugh was reaching the end of his rope. "I know what you mean. I had a lot of trouble with the law too—everywhere—big kickbacks to foreign officials as well as—as our own. And the cartels, you know. Looks like I won't have any more chance to work over the public in the USA, or anywhere else—no ships—no ports—nothing; everything gone—family and all. Well, maybe not all—maybe not my brother Victor. Maybe—there's a chance he's still alive. Say, how did you know he was down there?"

"Hell," Coco muttered. "I'm gonna die anyway. We're both gonna die—so I'll tell ya'. Me an' Chintsey was talkin' about it yesterday in a gin mill. We were gonna try an' spring Mike Rossi an' pull a coupla heists. Old man Rossi wanted your brother dead. There's a contract out on him. My daughter and her brother-in-law are after him on that cruise ship."

"A contract! For God's sake! Why?" exclaimed Hugh.

"He—saw somethin'—after a plane crash—in Panama. He saw—he saw—" Coco was slipping. Hugh grabbed at him, but his oily hands couldn't hold Coco back.

Hugh screamed, "What are their names! Your daughter and—" In Coco's exhausted condition, he couldn't struggle against the current. His nostrils drew in the slimy liquid. His breathing stopped. Hugh watched in horror as Coco disappeared into the murky water.

Hugh Daly silently hung on as the desk was borne along. Almost blinded, he clung desperately, expecting the end momentarily. But he did survive the disaster, and lived to recount, most vividly, the disappearance and destruction of the world's busiest seaport.

Overwhelming New York City and smashing down the great bridges took only a few minutes. When the violent swells subsided, Manhattan was anointed, from east to west, and from the Battery to the Bronx, with a thick layer of crude petroleum. Running down its proud steeples, and dripping from its walls and statues, the black liquid thoroughly saturated the borough.

As the hours passed, traffic on U.S. highways worsened. Great traffic jams developed, extending scores of miles on all routes leading to the west.

Exodus from coastal areas was badly blocked. Thousands of persons abandoned their automobiles and took off on foot across snow covered fields and hills, sleeping wherever they could find shelter. Blizzards hampered the movements of the hungry and frightened multitude.

Dying people were left to succumb on the snow. Epidemics of infectious diseases spread throughout the land. Domestic animals were abandoned. Unattended, and left to fend for themselves, many contracted rabies. Wild packs of dogs roamed everywhere. Some were shot. Others, along with the ferocious zoo animals which had escaped, terrorized the fleeing refugees, attacking and devouring some of them.

West coast cities and seaports of the Americas were all destroyed before nightfall, but millions of people, heeding emergency warnings, fled to the nearby mountains and escaped. Millions of others were drowned.

Similar to the fate of the Americas was that of many other parts of the earth. All over the ailing, corrupt and polluted world, millions of persons, suddenly faced with a common disaster, were seeking refuge within tall buildings of cities, and in the hills and mountains. Fleeing in droves from destruction by the relentless seismic swells, thousands grew weak with hunger and extreme cold. Many faltered and gave up. Only the strong survived.

Some seas, largely surrounded by land, such as the Mediterranean, Persian Gulf, Baltic, Black, Red, Japan, Java, and China seas, and others, did not suffer the direct impact of the ocean swells. But their waters rose rapidly, flooding their coastal areas and ports.

The coastal highlands of Africa afforded means of survival, but the great devastations of seaports and river valleys killed millions of luckless inhabitants and destroyed their fishing fleets. Famine and disease spread rapidly.

The vast Pacific Ocean was an easy highway for the unbridled seismic swells. In less than four hours after the earthquakes began, the swells impacted with tremendous fury against the rugged shores of New Zealand and Tasmania, demolishing their seaports.

Onward they rolled, demolishing in rapid succession the excellent ports of Australia. The giant angry crests rolled high over the shallow continental shelf of the Great Australian Bight, cast their awful might against the coast, and rolled on northward over the low lands of the Great Artesian Basin, stopping only when reaching the highlands near the Selwyn Range. Those vast areas, both east and west of the great range of mountains, were completely inundated, almost dividing Australia into two separate lands.

Completely surrounding Australia, the swells and terrible breaking crests surged around the Cape York Peninsula, and southward into the Gulf of Carpentaria. Unobstructed, they rolled up the river valleys.

The ports of Australia's west and northwest shores were destroyed, but the seas encroached very little on that rugged coast. Australia lost more than a fourth of its land.

Northward raced the colossal undulations against the shores of Madagascar, Indonesia, Ceylon and India, leaving destruction and death in their paths.

The islands of Polynesia, Micronesia, and Melanesia impeded the advance of the swells to some extent, but didn't stop them. These obstacles afforded a small measure of alleviation for the Philippines, Japan, and Korea, but not enough to prevent the destruction of many of their seaports.

The harbors and resorts of Hawaii fell rapidly to the onslaught. The swells moved rapidly northward, devastating the coasts of Canada and Alaska. Overwhelming the Aleutian Islands, they surged onward to the narrow funnel of Bering Strait. There the Pacific thrust came to an abrupt and violent halt.

The British Isles afforded a measure of protection to the North Sea, but not enough to stop the devastation of the seaports and offshore oil rigs. The low coastal areas of Northern Europe—France, Holland, and Germany—were destroyed by tremendous surges through the English Channel.

Lashing the coasts of Greenland, Iceland, England, and

Norway, the swells surged, unhindered, through the Norwegian, Greenland and Barents seas. Crashing violently against the islands of Svalbard, they spread far into the frozen wastes of the Arctic Ocean, heaving and fracturing its winter mantle of ice. That frozen polar ocean temporarily resisted the effect of the great Antarctic seismic undulations, but not for long.

In Baffin Bay, the swells met their end against the icebound coast of Greenland and the Queen Elizabeth Islands.

After the Antarctic Continent stopped shaking like a leaf, the mighty seismic swells subsided in all the oceans, but the tremendous flow of water from the disintegration and melting of Antarctica's seven million cubic miles of ice increased hourly, spreading and raising all ocean levels including the Arctic Ocean.

A canopy of vapor spread northward. As the year advanced, the sun brought its warmth upon the northern hemisphere. Warm waters of the tropics flowed rapidly into the Arctic regions.

Greenland also began to shed its formidable ice sheet. Slowly, the Arctic ice melted, greatly contributing to the rising level of ocean waters. Those seaports in Russia and other northern shores which had not been immediately destroyed by the swells, became inundated by the flooding waters.

The rising Arctic Ocean flowed rapidly southward into the northern territories of Canada, Scandanavia, and Russia. It inundated the coastal areas of the Barents, Kara, and Laptev seas, and large portions of the West Siberian Lowlands.

Radio news bulletins continually brought vivid details of the world's tribulation to the sorrowful survivors in the Antarctic at Palmer and on board R. V. *Quest* at Deception Island.

The news also brought more grief to the anxious passengers and crew of the M.S. *Sinbad,* many of whom had been obliged to abandon their comfortable quarters on the ship and camp, uneasily and precariously, on an iceberg.

8

BRENDA CLARK'S first remark, after she left *Sinbad* and entered Raft One on the iceberg, was, "Oh, boy, what a place to spend Christmas eve!" She sat down beside Marjory Dumont.

"I'd rather be here than on that sinking ship," said Marjory.

When the Destefanis entered the raft, Tony took a seat beside Brenda. Teresa had moved to the forward end of the raft. Tony remarked, "I don't think the captain really believes it's going to sink."

"It's supposed to be specially reinforced to stand a lot of pressure," said Al Norwood.

"You think Captain Gilbert would stay on the ship and go down with it if it sinks?" asked Al's wife, Helen.

Al said, "I hope he's got more sense than that."

Clarence Dearborn said, "I think he'd stay on board until everyone else was off, but he'd be crazy to go down with it. That's just old tradition. What good would it do?"

Dr. Barry tried to reassure them. "I don't believe it will go down. It's a very strong vessel. However, it's now 'nipped' and the captain is playing it safe so as to get all the people off in time if it does start to go down."

Filled to its legal capacity of twenty-five persons, Raft One, with its sides closed down, was dimly lighted inside by a small battery lamp in the center attached to the roof

215

or canopy. One of the seamen loosened a flap on the lee side and let in some light and air.

Their conversation was interrupted by loud voices from the other end of the raft. Teresa Destefani had taken a seat next to Victor Daly. After awhile, she left her seat momentarily to look outside. While she was gone, Emma Cavige moved over alongside Daly. When Teresa returned, she demanded her seat.

"You left it, so I sat down here!" snapped Emma.

"I know, but I was sitting there!"

"You got this seat reserved?" Emma's voice was getting a little louder.

"Vic is a friend of mine! We were talking!" Teresa's voice was also rising to a higher pitch. Emma didn't move. "You think because your husband's swimming in oil you can do anything you want! You get over an' lemme sit where I was!" screamed Teresa.

Others joined in with their own remarks. "Shut up!" someone yelled.

"Don't tell me to shut up," retorted Teresa.

"Hold it!" bellowed Phil Cavige. "Any fightin' in here an I'll throw ya both out!" Emma finally got up and took a seat farther away. Teresa sat down again next to Victor Daly.

All the passengers were finding the close quarters and inactivity uncomfortable. As their initial apprehension wore off, they became more talkative. Some went out and stood on the lee side, attaching themselves with short ropes to the lifelines. Others tried to doze.

Clarence Dearborn said, "Next time we come out here on this cake of ice, we better bring a bridge table."

Joyce Dearborn said, "I think you'd find it hard to play bridge with all this yak-yak going on. I wonder how long we'll have to stay here."

"Until they get the holes fixed in the bottom of the boat."

"The ship."

"OK, the ship."

216

Dr. George Barry sat beside Al and Clarence. "I have considered catastrophism," he pondered, "but I never expected to experience it to this extent."

"George," said Clarence, "you don't mind me calling you George, do you?"

"No, not in the least."

"George, I've been wanting to talk with you. Here we are in the Antarctic with a large piece of our world falling apart, according to the President's speech. We can even hear and feel the destruction of the ice sheet. How could it happen?"

"Yes," said Helen, "what could possibly cause such a tremendous upheaval? An area larger than the United States, all cracking up at once."

"It's so strange," said Al. "I can conceive of a few volcanoes and earthquakes, but a whole continent at once?"

Dr. Barry was silent for a moment. "Since it started, I've been trying to understand it, but I must confess, I don't know either. As a geologist, I can't justify it logically, but it's happening. I can only say that it must be the result of a combination of forces which science isn't yet equipped to comprehend."

"Do you think there could be some dislocation of the earth's interior core, or perhaps something like a nuclear explosion deep down?" asked Dr. Dearborn.

"Perhaps, but what force would start it?" replied Barry.

A voice near the other end of the raft said loudly, "God, maybe?"

"God?"

There was a sudden lull in the babble of voices around them.

"Whaddya mean God? Nobody can prove there's any God."

"Maybe you don't think so, but I do."

"You can't prove it."

"How do you think life began on this planet?"

"It just started up by itself billions of years ago."

217

"You can't prove that either."

The argument spread among the passengers in Raft One. The question of God's existence, an age old dispute, had polarized the group.

George Barry thought, "This is good. Let them argue and keep their minds off their troubles." An old hand at long, weary vigils in Antarctic camps, he knew that good argument and conversation could help relieve tensions.

Marjory said, "I wonder what the floods will do to England."

"London will be covered by water," said Dr. Barry, "like all the other seaports."

"Where will the people go?"

"They'll have to get onto land higher than two hundred fifty feet above sea level. Maybe higher than three hundred fifty if the Arctic melts too," replied Barry.

"How about getting on ships and boats?" asked Joyce Dearborn.

"Over eight million people? And that's only London—all the other seaports and a lot of the land will be under water."

"If some of them get on boats and ships, where are they going to get food?" asked Al.

Brenda said, "Fish. I'd catch fish."

"How about fuel? What will the ships do when they use up all their fuel?" pondered Helen.

"Buy some more!" yelled Cavige.

"The oil storage tanks around the coasts will be under water. So will the banks in London and New York and all major cities on the coasts," said Barry.

Al said, "Come on, let's not try to solve the world's problems—we got enough of our own."

So the evening passed, uncomfortable, but bearable. At midnight, the group C people began climbing to the life rafts. And, in due time, group B was assisted back to the ship. Daylight still remained although diffused by smoky clouds overhead flowing northward away from the south polar area.

At 0800, group B returned to the iceberg, and group A went down for a hot breakfast and eight hours on board. The worst part, Helen thought, was getting down the Jacob's ladder and across the narrow chasm between the side of the iceberg and the ship. Several hands helped, and they all made it safely.

How good it felt to get into their cabins and get a warm bath! After breakfast, many of the group A passengers went back to their berths for a few hours of rest. They slept fully clothed with their life jackets loosened only enough to be comfortable.

Sinbad's cook had prepared a sumptuous Christmas dinner which was served to group A at 1330. Free booze was available at the bars all day, and champagne was served at dinner. A real Christmas party evolved in the main lounge during the afternoon. The orchestra whooped it up, and many passengers, their tensions and anxieties temporarily abated, indulged themselves in a short interval of spirited glee. That was soon over however, because promptly at 1530, the orchestra stopped playing and group A was ordered back to the iceberg. It was time for group C to return to *Sinbad*.

It was a difficult maneuver. Many en route to the iceberg were in varied degrees of inebriation. Some tried to carry bottles or drinks with them, others forgot their life jackets, some persisted in singing, and a few didn't turn up at the Jacob's ladder at all. They stumbled to their own or to someone else's cabin.

Among group A passengers failing to get off the ship, were Teresa Solare, alias Mrs. Anthony Destefani, Emma Cavige, and Victor Daly. They weren't found immediately, and rather than hold up the embarkation of group C, they were left on board. Later, Teresa and Victor were flushed out of his cabin by the chief purser. After much drunken argument, he got them dressed and led them, amid a torrent of loud and virulent profanity, along the corridors and up to the boat deck where they were turned over to the mate and finally hoisted up onto the iceberg.

219

They went into Raft Two. Meanwhile Mrs. Cavige had staggered into the dining room where group C passengers were gathering for dinner. She sat at a table, but promptly went to sleep with her head on a plate. It took four stewards to carry her to the boat deck.

Group C members were finally all on board *Sinbad* by 1700. As soon as they got cleaned up, many went to the bar in the main lounge for their free drinks and then to the Christmas feast. Their eight hour sojourn on the ship was to be a big Christmas celebration. Most of them started by proceeding to get themselves well oiled. When dinner was over, group C passengers collected in the main lounge and continued their boozing around the gaudy Christmas tree.

At about 2200, *Sinbad* trembled and took a sudden list. A shift in wind and current had loosened some of the grounded icebergs. The movement of ice immediately released some of the pressure on *Sinbad*'s hull. There were several loud reports like gunfire as some anchor cables, with which the ship was secured to the camp iceberg, snapped. Crew and passengers scrambled toward the boat deck. Drunken people tried frantically to get up slanting stairways. The Christmas tree toppled, and furniture slid across decks. The ship continued to list sharply to starboard as the icebergs moved. Within a few minutes, all the cables snapped and the space between *Sinbad* and the camp iceberg widened.

Crewmen on the iceberg tossed heaving lines to some of the passengers who wore life jackets, and hauled them up onto the iceberg. The captain's voice was heard giving orders to the crew to stand by to launch the inflatable rafts and the motor life boat, one of which had been left on board. "Abandon ship," was sounded on the alarm bells throughout the vessel. Deep tones of the siren echoed along the rocky canyon walls. As the ice jam loosened, *Sinbad* slowly righted itself, but the camp iceberg, carrying over two-thirds of the passengers and crew, rapidly drifted away from the ship, and was soon lost to view. Other large bergs came between them.

Captain Gilbert's voice was heard again. "Attention, ladies and gentlemen! All passengers please assemble immediately on the boat deck with your life jackets. You will stand by to abandon the ship in the remaining rafts and motor life boat in case it becomes necessary. The ship is *not* sinking. I repeat—the ship is *not* sinking. We must be prepared to abandon, however, until we are in a safer situation. We will endeavor to stop the leaks from the outside as soon as possible. Meanwhile, there is danger from moving icebergs and you *must* remain on the boat deck. Thank you."

Disturbed glacier icebergs had crashed against the larger camp iceberg and had dislodged it from the rocks on which it was grounded. The sudden shift of wind and current carried the camp berg northward away from *Sinbad*. The big floating camp moved along with the mass of ice toward Gerlache Strait.

A count showed seventy-one passengers and fifty-seven crew members, a total of one hundred twenty-eight persons, rapidly floating away on the flat-topped berg surrounded by hummocked pack and crashing ice of many sizes and shapes.

Terror seized many of the passengers on the iceberg as they drifted farther away from *Sinbad*, nearly lost to view behind large bergs. Soon only the top of its mast showed above the ice. Dr. Barry and the ship's officers and crew went among the frightened people with assurances that they weren't about to be drowned.

With his portable radio on the iceberg, Ole Magnussen hurriedly transmitted the "Mayday" message which Enrique had received on *Quest*. Both Palmer Station and *Quest* had responded immediately, but neither could render assistance to the drifting camp.

On board *Sinbad* the second mate also transmitted "Mayday," but even with the greater range of the ship's radio, no station offered assistance. Finally, the Argentine Antarctic Vessel *General San Martin* answered, but informed *Sinbad* that they, too, had much damage, and were trying to get back to Argentina after evacuating some Argentine polar stations. They also said that Buenos Aires, Montevideo, and all other seaports were destroyed. They were having difficulty navigating, locating their position, or making any landfall and couldn't possibly return against strong currents and the great flow of icebergs to aid *Sinbad*.

The only hope of the people on the iceberg seemed to be the possible repair of the helicopter at Palmer, and their removal to some place onshore, unless they could get off in their own rafts.

As the floating camp drifted farther away, they gave up all hope of trying to get back to the ship. The undercurrent, moving the deep camp berg along, wasn't affecting *Sinbad* which was still held by too much ice to move in any direction.

As it was borne along, the camp berg was frequently jarred by collisions with other icebergs. Most of the passengers were too frightened to go outside the covered rafts. Some became seasick from the motion, some moaned, some prayed and others implored the mates and seamen to get them back to the ship or ashore somewhere.

Others, more daring and calm, such as Bill Bush, Al Norwood, and Jerry Connally, took the situation in stride, even venturing outside to watch the progress of their frozen ark. They were cautioned to keep themselves secured by lifelines. They had their cameras, and when the weather permitted, took some pictures of their camp, the people, birds, seals and penguins. To the best of their ability, the courageous tried to comfort the frightened.

Occasionally, squalls drove everyone inside. The rafts then resounded with moans and hysterical cries, mingled with curses and a few shouts to "please shut up" or "knock it off." As time passed, tension mounted and the crewmen had to restrain some of the passengers, aided by Dr. Barry. Al Norwood, Jerry Connally, Bill Bush, and some of the younger men, including Ed McCaughlin, and Tony Destefani.

Later, during a relatively calm period, a small group from Raft One gathered outside with Dr. Barry. He said, "What is most difficult for me to comprehend is the magnitude of the force, or combination of forces, which has caused a change in the angle of the earth's axis. Since the earth's rotation seems to be still going on, that is, I presume it's still rotating as usual, what great force could cause it to—how shall I put it—wobble?"

"Wobble?" asked Jerry.

"Yes—wobble."

"I don't feel anything," said Al.

Dr. Barry smiled. "I don't either, but I can see some signs. Take for instance, the sun. It never gets this high down here. And it seems to be getting higher each noon, whereas now it should be getting lower, since December 22nd. If the Antarctic ice is breaking up, and the great weight of seven million cubic miles of ice were spread all over the earth in the form of water, it would seem to me that the earth's rotation would be affected because the larger part of the land masses lies in the northern hemisphere."

"Do you think that would cause the earth to wobble, like the tail wagging the dog?" asked Ed McCaughlin.

"Something like that. If the Arctic ice all melted too, that could make a difference, but it would still be off balance," said Barry.

"Well, suppose it does wobble some, what then?" asked Jerry.

"I wonder. I'm just mystified by the cause of all this. You can get some idea. Take a gyroscope, for example. After all, the earth whirls like a gyroscope. You take a gyroscope and set it whirling and hold it on your hand. You've done this when you were a kid, a gyroscope top?"

"Yes, I sure have," said Connally.

"Well," continued Barry, "you know how you can move your hand around and the top stays at the same angle you set it. If it could be left without support, as the earth hangs in space and rotates, and if you pushed against one side of it, you would expect it to move away from where you put pressure on it, but actually it would move at right angles. That is called precession."

"Precession?" asked Marjory.

"Yes. The earth is whirling like a gyroscope, and it would take a force beyond our comprehension to cause a change in its stance in space, but that must be happening. I hope we live to see what's going to happen next."

"What do you think our chances are of getting off this iceberg and onto land?" asked Al.

"Now, about that, I *am* optimistic. If this berg holds together, I think it will probably run aground several times before it's carried out to sea. Sooner or later we may be able to launch these rafts and get ashore."

The small group, who had listened to Barry's remarks, withdrew, and Dr. Barry returned to Raft One. The iceberg jolted incessantly and frequently collided with other large icebergs as the current carried them all northward through Gerlache Strait.

As tension among the passengers increased, Victoria continued to be obsessed with the suspicion that Brenda Clark had stolen her brooch. She made frequent threats against Brenda in the close quarters of Raft One. Victoria didn't let anyone forget the incident, nor her disdain of the travelettes in general, and Brenda in particular.

"Six sousan' dollars," Victoria muttered, over and over again. "Zat brooch is worse six sousan' dollars. Who let zem low-type travel *femmes des chambres* on zis cruise? Zat Brenda geefs me back my brooch, or I bump 'er dam' nack." Victoria made a karate chop gesture to show what she intended to do to Brenda. At the other end of the raft, Brenda sat quietly. She didn't fear the older woman, but on top of everything else, the situation was annoying, to say the least.

Dr. Barry, who had taken a seat near Victoria, was getting fed up with the woman's threats. He knew that Teresa Destefani had taken the brooch, and finally he decided to confront Teresa with the truth. He waited for an opportunity to talk privately with Teresa and Tony. He asked Tony to step outside and got Teresa out of Raft Two.

"Mrs. Destefani," Barry soberly began, "I wanted to talk to you and your husband to let you both know that I saw you pick up Mme. Degrelle's brooch when she was quarreling with Mrs. Cavige." Teresa grew tense. Dr. Barry continued. "You've heard Mme. Degrelle blaming Miss Clarke. I think you should return the brooch to Mme. Degrelle, and put an end to all this trouble."

Tony said nothing, but Teresa clenched her fists and loudly replied, "I never took her damn brooch! I wouldn't wear that cheap buncha glass! I didn't pick it up! I don't know who got it! I didn't!" Her voice became louder and more shrill with each word. Dr. Barry and Tony tried to calm her. Actually, she feared she had lost the brooch before they came on the iceberg, but she insisted she never took it.

Unknown to Teresa, Tony had found the brooch in her belongings before they left *Sinbad*. He had said nothing about it to Teresa, but quietly returned it to Victoria's cabin, slipping it into the pocket of a robe hanging in Victoria's clothes locker. He expected that Victoria would find it there, and stop blaming Brenda. But Victoria hadn't found it, and she didn't take the robe with her onto the iceberg.

So loud was Teresa's denial that it reached Victoria's ears inside Raft One. When Victoria realized that Dr. Barry had seen Teresa take her brooch, she came outside immediately and transferred her vehemence from Brenda to Teresa, firing a barrage of high fequency expletives at Teresa. Tony and Barry kept the women apart, but the entire iceberg community became acutely aware of the squabble, and Teresa's implication in the robbery. Everyone was, in fact, so jittery anyway that arguments and altercations were touched off at the least provocation. There was no way of proving anything however, so the matter of the stolen brooch had to be dropped. Tony, not wanting to become involved in the fracas, kept his mouth shut about his part in finding the brooch and returning it to Victoria's cabin. Victoria believed Dr. Barry, and Brenda was glad of that. Teresa returned to Raft Two, and for a time, things quieted down.

Ole Magnussen continued talking to *Sinbad*. The ship was still afloat and able to move occasionally as the mass of icebergs loosened. Captain Gilbert informed Ole that the engineers and deck crew were ready to go over the side and into the water to attempt to plug the leaks as soon as the danger of being crushed by the ice was over. They had already succeeded in getting collision mats down over the worst leaks, which had stopped some of the water coming into the hull. Captain Gilbert was optimistic. He felt they could save the ship, and go after the people on the iceberg.

When Ole passed the news to the worried groups, there were shouts and sighs as tensions gave way to hope. They were already over thirty miles from *Sinbad*, and still rapidly moving northward along the Danco Coast. Chief Mate Eric Sorensen kept a close plot of their movement.

By the next morning, the surface wind had abated and thick fog blanketed their iceberg. Outside the rafts, people moved unseen to and from the rest room tents and around the camp, secured by snap hooks at the end of short ropes around their bodies below the arms. People and objects twenty feet away couldn't be seen through the thick fog.

With difficulty, the crew served breakfast at the mess tent. Some of the tired passengers sprawled awkwardly in their habitats. They had slept very little since leaving *Sinbad*. The faces of the men were turning dark and rough with beards, and both men and women had lost their smart and well-groomed appearances. Notwithstanding their plight, they managed to take nourishment. The food which the ship's cook had prepared in the galley tent wasn't as fancy as it had been on board *Sinbad*, but it was edible and sufficient, and there was plenty of coffee.

During the long day, the passengers became restless. Helen whispered to Al, "I told you that Destefani guy was hanging around Brenda a lot. See? He's managed to stay near her all night, right here on this raft."

"Yeah, where's his wife?"

"I think she's over in one of the other rafts with that drunk. They brought them off the ship together," said Helen. "I said I thought she was a phony."

"Tony seems to be pretty straight," replied Al. "But I'll agree he doesn't get along very well with his wife. She hangs around that Victor Daly a lot, and Tony doesn't seem to mind."

"Yes, I know," murmured Helen. "And that's another thing. Daly was chummy with that man—Bailey, the one they say committed suicide. You know, the one that jumped overboard." Helen cupped one hand over her lips and leaned her head close to Al's ear. "Ever since that happened, Daly and that woman have been hanging around together."

"So what?" said Al.

"Who knows!" Helen shrugged her shoulders.

As *Sinbad*'s iceberg community drifted on a northeastward course, other survival activity continued in the Antarctic. The USARPS at Palmer were hoping *Southwind* or *Quest* would ultimately come to their rescue. But *Southwind* would not return to Palmer. An agglomeration of huge icebergs, dislodged from the Ross Ice Shelf, swept northward, like the stampede of a monstrous herd, into the Pacific Ocean making it impossible for *Southwind* to enter the Ross Sea.

Maneuvering his rolling vessel carefully and expertly, *Southwind*'s skipper, Commander Charles Dillon, managed to prevent it from being crushed. Removal of the eight men from McMurdo had been accomplished at great risk by *Southwind*'s one remaining helicopter. They had been lifted by hoist from a veritable inferno, and flown out to the icebreaker far offshore.

Once the survivors were on board *Southwind*, a course

had been set north toward New Zealand rather than risk a return through turbulent ice-filled seas toward Palmer. Cmdr. Dillon wanted to get his ship as far away from the Antarctic Continent as possible. His action was approved by USCG headquarters. After all, Dillon was an expert in Antarctic navigation and he had nearly two hundred persons on board, including two dead.

When the battered chopper returned to *Southwind* from McMurdo, delivering six badly injured and burned men and two dead ones onto the rolling and pitching icebreaker, the survivors had a harrowing tale to tell.

As the chopper had approached what was left of Ross Island, the men saw great upheavals and tremendous explosive eruptions of Mount Erebus and Mount Terror. In fact, nearly all of Ross Island was erupting and, except for the tops of those two volcanoes, much of the island had collapsed into a seething fiery maelstrom.

All the great glaciers pouring down from the erupting mountains along the Dufex, Shackleton, Hillary and Scott Coasts were rapidly pushing onto the broken Ross Ice Shelf. Huge masses of ice from such tremendous sources as Beardsmore, Shackleton, Amundsen, Scott, Byrd, and hundreds of other glaciers, were plunging down the tortured slopes, violently shoved by the shattering and dislodging of the mile-thick ice sheet above.

Low-lying Hallet Station, long since evacuated, had disappeared entirely with the first earth shocks. The whole flat terrain on which it stood was overwhelmed by the sudden surge of the sea and avalanches of snow and ice from the heights behind it.

A small portion of Ross Island remained, but a great rift was widening toward Hut Point. Hills and buildings were toppling as *Southwind*'s helicopter hovered over the group waiting to be rescued. The injured, writhing on the hot ground, were hoisted first. A vast upheaval occurred soon after the group was brought up to the chopper. The rift widened suddenly, and all that remained of Ross Island, including McMurdo Station, New Zealand's Scott Base,

Observation Hill, and other installations, plummeted into a bottomless smoldering abyss.

The helicopter was tossed high into the sky by the awesome blast that followed, its occupants violently thrown against the top, sides, deck, and against each other like dice in a *cacho* cup. Some were knocked unconscious. Yelling and clawing, the men were rolled over and over. The helicopter tumbled like a pigeon blown higher and higher on the crest of a hot blast of steam and smoke.

Fiery incandescent fragments of molten rock smashed against the fuselage. Heat seared the flesh of the helpless souls inside. The pilot and co-pilot were securely strapped in their seats, but there had been no time to secure all the evacuees before the explosion. Two of the severely-injured succumbed. Finally, at the peak of their upward toss the pilot regained control and succeeded in uprighting the battered "horse." They flew off out of the holocaust toward *Southwind*.

It had been a cataclysmic eruption of the whole of Ross Island combined with a great convulsive earth shock. The entire area was swallowed by the deep fiery rift which opened in the earth's crust. Everything fell into the great conduit, and an enormous mass of rock, ice and water poured into the chasm swallowing the entire McMurdo complex.

Sinbad's passengers and crew on the iceberg, preoccupied with their own situation, were totally unaware of the details of the daring and courageous rescue of the men at McMurdo. The iceberg camp had been carried northward through Gerlache Strait past the east end of Anvers Island. There, a strong current swept it westward past the Waifs into Schollaert Channel. Skirting the Hulot Peninsula, it drifted with the sea of moving bergs. Before the middle of January, the iceberg camp grounded off the eastern end of Gand Island which, itself, was almost submerged.

In the distance, toward the north, could be seen what

was left of the Melchoir group of Greek letter islands. Greatly reduced in size, only the heights of Eta and Omega were visible. Identifying islands and shores had become much more difficult since the waters had risen and partially covered some of them.

Hoping each day for some safe way to get on land or on a ship, the occupants of the berg were growing desperate, fearing they would suddenly be swept into the maelstrom of pack ice and growlers whirling around them, or that their iceberg would capsize, or be carried north into the Atlantic Ocean. They were terrified as gales howled around their plastic habitats, causing them to tremble and strain against their cables.

The crew carefully tended the anchors and safety ropes. They required constant attention because of the melting of the iceberg surface and the shifting of the winds. Several of the passengers, both men and women, willingly assisted the crew.

Sometimes the atmosphere cleared enough to give them momentary glimpses of the mountains and valleys along the Danco Coast, or the rugged features of Wiencke and Anvers Islands. Much ice and snow had plunged into the sea and large areas of bare land and rock could be seen whenever the fog lifted.

Chief Mate Eric Sorensen, appointed by Captain Gilbert to be in charge of the iceberg camp, kept searching the shore and sea around them with his binoculars, looking for any possible opportunity to get his people off the iceberg and safely on land. They couldn't attempt to leave the berg until they had some open water in which to launch their motor lifeboats. The ice was closely packed, but moving around them. It piled up in pressure ridges and hummocks, but was unsafe for walking. There were no open leads to shore. Eric told Dr. Barry he thought their iceberg was drawing about forty-five fathoms.

While the iceberg occupants kept a daily vigil, seeking a way to get onto land, the USARPS at Palmer had continued their slow trek to higher ground. After the first big surge of ice off the peninsula and the islands, the level of the sea rose more slowly. But because of the rising waters, the men had to keep on the move. They couldn't stop to repair the helicopter, but they didn't allow it to become flooded. The raft they had built with oil drums and lumber kept the chopper afloat. Hank Osborne had cleaned up an outboard motor which had fallen from a zodiac. The USARP's kept the raft moving with the aid of the motor and hoist cable, toward a new camp site farther east and higher up in the foothills of Mount William.

All hands worked each day as much as their injuries would allow. It was a most difficult task on extremely rugged terrain, over hills and hollows, along a rockbound coast with ice sliding down.

So passed days of strenuous and sometimes frustrating effort. The men became exhausted before they had reached a place suitable to establish an adequate or sufficiently elevated camp, but they kept on struggling.

During that period, *Sinbad*'s situation improved. The rising waters released the pressure on the hull and the ship's engineers succeeded in stopping nearly all the leaks. Finally, the vessel was moved, slowly and cautiously, out of Lemaire Channel toward Biscoe Bay. Captain Gilbert, in constant radio communication with his crew and passengers on the iceberg, and with Palmer and *Quest*, decided to seek an anchorage as near as possible to where the Palmer group expected to camp. He would try the inundated slope of Anvers Island, moving in carefully and sounding until in anchoring depth. He wished to get his few passengers ashore before attempting to take his damaged ship through Gerlache Strait toward the iceberg camp, hard aground near the eastern end of Gand Island.

At that point, *Quest* was ready to move out of Deception. As weather and floating ice permitted, a zodiac was run out to the Neptune's Bellows opening where soundings were taken. Constant radio contact with Palmer, *Sinbad*, and the floating camp iceberg kept Captain Pack and the crew alert to the possibility that *Quest* might still be put to a further test against the elements. The probability that *Quest* would go to the rescue of the passengers and crew on the iceberg increased day by day.

Icepack, Elbow, and I made frequent hikes up the hill to look over the sea outside. As time passed, it seemed that the number and size of the icebergs were decreasing. We could see more open water, and less broken ice was coming into the Deception caldera. The current had abated somewhat. Ice on the northwestern slopes of the peninsula was gradually disappearing. The mountains and valleys along the Danco Coast were then dark gray instead of white. There were splotches of green and red, evidence of copper and other ores.

Bransfield had reported much difficulty in reaching the Orcadas, but the ship had finally managed to get through the mass of icebergs flowing out of the Weddell Sea. That flow would probbly go on for months, perhaps years. *Quest* had actually been trapped in a safer area, protected from that great flow by the peninsula itself. All of us on board *Quest* were extremely aware of how lucky we were. We were certainly better off than the others. After all, *Quest* wasn't as badly damaged as *Sinbad*, and we weren't trying to keep a helicopter afloat like the men at Palmer, nor attempting to get onto land like the passengers and crew of the floating berg. Of course, none of us were yet aware that the perilous situation on the iceberg had been compounded by the possibility of foul play.

Tensions and fears mounted at the iceberg camp. A seaman, who had discovered two abandoned security ropes with snap hooks attached, and an empty whiskey bottle on the ice near the rest-room tents, reported the matter immediately to the mate, Eric Sorensen. Eric made a head count and soon determined that there were, indeed, two persons missing; however, it wasn't immediately known who they were. He asked the occupants of each raft if they had noticed anyone missing.

Finally, after much questioning, one of the travel girls,

Sally McMurray, of Raft Two, said, "I think those two people—the tall man with the—well, I *think* he had a mustache—or used to have, and that woman who hollered so much—you know, the two who came off the ship drunk?"

A man's voice interrupted. "He didn't have a mustache. He had a beard like all the rest of us."

Sally continued, "Well, he had a mustache *before* he had a beard, but it got lost in the beard." She hesitated, then went on saying, "You know the two I mean—aren't they in one of the other rafts? They were in here for a while. She had an argument with another woman. They went out at some point or other." Sally moved away from Eric, but he pressed her for more information. Reluctantly, she said, "They went out with that good looking guy—I think he's her husband or something. The one in Raft One. I saw him this morning. He had a bottle hidden in his jacket. I guess he asked them to have a drink—or something."

"You want to come with me and show me who you mean?"

"No. I don't want to get involved in anything."

Eric persisted, however and finally she consented. They hooked themselves together and to the lifeline and went over to Raft One.

"That's who I mean," Sally said softly, indicating Tony Destefani.

The mate accompanied Sally back to Raft Two. He didn't question Tony directly. He rememberred the incident on board *Sinbad* when Teresa made a scene and Tony had threatened to hit her. Eric also knew about her coming off the ship late with Victor Daly when they were both drunk. Eric was a cautious man. He decided that he must determine beyond a doubt that Teresa and Daly were actually missing before asking any further questions. He made his way from one raft to another searching for Teresa. He recalled her face quite well. But the faces of the men, all with beards, were harder to recognize. He

233

couldn't find Teresa. Finally, he decided to question Tony. He went back to Raft One and asked Tony to step outside.

"Yes," said Tony. "They were in Raft Two. I went over there and they came out with me and got to drinking over there." He indicated the rest-room tents barely visible through the fog. "Aren't they in Raft Two?"

"No," replied Eric.

"Raft Three?"

"No."

"Nowhere?"

"No. I couldn't find them. Two safety lines were found unsnapped and an empty whisky bottle near the edge of the iceberg over by the rest tents," explained Eric.

"Think they fell overboard?"

"I don't know. I thought *you* might know."

"No. When I left them, they were OK."

"Were they snapped onto the lifeline?"

"Yes, I think so," replied Tony. "It was very foggy."

"I must report this by radio to Captain Gilbert on *Sinbad* unless we can find them somewhere around the camp," said Eric.

They went searching together without result. Tony returned to Raft One. The mate noted Tony's lack of anxiety over the apparent disappearance and possible drowning of a woman he assumed to be Tony's wife. It was, indeed, a strange attitude.

"Murder?"

"Not so loud! Shhhh! Yes, murder," Al Norwood and Bill Bush were standing on the lee side of Raft One. Thick fog still surrounded them.

Al lowered his voice. "That's what Eric thinks. Eric questioned us again this morning. He says they can't prove it. Nobody saw anything in the fog. Someone heard them singing and laughing over there near the rest tents. They were polishing off that bottle of liquor."

234

"Maybe they just got to dancing around and slipped off the edge," said Bill.

"Eric thinks Tony could have pushed them off. Brenda says he was sober when he came back and sat beside her. She didn't smell any liquor. His wife and Daly must have killed that bottle." Al spoke softly, scarcely above a whisper.

Rumors spread through the camp during the bleak foggy morning. Furtive glances were directed toward Tony Destefani. Could it be they had a murderer in their midst? Was he really a killer? He certainly didn't appear dangerous, yet how could one be sure? Would he strike again? What could have been his motive? Jealousy? Obviously not. He had shown no concern about his wife's affair with Victor Daly. Maybe Tony just wanted to get rid of them. Someone remembered his interest in the question of court jurisdiction here in the Antarctic.

Joyce Dearborn and Helen Norwood thought they should try to move to another raft.

"I'm trying to recall," Helen mused. "I think it may have been Dr. Barry. Anyway, it was when we were back there on *Sinbad*, we got to talking about those graves. Someone said that if a murder was committed here the trial would be under the jurisdiction of whatever country the ship is registered in."

"Icebergs? How about on an iceberg?"

"That's it. Looks like, if it really was murder, he could get away with it, doesn't it?"

"I really don't know," said Joyce.

For a short time, Victoria Degrelle was suspect too. Emma Cavige was most vocal in the matter. It seemed preposterous, but it wasn't without some merit. Emma reminded everyone of Victoria's verbal attack on Teresa concerning the stolen brooch. Emma thought that perhaps Victoria had confronted Teresa again, in front of Daly, and killed them both by pushing them off the iceberg. Victoria emphatically denied the allegation, and the idea was soon discarded. Several people in Raft One vouched for Victoria, and remembered that she hadn't been outside, or alone at all, during the time in question. Once again, suspicion centered solely on Tony.

Helen said, "I have an idea. We have to get a place ready for Lucille Connally. Her baby's due any day now. Joyce, why don't you and Clarence and I move to the one we're going to use for a maternity raft and start getting things ready so Lucille can be moved to it? I'd rather not stay around Tony anyway, just for now. We'll get the nurse, Lorraine Jackson, to come with us. You talk to Clarence."

The fog lifted slowly during the morning. Gradually, the silhouettes of people moving around, and dark shapes of rafts and tents appeared. Eric made his rounds, and when he came to Raft One, Dr. Dearborn and Jerry Connally got his approval to start preparing a raft for Lucille and the new arrival. The group moved without delay.

Suddenly, there were shouts from the direction of the rest tents which could then be seen clearly. The fog had cleared and several of the crew were seen gesticulating and pointing over the edge of the iceberg.

The body of Teresa Solare, alias Mrs. Antony Destefani, shrouded in her orange-hued flotation jacket, lay face down upon a large level floe a few meters from the iceberg. A thin pool of blood, mixed with melt water, spread outward around her head. One fur-lined boot was missing.

Eric shouted for a heaving line. One was brought to him quickly. "I'm going to see if I can get an eye around her and pull her up." He tied a small bowline in one end and made a slip eye. He carefully tossed it at the woman's body, but it fell to one side. After several attempts, he succeeded only in getting it over one foot, but when he pulled, the rope slipped off. The floe on which Teresa lay was drifting away. Eric gave up trying to get her with the rope.

The horror of the camp occupants was surpassed only

by their curiosity. They ventured as close to the edge as safety lines would allow to gaze down on the lifeless form moving away on its frozen bier. A few skuas, the scavenger birds of the polar seas, flew around over the body, waiting to alight. Occasionally a leopard seal breached the surface where water appeared between the bitsy bergs and loose pack ice. Animals, confused at the strange happenings, had to find food. Teresa wouldn't lie undisturbed for very long.

Tony and Brenda undoubtedly had something going. Brenda was not sure what it was, nor to where it might lead her, but since they were on their way, perhaps to eternity, on a chunk of ice, she had found Tony's attentions nearly irresistible. Majory cautioned her several times about the possibility of a disagreeable situation with Tony's wife, and getting involved with a married man. With Teresa off on her own cool journey, and very dead, Brenda sought some answers from Tony. He was emphatic in his denial of any guilt in the tragic end of Teresa and the disappearance of Victor Daly.

Brenda's inquisitive attitude caused Tony some concern, but he decided she should know something about his background. Because of the probability that his father and brother, and possibly all his other connections in New York, had been washed out by the swells which hit Manhattan, perhaps Tony might be able to live normally without any clandestine obligations, even make a living by applying his education to a legitimate endeavor.

Tony and Brenda found a spot where they could talk quietly and confidentially. "In the first place," said Tony, "I didn't kill anybody, and I never have! I'm going to tell you about my family and my reason for being on this cruise. It's a long story, and I'm not proud of it, but here it is." Tony made certain that they weren't being overheard, and then continued. "Brenda, Teresa wasn't my wife. She was my older brother Leo's wife. My father and Leo made a lot of money in the rackets and sent me off to Europe for my education. I was to get training which would open the doors to the upper brackets of society, and they spared no expense to put me up there.''

Long ago, Tony had his name legally changed from Andrew Rossi to Anthony Destefani. The change had been suggested by his father, Mike Rossi, who, with his other son, Leo Rossi, was spending bitter years in a prominent federal institution.

Tony continued his story. ''About three years ago, there was an airplane crash in Panama. My father and my brother Leo were on that plane, but they weren't injured. Many others were injured and some were killed. Several walked away from the crash with only minor bruises. Dismembered bodies and baggage were scattered over a wide area.''

''Ugh!'' Brenda grimaced.

''Several passengers who could walk went off looking for help. My father and Leo began searching among the victims to see what they could pick up. It was definitely their day. Leo found a woman's hand. There was a big diamond ring on one finger. He couldn't remove the ring from the rigid finger, and not having a knife to cut the finger off, he wrapped the whole hand in a red shirt he found in the debris. While Leo was doing that, my father, Mike, stumbled across another find which changed their lives.'' Tony glanced around to make sure nobody was listening.

''Go on,'' said Brenda. ''What was it?''

''A strong plastic satchel with a small chain slung around a dead passenger's arm. It was half covered by his body. Dad suspected that it contained valuables, and he searched the man's pockets for the key. Unknown to my father, he was being observed by another passenger who had just regained consciousness. He was lying on the ground about twenty feet away, slightly injured. Mike found the key and opened the satchel. There, right in his big hot fist was what he described to me later as a fortune in jewels. He took a quick glance around, locked the satchel, and slipped the chain off the dead man's arm. Leo was still searching. Dad called him, and they took off in a hurry, just as the rescuers arrived," Tony paused.

Brenda asked, "What happened then?"

"Well, in his haste, Dad lost the key to the satchel and couldn't show Leo what was in it. Leo tried again to get the ring off the finger of the hand he had found, but didn't succeed. Among some trash, they found a rusty metal box and Leo stuffed the hand in it. One hinge was broken so they wrapped some wire around the box. It was loosely fastened, slightly open, but the hand would stay in. They reached the waterfront and stole a small boat. They dropped the satchel of jewels, and the box with the hand, overboard in a depth of about thirty-eight feet. My father told me the details of this escapade during the months that followed. He showed me the points of land he used for reference to mark the location of the jewels. I have a small map." Tony tapped his wallet pocket.

"Do you think you can find it?" Brenda asked.

"I don't know," replied Tony. "The coastline is probably changing now with the floods, so maybe my map is no good." He lowered his voice. "Later, they found out that the man who had seen them take the stuff was none other than our friend, Victor Daly, on vacation in Panama, the same Victor Daly who disappeared from this iceberg a few days ago."

Brenda gasped. She was intrigued by the story. Tony resumed his account.

"At his first opportunity, Daly obtained the plane's passenger list. He then traced my father and Leo in New York. There he confronted Leo with looting and the theft of a woman's hand and ring, thinking that by doing so he could force disclosure of its hiding place and also the satchel."

Tony paused. Brenda was spellbound. "Did it work?" she asked.

"No, his attempts at blackmail were unsuccessful so Daly decided he would inform the police about the looting of the plane's baggage to see if any investigation would disclose any information about the satchel. Nobody besides Daly knew about the satchel, and Daly didn't mention it at the trial. Dad took notice of this, but said nothing. The whole case concerned looting in general. They both got four years.

"My father told Leo's wife, Teresa, about Daly, and gave instructions that she was to get me to go with her and see if we would make a deal with Daly. Dad wanted out of prison and also to get rid of Daly if we couldn't make a good deal. So we followed Daly on this cruise. Teresa got to playing around with him until they fell off this iceberg. I don't really know how they happened to slip off. I didn't have anything to do with it. Maybe she pushed him off and slipped off herself. It would be just like her to do that. She was always bungling things." Tony told Brenda that he thought Teresa had confused *Sinbad*'s suicide victim, Gordon P. Bailey, with Victor P. Daly at the beginning of the cruise and had pushed the wrong man overboard. Tony also cleared up the matter of Victoria's missing brooch and told Brenda he had returned it to Victoria's cabin.

After a short pause, during which Tony seemed to be making some sort of difficult decision, he looked intently at Brenda. "You know we've become close lately," he said softly. "I feel we may even be closer if we live through this calamity. Please don't say anything about the things I've told you."

"All right, Tony," Brenda replied. "You can trust me."

"Now, with Leo's and my father's probable deaths," Tony said, "and Daly gone, I don't believe anyone else alive knows anything about those jewels. If we ever get out of this situation alive and recover them, maybe we can get a reward. At any rate, if we never get to Panama, or if we never leave Antarctica, I hope we can spend a lot of our future together."

Brenda was impressed. She certainly liked Tony. Time would bring an answer to some misgivings she still had about him, but she saw no reason why she shouldn't continue their relationship. But she still wondered about the death of Teresa and the disappearance of Victor Daly. Could it be possible that she and Tony might recover that "fortune in jewels" some day? Brenda was never one to turn down a proposition that might be of financial benefit, whether or not a good looking hunk of man went with it.

No trace of Victor Daly was found. Eric carefully examined all the surrounding ice with his binoculars. He and other members of the crew peered over the edge all around looking for Daly. There were many other bergs near them and it was assumed that, if he had met the same fate as Teresa, he might have slipped off into the water, or possibly drifted behind some other icebergs out of sight.

Another week of anxiety passed. Frustrated and distraught, suffering from lack of customary comforts and amenities, fearful for their lives and anxious about their homes and relatives, many occupants of the floating camp were beginning to break under the strain. Unkempt, malodorous, with only ice water for washing, eating only canned food, getting little exercise, and developing much animosity, the iceberg camp was rapidly turning into a drifting madhouse.

At last Eric, Dr. Barry, Dr. Dearborn, Bill Bush, Al Norwood and Jerry Connally appointed themselves as a committee to try to bring reassurance to the groups at each raft, and to restore confidence that they would surely be rescued. The loss of two of the passengers, and the morbid afterthoughts of the grim scene of the week before, didn't help. Eric reported the situation by radio to Captain Gilbert on *Sinbad,* but there was no way Gilbert could help. Matters would have to take their course, whatever they might be.

Ole Magnussen monitored all radio broadcasts and kept everyone informed to the best of his ability. News from home was appalling. The self-appointed committee members held their first meeting inviting all to attend. They sought to determine the best means of handling the grave situation in the camp.

"I have in mind the possiblity of giving some brief lectures," said Dr. Barry. "We're getting these radio reports and perhaps each of us can take a subject—get everybody to assemble together outside the rafts when the weather permits. I can discuss 'Survival on New Land.' "

"I can work up some health information," volunteered Dr. Dearborn. "Let's get it up for this afternoon."

Eric said, "I'll discuss procedures for getting off this berg." That statement met with applause.

"Al," remarked Dr. Barry. "You heard that last broadcast. How's about your discussing how the refugees are getting out of the big cities?"

"OK," agreed Al. "Maybe that will take our minds off our own troubles for awhile."

Jerry Connally said, "The first topic that comes to mind is Noah, but I must look out for Lucille now. Suppose I discuss later what we might do when we finally get ashore —how we can organize our living conditions—some rules to live by."

"Sounds good," Eric said.

"I'm not much at talking, but I used to sing a lot; so does my wife, Jean. I'll try to organize a couple of singing groups," offered Bill Bush. "We've heard some singing in the rafts. A couple of the ship's orchestra members are here. I think there's a violin and an accordian. Let me ask right now for a show of hands. Who would like to sing with us?" Over thirty hands were raised.

"Ok, that's fine," said Bill. "If the weather is good, we'll meet right here after lunch. Everybody write down some favorite songs. What do you think about dividing into three groups of about ten each? You can pick out names for each group, and we'll have a competition. The prize will be Phil Cavige boiled in hogwash!"

"I won't taste good," said Phil, grinning through his grey beard.

242

Someone hollered, "Boil him in oil!"

"Yeah! Texas snake oil!" yelled another.

"OK, come on," said Bill. "Suggest some names for our glee club."

"The Icicles?"

"Hell, no! Let's forget about ice!"

"I know," volunteered Phil Cavige. "Call us the Polar Punks." The name stuck to his group.

"How about the Fog Horns?" said Al Norwood. There was a sudden silence. Tony winced.

"OK, Fog Horns," echoed Bill. "One more."

Marjory said, "Let's name one especially for the girls. How about Stormy Petrels?"

"Good," said Bill. "We'll meet here after lunch then, and start singing."

The weather was fair with a southeast breeze in the early afternoon, although vast clouds of vapor continued to blow northward high overhead. The prospective singers gathered between Rafts One and Two about 1330. Led by Bill and Jean, they got themselves into questionable harmony, and after an hour of practising, the Polar Punks were given the "stage" and the others listened. They made a good start and by the time it was over, they had a fair "barbershop" sound.

Next came Dr. Barry's lecture. He was in good form, but the wind had freshened from the southeast and he had to speak loudly.

"I've been doing a great deal of thinking about our situation, and about the reports we have been getting from the United States and other parts of the world. I think we must try to analyze these events very carefully. The more we understand what is going on, and what may be expected to occur, the better we can cope with our own troubles. We have all been anxious and several here have had what we may politely call 'nervous disorders,' like, say, coming unglued—blowing our tops. I can sympathize with that, but I certainly won't follow suit because I, for one, have spent many years in the Antarctic, and I am convinced we will go *safely* through these events."

The crowd broke into instant applause. When it quieted, Barry continued. "In contemplating the conditions elsewhere in the world, I have tried to imagine the worst. For example, the eventual scattering of all polar ice, the flood of ocean water over the entire globe, the rise of land masses of the Antarctic Continent and the eventual spread of humanity down here into this vast region." Dr. Barry had to speak louder as the wind became stronger. "Development and growth of a wealth of flora and fauna in that virgin land is a great part of such a future, and fires the imagination. Another important consideration as we try to analyze these events, is the inundation of extensive land masses and all the seaports of the world."

The groan from his listeners were audible even above the noise of the wind.

"Something else, too," George Barry continued, "is the possibility of the end of nationalism as humanity is confronted with this common and overwhelming disaster." He paused for emphasis, and looked carefully into the faces of several near him. Could he really put his feelings on the line? His object was to allay their fears. Would his words have the opposite effect?

"Let us consider such a hypothesis," he continued. "As the flood waters creep onto the coastal areas, the national authorities of the world are already finding it difficult to cope with the problems caused by masses of humanity fleeing toward the interior. We have all listened to these reports. We're all beside ourselves wondering what may happen to our families and friends. However, it won't do any good to worry. Most intelligent humans are resourceful, and will find a way to save themselves. We have heard that local, state and federal employees, including law enforcement personnel, have joined in a massive exodus to higher ground."

The wind kept blowing. So did Dr. Barry. He was just warming up. "Seaports, fuel and other operational facilities for the costly, burdensome and destructive military establishments of the world are crumbling. Arms races by the major powers, supported by the vast and powerful munitions manufacturing interests, their lobbyists, and their congressional puppets, are bound to collapse.''

Phil Cavige refrained from giving his usual "hogwash" comment. Bill Bush suddenly interrupted. "You know, something just occurred to me. How about all those nuclear submarines? Couldn't they send a couple down here to rescue all of us? They must have plenty of fuel.''

"Yes," responded Barry, "but they need seaports, charts, and other navigational aids to operate with, and they need governments to give them orders. Who's going to tell them anything?''

Al Norwood joined in the discussion. "We've been hearing so much about hand guns—Saturday night specials, et cetera, in the hands of 'goons.' How about warships, war planes and nuclear subs in the hands of inept and self-serving political goons? Show me one national government above corruption and greed.''

"You can say that again!" Barry responded. "Areas of all continents high enough to show above the water must receive the hordes fleeing from the great cities and towns and rural areas which have been flooded.''

Jean Bush said, "The people who live in the inland and higher elevation areas are going to resent the crowds of people pouring in, especially in the cold parts of the world. Undoubtedly the law enforcement organizations will collapse under the strain of masses seeking food and shelter.''

"Disaster? I'll say!" commented Ed McCaughlin. "Radio newscasts already report millions drowned, and more are dying hourly from lack of food and shelter. Mass graves are being dug, but even so, many bodies are left to decompose. Disease and starvation is sweeping the world. The plight of the refugees on the roads of Vietnam was nothing compared to this.''

"I think we're better off here in these Antarctic regions

where it's uncrowded, to say the least," said Eric.

"We must find out about our families," someone said.

"Yes," echoed several voices. "Get us information!"

"I wonder sometimes if I want to go home to so much trouble," reflected Helen.

"I want to go home, but I'd consider coming back here if we can get a farm started," said Bill Bush.

Jean added, "We could have some beautiful farms and gardens. Look how well everything will grow here in virgin soil."

"Ugh," grunted Victoria Degrelle. "Zis place makes me seek. I would not stay here eef my life depended on it!"

Emma retorted, "What makes you think it doesn't?"

Before Victoria could answer, Ed McCaughlin said, "I'm going to try mining some gold."

"Gold? Yeah, there may be a lot of gold here," said Phil Cavige. "Black gold—my kind."

"Yes. Maybe we can get that too," agreed Ed. "But I mean yellow gold. Maybe it'll be as cheap as any other metal with all the gold we may find here. We won't have any use for money around here, will we?"

"There wouldn't be any use hording gold to take it back home," declared Bill. "It won't be worth any more than silver or copper, will it?"

Marjory said, "I understand that there are no more national boundaries. All the custom houses are being destroyed in the floods."

"Who needs them? Let's have one world—no barriers," said Jerry Connally. "People will have to help themselves and each other now. No more welfare. With nearly all fuel supplies gone, travel will slow down to a trickle. Airlines and railroads are greatly curtailed. Very few automobiles are moving. Very little gas, and many electric power plants are shut down. There's no diesel fuel for locomotives to haul the coal. They'll have to go back to steam!"

"Can we really be objective now?" resumed Dr. Barry,

almost shouting. "Let's consider our situation. We must set up some kind of rules—" Barry stopped. "Let's go in —too much wind. Suppose we get every—" Eric interrupted him.

"Looks like a big storm coming. Let's get busy on these anchor lines and secure everything."

All who could do so helped the crew attend to making the rafts and ice anchors as secure as possible. Everyone seemed to be in a better frame of mind as the camp was secured against the wind. For a change, there had been no serious arguments during the afternoon.

Dr. Dearborn and nurse Lorraine Jackson made final arrangements in the "maternity" raft. Lucille Connally's time was getting close. She was ready for the event. Word was passed throughout the small community, and everyone awaited the birth with much interest. Jerry was happy and grateful for the solicitude and help.

As Lucille lay on her improvised inflated bed, she heard the singing and laughter outside. She slept on and off during the afternoon. Between naps and labor pains, she heard the wind and fragments of Dr. Barry's speech. Gradually, Lucille became aware of another sound. Was it just her imagination, or possibly her own heart murmuring? She listened as it kept on, seeming to grow stronger. What Lucille felt and heard was a sort of deep grinding vibration. No one else was yet aware of it.

Jerry was seated beside his wife, holding Lucille's hand. When she stirred, he placed his hand on her forehead. A babble of voices and shouting penetrated Lucille's thoughts. Dr. Dearborn and Lorraine, who had been outside helping to secure the raft, came inside.

"The iceberg has started to move again!" exclaimed Lorraine.

"But don't worry! Dr. Barry said it's all right and we'll be safe!" said Dr. Dearborn.

The vibrations and grinding which Lucille had heard

and felt before anyone else was the bottom of the iceberg moving off and scraping against the rocks on which it had been aground.

Dr. Dearborn repeated his statement about their safety. "Everybody is watching now to see where we are going to drift next. Maybe we'll get someplace where we can get ashore."

The four "wire men," Enrique on *Quest*, Arthur and Ira at Palmer, and Ole on the iceberg, had frequently held three-way radio conversations. They agreed early that Ole's emergency radio should use the call letters, CC, which they said stood for Camp Courage. The inhabitants of the camp had other names for it, such as Camp Calamity and Camp Crisis. Phil Cavige had some choice names for it which don't bear recording.

Whatever the name, Ole usually responded to CC when called. With some difficulty, he gave frequent reports to Captain Gilbert on *Sinbad*. Everyone knew of the troubles at the camp. Ole's transmitter had to be cranked by hand, an irksome job. One of the seamen helped with the chore. At times, the other stations had difficulty hearing Ole. Sometimes he wasn't heard by anyone. Enrique called Ole at prearranged scheduled times, but didn't always receive an audible response. Ole's transmissions were getting weaker with each day.

When the iceberg was suddenly dislodged from its position aground off Gand Island, Ole immediately called the others to tell them of its drift toward the open Atlantic Ocean. His efforts were almost futile. He could hear *Quest* calling, but Enrique heard Ole only faintly. He was aware, however, that Ole was sending an emergency message. Enrique told Captain Pack his suspicions.

As the hours passed, the weather grew worse. The iceberg, carried by the current, began to move faster in a northerly direction toward the Atlantic. The surrounding pack ice and other bergs were moving also, and the sea became more agitated and turbulent as they drifted northward. Soon, large ocean swells were felt rocking the iceberg camp. The wind rapidly increased, and tore at the improvised lodgings with great force.

Suddenly, a shattering storm was upon them. The terrified occupants huddled inside, clinging to one another and to their fastenings. Within moments, a tremendous gust tore away the entire camp. Anchors were pulled loose, and rafts were blown violently over the edge of the iceberg, rolling and tossing like leaves in a gale. Some rafts fell on ice, and some in the angry sea itself. Screaming and bruised, the people clawed and grabbed at whatever they could grasp as their habitats kept rolling and twisting, some bottom up, some on end as their loads half submerged them.

The frightened people inside the "maternity" raft were all securely lashed by the seamen aboard. Great swells and heavy seas laden with ice dashed against the sides and hull of the raft. As it was tossed and hurled mercilessly by enormous waves, little Joseph Connally was born. His first weak cries were lost in the howling of the wind. While the people struggled to hold little Joe safely, and gave aid and comfort to Lucille, a faint sound of escaping air reached their ears. Their inflated raft was losing air and sinking.

9

EARLIER ON the same day that *Sinbad*'s rafts were blown off the iceberg, there had been a shift in wind at Deception where *Quest* was trapped. It freshened from the south, blowing much ice away from the vicinity of the caldera. There was more open water, and more space between the icebergs.

After viewing the situation for the umpteenth time, Icepack decided to take *Quest* out of Deception. He summoned all hands, and spoke to them over the squawk system. "This looks like the day we've been waiting for," he said hopefully. "Things are so bad on that iceberg camp, I think we should try to get those people off before they're all killed. Let's see if we can make it. Stand by to get underway!"

There was a gleeful shout throughout the ship as the crew took their stations. Harry King climbed to the fo'c's'le deck, and tried out the windlass. Two men went below to the chain locker. Paul Shelley and a couple of seaman hoisted the zodiac. "Crankshaft," Lytel warmed up the main engines, and Ray Godney started a fresh pot of coffee.

Elbow Larsen, Beebee Abbey, Carol Moore, Arnold and Nancy Varnay and I suspended laboratory duties and all other activities. We gathered out on the charred forward deck to lend our moral support to the crew.

Quest had been riding at anchor in Whalers Bay over three weeks. During that time, the water had risen several meters. Harry had raised the anchor a couple of times to see that it was clear. There were four shots of anchor chain, or about a hundred and ten meters.

The chain came up slowly, clattering and thumping over the wildcat. Captain Pack waited apprehensively in the wheelhouse, where I joined him. He remarked, "The bottom of Whalers Bay is foul with old moorings. I recall a conversation I had with the captain of the British Research Vessel *Shackleton*. Once he had a lot of difficulty getting his anchor up. He told me that he dragged a piece of heavy mooring all around the bay and out, almost over to Collins Point across the caldera, before he was able to clear his anchor and get it up. It took him a long time to get clear."

Forward, three bells were struck by Harry as the forty-five fathom link came in view. He signalled the direction of the chain. The links slapped loudly as they adjusted to the wildcat. Pack watched the mate. Harry struck two bells as the thirty fathom link appeared. Pack murmured, "It won't be long now." The wind was getting stronger.

Suddenly, the chain tautened. *Quest* slowly swung to starboard. The mate signalled and moved back along the starboard rail. The ship continued swinging, pulled by the shortening chain. But it kept coming up—soon we would know; was it just the anchor which needed breaking out, or were we to have some trouble?

Pack swore he would *not* lose an anchor. He would get it up at all costs. As the links came slower over the windlass, he knew something heavy was fouling the anchor. The strains increased and the windlass turned slower. Harry stopped heaving to allow the anchor to break out—but was that all it needed? It would not budge. It was, indeed, fouled by some heavy old moorings, possibly down there for the past century or longer, embedded in the mud.

They kept a strain, and after a few minutes, tried to heave some more. They got a few more links and stopped again. Whatever was down there had to be given time to break out. By heaving and stopping several times, they finally brought the anchor to the surface, and saw that an old heavy stud chain was over one fluke. Pack went forward to look at it. Harry got the end of a mooring line under it and held it while he slowly backed out the anchor. Then they let go the line and the old stud chain dropped off.

Quest was free, anchor up, and clear. We turned and headed toward the open sea, carefully sounding as we passed over the obstruction at Neptune's Bellows. Pete's Pillar was no longer visible. It had been toppled by the earthquakes. The wind was increasing, and outside the sea was rough.

As we departed Deception and headed for Brabant Island, the storm that had blown the rafts off the iceberg struck *Quest* with all its fury. Pack maneuvered carefully to avoid collision with heavy ice and drifting bergs. As the hours passed, Enrique repeatedly called CC, but no response came from the iceberg camp. Unknown to us, its rafts were scattered widely on the angry sea, its people frightened, sick, injured, or dead.

On orders from the skipper, Sebastian Lund, AB, climbed the rigging to the crow's nest on the swaying foremast with a pair of binoculars hanging from his shoulder. Several hours passed. Suddenly, Sebastian shouted and pointed to something about two points off the starboard bow. Paul, who was in the wheelhouse with Icepack, took the compass bearing of the direction in which Sebastian was pointing. Icepack went up into the upper conn. Soon he spotted a tossing gray raft. One end was deep. It was being battered by the heavy sea, but it was afloat.

Pack maneuvered *Quest* carefully to windward of the raft and drifted down broadside toward it, forming a lee. Harry and Paul, assisted by everybody on deck, managed after several attempts to get a hook into a ring on the raft and hold it steady while the terrified occupants were hoisted aboard *Quest*.

Of the seventeen persons who were hauled out, only two could stand. They told us they had been blown off the iceberg. They were all carried below and given the best attention Dr. Varany and his hospital staff could provide with the ship rolling and pitching as if we were riding a three-legged camel.

"There's another!" shouted Sebastian, pointing northward.

Pack quickly turned *Quest* and moved as rapidly as possible toward a dark spot showing briefly, from time to time, some three miles away.

"Two more!" yelled Sebastian, holding his arm in the direction of the port beam.

Quest raced from one raft to another and brought the hapless victims aboard, stacking the empty rafts on the forward deck. Some of them were already partly deflated. The people were completely so, and worse still, after the first four rafts were retrieved, nine lifeless bodies lay in a row, side by side, covered and lashed down on *Quest's* forward hatch.

It was learned from a coherent survivor that somewhere out there on the sea there were three more rafts, one of which was the "maternity" raft. The search continued. All eyes searched the horizon intently as the vessel moved northward. Pack assumed that the missing rafts would be found in the direction toward which the wind was blowing.

Before the short polar night came, two more rafts were found and three more victims added to the row of dead on the hatch. All of *Sinbad's* rafts had been found except the "maternity" raft. Among the ninety-nine survivors, in various stages of illness and injury, were Al Norwood, Dr. Barry, Phil Cavige, Bill and Jean Bush, Brenda Clarke, Marjory Dumont, Victoria Degrelle, Sally McMurray, and Edward McCaughlin.

Questioning the last survivors, those able to speak said that the "maternity" raft had only a few persons in it. I managed a short talk with Eric Sorensen, who had been in the last raft. Sorensen said he thought the "maternity" raft, having such a light load, had probably been blown faster to the northward, and therefore could have been farther away than the others.

Twilight came a little before midnight. Pack kept *Quest* heading slowly along with the wind so as not to pass the missing raft, and we hoped we would see it when the sun came about 0200. Meanwhile the searchlight was kept on and its beam constantly swept the stormy ice-strewn sea in all directions.

Gradually the wind abated, and the sea became less agitated. *Quest* was crowded with people in various stages of vitality and inertia, many with fractures and lesions. All those able to assist made great effort to ease the suffering of the injured. Space for so many to lie down was limited, but we managed to get through the short night without any additions to the sad row on the hatch. Among that still group lay Mrs. Emma Cavige. Her fingers, usually loaded with jewelry, were bare, as were her ears and neck. Phil Cavige was in such bad shape he was not immediately told about his wife.

Icepack, who had been in the wheelhouse constantly since leaving Deception, increased *Quest*'s speed as much as ice conditions would permit, heading northward with the wind, continuing the search for the "maternity" raft without result. The sea was no problem then, and *Quest* was steady. Everyone looked for the raft. Several seamen climbed the rigging of both masts to watch.

For three more hours *Quest* continued the search northward, then headed west for about four miles and turned back south. No sign of the raft could be seen in any direction. Captain Pack was reluctant to give up, and we covered the area again and again. He was also mindful of the crowded situation on his ship and the plight of the injured, of which there were more than sixty of the ninety-nine survivors already picked up by *Quest*. Should another storm develop, he knew more lives would be lost. He had to make a decision as to how long we should continue the search for the "maternity" raft.

It was daylight again. Joe "Cajun" Melba was then on lookout high in the crow's nest. His ample girth filled the round enclosure and his black beard hung over the edge. Suddenly, his eye caught sight of a tiny object far to the southwest. He shouted and pointed. Harry King was in the wheelhouse, and Captain Pack was taking a short rest in his chair in the upper conn.

"Looks like somethin' about three points!" yelled Cajun and motioned off to port. "Looks like another one!" he shouted. "Like a small one!"

Harry hollered up to Cajun. "Another what?"

Cajun had his binoculars up and fixed on the object which was not visible to those below. The thing he saw disappeared briefly, then came back into view. Finally, in the dim morning light, Cajun saw it more clearly. It was another raft, partly sunk, with one end sticking up above the water.

"Looks like a sinkin' raft!" he yelled.

Quest came around onto a course toward the raft. It was growing lighter to the northeast, and Pack speeded up as much as safety allowed, crunching through the ice and around the bergs.

As we got closer, we saw with alarm that it was, indeed, one of *Sinbad's* rafts. *Quest* approached as rapidly as possible. Soon we had the raft alongside. To our horror, no people were found in it. Eric identified it as the one which had been called the "maternity" raft. Evidently the occupants had all perished. Al Norwood, only slightly injured, was at *Quest's* rail when the raft was recovered. He was stunned by the knowledge that his wife, Helen, had drowned. Dr. Barry, and Jean and Bill Bush moved to the rail to comfort Al.

Captain Pack said wearily to his mate, "Harry, take her to Gerlache. Keep a good lookout for bodies. We'll try to get through to Palmer if Gerlache is open. I don't want to go around outside unless we have to. Enrique?"

"Yes, Captain."

"Tell *Sinbad* and Palmer we have recovered all the rafts and are proceeding toward Palmer. Paul, you and Eric Sorensen get a head count and let them know the names of living and dead. See if you can find out who was in that empty raft. I'm going to get a couple of hours in the sack."

"Yes, Sir," said Paul.

Icepack made his way down the companionway and along the alleyway stepping over people. As he neared his door, he met Beebee Abbey. She put her hand out to detain him. "Sorry, Captain, your room is full. We had to put an injured woman in your bunk, and five more are lying on the deck. You can't even find a place to step."

Pack smiled wanly and said, "OK, Dr. Abbey, I'll just go back and rest in my chair up top." He climbed slowly to the wheelhouse and on to the upper conn. Someone was already in the chair with his feet up on a window sill. Pack went out, and after searching around, found a spot where he could stretch out. He lay down upon the steel deck with a life jacket for a pillow, and was soon asleep, lulled by the rhythmic pulsations of the main diesel exhausts atop the funnel above his head.

Second Mate Paul Shelley pulled himself together, and went to look for Eric Sorensen to help prepare a list of survivors and dead. Eric wasn't much help. His injuries were too severe.

"Better get someone else to help you," Eric said. "By the way, there were one hundred and twenty-eight altogether." He remembered Teresa and Daly. "No, a hundred and twenty-six."

"You sure now?" Paul asked. "When we got the Mayday, it was a hundred and twenty-eight."

"I'm sure." Eric told Paul about Teresa and Daly.

Paul started with the lifeless forms spread out on the hatch, reasoning that, since there was no means of preserving them in that temperature, he better get them identified before they might have to be jettisoned. It was a horrible thought, and an action which certainly wouldn't have been necessary in the previous freezing Antarctic climate.

Paul began his gruesome task assisted by AB Sebastian

Lund and OS Charlie Stern. They carefully pulled off the tarpaulin covering the bodies. *Sinbad*'s survivors crowded around them.

"Look at that one!" Charlie exclaimed. "We put them all face up! She's rolled over!"

They hastily stepped over the other bodies to get to the woman. Paul turned her over and put his ear to her chest. There was a faint heartbeat. He yelled for Dr. Varany. Dr. Varany and Nancy came quickly. They soon confirmed that the woman was alive, and immediately set to work to bring her around. As they worked on her, she began to moan and cough. Emma Cavige had survived! That brought the count of survivors to one hundred with eleven dead. In all, not counting Teresa and Daily, fifteen were missing and it was assumed that they had drowned in the storm.

Those of *Sinbad*'s passengers and crew members who were able to stand moved closely around the hatch. Some were curious to see who was dead. Others were fearful that friend or spouse might be found there. Emma Cavige was quickly removed and carried to the fo'c's'le deck for better air. She was unable to speak, and after her breathing became more normal, she fell into a deep slumber.

By his tall figure, Tony Destefani was quickly identified. His handsome features were distorted and his head was bloody. His clothes were in shreds and his shoes were gone. His neck was broken. Marjory Dumont gasped when she saw him. She immediately thought of Brenda asleep with a high fever, on the after deck. She gave Tony's name to Paul and then carefully made her way to Brenda. She would tell Brenda, quietly and gently, about Tony when she awakened. Majory felt that Brenda's greatest problem had then resolved itself. She had never been in favor of Brenda's relationship with Tony.

Despite his bruises, Dr. Barry was at the hatch when the bodies were uncovered. He identified some of the lifeless forms. After giving the names to Paul Shelley, Dr. Barry made his way forward. With much difficulty, he stepped around and over the people lying or sitting crowded together on *Quest*'s forward deck. Climbing laboriously up the ladder to the fo'c's'le head, he sought Beebee Abbey who was attending to Emma Cavige.

Barry whispered softly in Beebee's ear. "Mr. Cavige is looking for his wife. Shall I bring him?" He pointed to Emma's left cheek. "Did you look at that?"

"Yes, it's OK. She's got a shiner."

Dr. Barry recalled the altercations between Emma and Victoria. He wondered if Victoria was responsible for the shiner. He said, "Shall I bring Phil Cavige?"

"Let her sleep awhile," answered Beebee. "She was nearly dead."

George Barry went back to the hatch to watch the progress of the identifications. He stood silently for a few minutes, his eyes glistening, a lump in his throat, and then he left to find Phil Cavige. He decided to say nothing to Phil about Emma's condition, but to tell him only that Emma was alive and sleeping. Phil's ticker wouldn't take any more shocks just then.

After making positive identifications of all the dead, Paul had them covered again with the tarpaulin and started his list of the survivors. He made columns on his sheets and listed them alphabetically. Within an hour, he had all their names and home towns listed. He then went up to the wheelhouse.

As the tumultuous days of January passed into history, the western slopes of the Antarctic Peninsula became divested of their accumulations of ice and snow. Bransfield and Gerlache straits were slowly disgorging their masses of icebergs into the Atlantic Ocean. Here and there, open water appeared momentarily. Great clouds of water vapor rapidly spread northward high overhead. Frequently the surface atmosphere became laden with mist and fog, but there were occasional shifts of surface winds and short periods of better visibility.

On the broad western rise of Anvers Island, from Cape

Monaco to the foothills of the eastern mountains, large areas of land appeared. The Marr Ice Piedmont, flowing off into the sea, disclosed patches of soil and smooth boulders which had been covered with ice and snow for many centuries. Nine thousand foot Mount Française stood as a headless sentinel over that strange new land, its peak almost constantly shrouded in clouds.

Reduced in area by the rising waters which encroached upon its western shores, Anvers Island still maintained its formidable identity by those sturdy ramparts, the Bull Ridge and the Trojan Range.

The five miles that the Palmer Station survivors had to move to the foothills of Mount William seemed more like a hundred to those exhausted men. The ever-rising and menacing water continuously swirled and lapped at their supplies, threatening at any moment to overwhelm them and their entire operation. They couldn't move their equipment fast enough, and as the days passed, the USARPS had to abandon many things. They endeavored to secure mark buoys with long lines on some articles which they hoped could be salvaged later. Nights grew longer and tempers shorter as austral midsummer passed.

One morning, as they were taking a short break from their strenuous labors, they heard an excited shout. Bitsy was standing on a rock near the water's edge yelling his head off and waving toward the south. There, across Bismark Strait, was a wonderous sight. Sides rusted from scraping icebergs, and a cascade of sea water gushing from its hull, the luxury liner *Sinbad* came in glorious magnificence toward the weary Palmer group.

With shouts of joy and cries of relief, the men stumbled to the water's edge, waving as the ship approached. Moving cautiously, and sounding constantly, Captain Gilbert brought his vessel toward the new and uncharted shoreline.

The harried USARPS watched with growing excitement as *Sinbad* anchored near them. They shouted and waved with glee. The splash of *Sinbad*'s anchor and the rattle of her chain came loudly like music to their ears. Here was the answer! An elegant floating home with all facilities for living in sumptuous comfort!

As *Sinbad* anchored, a message was received from *Quest* advising Captain Gilbert that the survivors of the iceberg camp had been picked up and that *Quest* was bound for Palmer.

Within a few minutes after anchoring, Captain Gilbert ordered their remaining motor lifeboat over, and brought the exhausted Palmer group aboard. While the USARPS were resting and getting back their strength, the crew succeeded in hoisting the helicopter aboard.

Repairs to the rotor blades rapidly continued with the help of *Sinbad*'s engineers and the use of the ship's fine machine shop. After a few days, Lieutenants Thompson and Stefano took the chopper up for a short trial flight.

Captain Gilbert was unable to contact *Sinbad*'s owners. He decided that, due to the damange to the hull, and the hazards of ocean navigation without accurate positions of celestial bodies with reference to Earth's equator, the ship should remain at anchor where it was.

On board *Quest*, Chief Mate Harry King had laid a course for Dallman Bay. He had intended to take the ship between Brabant and the Melchior Islands, then out through Schollaert Channel into Gerlache Strait. As he approached Brabant Island, he realized that great changes had occurred in the appearance of the coastlines. Islands were smaller and some of them no longer appeared above the surface of the sea.

Harry was finding navigation difficult. Radar gave him his range off the new shorelines, but he couldn't plot his position from "them dam' shores" because "them dam' charts" showed only the old shores. He took bearings of Mount Parry and used its eight thousand foot peak as a guide. He shaped his course to pass well to the west to avoid the rocks which lay off Cape Roux. He need not have worried about those rocks. They were covered by nearly seven meters of water, but it was hard to get used to "this here crummy situation."

"What about th' Melchoir Islands?" asked Paul. "I wonder what happened at Melchoir Station." He referred to the Argentine Base on Gamma Island. "I understand th' *General San Martin* evacuated them right away at th' first news of th' tippin' of th' axis, long before th' earthquake."

"Yeah," Harry said shortly. "Why the hell didn't they evacuate Deception while they were about it?"

"You said it! The way I see it—what I mean is, they had those guys in there to study volcanoes an' such an' they waited to see what would happen."

"They saw all right. They nearly got roasted an' us along with 'em!"

"Well, Harry, it's a good thing we were in there after all. We coulda been smashed up outside. An' look at th' bunch a people we saved!"

Carol came to the wheelhouse door. "Can I come in?" she asked.

"Sure," said Harry.

"It won't be long now," Paul said knowingly.

"Where are we?" asked Carol.

"He's havin' a hard time findin' his way. It has nothin' to do with me this time," Paul said, "nor th' sun. It's Harry's fault—he can't find any islands. They're all sunk."

"That's all right," said Harry. "I can find my way. Don't worry. See that thing stickin' up back there?" He pointed off the port quarter. "That's the Astrolabe Needle. It's not as high as it used to be, but it still makes a good mark. An' I can go by that big peak—that's Mount Parry, over eight thousand feet high."

"Oh?" Carol said soberly. She seemed distracted. *Quest* was heading back toward Palmer where she had seen Larry for the last time.

They were all quiet for a long time as *Quest* moved southward. Harry thought that Carol must have been crying earlier, but it was no wonder, with the loss of Larry, and then working with all the injured survivors from the iceberg. He tried to lift her spirits. "You see that land ahead, Carol? That's Anvers Island. Don't worry. I'll get us there, you can be sure of that. Paul can have his sun an' stars. I'll take my mountains."

"OK," said Paul. "Y'all keep your mountains! Hey! What's that!" Paul was looking through binoculars at what was left of the Melchoir Islands. He thought he saw something red on the shore a little above the water. He searched the shore intently, but whatever it was seemed to have disappeared. Harry picked up the long glass and, steadying it against the side of the open window, swept the island where Paul was looking.

"Red?"

"Yeah."

"I don't see nothin' red."

"I could be mistaken, but somethin' red showed up over there—that's Omega Island, ain't it?" Paul looked at the chart.

"Yeah, but I don't see Gand Island," said Harry. "Looks like it's flooded over." He checked the Brabant coast and islands by radar.

"It's all off now—none of the charts are any good for th' coastlines any more," mused Paul.

"There it is!" Harry spotted something red through his long glass, but the motion of the ship made it hard to keep the object in view. "There! Looks like it might be somebody in a red jacket!" Carol breathed heavily. Her heart skipped a beat. Both men peered at the chart. The tall pointed monolith called Astrolabe Needle, then astern, was a reliable radar target. It served to fix *Quest*'s position and the approximate location of the red object on greatly reduced Omega Island.

"There's a lot of foul ground in there, or there used to be. Maybe we can get in closer now. Maybe we better go in and see if somebody's there." Harry altered course toward the island, about four miles distant. He headed *Quest* for the south end of the island. "If we make out it's a live person, we'll sound our way in an' send a zodiac an' you can see who it is."

Paul took the long glass and kept it focused on the red spot. Carol closely watched the shore, but she couldn't see anything. Paul handed her the long telescope. She put the wrong end to her eye. Everything, including the bow of the ship and rigging, appeared in miniature. She quickly turned the telescope around. She lived with microscopes—she was glad the men hadn't noticed her error. She finally saw the red spot on the shore right ahead.

Harry said, "I don't want to use the squawk box, Paul. I don't want to scare a lot of those sick people. We'll just find out first if anybody is in there. You go down an' get a coupl' a boys an' get a zodiac ready an' I think if it is somebody in there, you should go in and see, but we'll wake up the skipper first. Let him tell you what to do."

The ship was getting closer. Harry switched on the sonar and checked the depth. He slowed the speed as the depth decreased. They continued to look closely at the red object.

"It looks like a flotation jacket," said Paul, "but it's not movin'."

"It looks like it's draped over a rock. Maybe it just floated in there during those swells. It's well up from the water. Paul, call the skipper. I think we should send the boat in."

"Where's the skipper?" Paul lasked. "Beebee told me he couldn't get to his room."

'He's lyin' out aft there on deck somewhere."

Paul found Captain Pack still sound asleep with his head on a life jacket. He hated to wake him after the long rescue operation they had gone through, but here was another possible rescue. He gently shook him.

"Cap—Cap."

"Yes." Pack opened his eyes and looked up at Paul.

"Cap, we see somethin' on shore—on Omega Island, near the south end. A red jacket. Harry thinks we should send a zodiac in. Maybe somebody's in there."

Pack was awake. "Go ahead, but do it fast. We want to get this crowd down to Palmer as soon as possible." The skipper wearily got to his feet and went to the wheelhouse with Paul.

"Hello, Carol," Pack said.

"I hope you feel better," said Carol.

"Nope. Not much, but there's nothing the matter with me that about a week's solid sleep wouldn't fix. Now, where's that thing you see?"

Harry had stopped the ship. He pointed toward Omega Island.

Captain Pack blinked. "Omega? That's Omega? That little chunk?"

"Yes, Sir, that's Omega—what's left of it. It used to be over six hundred feet high at this end," replied Harry.

The skipper looked around in all directions. He saw Mount Parry. "Where are all the small islands around here?"

"No more," said Harry.

"Go ahead, Paul," Pack said finally. "See what's in there." He had a fleeting thought that they might find some survivors of the empty "maternity" raft, but he dismissed the idea as very unlikely.

The zodiac was soon speeding in toward shore with Paul, Sebastian Lund and Charlie Stern. Ice was a problem, but it was well broken up, and they soon stepped out onto the shore near the red jacket. They climbed up to it, and saw it had been carefully draped over a rock with the sleeves tied together to keep it from blowing away. "Somebody could be alive here!" exclaimed Paul. He sent Sebastian and Charlie northward, and he started off around toward the south.

Stumbling along the rugged shore among boulders and climbing over jagged broken rock, Paul made slow progress. He was about to give up and turn back toward the zodiac, when something caught his eye higher up the craggy slope. A woman's boot protruded from between the boulders. Paul climbed with difficulty up to the spot and picked up the boot. He put it in one of the deep pockets of his jacket, and carefully made his way down to the water's edge. He intended to go on farther, but just then he heard shouts from Sebastian and Charlie. Paul quickly turned and went back. The two men motioned to him to follow them around the curve of the shore.

Lying well above the water, were the remains of a man—just a skeleton. Very little flesh remained. Hungry skuas and possibly other predators had been there. The man's clothing was in shreds. Except for a belt and shoes, hardly any clothing remained. The buckle of the belt bore the initials "VPD."

Around the flotation jacket, they found a few empty cans, all of which were labeled in Spanish. Some had contained preserved meat, also *Galletas Terrabusi* and *Yerba Estrella*. Undoubtedly they had been washed over from the submerged Argentine base on nearby Gamma Island.

Paul and Charlie removed the belt and left the skeleton where they found it. Evidently the man had reached the island alive, but hadn't survived the rigors of the elements. All three men searched the island, but found no other human occupants or remains. They returned to the ship with the belt, the flotation jacket, and the woman's boot. Identification was made by Eric Sorensen and confirmed by Dr. Barry and several of *Sinbad*'s passengers. Paul made a suitable entry in *Quest*'s log book. Victor P. Daly was officially dead.

The boot was thought to have belonged to Teresa. Conjecture became rife among *Sinbad*'s passengers and crew.

"Maybe they were dancing around in the fog and he slipped over the edge of the iceberg with her boot in his fist."

"Why would he have her boot in his fist?"

"Maybe he grabbed at her foot as he slipped over and her boot came off."

"Maybe she pushed him off and he pulled her over with him."

"How come she got killed and he didn't?"

"Maybe she hit the ice, but he fell in the water and floated to that island. The water's not so cold now, huh?"

"Well, whatever happened, we'll never know with Tony Destefani dead."

The matter seemed to end there. The attention of the passengers was switched to getting to Palmer and the comfort aboard *Sinbad*.

The expected arrival of *Quest* with the *Sinbad* iceberg survivors had the USARPS and the crew and other passengers on board *Sinbad* in an overwhelming flurry of excitement. Eagerly listening to radio reports and conversations between Enrique and *Sinbad*'s second mate, they planned a whopping reunion with their shipmates and survivors of iceberg Camp Courage. Staterooms on board *Sinbad* were made ready and neat by the room stewards, and *Sinbad*'s cooks planned a feast for those who could enjoy it.

All cabins on the deck where the ship's hospital was located were reserved for the sick and injured. Dr. Schaeffer of the Palmer group assisted Dr. Raymond in those preparations.

After many hours helping the survivors on *Quest*'s decks, Carol sought an opportunity to relax. She took down the visitor's book from its place on top of a locker in the mess room. She had never looked at it before. Turning its pages, she noted the names of some of the persons who had visited the ship during the years. There were numerous phrases such as "best wishes" and "happy returns." There were also some humorous verses. One read: "To the brave crew of the *Quest*

May you never be distressed,

Keep your ship away from rocks,

And come back safely to our docks."

Another read:

"If storms and gales rip off your sails

Hitch up your ship to a couple of whales."

Carol was about to close the book when another entry caught her eye:

"Keep in mind, when success you find
It is wise to meditate,
On questions to Job, about our globe,
In Chapter Thirty-eight."

Her curiosity aroused, Carol decided to see what those "questions to Job" might be. On one of the ship's book shelves, among a profusion of confession magazines and murder mysteries, she found a Bible. She took it to her room, and found the Book of Job. Turning to chapter thirty-eight, she read it verse by verse. She was intrigued by the references to great global forces, and noted with special interest the twenty-second and twenty-third verses, which she copied on a pad:

"Have you entered into the storehouses of the snow,
Or do you see even the storehouses of the hail,
Which I have kept back for the time of distress,
For the day of fight and war?"

Although Carol held no disrespect for the Bible, she had never read it. She had little regard for religion in any form. She had been raised in a Catholic family and had, for a time, attended parochial school as a child, but that was the extent of her religious experience. Nevertheless, she wondered what significance, if any, those verses might have with regard to the great events in which she and her companions had been involved. She thought of the great masses of ice and snow which were being cast into the oceans by the shattering of the Antarctic ice sheet. Had it all been "kept back" purposely, to be released in "time of distress?" She thought of the disturbing news reports that had been flowing constantly by radio from the U.S.; the energy shortage, millions out of work, widespread starvation, corruption in government, nations at war, violence, pollution and disease. Certainly, as never before, this was a "time of distress, fight and war."

Carol dismissed those thoughts. She had enough grief with the loss of Larry. She might consider those verses again sometime, but just then she must do all she could to help with the shipload of survivors.

Quest moved on under the guidance of Harry King for the next hour. At noon, Paul relieved him and carefully took *Quest* through Schollaert Channel, keeping close to the south end of Brabant Island, and out into Gerlache Strait. Progress was slow. There was still much ice to dodge.

With our sad burden of injured, ill, and dead crowded closely together on the vessel's scorched decks, every moment was filled with anxiety. As we entered Gerlache Strait and turned southward, a breeze began to agitate the wide expanse of water and ice into a beam sea which caused *Quest* to roll.

The people on deck held on to one another, and on to everything available to keep from sliding all together in a heap against the starboard bulwarks. Occasionally, a wave would slap against *Quest*'s low freeboard, and a mass of briny spray and pieces of ice would wash over the crowd. Captain Pack ordered everyone who could to get below, but there the crowd was thicker. As the vessel continued to roll, many more became seasick.

"Good grief!" exclaimed Jesse Lytel. "My engine room is getting to be a garbage dump. If we don't stop rolling soon, we'll all suffocate down there below. It's like we are being shook up in a blender."

Icepack was back on the bridge and trying to figure out some way to ease the situation. He wanted to continue on toward Palmer as fast as possible, but conditions on board were getting unbearable. He slowed *Quest* to ease the motion, but she still rolled too much. There was more weight topside than usual, just too many bodies on deck. He was reluctant to dump the dead. Pack altered the course toward the Danco Coast. He thought he might find smoother water nearer a lee shore.

Without charts to show the new coastline, navigation close to any coast was too dangerous. Pack finally hove to with *Quest*'s blunt bow into the swells. He waited awhile for a possible shift of wind.

The long afternoon passed slowly with little change of

wind. Ray Godney and *Sinbad*'s cooks and stewards did what they could to provide coffee and sandwiches for the crowd. Few could eat anything. Everybody able to do so tried to help others. They were thankful to be alive and yearned to get back to the comfort of *Sinbad*.

As the polar night brought darkness, the wind subsided. Pack resumed the southerly course, moving cautiously, sounding constantly, and checking all possible radar targets. He stopped frequently as the baffling shorelines made progress too dangerous. He would take no risks with his precious cargo.

The short night finally ended and the grey dawn brought the outline of the high peaks of Wiencke Island into focus off our starboard side. *Quest* picked up speed as Captain Pack guided her between bitsy bergs and heavy pack ice with a practised hand.

Finally, we rounded Cape Errera and headed toward Biscoe Bay. When *Sinbad* came into view, there was a great shout of joy by everybody who could stand up and look over the bulwarks. As we came closer, each ship sounded three long blasts of welcome. Pack moved *Quest* in slowly, seeking a good anchorage. Everyone on *Sinbad* was standing on her decks waving. There, in the morning mist, the whole surviving throng of passengers, scientists, and seamen, from ships and shore, shouted and waved.

There were laughter and tears on the faces of many. One of those weeping was Carol Moore, holding tightly to the rail of the forward deck. I knew it was very difficult for her.

When *Quest* anchored, all those passengers still alive were quickly taken to their staterooms on *Sinbad*. The dead were buried on Anvers Island, their graves marked with stones instead of crosses, since wood was scarce. There were no trees in the Antarctic, and we had no idea when any lumber might be obtained. Forests would probably rise some day, but for the present, we had to save all the wood we had.

The lofty ramparts of the peninsula provided a protected area for the USARPS and the two ships. They had been a defense against the worst of the swells which emanated from the Wedell Sea and the rest of the continent. But for that, our lives would have been lost.

The joyous reunion of scientists, passengers, and crews of *Sinbad, Quest,* and Palmer was an event for Antarctic historical records. In a region noted for its hospitality at lonely research stations never had there been such a celebration. Never had so many inexperienced persons survived such perils and hardships in polar seas. But despite the celebration, we were all painfully aware of the missing and the dead. Al Norwood, Carol Moore, and many others didn't participate in the festivities.

Sharing with the others a great feeling of relief and exhilaration, I busied myself with camera and notebook. Beebee happily accompanied me with her cassette recorder, and together we interviewed survivors. Talking first with the Palmer men, we recorded the full story of their harrowing experiences. Captain Gilbert filled in some of the gaps in my *Sinbad* story. He told of the heroic efforts of the crew which had managed to slow the flow of sea water into the ship so that the pumps could keep it afloat. He praised the passengers for their understanding and cooperation, and deplored the loss of lives of those who were blown off the iceberg.

Much later, I learned the details of Larry Field's disappearance from Palmer Station during the earthquakes. When he crawled into the collapsed, shaking building to search for the two graduate students, he was followed by the dog, Princesa. He struggled on, hoping to find the boys and save them, but he found no one. As he reached the area from which he thought their cries had come, he saw only a wide gaping chasm into which parts of the building and furnishings were sliding. He tried to turn back, but suddenly, a tremendous surge of ice laden water swept him toward the rift.

Among many objects dashed into the wreckage were the inflated zodiac, which had lost its outboard motor, and an empty oil drum. The zodiac came down on Larry and

Princesa. It cushioned the impact of the oil drum and other debris. Larry grabbed the stout rope painter of the boat and wrapped several turns of it around his body, tying it securely. He held the frightened dog under his strong left arm, and together, they were dragged into the rift with the zodiac. The great surging wave bore them along through the rift to the opposite side of the point, and out into ice-filled Arthur Harbor.

Fastened securely to the inflated plastic boat, sometimes on it, sometimes under it, man and dog were whirled, battered, buffeted, and nearly drowned. The great white ice-laden crests lifted and swept them northwestward toward Cape Monaco. Larry clung desperately to the rope, but as the hours passed, his strength waned. There was no respite from the tortuous swells.

Nearly unconscious and about to lose his hold on Princesa, Larry was beginning to give up the struggle when they were violently dashed upon the barren, rocky ground near the Cape. Larry was knocked unconscious, his collar bone cracked, his left leg broken. Princesa was beside him; the zodiac, bottom up, on top of them. They would surely have been bashed to death were it not for Larry's heavy clothing, Princesa's thick fur, and the inflated boat. As the swells subsided, they lay drenched and almost lifeless beneath the zodiac.

With the passing of the short period of semidarkness, and the dawning of day, Princesa began to stir. She wriggled out from under the overturned boat and limped, holding one foot off the ground, around the zodiac, sniffing at their strange surroundings. She went back under the boat several times, whimpering and trying to arouse Larry. He was so near death that he made no effort to respond to the dog's attempt to revive him.

So passed the day with Larry and Princesa on the coast of Anvers Island, some six miles west of Palmer, a bleak and forbidding area facing the turbulent Atlantic Ocean. The vast Marr Piedmont slope was still covered with snow and ice, moving fast toward the sea. Another day passed slowly, and Larry, breathing a little easier, found he could move one leg and one arm. He put his hand to his head and felt blood caked in his hair. He wiped the mixture of blood and salt from his cheeks. He heard Princesa outside, and tried to call to her, but couldn't make a sound. He heard the rush of water and ice down the slopes, and he shook with cold.

Gradually, Larry began to realize his perilous situation. With great effort, he succeeded in rolling over to a slightly higher part of the ground under the zodiac, where for the time being he got his broken leg out of the flow of water. As the days passed, Larry often thought of Carol, and despaired of ever seeing her again.

Larry didn't have the slightest idea of where he was. He suspected that he and Princesa were on some part of Anvers Island, but he couldn't be sure. He had a pocket knife and a lighter, so they wouldn't starve. Princesa searched the area for food. She found dead birds, seals, and some fish which had been washed up onto the land. By the time Larry was sufficiently recovered to drag himself out from under the zodiac, the dog had brought several carcasses of dead animals to their location, but it took Larry a long time to adjust his mental attitude and sample the dog's trophies.

Each day, Princesa wandered father away from Larry during her search for food. One day she came across a group of people, the survivors of the "maternity" raft and the motor lifeboat.

The storm had blown the motor lifeboat off the camp iceberg. Its anchor had dragged across the berg, and when it went over the edge, it hung vertically for awhile. The boat finally slipped down into the loose pack ice. There, in the lee of the iceberg, the two seamen who had sought shelter in the boat managed to float it upright.

After drifting awhile, they found themselves near the partly deflated "maternity" raft. With much effort, they succeeded in getting the motor started in the lifeboat. They took all the passengers out of the raft, including little Joe.

They weren't sure of where they were, but they could see land and a lee shore to the southwest. One of the seamen thought he recognized the mountains of Anvers Island, so they decided to go in that direction. It was a terrifying trip, pushing through rough pack and around large bergs. They finally got their boat to the Anvers coast at a point west of D'Abnour Bay, a forbidding shore, bordered by ice cliffs, and fringed by submerged rocks which the boat struck several times. By the time the survivors found a place where they could get ashore, the boat was leaking so badly that it was nearly swamped. Before it sank, they tossed the boat's equipment ashore— the remaining emergency provisions, cans of water, masts, boom and sail. They were on a small peninsula of barren rock worn smooth by glacier ice. Using the boat's sail and mast, they fashioned a scant shelter.

There were eleven survivors—six men, four women, and baby Joe Connally, a new native Antarctican. The men were Dr. Dearborn, Jerry Connally, and four seamen. The women were Joyce Dearborn, Lucille Connally, Helen Norwood, and Lorraine Jackson.

They soon saw that they had to find a means of moving farther in from the sea. The men examined the ice cliffs and found a place where, with great care and effort, they managed to get the party through the slopes beyond. They were on the northern end of Anvers Island, about thirty miles from Palmer. Day by day, they made a difficult southward trek over the melting snow of the Marr Piedmont, camping wherever they could find a suitable spot somewhere clear of ice. They had to take a circuitous route parallel to the island's west coast, carrying Lucille on a stretcher improvised from the sail.

One morning, when they were near Cape Monaco, they were suddenly startled by the barking of a dog. It was Princesa.

Jerry shouted, "Look! Look over there! It's a dog!"

"Be careful! You don't know where it comes from! It might be mad!" cautioned Dr. Dearborn.

But in a few minutes, their fears were dispelled. Limping and whimpering, Princesa came joyfully toward the party. She went from one to another trying to identify them. They were all strangers to Princesa, but she was happy to see anybody. They all hugged her and wondered where she had come from on the barren piedmont. After she had sniffed at each one, Princesa limped off a short distance and looked back at the group watching her. Then she came back to them. In a few moments, she went off again in the same direction, stopped and looked back. After she had done that a few times, Jerry said, "She wants us to follow her. I'm going to see what she wants."

"Don't go alone, for goodness sakes!" exclaimed Joyce.

A seaman went with Jerry and Princesa. Soon they came upon the overturned zodiac and Larry Fields, who was nearly dead, unable to move or talk. Jerry rushed back and shouted for Dr. Dearborn. Within a few minutes, he and nurse Jackson began to examine Larry and make him more comfortable.

The group moved to Larry's location and established a camp there. They ministered to Larry, giving him the best care they could. Dr. Dearborn also took care of Princesa's injured leg. The next day Larry was very weak, but he was able to talk. The party learned that he had been at Palmer Station when the earthquakes occurred. He didn't know whether Palmer Station still existed.

"I remember hearing about the radio reports when we were on the iceberg. There are men at Palmer. They're trying to move a helicopter to higher ground," said Jerry.

"What about Deception Island?" Larry's voice was very weak. "What have you heard about Research Vessel *Quest* in Deception Island?"

"Only that the ship is trapped at Deception Island, but safe," answered Jerry.

"My girl's on it." Larry struggled to get the words out.

"Carol. She—she probably thinks I'm a goner."

Dr. Dearborn and Jerry exchanged glances. Dr. Dearborn said, "OK, that's enough talk for now, Larry. You've got to get some rest. You've been through a lot."

Dearborn, Connally and the others decided that if they could take Larry, they would push on toward the former Palmer Station site to see what had happened there. They knew the USARPS had a radio.

"I've got to know what happened to Al," said Helen. Tears were in her eyes. "If only he had been with us in the 'maternity' raft!"

Joyce tried to comfort her. "Try not to worry, Helen. They've probably all been picked up by a ship by now."

The group made preparations to carry Larry on another improvised stretcher. With the help of the four seamen, the party started toward Palmer, some six miles away.

Suddenly, they heard a helicopter and saw it in the distance. It was *Southwind*'s chopper which had been repaired on *Sinbad*. The survivors waved and shouted. They soon knew that they had been seen. The chopper changed course and came toward them. Within the next hour, they were on *Sinbad*'s boat deck.

Word of the rescue was shouted from one end of the ship to the other. Carol Moore was asleep in one of *Sinbad*'s cabins when Larry was lifted out of the helicopter on a stretcher. All he could say was, "Carol—Carol—where's Carol?"

Beebee was with the crowd which surrounded the helicopter when Larry was lifted out. She nearly fainted when she saw him. She rushed to the cabin and awakened Carol.

"Carol—Carol," she shouted. "Carol, get up! Get up quick! Go up on the boat deck!" Carol thought Beebee had gone berserk. She quickly smoothed her clothes and straightened her hair and climbed the stairway to the boat deck. The moment she stepped outside, she heard Larry's voice calling her. She rushed aft and pushed through the crowd standing around the chopper and Larry's stretcher on the deck. In a moment, Carol had Larry's head in her arms, laughing and crying.

"Larry! Oh, my God! Larry! Oh, my darling! Are you all right? I—I thought you were—Oh, Larry!"

Princesa limped over to Carol, whimpered, and licked her face. Carol hugged the dog.

Dr. Dearborn told Carol that Larry would be all right, and would soon walk again. He said, "You have that dog to thank. She saved his life."

Carol kissed Larry's face, and hugged Princesa over and over again. Larry was taken to the ship's hospital where Dr. Raymond and Carol took over his care immediately, giving nurse Jackson and Dr. Dearborn a much needed rest.

Al Norwood, who was ashore, came running to the landing place. He saw Helen at *Sinbad*'s railing. They waved and shouted happy greetings across the water between ship and shore. Within minutes, Al got out to the ship. It was a while before he could find Helen. She had gone down one stairway as he went up another. They went up and down and through alleyways on opposite sides of the ship calling each other. Al got himself completely lost and wound up in the ship's laundry, where the Chinese laundrymen were eating their lunch with their chopsticks, sitting cross-legged on the deck around a large bowl of food. Al stumbled and fell into the bowl in his haste to get out of there.

Meanwhile, Helen had gone back up to the boat deck looking for him. Several other passengers joined in the search. Finally, Al appeared in the main lounge, smelling of sweet and sour pork. Helen wiped off his face with a napkin and kissed him.

Al said, "Where the hell have you been?" Helen didn't smell very good either, but after a few belts of bourbon, neither seemed to mind.

Later, when Larry Field was stronger, I interviewed him about his ordeal with Princesa on Anvers Island. I also interviewed Jerry Connally and Dr. Dearborn and recorded the details of their rescue and long hard trek across Anvers Island. Their little group, which had been blown off the iceberg in the "maternity" raft, hadn't suffered many injuries due to the excellent foresight of the two *Sinbad* seamen in their raft. The seamen had lashed them all securely as the storm came upon them. Joined later by the two hardy seamen with the motor lifeboat, they had all made their escape safely from the treacherous sea. Little Joe Connally, "son of the storm," weathered the escapade with great success. He yelled his head off most of the time, giving his little lungs a good start for a useful life ahead.

One night, Elbow Larsen, Art Allen and I were sitting in the *Sinbad* main lounge having coffee when Brenda and Marjory happened to stroll in out of the darkness.

"Come and sit with us," said Elbow. "We need some good-looking company."

"Don't look at me," said Brenda. She had finally recovered from her illness but was still pale and thin. She and Marjory ordered soft drinks and sandwiches.

"You look much better than when you came aboard *Quest*," remarked Elbow.

"I hope so," said Brenda. "Don't remind me."

"She's doing fine," said Marjory.

Beebee Abbey walked by our window taking a stroll on deck. I saw her profile for a moment by the light from our window. *Sinbad* had only a few deck lights on in order to save fuel.

I said, "I wonder where Beebee's going?"

"Who knows, Jamie," said Elbow. "Probably off to tell somebody about worms or shrimps or something else she's pulled up off the bottom. She told a good one last Christmas on *Quest* when we were in Deception. Remember, Jamie? She said she was out in a small boat with her friends. They were collecting marine biological specimens somewhere around the Panamanian coast. They were using a small dredge or grab, and they pulled up a woman's hand with a diamong ring on it."

Brenda choked on her sandwich. Marjory patted her on

the back. Art called the steward for a glass of water. Brenda took a few swallows and regained her composure. "Who was it—said that?" she gasped when she got her voice back.

"Dr. Belle Abbey—Beebee—she just went along the deck," replied Elbow.

Brenda said, "Oh, I—I don't know her."

"She's a biologist who was on board *Quest.* A fine person. If she comes back this way, I'll introduce you," I said. Beebee did come back through the lounge in a few minutes. I called to her. "Come on, Beebee, and join the party."

"Coming," said Beebee.

Elbow, Art, and I rose and made the introduction. Beebee sat down and ordered coffee.

"You folks getting rested up?" asked Beebee. "You're looking better, Miss—ah—?"

"Clarke. Brenda Clarke," said Art. "She's from New Orleans."

Elbow smiled and said, "Dr. Abbey has a reputation for telling stories. She told us some good ones while we were stuck in Whalers Bay."

"Well," responded Beebee, "we have to get some fun out of work. I keep so many records and make so many dull reports that I have a lot of material to draw on for stories."

Marjory asked, "When you pick up specimens from the bottom of the sea, do you keep records of all your work— like what they are, and where you find them?"

"We sure do," replied Beebee. "We even put down the latitude and longitude. I have a record book dating over five years back showing exactly where we've worked, mostly here in the Antarctic and in Panama where I have a home, or should I say, *had* a home. I'm afraid it's washed away, or flooded over now."

Brenda said, "That's awful. I hope not. I wish I knew more about oceanography. It sounds so interesting."

Beebee said, "You should get acquainted with my assistant, Carol Moore. She's pretty good on worms. Got a big one on her hook right here.''

"Carol Moore?"

"Yes, she's about to get married, it seems. I'll introduce you, if she and her fiancé, Larry, come around. He's still on crutches.''

Brenda was thinking hard. Maybe Dr. Abbey had a record of where she found that hand in that book she mentioned. Maybe, just maybe, that satchel with all the jewels could be located. Aloud, she said, "I wonder about our homes. Marjory's from London and I'm from New Orleans. I've heard they no longer exist.''

Elbow said, "You may as well think about settling down here. All you travel girls can help increase the population here. Anyway, it's going to be a long time before we can go anywhere, and from what we hear, the whole world is coming apart right now, except here.''

"This is OK in the summer,'' said Beebee, "but I like lots of sunlight, and we'll only have it here for about half of the year.''

"I don't mind the twilight,'' said Art. "Especially now that it's warm. When we used to have real darkness with the temperature below zero, and blizzards, and high snow drifts, that was grim, but this nice spring climate is fine. I wish my family was here to enjoy it. They're all alive. They were taken out to sea by a friend on his ship and stayed in the Bermuda Triangle. When I finally got through by radio, and talked with my wife, Marilyn, she told me all about it. I wouldn't mind bringing my family here and help develop this fine land when we get some transportation again.''

Marjory said, "I'd like to go back to England for a while to see my family. I imagine they were all in the floods, and I don't exactly know whether they got out in time. The radio operators have had great difficulty in arranging communication with England. I pray that my family is all right. I wouldn't mind coming back here, but I would like to go home for awhile.''

Brenda was silent. She was thinking about the possibility of getting information from Beebee, or from Beebee's records, about where she picked up the woman's hand.

Elbow urged, "Beebee, why don't you tell us more about finding that hand with the diamond ring on the finger. You took it to the police, didn't you?"

"Yes," said Beebee. "I don't think I mentioned, though, that we also pulled up a small satchel full of jewelry. It came up at the same time as the hand. The hand and the satchel belonged to a costume jewelry salesman killed in a plane crash, and both the diamond ring and the jewels were phony. The hand was plastic. I didn't get a chance to finish the story Christmas night in Whalers Bay."

Brenda didn't choke on anything that time. She simply shuddered, got goose bumps all over and didn't say a word.

I had noticed Brenda's reactions all through Beebee's story. At the time, I didn't think anything of it. But as the days passed, I learned that Captain Gilbert had received an urgent radio message from a Hugh Daly somewhere in the United States. Daly was concerned about his brother, Victor. He told Gilbert about the threat on Victor's life which Hugh had learned from Coco Solare. He also confirmed reports about the devastation of New York City.

Gilbert recounted the events surrounding Victor's strange disappearance and the subsequent discovery of his skeleton. The exchange of information between Captain Gilbert and Hugh Daly prompted a further investigation into the deaths of Victor P. Daly, Teresa Solare Rossi, and Anthony Destefani. The investigation resulted in Brenda's admission of the information Tony had given her about Bailey's death, the return of Victoria Degrelle's brooch, and the contract on Victor Daly. The details of Teresa's and Victor's deaths were never resolved. There remained many questions in Brenda's mind about Tony. Perhaps it was he that pushed Bailey over the rail. Maybe Tony had lied in saying he thought he saw Teresa do it. And maybe Teresa had had second thoughts about the brooch and returned it herself to Victoria's cabin. Maybe Tony had lied about that too. Brenda would never know the truth. Her memories of the late Tony Destefani would be shrouded in doubt forever.

10

LARRY FIELD hobbled along *Sinbad*'s promenade deck on his crutches. He had an important matter to discuss with the captain—namely marriage.

"Marriage?" echoed Captain Gilbert. "You want to get *married*?"

Larry had decided to ask Captain Gilbert if he would consider tying Carol and him together with a real seaman-like hitch, or, say, a nice reef knot.

"Why me?" asked Captain Gilbert. "Why not our minister, Mr. Connally? He can do a better job than I can."

"Well, you see, Captain," Larry said with some discomfort, "it's like this. Carol's a Catholic and I'm a Protestant. I was thinking, maybe, we should just have a sort of civil wedding, and leave religion out of it."

"Hmm," murmured the skipper. "Let me think about it awhile. I suppose if I performed the ceremony and entered it in the ship's log book, it might be considered legal—that is, if we were out at sea. But here, we are in the Antarctic, and no country has any territorial jurisdiction. There's really no civil government here. So how can you have a civil wedding?"

"Isn't it the same as being out at sea?" asked Larry.

"Well, I wouldn't say so really. We are anchored at Anvers Island."

"Isn't there any authority here, or say, here on the ship

—I mean civil authority? Aren't you the civil authority on board your ship?''

"Hmm—ah, yes, I'm the authority here, and I suppose you could say I'm 'civilized,' or I try to be. But you—you are not really on my ship. You are neither a passenger nor a member of the crew. I would say offhand, that you don't come under my authority. You are a—a—you are really an Anti-American, I mean an *Antarctic*-American—wouldn't you say? My ship is under Norwegian registration—the Norwegian flag. I don't think I could rightfully marry a couple of Americans. Maybe George Reszke could help you. Or try Captain Pack. He's a real stout character, you know, real stout,'' Gilbert laughed.

"Jumpin' jupiter!'' exclaimed Larry. "What complications! Well, thanks, Captain. I didn't know we'd run into such difficulties. I'll see what I can do with George Reszke. Thanks just the same.''

Captain Gilbert hated to disappoint Larry, or anyone else, but he didn't want to be involved in any matter in which there was some question of legality.

Larry left *Sinbad* and sought out George Reszke. George was in charge of Palmer Station, now many feet below the surface, but George was still in charge of the Palmer personnel. Could George be considered the civil authority? Larry decided to talk to him.

"I wouldn't go so far as to claim that,'' said George in reply to Larry's question. "I haven't been authorized by the U.S. Government to act as civil authority. I was manager of Palmer Station, that's true, but the station no longer exists. Even if it did, I don't think I ever had any authority to perform marriages.''

"Holy smoke!'' said Larry. "How can anybody get married around here?''

"I'm sorry, Larry,'' aid George. "Maybe you'll just have to postpone it until you get back home.''

Back home, thought Larry. Who knows when, if ever, that will be! His plans for a quick wedding were beginning to crumble. He had hoped for a nice wedding ceremony, a reception on board *Sinbad*, and to have all arrangements settled as soon as he could walk without crutches. Now he would have to start all over again with Captain Pack. He wondered what the answer would be. He didn't even know what Carol would say, but he lost no time in asking Captain Pack if he would perform the wedding ceremony.

"Now, Larry," Captain Pack said solemnly, "I would be glad to do anything I could for you and Carol, but I can't handle a matter of that kind. The law would permit me to marry someone at sea, but not in port. I'm sorry, but that's the situation. I suggest you try *Sinbad*'s minister, Mr. Connally."

Larry explained his reason for not wanting a religious wedding. He didn't get much sympathy from Icepack on that score. It looked to Larry as if he would have to see Jerry Connally after all, but first he had to talk it over with Carol.

Carol said she didn't see why it mattered. "If Mr. Connally will marry us, it will be fine with me. Go ahead and ask him."

Larry went back on board *Sinbad* to find Jerry Connally. He was told that the Connallys were in the main lounge. Larry shook hands and sat down at Jerry's invitation.

"I'm sorry to bother you," Larry began, "but I have a problem, and possibly you can help me solve it."

"I will be glad to try," Jerry said cordially.

"Well, my problem is this. I'm Protestant, and my fiancée is Catholic. We want to get married, but we don't want a religious wedding—if you know what I mean."

"I don't see that as much of a problem," Jerry was encouraging.

"No?"

"No, I don't. I will be glad to perform a nonsectarian marriage service. Just you name the date and time."

Larry exclaimed, "That's great! Maybe you know my fiancée. Her name is Carol Moore."

"Sorry, Larry, I don't think I met her. I've had my

hands full helping with the care of the injured people, as well as my wife and new son."

"Well, anyway, I'll bring Carol on board and we'll arrange all the details."

Jerry said, "That's fine. I'm an ordained minister licensed by the State of New York to perform marriages. You and Carol just bring me your marriage license, and it won't take long."

"Marriage license?" Larry was bewildered. "You mean we have to get a *marriage license?*"

"Yes, Larry. I can't marry you unless you show me your marriage license."

You could have knocked Larry over with a snowflake. "Marriage license! Where the heck can we get a marriage license around here, for Pete's sake?"

"You have to go to the civil authorities, whoever they are. I'm sorry, Larry. I haven't been around here long enough to know anything about that. You'll have to handle that part yourself." Larry thanked Jerry and hobbled off in a perplexed state over the marriage license question.

As *Sinbad*'s "sky pilot," it had been Jerry Connally's duty to conduct a nonsectarian service on Sundays. The services had been suspended during the emergency situation, but with everything under control, they were again scheduled on a regular basis. Jerry planned a Sunday service for all the *Sinbad* survivors, Palmer USARPS, and *Quest* personnel together for the first time. He posted a notice on the bulletin board that the service would be held at 1400.

After lunch that Sunday, I joined Elbow Larsen, George Barry, Clarence Dearborn, and John Powell, Palmer's meteorologist, who were strolling on *Sinbad*'s promenade deck. Our conversation was animated.

"I'm wondering about the temperatures," reflected Dr. Barry. "Since the poles will be receiving more direct heat from the sun and the temperate climate in the U.S. will receive less, my opinion at first was that it would be abnormally cold in the northern states."

"So it is," said John. "From the radio reports we've been getting, it's much colder than ever before. But I have some thoughts, too, about the long range effect of this change."

"So have I," said Barry, "but go ahead."

"Well, as we know, ever since the earthquakes and outpourings of volcanic heat, we have seen those clouds of vapor racing northward."

"I know exactly what you're coming to," said Larsen. "At least, I think I do."

"So," continued John, "they must be carrying a lot of heat. Maybe we'll have a steam heated planet!"

"Yes, but how long will it last?" I asked.

Dr. Barry said, "it will eventually drop to the surface."

"Sure," said John, "but more keeps rising, too. The sun pulls, I believe, some sixteen million tons of water vapor per second up off the earth's surface into the atmosphere. Now, I may be wrong, but I'll venture to say this much: our planet will probably acquire a more temperate climate all over."

"Yes, you may be right—the greenhouse effect!" declared Clarence. "We may have an atmosphere somewhat more dense, which may tend to distribute the heat more evenly over the entire surface of the earth, like a canopy."

"It shouldn't take too long to find out," said Dr. Barry. "We're getting closer to the vernal equinox. It's cooling off some now, but only a few degrees. We're not having the cold we would normally have here. Actually, this is a very comfortable temperature, and if all the ice melts, it will probably remain temperate all winter."

"Remember, there were some seven million cubic miles of ice here," stated Larsen. "It will take some time for all of it to melt and spread over the world. Then there's all that ice in Greenland and over the Arctic Ocean. The sun will heat that up some too. I wonder if there will be other forces such as we have had here — earthquakes and volcanoes.

"We'll just have to wait and see," said John.

"Meanwhile," said Barry, "we should plan our future. I, for one, intend to stay right here. As a matter of fact, it will be a long time, maybe years, before we can go anywhere else, even if we would like to, with all transportation stopped and ocean navigation so difficult for our ships."

As we walked along the deck and the scientists aired their views, trying to analyze and comprehend the tremendous events which had taken place, people were gathering on the boat deck to hear what Jerry had to say.

Elbow suggested, "Let's go up and listen to Jerry."

"I'm with you," said Dr. Barry.

"Lead on," said John. We went up to the boat deck.

As two o'clock drew near, the boat deck was filled to overflowing. Never before had so many passengers showed up for Jerry's talks. There were, of course, a number who had no use whatever for such events, but that time even the skeptics came. There were many bandages among the group. Several people were on crutches made by *Sinbad*'s carpenter. Others were too severely injured to leave the hospital.

Nearly all the Palmer survivors came, and the crew of *Quest* was well represented. Captain Pack and Captain Gilbert stood together at the after end of the deck.

Jerry started with a short prayer of thanks, something in which we could all participate with good reason. He began his talk by recalling Dr. Barry's lecture at "Camp Courage" on the iceberg. Jerry smiled and waved to George Barry and Elbow. "Many of us have wondered about these events which Dr. Barry had chosen to call 'disaster.' According to my way of thinking, and from my studies during several years, I cannot subscribe totally to Dr. Barry's terms.

"Undoubtedly, these events—the increased tilt of the

earth—the earthquakes and eruptions—on such a large scale are, to my thinking, a manifestation of the tremendous power of God." Jerry glanced at Phil Cavige, but Phil kept quiet.

"Diaster?" Jerry remarked. "It depends on several factors. For some it may be just the opposite. Let's look at the bright side. We have heard these broadcasts from home about the terrible floods, but what have we had during the past several decades? Look at the flood of wars since nineteen fourteen. We are hearing now that the mechanized military forces, the navies, armies and air forces of the world may no longer be any threat to world peace because of fuel shortage. That, to me, is no disaster, but just the opposite. Some of us have heard the scientists mention that the temperate climates, such as we have in our northern states, may turn much colder in winter. Living there could be almost impossible, with the sun moving so much farther from the equator each season. I understand that many of you do not take that seriously, however. But I just want to mention something which I think you may find interesting. According to Scripture, at one time a vast canopy of water vapor existed in the atmosphere. Now, I don't pretend to be a scientist, but I understand such a canopy might cause a 'greenhouse effect,' a diffusion of the sun's heat, so that it would be scattered more evenly over the whole surface of the globe, giving it all a temperate climate, including both the Antarctic and the Arctic regions. Just look up there now, at all that mist and vapor flowing away from this polar area toward the north." He motioned with a wide sweep of his arm to the great expanse overhead where a steady movement of vapor could be seen moving northward across the sky.

Already veiled from the sun's rays, the temperature remained in a comfortable range of fifteen to twenty degrees Celsius under the warm vapor cover when norm   the temperature in the polar regions would be freezing. Indeed, there had already been a marvelous and comfortable change.

Jerry experienced a surge of enthusiasm and confidence, a sudden new strength of purpose. It seemed to him that he was being directed by an unseen prompter. He stood tall in his open-necked sport shirt and slacks, on a wooden grating about a foot above the deck. He looked like any other young man; somebody who might mow your lawn, deliver your groceries, or sit at a bar and have a highball with you. He looked more like a cowhand than a preacher. A small Bible stuck out of his hip pocket, which he said was more potent than a pistol. He made a "fast draw" and, turning its pages, he read some passages such as *"vapors to ascend from the extremities of the earth,"* and *"anguish of nations, not knowing the way out because of the roaring of the sea and its agitation."*

Jerry's audience seemed unimpressed. Phil Cavige exploded a loud "hogwash" and some people started to leave. But Jerry had a full head of steam, and believing so intensely in this theme, he was conveying his enthusiasm to some of the blasé listeners, even against their inclinations.

"And now," Jerry continued, "I don't claim that what I have just read refers specifically to what we see today, but it does mention anguish, which means trouble, and believe me, our globe is sure having that, and more! I can't say it will happen, but I believe my theories point to a happy future for humanity."

Some of those about to leave sat down again. Could it be that this guy had something worth listening to?

Jerry resumed with a broad grin. "I think we may have, in the end, a very desirable situation on this planet. With the rise in ocean levels, and flooding over all seaports and all coastal areas, the people who managed to survive will surely have experienced such distress that they may become less greedy, less nationalistic, and more reasonable. Faltering governments, incapable of making war, may bow to an upsurge of honesty and cooperation. We have heard that great famines and pestilence are destroying vast populations. Much land has been inundated, but with the diffusion and spreading of the sun's heat, much land in both polar regions will again become inhabited as it was at some time in the past, according to well documented scientific records. As for me and my family, we will be glad to stay right here in the Antarctic and help in the development of these beautiful lands. To that end, I would like to make a few practical suggestions. I think we should form a temporary committee to supervise the establishment of a more permanent governing body. Whoever would like to do so, please volunteer or suggest the names of persons you would like to have on that committee. Let me have a show of hands and I will write down the names now."

Several hands went up. Those who volunteered or were named immediately included Dr. Clarence Dearborn, Captain Ivan Gilbert, Arthur Allen, Dr. George Barry, Dr. Beebee Abbey, Captain Isaac Pack, Dr. Elbano Larsen, Alfred Norwood, Jerry Connally and George Reszke. Upon hearing their names, the captains of both ships declined, excusing themselves because of their responsibilities to their vessels. That left a preliminary committee of eight with Jerry as temporary chairman until such time as a more permanent supervisory body could be elected.

The committee held its first meeting immediately after Jerry had finished his talk. The first order of business was to ask for nominations for a permanent chairman. Al Norwood immediately nominated Dr. Barry and his nomination was seconded by Arthur Allen. Arthur himself was nominated by George Reszke, and seconded by Dr. Barry, and so it went. Finally, the nominations of Barry, Allen, and also Reszke, were put to a vote. It was obvious that Dr. Barry would be favored because of his years of experience in the Antarctic. He immediately appointed committees to handle pressing matters.

The meeting was held with all the people present, and

Dr. Barry briefly stated his views and asked everyone to cooperate and to make their desires known to appropriate committee members.

"First, I wish to thank everyone for the confidence you have shown in me by electing me chairman. We will continue to hold meetings and decide our future procedures. Please feel free to express your views. I hope all of us can work together to make our lives safe and comfortable."

His words drew applause, and there seemed to be unanimous approval of Dr. Barry for the chairmanship. The governing body immediately set to work to list the various problems and items for discussion. One of the most important and urgent was to establish an area onshore where all of us could find safety in the event of having to abandon *Sinbad* and *Quest*.

The Antarctic Continent was still in a state of instability. Ice and snow was disappearing from the peninsula and the islands, but the vast plateau still held a great quantity which was melting and flowing away in torrents from all sides. We decided to continue with the establishment of a village on the slopes of Mount William where the USARPS were already camped. Later, the helicopter would be flown over the mainland, and a survey would be made of the conditions there.

Dr. Larsen, Arthur Allen and George Reszke were appointed a committee to establish the shore facility. Al Norwood, Dr. Dearborn and Jerry Connally were appointed to draw up a list of matters to be considered in order of priority. Everyone was anxious for more information about conditions at home and that was first on the list. The three industrious "wire men," Ole Magnussen, who had also survived the ordeal of the iceberg camp, Ira Mason and Enrique Salaverry, were urged to pool their expertise and make every effort to establish a reliable channel of communications through ham or other broadcasting operations, wherever they could. Ed McCaughlin, because of his family ties in broadcasting, offered his services and knowledge of the industry to obtain and disseminate information regarding families, friends, and conditions at home and prepare news bulletins. It was because of Ed, and through his contacts in the United States, that I was able to find out what had happened in Washington, New York, and in many other parts of the country, as well as the world.

Both Captain Gilbert and Captain Pack had turned down all suggestions that either ship attempt to reach South America or any other continent. Even if their ships hadn't been damaged, they considered it highly imprudent to attempt voyages without accurately tabulated positions of celestial bodies. And even if they had such tabulations, there were no ports to which they could take their ships. Extensive uncharted alterations in coastlines would make approaches to any land very hazardous. All charts were obsolete. Until more information became available, both captains considered their vessels and people in safer waters where they were anchored.

Within a week, with the help of many willing hands, a small village was established within a quarter mile of the anchorage, on the western slope of Mount William. It was determined that the location was about three hundred feet above the original sea level, between what had been Biscoe Point and Access Point. Both those points of land on Anvers Island had disappeared beneath the rising waters. It was considered that even if all the ice of the Antarctic should melt, which seemed quite likely, our refuge would be above water. With the five thousand foot heights of Mount William sloping toward Cape Lancaster to the southeast, and Mount Moberly to the north, we seemed to be protected from disturbances over on the mainland, and we could quickly move higher if necessary.

Dr. Barry, Dr. Larsen, and Dr. Enrico Monelli, Palmer's geologist, formed themselves into a committee to find, when possible, a suitable location on the mainland to establish a permanent living area. There had to be land on

294

which to grow crops. Arthur Allen made a suggestion which was immediately put into practice. Seeds would be carefully removed from vegetables and fruits before cooking and would be kept for planting. Considering the large supplies of provisions on each ship, enough for over a year, we would have a fair quantity of seeds to plant whenever a suitable area was chosen.

An appropriate name for our first village on Anvers Island was discussed at length. Many names were suggested. The most acceptable turned out to be Palmer Village.

One day, Ed McCaughlin, Joseph Melba, John Panola, and Jerry Connally were busy with shovels and picks digging steps out of the hard ground to make access from the water's edge up the village.

"We'll have to get Hank Osborn to rig us up a flagpole," said Joe.

"What for?" asked Ed.

"What for? For flying a flag, of course."

"What flag?" Jerry asked.

Joe hesitated. "Well, the American flag, I guess. What else? We're Americans, aren't we?"

"Yeah, but as I understand it," said Ed, "no country has any territorial right here in the Antarctic."

They were joined by Dr. Barry and John Powell. "That's right," said Dr. Barry. "And any measures of a military nature are prohibited by the treaty signed in nineteen fifty-nine by twelve governments."

"You mean we can't even fly a flag?" asked Joe.

"No, I didn't say that," replied Dr. Barry. "But we come from so many different countries, which flag would we fly? We have people here from England, France, Germany, Russia, China, Japan, Argentina, Chile, Mexico and other countries, as well as from the USA. *Sinbad* is a Norwegian ship. So I really think we're better off without any flag. If we put up an American flag, someone might resent it."

"That sure makes sense," said Jerry. "Flags represent

nations, and from what we see in the news bulletins, nations and countries are folding up—governments are dying.''

''How's about designing our own flag?'' suggested Ed.

''That's a good idea,'' said John.

''Flags don't unite people,'' Jerry said. ''Any more than the United Nations ever united people. Flags and nations are like religions; they don't unite people. On the contrary, they separate them.''

''Maybe we could design a flag that would represent the whole world,'' said John. ''Something like the United Nations' flag.''

''Yeah,'' Joe said. ''Only that never included all the nations. Some were in and some were out, and they never could agree.''

''Well, you try to figure out some flag or emblem which stands for world peace, and I'll certainly go along with you,'' agreed Jerry. He then went on up the hill.

John, deep in thought, made circles on the ground with the toe of his boot. ''You know what I'm doing?'' he said with a grin. ''I'm designing a flag.''

''Looks like a bunch of basketballs to me,'' laughed Ed.

''Basketballs!'' John snapped his fingers. ''That's it! Basketball! Swimming! Diving! Gymnastics! The Olympics! That's it. The Olympic flag!'' John was excited, ''Why not?'' he shouted. ''That's our flag! Why not adapt the Olympic flag with its five circles? They represent continents, not nations. They stand for peace and cooperation, don't they?''

Dr. Barry was delighted with John's suggestion. He said he would get the full approval of the governing body at the next meeting. ''Only I think there should be six circles in our flag, one for the Antarctic,'' he said. ''Six circles would then include all the continents.''

Helen Norwood designed the flag. It featured six entwined circles of various colors forming a larger circle on a sky blue field.

Surprisingly, Palmer Village took shape rapidly. Using

dunnage lumber, pallets, and canvas from *Sinbad*, huts were erected. We had our problems, but we had people of many trades and talents among the scientists, passengers, and crews. I kept busy every day interviewing people and chronicling our progress and the events that occurred. I overheard many discussions about a variety of subjects.

One morning, Doc Schaeffer was making his rounds of the village. As the official medical officer at Palmer Village, he made certain to visit his charges each day and check on their health. I accompanied him on some of his rounds.

Hank Osborn was sounding off in front of his small machine shop. "Why don't you people talk about something else? I've had enough about floods and disasters. I've lost all my people too, but I'm thinkin' about the future. We all know the earth has had a bad time."

"Yup, I'll say," Doc Schaeffer agreed pleasantly. We watched as Hank wired an electric light socket to a pipe. He was setting up a row of lights along the main path. Daylight was limited to about five hours per day. The Antarctic would be in semidarkness until the following September. Then the sun would return and gradually bring light again. Meanwhile, Palmer Village had to have light, and *Sinbad*'s generators would supply the current until Palmer's generators could be salvaged.

Doc said, "Hank, you better come by the clinic in a little while and let me change that bandage."

"Right, Doc."

We then went next door where Art Allen had a small laboratory with the precious stock of seeds stored in plastic containers. Art, in his usual orderly manner, had the containers all clearly labelled and arranged on shelves. Each day he received a new supply of seeds from the cooks on the ships. He carefully dried them and added them to the stock. Art said hopefully, "They'll provide a good garden when the sun comes back, say around September."

Dr. Arnold Varany, Dr. Nancy Varany and Jean and Bill Bush were also enthusiastic gardeners and worked along with Art in the necessary agricultural effort.

"Arnold, how ya doin'?" Doc asked cordially.

"OK, Stan," replied Dr. Varany. He held a small container of soil which he and Art had been testing. "You will be pleased to know that we think we may have picked out a good spot for a garden. There used to be a penguin rookery on Biscoe Point, and I think this area is well fertilized."

"Good," said Doc. "We need good news."

Our next call was on Ira Mason and Ed McCaughlin who were busy at the shore radio station a few short steps up the hill. Ed showed Stanley Schaeffer the last radio news bulletin. Doc passed it to me. As usual the news was all bad.

Dr. Schaeffer, remembering Hank Osborne's remark, said, "Ed, why don't you keep these bulletins to yourself. Our people have heard so much bad news from home, why not just hold off for a while and let them rest their minds? It may do them some good."

Ed was silent for a moment. "I hope I won't be accused of withholding the news," he said. "What do you think, Jamie?"

"Well, that's hard to say. But Doc does have a point," I said.

Dr. Schaeffer smiled, "You mean I might be interfering with—ah—the 'freedom of the press'?"

"Well, no, not exactly," replied Ed.

"No," said Doc, "I'm just referring to all this disaster news which has overwhelmed us for so many weeks now. Any special emergency items might be handed to Dr. Dearborn and Dr. Raymond on *Sinbad*, or Captain Pack on *Quest*, and to me here on shore. We might just hold it from certain individuals until they have recovered. The anguish of the past few weeks has been too much for some of them."

"OK," said Ed, "we can try it. I think it might be a subject for the committee to discuss so there can be no mis-understanding about it. Here's an earlier bulletin. Take it along with the one I just gave you and see what the others think about it."

The good doctor and I read over the bulletin. It was a continuation of news about the virtual destruction of the world. Practically all governments had collapsed. Chaos and ruin stalked the whole of planet Earth—except the Antarctic. It would take years to make even a rough estimate of the number of persons killed. Perhaps many of those now at Palmer Village would never learn the facts about their relatives or friends.

Dr. Schaeffer put both bulletins in his pocket and continued his calls. Our next stop was at John Powell's weather station.

"How's the weather, John?"

"Don't ask me, Doc. I thought I had learned something about meteorology, but this is something the book scribblers never conjured up." He pointed to his temperature graphs. "We haven't had over six degrees drop in temperature since the sun left us last month. Right now, it's fifteen degrees Celsius, and we're near the middle of winter!"

Palmer Village grew and prospered. The long flat slope of Anvers Island was cleared and produced a good vegetable crop. The ship's reefers were filled, from time to time, with fresh edibles from both land and sea.

As months went by, the earth began to recover and the survivors busied themselves with the work of rehabilitation. The scars of their ordeal were deep and their attitudes were changed. Vice and corruption weren't resumed because the people had no inclination to return to their former brutal and competitive methods. Military organizations were abolished, and the terrible threat of war and profit from manufacture of military equipment were eliminated.

The great burdens of nationalism and religion were angrily attacked by those very forces on which they had thrived. Their false and idolatrous edifices, images, and treasure hoards were destroyed. No longer did the people salute their flags and intone, "One nation under God." Instead, it was, as in the beginning, "one *world* under God."

As time passed, we all became aware that our attitudes toward one another were changing. Personal animosities were forgotten, and an atmosphere of cooperation and mutual respect prevailed. Phil Cavige couldn't resist an occasional "hogwash," but he no longer sneered when he said it. Dr. Barry was relieved to see Emma Cavige and Victoria Degrelle playing bridge peacefully. Victoria's brooch was back in her possession. Harmony prevailed at Palmer Village. There was really nothing to quarrel about any more.

Oh yes! Larry and Carol finally got married. After Dr. Barry was appointed chairman of the governing body, he issued them a marriage license. When Larry asked him about it, Dr. Barry said, "With such a large collection of PhDs around this place, I don't see why we can't come up with some scheme to get you two spliced. This PhD is going to do something about it PDQ!" So he sat right down and wrote out a marriage license for them.

Jerry Connally performed the ceremony in the small Palmer Village square with the entire population of the great Continent of Antarctica present at the wedding. An uproarious reception followed in *Sinbad*'s main lounge. The activity touched off an epidemic of weddings among the *Sinbad*, *Quest*, and Palmer "Antarcticans." Beebee and I were among the first. Our wedding was another excuse for a wild celebration. There was a lot of good natured conviviality spiced with facetious remarks. Harry King, *Quest*'s mate, said I only married Beebee for her cassette recorder. Capt. Pack said Beebee only needed me to help her stuff worms in her jars, now that Carol had caught herself a worm of her own, too big to classify.

The demands on Jerry Connally to perform weddings was so great that they had to be scheduled a week apart, so that the rest of us "Antarcticans" could recuperate between them.

Ed McCaughlin's marriage to Marjory Dumont was followed by that of Brenda Clarke to Jon Rankin. Brenda's torch for Tony Destefani had quickly burned out when she met Jon. Victoria Degrelle's interest in marriage had apparently been abated by her five previous attachments, but she maintainted a constant preference for Dr. Barry. He had other matters on his mind however, and did not encourage her.

Mike Vogt finally took me into his confidence, and told me what his differences with Per Thysen had been all about. "I haven't heard anything about my sister in New York," Mike said. "She was married to Per Thysen's twin brother, who was arrested for smuggling a few years ago. They split up. Thysen and I often argued about them. He claimed his brother was framed. I wonder if my sister is still alive."

My love and admiration for Beebee grew stronger day by day. We enjoyed each other's company, and spent many happy hours exchanging pleasantries and philosophical reflections. But we knew that, sooner or later, when transportation could be restored, we would travel to other parts of the world, to write our stories of the great upheaval and tribulation, and the miraculous changes for the better in the attitudes of the earth's human populations: the determination of all that henceforth there would be peace.

"Looks like the world is getting a fresh start," Beebee observed one morning as she read over Ed McCaughlin's news bulletins. There was then so much good news coming in from the outside world that the committee of doctors abandoned their news censorship. Beebee was thrilled at the thought of a brave new world where national boundaries no longer existed, where crime and corruption were gone, and where both wealth and poverty had disappeared.

In time Antarctica would become further inhabited, and much new and fertile land would replace the polluted areas lost by inundation from other continents.

Our beautiful Earth would be a happy and peaceful planet once again.

THE BEGINNING